TASTE OF EVIL

TASTE OF EVIL

A NOVEL

By

Tony Aspler and Gordon Pape

Library and Archives Canada Cataloguing in Publication

Title: Taste of evil / Tony Aspler & Gordon Pape.

Names: Aspler, Tony, 1939- author. | Pape, Gordon, author.

Description: Translation of: Bienvenue en Afrique.

Identifiers: Canadiana (print) 20210184485
              Canadiana (ebook) 20210184566

ISBN 9781771615808 (softcover) ISBN 9781771615815 (PDF)
ISBN 9781771615822 (EPUB) ISBN 9781771615839 (Kindle)

Classification: LCC PS8551.S65 T37 2021
              DDC C813/.54—dc2

Published by Mosaic Press, Oakville, Ontario, Canada, 2021.

MOSAIC PRESS, Publishers
www.Mosaic-Press.com
Copyright© Tony Aspler & Gordon Pape, 2021

Cover Design by Rahim Piracha

ONTARIO ARTS COUNCIL
CONSEIL DES ARTS DE L'ONTARIO
an Ontario government agency
un organisme du gouvernement de l'Ontario

Funded by the Government of Canada
Financé par le gouvernement du Canada

ONTARIO CREATES

MOSAIC PRESS
1252 Speers Road, Units 1 & 2, Oakville, Ontario, L6L 5N9
(905) 825-2130 • info@mosaic-press.com • www.mosaic-press.com

to Esther, with Love
Gordon

to Survivors, everywhere
Tony

Foreword

This is a book of fiction based on facts. The reader will recognise the names of some of the historical characters; the others spring from our imagination.

Adolf Hitler had fourteen women who tasted all his food; but Gretchen von Bismarck was not one of them. Of the real women who did this dangerous job, only one survived the war.

Apart from the fictional aspects of our story, we have tried to be as historically accurate as possible in terms of the major events in WWII, even to the timeline of the war.

We are indebted to the following authors whose works provided us with information and the direct quotes we have used in the narrative.

Adolf Hitler: *'Mein Kampf'*; Albert Speer: *'Inside The Third Reich'*; Antony Beevor: *'The Second World War'*; Christa Schroeder: *'He Was My Chief: The Memoirs of Adolf Hitler's Secretary'*; Hugh Trevor-Roper: *'The Last Days of Hitler'*; James P. O. Donnell: *'The Bunker'*; Jean-Denis G.G. Lepage: *'Hitler Youth, 1922-1945: An Illustrated History'*; Jörg Friedrich: *'The Fire: The Bombing of Germany, 1940-1945'*; Joachim C. Fests:; *'Albert Speer: Conversations with Hitler's Architect'*; Jost Hermand: *'A Hitler Youth in Poland'*; Martin Kitchen: *'Speer: Hitler's Architect'*; Norman Stone: *'Hitler'*; Robert E Conot: *'Justice at Nuremberg'*; Stephen Halbrook: *'The Swiss and the Nazis'*.

And, of course, the Internet.

Potsdam, September 1, 1939

'Phew!' Gretchen turned away from the tin canister of flour in disgust.

'What is it, *liebchen*?' asked Cook, wiping her hands on her apron as she bustled across the kitchen. 'You look like you just sucked a lemon.'

'There are weevils in the flour,' Gretchen replied, backing away from the container on the counter.

'No, that can't be,' said Cook, dismayed. 'That can't be. I bought it two days ago. Let me see.'

She peered into the porcelain container. 'I don't see anything.'

'They're in there... I could smell their droppings.'

Gretchen watched Cook as she thrust her hands into the canister and stirred the flour. A moment later she hastily pulled them out.

'Ugh! It's swarming with them! They're all down near the bottom.'

She waddled to the garbage can and the contents disappeared in a cloud of white powder.

'What will your father say with food so expensive now with all the talk of war?'

She turned back to Gretchen, dusting her hands before putting them under the tap. She dried her hands on her apron and reached up to a shelf for a clean canister. It was standing next to a fat book totalling 720 pages, entitled 'Mein Kampf.'

'Why does your father insist on keeping that book of Herr Hitler's in the kitchen?' said Cook.

Gretchen shrugged. 'Daddy says every household in Germany must have a copy.'

What she didn't add was that she had heard her father telling her mother that he would not have 'Mein Kampf' in his library as it 'might pollute all of German literature.'

'How did you know the weevils were there, child?'

'I could smell them.'

Cook stared at Gretchen for a moment and shook her head. It wasn't the first time she had witnessed the girl's uncanny sense of smell. From the age of ten she could tell immediately if a particular herb was missing from the roast or if the milk was on the verge of turning sour. And the teenager's sense of taste was just as acute.

'I'll have to get fresh. And I did so want everything to be just right with that nice Herr Speer coming for dinner.'

Gretchen could feel the blood rising in her cheeks at the mention of Speer's name: she had a secret crush on the handsome architect. She was glad Cook hadn't noticed, as she made her way to the pantry to find another sack of flour.

Gretchen gazed around the kitchen. It was her favourite place in the family's rambling country estate in Potsdam – warm, cozy, and filled with mostly enticing aromas. One wall was dominated by a huge open fireplace, where roasts were slowly turned on a spit on cool days. An array of copper pots, ladles, spoons, and other culinary paraphernalia hung from an iron wheel suspended above a long oak table.

Directly across the room was an ancient wood-burning stove that had been fired up in preparation for bread baking. The backsplash behind it was a mosaic depicting a group of hunters converging on a cornered wild boar. Gretchen had heard there were still a few feral pigs in the forest, but she had never seen one in spite of her solitary walks in the grounds of her father's estate at dusk. The head gardener had said they came out at that hour to gorge on the acorns that fell from the century-old oak tree.

Between the fireplace and the stove was a wall of cabinets and shelves filled with china, glassware, cooking utensils, and silverware, all neatly sorted and organised. The outer wall was dominated by a huge picture window giving out to a wide meadow that sloped down to the bank of the River Havel, about a kilometre away.

'Here we are. I've sifted through it and this lot's fresh and clean,' Cook said, setting a freshly scrubbed canister in front of Gretchen. 'Let's hurry along. The oven is just at the right temperature.'

As she kneaded the dough, Gretchen thought about how much she would miss this place. They were due to return to the apartment in Berlin in a few days, she to begin a new term at school and her father, Carl von Bismarck, to resume his work as the chief assistant architect to

Albert Speer. From table conversation, Gretchen understood that Herr Speer had been commissioned by the Führer to construct a series of grandiose buildings and promenades that would transform the city into 'a wonder of the world.' Gretchen was proud that Speer had chosen her father, one of the country's most prominent architects, as his chief aide.

Once the bread was in the oven, Gretchen sat and stared out the window, inhaling the fragrant aromas. If there was anything in the world that smelled better than baking bread, she had yet to encounter it. Outside, the dew on the grass sparkled in the morning September sun. Later, she would stroll down to the water and feed the ducks, she thought. Cook had told her that there was an army base across the river, and that there had been more activity than usual in the area in recent days, with tank columns seen on the roads. Gretchen had never seen a tank. Perhaps she would today.

'It's done.'

Gretchen was wakened from her reverie as Cook pulled the loaves from the oven. 'Go get some fresh butter and honey from the pantry. As soon as it's cool enough, you can take some in to your mama and papa.'

The moment she entered the stately drawing room with the tray, Gretchen knew that all was not right. Her father and mother were bent over, heads close to the radio speaker. She could see by the tension in their bodies that something was wrong.

Setting the tray on a table, she hurried over to them. 'What's the...'

'Shush,' her mother commanded, at the same time as her father waved her to be quiet. Gretchen moved closer.

'*Latest reports are that our forces have met little resistance and are making rapid headway,*' the radio announcer was saying, his voice unable to maintain the neutral tone habitual to newsreaders. '*To repeat, early this morning forces of the Wehrmacht* crossed the border into Poland to assist our German compatriots in Prussia, Upper Silesia, Poznan, and Danzig to free them from the tyranny *to which they have been subjected since the infamous Treaty of Versailles. Our heroic forces are advancing on all fronts and have suffered minimal losses. The War Office expects the campaign to be over in a few days. A statement from the Foreign Ministry has assured the world that Germany's only interest is to protect the rights of its people and that we wish only to see a lasting peace established. Heil Hitler.*'

Her father snapped off the radio and turned to Gretchen. She had never seen his face look so grave. 'Go and pack your clothes, child. We're returning to Berlin tonight.'

'But Papa, Herr Speer is coming to dinner.'

'We had a telephone call from Herr Speer, Gretchen. He is other-wise occupied.'

As if to himself, he added: 'I don't know when he will grace this house again.'

Berlin, September 1, 1939

Albert Speer, dark-haired, dressed in his grey field uniform, as handsome as a matinee idol, pored over a set of architectural drawings. He would build the largest edifice in the world – Hitler's power centre. The assembly hall alone would accommodate 180,000 people standing, all for the ultimate glorification of the Führer.

Speer had joined the National Socialist Party in 1931 and had endeared himself to Hitler by designing the Nuremberg Parade Grounds. He smiled to himself as he remembered how pleased Hitler had been when the leader drove into the grounds to the deafening roar of the crowds, a roar that could be heard as far away as the airport. To stage-manage the rally, Speer had created a cathedral of light formed by 130 anti-aircraft searchlights pointed skywards: Hitler, in a blue Daimler-Benz, standing next to his driver, all five foot-eight of him, his left hand resting on the windshield, his right arm extended in acknowledgement of the adoring throng.

He recalled how Goering had fumed over his appropriation of the searchlights, but Hitler had overridden the strenuous objections of the Commander in Chief of the Luftwaffe.

Speer, now 34 years old, secure as Hitler's protégé and confidante, could afford a little self-congratulation. He turned to his secretary Annemarie Kempf who was hovering at his elbow, pencil poised over her notebook.

'Call von Bismarck. Tell him I regret I cannot dine with him tonight. We will meet in my office tomorrow.'

He felt a qualm of regret at not being able to accept his assistant's dinner invitation. Von Bismarck's cook was as talented as any chef in

Berlin and his beautiful daughter was a delightful dinner companion with her corn-blonde hair and China-blue eyes.

Speer had noticed how she lowered those eyes every time he looked at her; but she was a child and he had always been faithful to Margarete since their engagement when they were both nineteen. And how long it took for his mother to accept their marriage! It was seven years before they were invited to stay over at his parents' house in Mannheim.

Yet, there was something about her – Gretchen von Bismarck, that was her name – there was something about the girl that fascinated him. The way she savoured every forkful she lifted to her mouth, sniffing before she ingested it, as if she were making love to her food.

Gretchen, yes – how Hitler would love her, he thought; a poster child for the new Germany, exuding health and vitality.

But his energetic mind dismissed the image of the girl to concentrate on the work at hand. He conjured up the memory of his last meeting with Hitler. It was at the Führer's house in Obersalzberg, where he lived discreetly with his mistress Eva Braun. They had been reviewing the drawings for the new Reichstag when Hitler confided in him the details of 'Case White,' the code name for the invasion of Poland.

How proud he had been of his leader and of Germany at that moment. The only cloud that cast a shadow on the future was the inevitable war with England, and how this might mean funds for his architectural vision might be diverted to support Germany's war efforts.

And how pathetic the British Prime Minister had been a year earlier, returning to from his visit to Hitler in Munich and waving a piece of paper, yelling, 'Peace for our time.'

There would be no peace until Germany took its rightful place as the leader of Europe and ultimately of all the White races.

The telephone jangled on the desk breaking his train of thought. The secretary took the call.

'Herr Speer, it's your wife.'

He took the receiver and without waiting for his wife's voice, said: 'Did you hear the news?'

'You mean our news?'

'No, the news about Poland. We have liberated Poland. It's all over the radio. Aren't you excited?'

'Albert. I have news myself. You know I've been feeling…well, not like my old self. I went to see Dr. Hofstetter today and…are you sitting down?'

'I'm working, *liebchen*. You know I always stand.'

'Well, you're going to be a Papa! I'm pregnant. Finally.'

It took Speer a moment to let the information sink in.

'Are you there, darling? I'm sure it's a boy and if it is, we'll call him after you.'

Speer handed the receiver back to the secretary and sank into a chair. He buried his face in his hands so that she would not see him cry.

Berlin, September 15, 1939

Gretchen was not destined to stay long in the family penthouse apartment on Berlin's Petersburger Strasse. Her parents, fearful for her safety, would pack her off to a Swiss finishing school, where they hoped she would stay for the duration of the war. According to the Nazi television news, the Fatherland would triumph before the next harvest.

Berlin was the first German city to have television broadcasts in 1935. The sets were expensive, so the city set up communal rooms around Berlin where the citizens could watch for free. The von Bismarcks felt that the investment was worthwhile, so they became the proud owners of the first TV set in their building.

At first, Gretchen was captivated by the daily cooking shows though she began to feel uneasy about the subtle undercurrent of racism expressed by the female host. Her references to 'Jew food' and sneering remarks about the Judaic prohibition against eating pork made the young girl question the antipathy towards Jews.

Her father was reluctant to address the subject, and Gretchen could tell from the glances he exchanged with her mother that they were uncomfortable with her questions.

When she brought up the subject again, her mother immediately shifted the conversation to Gretchen's imminent departure for Switzerland.

'Have you packed your suitcase? And, dear, remember to bring your pillow. You know how your allergies act up at this time of year... Are you going to bring Teddy?'

'Mama, I'm a sixteen year old. I can vote in the State elections.'

'I just thought Teddy would remind you of home,' she replied, reaching for her handkerchief. 'I'd like you to take Daddy's Leica so you can take some photos of the place.'

Carl von Bismarck glowered at his wife but said nothing.

His wife, picking up the visual cue, added: 'But you must be very careful with the camera. It's very expensive.'

They drove in silence to the railway station, each wrapped in their own thoughts. Her father wondering if he would ever see his daughter again; her mother, clutching her hand bag to her chest, images of Gretchen as a baby flashing through her mind. And Gretchen, fearful and excited at the same time, sad to be leaving the family mansion, the only home she had ever known; yet excited by the prospect of living like an adult in another country.

Her parents had chosen a small, well-established girl's school near Bern on the recommendation of the family lawyer whose daughter had attended it. They thought Gretchen would be more comfortable in a German-speaking Canton as the students were more likely to share a similar upbringing. They had heard stories of a finishing school in Lausanne where girls came home pregnant; but what would one expect with the influence of the French?

Herr von Bismarck pulled up the car by the curb at the entrance to the station. Standing on either side of the door were two helmeted soldiers carrying Mauser-Werke Gewehr 98 rifles that he recalled his father had used in the First World War. He opened the door so that his wife and daughter could alight and then went to the trunk for the suitcase.

'You have your ticket in a safe place?'

'Yes, Mama.'

'You'll be met at the station in Bern by one of the teachers. Her name is Hanna Seigert. She will have a sign, Lyceum Bern. And you will write as soon as you're settled.'

'Yes, Mama.'

'It's a nine-hour trip,' said her father, placing his hands on Gretchen's shoulders like a blessing. 'Your mother has packed food for you so you don't have to go to the dining car. And you have a single berth. You'll find it easy to sleep. The rhythm of the train is like a lullaby.'

He hugged Gretchen to him, hoping his daughter would be safe in the oldest democracy in the world. Her mother took her hand and pressed two 100 Reichsmark bills into her palm. Unused to showing affection, she stood back staring at her daughter, both hands pressed against her mouth to stop herself from crying.

Unbeknownst to the girl and her parents, as they were saying their 'goodbyes,' two Gestapo agents in black leather coats were leaning against the wall, taking particular interest in the scene. They nodded to each other and one followed Gretchen to the platform from which her train to Bern would leave, while the other watched the von Bismarcks head back to their car, noting the licence plate number.

Berlin, September 15, 1939

It was a twenty minute drive from Albert Speer's private office on Lindenallee in the West End of Berlin, near Adolf Hitler Platz, to his modest house in Berlin-Schlachtensee. There was hardly any traffic on the road at that late hour and as tired as he was he enjoyed this time of solitude that allowed him to think. When he got home he could relax with Margarete – the love of his life whom he called 'Gretel' in their intimate moments – and she could tell him about her day and her visit to the doctor.

He had been concerned that their unborn child might be prone to the same dizzy spells he had suffered as a youngster, dizzy spells that sometimes caused him to faint. He wondered if the condition that the family physician described as 'weakness of the vascular nerves' was hereditary.

But whenever such gloomy thoughts invaded his mind, he recalled the triumph of his ambitions as an architect. He was now Hitler's chosen man, one of the most powerful men in the Reich and a builder of the New Order.

As he drove through the darkened city, he thought back to the first time he had met the Führer. The date was engraved on his heart: July 27, 1932. He had joined the National Socialist Party a year earlier, enthralled by Hitler's speeches.

Speer recalled that December night in 1930 when he went to a beer hall in Hasenheide to hear Hitler speak for the first time. He came away mesmerised and determined to answer the Führer's call to action and help build the new Germany. *Ein Volk, ein Reich, ein Führer.* He had turned a blind eye to the subsequent violence in the streets and excused Kristallnacht as an aberration. You could not create a Thousand-Year Reich without a little bloodshed.

As an inconsequential member of the party in those days, he was chauffeuring a courier to Berlin-Staaken airport who had an urgent report to deliver to Hitler. The Führer was throwing a tantrum because the car for his entourage had not arrived. He was marching up and down the airport lobby thrashing a dog whip against his high boots and snapping his fingers. Speer had come to learn that snapping fingers was the first sign that the Führer was about to work himself up into a frenzy.

But how proud his father and his grandfather – both eminent architects – how proud they would be were they only alive to see how favoured he was by a leader who would restore Germany's pride. 'And my buildings,' he said to himself, 'will be a testament to the world of Germany's greatness.'

He had not forgotten how hungry he had been as a young boy growing up in Mannheim after the Great War and the roaring inflation of 1923. Hungry enough to devour a whole bag of stale dog biscuits. But those days were long gone and the future was as bright and shining as a naked sword.

Two years ago Hitler had commandeered the Academy of Arts on Pariser Platz for my offices and my ten associate architects, he remembered, smiling, and he made me his Inspector General of Buildings. My leader had selected this building because he could walk through the ministerial gardens out of sight of the public.

At their last meeting, Hitler had requested Speer to design a staircase for the new Chancellery, 'as magnificent as the one in the Paris Opera.' Hitler had confided that the Vienna Opera House was also one of his favourite buildings, in fact one of the most resplendent opera houses of the world.

What the Führer had told him about was the fate of its architect, which had given him pause for thought. When it was finished in 1848, Eduard Van der Nüll's design for the Vienna Opera house was subject to scathing criticism, so much so that Nüll thought his building was a failure. On the day before the opera house opened with Mozart's 'Don Giovanni,' he put a bullet in his brain.

Nor was Speer unmindful of the fate of the well-known cabaret comedian Werner Fink. Fink sailed too close to the wind in his mockery of Hitler's building projects. He had been taken off to Esterwegen concentration camp the day before Speer had booked to see Fink's show. He heard that Fink had taunted Gestapo informers in the audience by telling them to write down his every word. He had picked out one member in the front row, saying: 'Am I talking too fast? Can you follow me or shall I follow you?'

Albert Speer, for all of his pride in being Hitler's architect, knew that he had to watch what he was saying. And to watch for the first incidence of snapping fingers.

Bern, September 16, 1939

G retchen lowered her suitcase on to the platform and looked around for a woman holding a sign. She waved when she saw Hanna Seigert, a strikingly tall woman in her mid-forties, dressed in wide slacks, a pale blue twin-set and pearls.

She held a square of white cardboard with Gretchen's name printed on it in large letters. Beside her, a good head shorter, was a man with closely cropped hair in khaki pants and a white short-sleeved shirt buttoned to the neck. He appeared to be wearing army boots badly in need of polish.

'Welcome to Bern, Fraulein. Jorg will take your suitcase. I trust you had a pleasant journey.'

'Thank you, Frau Seigert,' replied Gretchen, extending the case towards the man who took it in his left hand. She noticed he had a tattoo that ran from the inside of his wrist to his elbow: crossed rifles above a legend in Gothic script she could not read.

'We have a half-hour drive to the school which will give us time to get to know one another. I'm sure you will have questions,' said the woman, striding ahead towards the car, a funeral black landau with white-wall tires that looked as if it might have just driven off the lot of an American gangster movie.

Jorg held the door as Hanna Seigert slid in the back and patted the seat for Gretchen to join her. Jorg opened the trunk and deposited the suitcase inside, then took up his position behind the wheel.

Strange he's not wearing a cap, thought the girl. The von Bismarck's chauffeurs always wore caps.

'So, Gretchen, this is your first time in Switzerland?'

'Yes, Frau Seigert, I'm very excited. My parents took me to Biarritz one summer. That's the only other place I've been to outside of Germany.'

Immediately she said 'Germany' she could see Jorg's head snap backwards. She met his gaze in the rear-view mirror. He was staring at her with such hatred in his eyes she was forced to look away.

'Jorg!' barked Frau Seigert. 'You missed the turning for the highway. Please concentrate on your driving.'

'My apologies,' mumbled the driver and put the car into reverse.

'Now I shall tell you about your sleeping arrangements. You will be sharing a room with a debutante your age from Zürich. We thought you would be more comfortable with a young lady who speaks your language. Her father owns a very fashionable medical clinic.'

Gretchen nodded to convey she was as impressed as Frau Seigert was by the information.

Gretchen's eyes flicked up to the mirror and again she saw the anger in Jorg's gaze.

'What's her name?'

'Shona. Fraulein Shona Rosenberg.'

Sounds Jewish, thought Gretchen. She had never actually met a Jew before.

'You will, of course, be taught French,' continued Frau Siegert, 'along with all the social graces a young woman should know these days – table decoration, floral arrangements, the art of serving afternoon tea. General etiquette and, of course, how to run a household.'

'What about cooking?' asked Gretchen.

'Cooking? All you need to know is what to *tell* your cook. We prepare our young ladies for the life you will lead when you marry well, my dear.'

'What's that building over there?' asked Gretchen, admiring the stone towers like witches' hats.

'That's the Bern Historical Museum. It was built in 1894 but it looks a lot older, doesn't it? The architect Andre Lambert loved old castles. Perhaps you'd like to see the old town.'

Before Gretchen could respond, the teacher leaned forward and instructed Jorg to cross the turquoise-coloured River Aare. The car trundled over the ancient cobbled streets of the old walled town.

'Stop, so we can get a good look at the Zytglogge,' ordered Frau Seigert.

Jorg pulled the car over and morosely began to bite his thumbnail.

'That's the Zytglogge, Gretchen. That clock tower was built in the thirteen century as a guard tower at the western gate of the city. You see the two clock faces. The lower one is an astrological clock with the signs of the zodiac.'

'It's so beautiful.'

Gretchen wished she had her father's camera handy, but it was carefully packed in her suitcase, wrapped in a sweater.

'We'll drive by the Bärengraben, Jorg, and then back to school,' said Frau Seigert. Turning to Gretchen, she added: 'The Bärengraben is a bear pit. The bear is the symbol of Bern. You can see it on our coat of arms.'

As the teacher droned on about the history of the city, Gretchen watched the passing scenery, wondering why Jorg had reacted so violently when she mentioned she was from Germany. And what was the significance of the tattoo on his forearm he made no secret of hiding?

Bern, December 2, 1939

Shona Rosenberg, dressed in a tennis outfit, sat cross-legged on her bed reading a magazine and smiling grimly to herself.

'What're you reading, Shoshy?' asked Gretchen, as she brushed her hair in the mirror.

The girls had given each other nicknames. Shona was Shoshy and she was Gretty.

Shona looked at the cover.

'It's a Swiss satirical magazine called *Nebelspalter*. Political cartoons and stuff. They poke fun at the Nazis. Very subversive.'

'Lemme see.'

Gretchen knelt down on the bed next to Shona who showed her a cartoon. It depicted a Nazi and a Communist officer embracing each other, dripping with blood and roaring with laughter. The caption read, 'The New Friends.'

'Where did you get it?'

'Jorg lent it to me.'

'Jorg? The driver?'

'Yeah. I sometimes sneak out to the gardening shed and smoke with him.'

'If you ever get caught Frau Seigert will expel you.'

'I don't care. I hate it here.'

'That tattoo Jorg has on his arm. What does it mean?'

'He told me about it once. The crossed rifles mean he's a marksman. An expert shot. Like most Swiss. It's their national pastime. And the writing is Switzerdeutsch for, 'Every one of us takes seven Germans.' If Germany invades, all the men will become snipers in the mountains.'

'He must hate us.'

Gretchen recalled the look in Jorg's eyes at the mere mention of the name 'Germany.'

'He hates the Nazis. Besides, he knows I'm Jewish and he knows what's happening to the Jews in Germany.'

'What do you mean?'

'The concentration camps. Jews are being sent off to concentration camps. There are trains full.'

'That's terrible.'

'Jorg told me. He's seen the trains. I think he's Jewish himself.'

'How do you know?'

'I saw it. He has no foreskin.'

Gretchen gasped and placed her hand to her mouth to stifle her giggles.

'You mean you did it with him!'

'No, I walked into the shed when he was having a pee. And I got a good look at it,' laughed Shona. 'He went beet red. I think he wet himself trying to put it away.'

'I've never seen a man myself,' Gretchen said.

'Believe me, you haven't missed much. Come on, we'll be late for class.'

Berlin, June 24, 1940

Albert Speer, reclining in his favourite armchair, poured himself a second glass of Riesling. As tired as he was, he was in jubilant mood. He had just returned from a three-hour tour of the captured Paris, invited by Hitler to drive in the Führer's own car.

'What's Paris like?' asked Margarete as she gave the baby his nightly breast-feed.

'The most beautiful city in the world,' her husband replied. 'The Führer told me Berlin must exceed it. His exact words were, 'Paris will forever stand in its shadow.' And Berlin will do just that, if I can realise my vision for it.'

Margarete said nothing.

'You know what he wanted to see first in Paris?' continued Speer, oblivious to his wife's silence. 'The opera house! Not the fortifications or the armaments the French left behind when they abandoned the city, but the opera house.... You know, last summer during the mobilisation he had all the draft records sent to his adjutant. And if they were artists, he tore them up. He won't send artists to die in the war. You know his chauffeur, Brecker, is a sculptor.'

Margarete sighed and remained silent.

'What's the matter, *leibchen*, you've hardly said a word since I got back.'

'Why don't you take off your uniform, Albert? You're at home now. You're becoming like one of them.'

'What are you trying to say?'

'I never see you. The baby never sees you. You are killing yourself with work.'

'I have a job to do for the German people.'

'Sometimes I think you're having an affair. Like Goering, seducing young actresses, with his painted nails and his pockets full of emeralds. And him playing with train sets, a grown man. And the morphine he takes.'

'You know he was wounded in the Beer Hall Putsch in '23. He's a war hero. He needs it to kill the pain.... Sometimes I wish I had time to have an affair,' laughed Speer. 'My only affair is with you, my darling.... Did I tell you the latest notion from Goering?'

Margarete shook her head.

'You know we need to manufacture trains to supply our troops. Well, in order to preserve steel for the war effort, for the armaments and tanks and such, well, Goering actually suggested to me we build trains with concrete. Concrete!'

'You know they're all jealous of you, don't you? You're the Führer's favourite. Have a look out the window. They're there all the time now.'

Speer rose from his chair, placed the wine glass on the table and crossed to the window. He pulled the curtain open and looked down on the street. There were two men standing in the shadow of a doorway.

'Gestapo,' he said. 'Himmler probably assigned them to protect me.'

'Are they guarding you, Albert, or spying on you? I don't trust any of them, particularly that club-footed, book-burner Herr Goebbels. And Bormann, always toadying up to Hitler. He appears to be so insignificant but he's ruthless, like a snake, a psychopath with a filthy tongue. There's nothing he wouldn't do to please the Führer.'

'Margarete! Be careful what you say. They have ears everywhere.'

'It's you, my darling, who has to be careful – for me and your son.'

'I have the Führer's ear, my dear. I'm his confidante. He treats me as if I were his son. Why only yesterday – and I'm telling you this in the strictest confidence – he told me of his plans to invade Switzerland. That miserable little country of chocolate and cuckoo clocks is completely surrounded by Germany and our allies. Twenty-one divisions of General lieutenant List's Twelfth Army should have no problem in taking it. It'll be just like Austria, another non-violent Anschluss…. This is an excellent Riesling, by the way. We should order some more.'

Bern, June 25, 1940

'The whole class was humming softly,' Shoshy said. 'Miss Myer thought the lighting was defective and rushed out to call the janitor. When he came, everyone was quiet. He looked at her like she was nuts.'

Gretchen almost doubled up with laughter at the idea of prissy Miss Myers being shamed by a janitor.

Their mirth was interrupted by the ringing of an alarm bell in the corridor. A female voice came over the public address system.

'All girls will assemble immediately in Big School for an important announcement by the Head Mistress. On the double, ladies.'

The hallway filled with girls making their way to the staircase that led down to the ground floor. Big School was a large room with a raised stage used for musical performances, the annual school play and graduation ceremonies. The fact that everyone had been summoned there caused a rush of excitement among the girls.

They filed solemnly into the room and took their customary seats, youngest in the front, the most senior in the back.

Frau Seigert sat at a table on the stage, flanked by three other teachers on each side of her. To her right was an easel from which a map of Europe hung. A teacher stood beside it with a pointer.

Shona nudged Gretchen and motioned her head to the left of the stage. Dressed in a grey battledress jacket with red flashes on the collar tips, Jorg stood at attention, staring straight ahead of him.

Frau Seigert tapped the microphone to ensure it was live. Her first words were drowned in the high-pitched howl of feedback. She pushed the mike a few inches away and began again.

'My dear young ladies. As you know Europe is involved in a war. A year ago Germany invaded Poland. As a result, Great Britain and France declared war on Germany. Frau Baumgartner will indicate on the map so you will understand the geography.... In April, Germany invaded Denmark and Norway...Norway, Frau Battig, not Sweden.... Last month Germany occupied Luxembourg, the Netherlands and Belgium. Then it was France. The Germans now occupy the northern zone of France and the entire Atlantic coastline. Switzerland has by international law remained neutral in this conflict. But we as a nation are surrounded by countries that have either fallen to German occupation or are Germany's Axis allies, namely Italy.'

There was a communal stirring in the room as the young audience processed the information.

'I am treating you all like adults by telling you exactly what has happened and what we will do to ensure your safety. I don't want there to be any false rumours flying around. I have heard from our ministry in Bern that German troops are massing on the Jura frontier, which as you see is to the northwest of us....'

The sound from the floor began to swell, a cacophony of sighs and high-pitched sobs.

'Now, be calm girls, take courage. Remember your school motto, *Nil Desperandum Auspice Deo*. Never despair and trust in God. We will be practising evacuation procedures this afternoon. The fire bell will summon you to the quadrangle and your senior monitors will guide you through the process. If you have any questions come to me or to Matron.'

A hand shot up in the back row.

'What about our parents, Frau Seigert?'

'Your parents have been contacted and arrangements will be made to ensure you are returned safely to your homes. That is, those of you who want to return home. Now go about your regular activities until you hear the bell. Dismissed. Oh, and Shona Rosenberg please report to office immediately.'

Shona and Gretchen exchanged glances. Shona opened her eyes wide and shrugged her shoulders to indicate she didn't know why she had been summoned by the head mistress.

****

While she waited for Shona, Gretchen took out her father's camera and loaded it with film.

When Shona returned she was in tears.

'What happened, Shoshy?'

'The cleaner found a packet of cigarettes in the drawer and she's going to expel me!'

'Expel you! I thought you wanted to leave.'

'I do, but my father will kill me. This will be the third school I've been expelled from. I don't know what to do.'

'I know. I'll tell Frau Seigert they were my cigarettes. I'm going to be sent home anyway.'

'You'd do that for me!'

'Yes, you're my friend, Shoshy. But first I have to take some photos. I promised my mother. Then I'll go and see Frau Seigert.'

'Oh Gretty, you are my friend for life!'

'I don't know what will happen, but we must keep in touch. We'll write to each other and when this is all over you can come and visit me in Potsdam, I'll give you my address and you give me yours.'

'Sisters,' said Shona, hooking her index fingers together.

'Sisters,' repeated Gretchen, mimicking the gesture.

The girls hugged each other and tears welled up in Shona's eyes,

'Now I'm off to take some pictures,' said Gretchen. 'If anyone asks tell them I've gone for a run.'

Gretchen changed into shorts and gym shoes and slung the Leica strap over her shoulder. She took the staircase to the ground floor and went out by the back door to the vegetable garden. She took the cover off the lens, and adjusted the focal length. She snapped photos of the back façade and then pointed her camera at the paddock beyond where the horses were stabled.

She walked around the ornamental pond where the ducks would land at twilight towards the woods.

She stopped and pointed her camera towards the bridge over a tributary of the River Aare. And then at the Bantiger Mountain to the north. Next, the arched stone bridge over the river at Bärengraben, the nearest village to the school.

In the distance she could hear the school bell ringing. She began to run holding the camera against her side. She heard footsteps behind her. Someone was running after her. She didn't look back and tried to run faster but whoever was pursuing her was gaining on her.

Once she had entered the school grounds Gretchen stopped suddenly and turned around, panting.

Running towards her was Jorg. He grabbed her by the arm.

'You're coming with me.'

His eyes blazed with anger.

'You're hurting me. Where are you taking me?'

Jorg said nothing but continued to drag the reluctant girl back towards the school.

'I wasn't doing anything. I know we're not allowed to leave the grounds without permission, but I was just –'

'Be quiet. You're going to see Frau Seigert.'

Meekly, Gretchen allowed herself to be led to the head mistress' office, mentally going over her excuses for leaving the school grounds.

Jorg knocked on the office door and without waiting for a response walked in, pushing Gretchen before him.

Frau Seigert looked up and took off her glasses.

'What is this about, Jorg?'

'I caught this young woman off the school grounds, Frau Seigert. She was taking photographs.'

'Photographs?'

'Yes, photos of bridges and roads. Photos that could be used by the Germans. I think she is a German spy.'

'I only wanted to show my parents what it was like here,' protested Gretchen.

'Give me the camera,' said Frau Seigert.

Gretchen took the camera strap from her shoulder and handed the camera to the head mistress.

'A Leica. This is not a camera for a child. Where did you get it?'

'It belongs to my father's. He lent it to me.'

Frau Seigert slid the catch to open the back of the camera. Then she pulled the cassette from its housing. She stretched the coil of film out to expose it to the light and dropped it in the wastebasket. She then closed the camera and handed it back to Gretchen.

'Jorg, thank you. You can leave us now.'

Gretchen scowled at the young man as he left the office.

'Gretchen, sit down.'

Frau Seigert opened a file in front of her.

'By coincidence, I was just looking over your record and this latest incident has decided me on a course of action.'

'I only wanted to show my parents pictures of the school.'

'Silence!...Several of my staff have told me that you have either been late for classes or you've missed some altogether. Do you have an explanation?'

'No, ma'am,' replied Gretchen, staring at her feet.

'It appears that you have more interest in what goes on in the kitchen than in the course of studies that has been laid out for you. You've been seen at all hours talking to the chef.'

'I wanted to learn his techniques.'

'Swiss chefs are renowned throughout the world, I grant you. But you are here to learn our curriculum.'

She rose from behind her desk and gazed out of the window at the field hockey pitch.

'There are German divisions at our border, Fraulein von Bismarck. I have to think about the safety of my charges. That is my primary concern. I can't have any fifth columns in my school. Do you understand?'

19

Gretchen did not know what a 'fifth column' was but she was too intimidated by the demeanor of the head mistress to ask.

'Before this latest violation of school rules, I had informed your father that you were not Lyceum Bern material. That you had flouted our rules and conventions too many times. Earlier today, I had advised Herr von Bismarck by telephone that I would allow you to stay with us for the remaining two weeks of the summer term. However, with this latest episode I think it best for all concerned that you leave us now.'

Gretchen realised she had nothing to lose now.

'Frau Seigert, the cigarettes that were found in my room. They were mine, not Shona's.'

She cast her eyes down to suggest contrition.

'And what was the brand?'

'I – I didn't look at the package.'

'So you bought cigarettes without looking at the package. And where are your matches?'

'I used them.'

'And how many cigarettes were left in the pack.'

'Three maybe, I don't remember.'

Frau Seigert pulled open the top drawer of her and took out an unopened pack of cigarettes.

'This is what was found in your room-mate's drawer. Fraulein, it is very noble of you to try to cover for your friend but I'm afraid rules are rules. Consequently, I will phone your father again to make arrangements for you to return immediately to Berlin.'

Bern, June 26, 1940

F rau Siegert was waiting for Gretchen at the bottom of the staircase when she descended with her suitcase. She had said a tearful goodbye to Shona Rosenberg, the two girls hugging each other and vowing eternal friendship.

'You have my address,' said Shoshy. 'We will keep in touch and one day we will see each other again. Promise?'

'Promise.'

Frau Siegert tapped her foot, impatient to see her errant pupil off the premises.

'I hope this will be a lesson to you, young lady. Here is your train ticket. Your parents have been informed of your arrival time. Now, Jorg will drive you to the station. Goodbye, Gretchen. And good luck.'

Jorg emerged from the shadows and grabbed the suitcase from her.

Once out of earshot of Frau Siegert, he said: 'Good riddance.'

Berlin June 27, 1940

The train trip from Bern to Berlin normally takes eight hours. But these were not normal times. Gretchen's train was shunted onto a siding at the German border and held for six hours to allow troop trains to pass.

When she finally arrived in Berlin she was exhausted, not having slept the whole journey. The platform was filled with uniformed soldiers and their kits. Gretchen stood on her suitcase peering over their heads to catch sight of her parents.

She saw her mother pushing her way through the crowd, beckoning imperiously for the chauffeur Fritz to follow her.

When Greta von Bismarck locked her eyes on her daughter, she stood a few paces away from her, her hands on her hips.

'This is the way you repay us? This exploit of yours, Gretchen, has cost your father a pretty penny.'

'Where is he?'

'He's in bed with gout. No doubt brought on by the thoughtless behaviour of his daughter…. Fritz, take the bag.'

They drove back to the Potsdam estate in silence, Gretchen taking in all the familiar landmarks.

It was getting dark when they arrived at the house. Cook was waiting at the front door. There were no lights in the windows.

'Are you hungry,' asked Cook after Gretchen embraced her.

'A bath and bed for this young woman,' said Greta. 'Cook, please draw her a bath.'

Gretchen closed the door of her bedroom with a sigh of relief. It was comforting to be at home again with the stuffed animals lined up along the pillows and the silver-backed hairbrush standing next to the row of nail polishes on the chest-of-drawers.

She stood by the window looking out at the darkening sky, relishing the silhouette of the ancient oak tree in the distance whose acorns fed the wild pigs that roamed the wood lot beyond. It was good to be home.

Her thoughts were interrupted by a knock at the door.

'Come in.'

The door opened and her father stepped into the room, supporting himself with a cane.

'Gretchen.'

She rushed to him and clasped her arms around him, burying her face in his chest. He had never seemed so frail.

'Oh, Papa, I'm so sorry.'

'Shush. Get me that chair and let me sit.'

She pulled the chair from her desk and turned it towards the bed. Her father folded himself into it with the sound of air rushing out of a tire.

Gretchen perched on the end of the bed. How old her father looked, how tired and sad.

'So..., what's all this about cigarettes, young lady? You're not smoking now are you? The next thing you'll tell me you got a tattoo.'

'No, nothing like that, Papa. My room-mate, Shoshy....'

'Shoshy?'

'Shoshy, my friend, that's what I call her. Her real name is Shona. I wrote to you about her. The Jewish girl from Zurich whose father has a medical clinic. She had a pack of cigarettes in her drawer and the cleaning lady found it. They expel girls for smoking at the Lyceum. Anyway, Shoshy would have gotten into terrible trouble with her father, so I told the headmistress the cigarettes were mine.'

'I see,' said Graf von Bismarck. 'So you were trying to help a friend.'

'Yes, I'm sorry I disappointed you.'

'Come here and sit by me.... What you did was foolish, but it was also self-sacrificing and for that I cannot blame you. What happened to this friend, Shoshy?'

'Well, Frau Siegert didn't believe me that the cigarettes were mine, so Soshy got expelled too.'

'Ah. So your false confession was all for naught. Then there was the episode with the camera.'

'She told you about that?'

'Yes.'

'I was taking photos of the school and the grounds as Mama had asked and someone caught me. They accused me of spying for Germany. Frau Seigert took out the roll of film out and exposed it. But she gave me back the camera.'

Graf von Bismarck nodded, 'But now you are home and we must decide what to do with you.'

'Papa, don't send me to another school like that, please. I want to be a chef. I want to learn how to cook. I mean really learn. I want to work in the kitchen of a famous chef. You know how much I love cooking.'

Carl von Bismarck sighed.

'Well, if that is what you have set your heart on...I will speak to your mother.'

A knock at the door ended the conversation.

'Gretchen,' called Cook. 'Your bath is ready.'

'Have your bath, my dear. You look very tired. You must sleep. We'll discuss this at another time. Good night my dear.'

Berlin June 28, 1940

The next morning, when Carl von Bismarck reported for work, he asked Frau Kempf if he could have a word with his employer, Albert Speer.

He had hardly settled in behind his drawing board when Speer appeared at his side.

Von Bismarck rose from his chair. 'Could we have a word in private?' he asked.

'Of course, my dear fellow. Let's go to my office.'

Once settled in the Bauhaus office chairs, which von Bismarck had always found extremely uncomfortable, Speer opened the conversation.

'And how is your daughter getting on at that Swiss school?'

'Actually, Herr Speer, she is back with us in Potsdam. The school sent the girls home because of the our military massing on the border.'

'Really? They should not have been so precipitate because I can tell you that there will be no invasion of Switzerland.'

'Are you sure?'

'I heard it directly from Captain Otto-Wilhelm Kurt von Menges in Oberkommando des Heeres who drew up Operation Tannenbaum.'

'Operation Tannenbaum?'

'Yes, the draft plan for the invasion of Switzerland. He told me our spies there reported that the Swiss army had retreated into the mountains. They had built kilometres of bunkers and mined all the key bridges and tunnels. We need those tunnels. They are our route to Italy, and if they had blown them it would have taken us months to rebuild them. It wasn't worth it.'

'So what happens now with Switzerland?'

'Germany will make a deal for their neutrality. To avoid being invaded they will allow us to use the passes and tunnels for transshipment of materiel and men between the Fatherland and Italy. They understood the cost benefit – and so did we.'

'I see,' said von Bismarck. 'War is really economics carried to a lunatic extreme, isn't it.'

'In the end, yes.'

There was silence between the two men before von Bismarck spoke again.

'My daughter has expressed a desire to become a chef.'

'A chef? She doesn't want to become an architect?'

'Unfortunately not. She wants to study under the best. I know little about this. Greta and I don't dine out much. Whom would you recommend?'

'Well, it's my impression that the large hotels have the best chefs. There's the Deutscher Hof in Nuremberg and the Hotel Diplomat in Frankfurt....'

'Is there nothing in Berlin?'

'There's the Adlon.'

'Yes, of course, why had I not thought of that.'

Berlin, November 26, 1940

'Take a letter Frau Kempf.'

Albert Speer paced up and down his office, while his long-time secretary Annemarie Kempf sat with notebook and pencil poised.

'To Reichsleiter Bormann…'

The mere mention of the man's name made his stomach turn.

'As you are well aware, the Führer has issued a decree concerning the buildings I have designed for Berlin be expedited, and in addition the reconstruction of the cities of Hanover, Augsburg, Bremen and Weimar be undertaken forthwith.'

He paused, wondering if the tone of his language gave away his utter distaste for the man. A man who could invite his mistress to stay at the family house while his wife was in residence. He wondered how the poor woman could put up with him.

'The cost of party buildings alone in these cities,' he continued, 'I estimate to be between 22 and 25 billion marks. Given this kind of capital investment at a time when all of Germany's resources should rightly be committed to the war efforts, I have asked our leader if it would not be prudent for me concentrate on the buildings for Berlin and Nuremberg – the buildings he is most interested in bringing to completion. He agreed. To respect his wishes, I have decided to resign all my party offices in order to concentrate fully on the task at hand. I look forward to your official confirmation of my request, which is supported by the Führer…. Sign it the usual way, Heil Hitler, but leave off my party titles, Frau Kempf. Thank you.'

Speer ran his hands through his hair. He had a headache, and he was troubled by the news he had heard on Reichs-Rundfunk-Gesellschaft, the German radio network, at breakfast. The RAF had bombed Berlin, no doubt in retaliation for Goering's Operation Eagle, the Luftwaffe's bombing campaign against Britain. But mercifully, the damage had been slight. Still, future bombing raids by the British could seriously disrupt his building schedule.

In the summer months, the RAF had dropped tiny incendiary devices – wooden and cloth strips coated with phosphorous – on the German countryside to try to burn down the harvest as well as the

High Harz, the Black and Thuringian forests. They had not met with success, but they would try other firebombing techniques and aim them at our cities next time, he thought.

There were other troubling sights for him in Berlin. On his drive to the office that morning, he had seen crowds of people on the platform of the Nikolassee Railway Station. He recognised them to be Berlin Jews about to be evacuated.

He felt a sense of uneasiness watching the shuffling mass of people with their suitcases and bundles. He tried to put the image out of his mind, but it kept returning. The Führer must have his reasons; in the bigger scheme of things we must accept this. 'I will bury myself in my work,' he said to himself.

A knock at the door broke into his train of thoughts.

'Come in.'

Annemarie Kempf entered carrying the letter he had dictated attached to a clipboard.

'It's ready for your signature, Herr Speer. Shall I mark it "Urgent"?'

'I suppose so,' he said with a sigh. 'Frau Kempf, you take the train to Nikolassee station every morning. Did you see Jews being transported?'

The secretary placed the clipboard in front of him and handed him a pen.

'I try not to look,' she replied.

Speer took the pen and signed his name to the letter.

'Can you get the drawings I was working on with Herr von Bismarck and ask him to come in.'

'Herr von Bismarck is not in the office,' said his secretary. 'He had to accompany his daughter to a job interview.'

Berlin, November 26, 1940

The Adlon on Unter den Linden at Pariser Platz was Berlin's most fashionable hotel. Built in 1907 by Lorenz Adlon, it occupied an entire city block. The eponymous owner was a successful wine merchant and coffee house owner who convinced Kaiser Wilhelm II that Berlin needed a luxury hotel at par with the Ritz in Paris and London. With the intercession of the Kaiser, Adlon was able to purchase the Palais Redem, which sat on the site of his chosen location. He had the palace demolished.

The construction of the hotel cost twenty million Gold Marks. When opened, it was the most modern hotel in Europe. Its sober façade belied the elegant extravagance of its interior. Huge square marble columns dominated the enormous lobby, adjacent to which was an indoor garden with a Japanese-themed elephant fountain and a palm court. It boasted of hot and cold running water.

Hotel Adlon was to be Gretchen von Bismarck's new place of learning after her hurried departure from Lyceum Bern.

At a loss as to what to do with their wayward daughter, her parents, at their wits end, finally gave in to her pleading to be trained as a chef. The von Bismarcks discussed in private the possibility of her apprenticing in some country inn in the Black Forest, far away from major cities and the industrial Ruhr Valley, which appeared to be the targets of the increasingly frequent British bombing raids.

But Gretchen had her heart set on the kitchens of Hotel Adlon ever since her parents had taken her there for tea on her twelfth birthday.

While she suffered through the mild reproofs for being expelled from Lyceum Bern, she knew that ultimately they would come around and would not deny their only child's heartfelt wish.

Reluctantly, the von Bismarcks accepted the fact that their single-minded daughter would not be deflected from the path she had chosen. They would pull what strings they could to ensure Gretchen's safety, knowing she would have to live in their Berlin apartment on Friedrichstrasse, a mere three blocks from the hotel, in a city that had already been bombed.

Gretchen was agonised over what she should wear for her interview with the Director of Food & Beverage, Herr Spangler. Should she wear trousers and look modern and fashionable or should she wear the tight-fitting oatmeal jacket with the cinched waist and the black skirt her mother had bought her.

She opted for trousers and a silk blouse, which she thought would give the impression that she was a woman ready to work. She had seen the factory girls coming home arm-in-arm, all of them dressed in trousers.

She could hear her heart beating with excitement as she walked with her father towards the hotel for her meeting with Herr Spangler. The weather was mild for November and Gretchen felt quite light-headed. She had never had a job before and now she would be earning her own money. She would be able to buy whatever she liked without having to consult her parents. She could have as many shades of lipsticks as she wanted. Or maybe buy some nylons on the black market.

As she approached the hotel, she could see workmen laying bricks on the sidewalk in front of the entrance. The wall was already waist-high.

'What is the wall for?' she asked one of the men.

'For the bombs,' was the laconic reply. The man's German sounded foreign. She had never heard that accent before.

'How high would it be?'

The bricklayer stood up and put his hand about two feet above his head, then turned back to his work, muttering to himself.

'Thank you,' she said. The man just nodded and dug his trowel savagely into a tub of mortar.

Once inside, Gretchen and her father headed to the reception desk and asked to be directed to Herr Spangler's office. The clerk behind the desk picked up the phone and dialled a number.

'Your names?'

'Carl von Bismarck. This is my daughter, Gretchen von Bismarck. She has an appointment for 10 o'clock. We're a little early, but I hope that's all right.'

The woman frowned and spoke into the phone. 'Herr Spangler, this is the front desk. I have a Herr von Bismarck and his daughter. She has an appointment with you at 10 o'clock. It is now 9.47.'

A pause. The woman nodded and said: 'Very good. *Heil Hitler!*'

She replaced the receiver and turned to them. 'You will take the elevator to the lower level where an assistant will meet you and escort you to Herr Spangler's office.'

Gretchen turned to her father and said: 'Thank you for coming with me, but would it be all right if I did this alone? I want to get this job on my own abilities. Perhaps you could wait here for me?'

Von Bismarck frowned, then nodded. His headstrong daughter was right. He found a chair and sat down.

The elevator that took Gretchen to the lower level was operated by a man who looked as if he could have been a jockey. He was dressed in a buttoned livery with a pillbox hat secured to his head by a chinstrap. He winked at her as she stepped inside.

Determined not to make eye contact, she fixed her gaze on the gleaming brass doors. She could feel the undersized man appraising her and was glad when the elevator stopped with a bump at its destination.

A sallow-faced man in a black jacket and pinstripe trousers awaited her as the doors opened.

'Fraulein von Bismarck, I am Joachim, Herr Spangler's assistant. Where is your father?'

'He is waiting for me in reception.'

Joachim clicked his heels and bent forward slightly at the waist. 'I see. Please follow me.'

He led the way along a red carpet to a large door at the end of the corridor. A brass plate on the wall to the left, above a bell, proclaimed that it was the office of Heinrich Spangler, Herr Direktor, Food & Beverage, Hotel Adlon.

Gretchen clutched her purse in both hands and took a deep breath as Joachim knocked discreetly on the door.

'*Kommen Sie herein!*' barked a voice from the other side of the door.

Joachim opened the door wide enough for Gretchen to squeeze through and closed it immediately she was inside.

Heinrich Spangler, in a winged collar and morning dress, sat behind an ornate desk. Above his head was a portrait of Hitler and the red Nazi flag with the central black swastika inside a white circle.

On the adjacent walls were framed photos of what appeared to be celebrity guests. Gretchen recognised Charlie Chaplin, Mary Pickford, Albert Einstein and Marlene Dietrich.

'Sit, Fraulein,' said Spangler, in a tone that sounded more like a command than an invitation.

Gretchen lowered herself into a leather chair in front of the desk. The sun shone through the windows, dazzling her, and she had to squint to focus on her new boss.

'So, you want to become a chef.'

'Yes, sir.'

'It is a noble calling, Fraulein. It takes years of apprenticeship and study. Are you prepared to work hard?'

'Yes, sir.'

'You realise that in spite of your illustrious name you will have to start at the bottom and learn everything that happens in the kitchen. And I do not mean just the creative aspects of food preparation, but the entire mechanics of food service.'

'I intend to learn, sir.'

'Good. Then we will start you off washing dishes....'

He could see the look of dismay on the girl's face. Gretchen had visions of herself dressed in an immaculate white chef's jacket preparing the perfect soufflé and Kaespatzle that melt in the mouth.

'The quality of a restaurant is judged by the cleanliness of its appurtenances, Fraulein. And the personal hygiene of its staff. Show me your nails.'

'My nails?'

'Your nails.'

Gretchen stood up, placed her bag on the chair and approached the desk holding out her hands before her.

'Good. Very satisfactory. They are clean, but they are too long. You will keep them shorter. When you are preparing food, it is imperative that your nails are pristine. Understand?'

'Yes, sir.'

'Now tell me why you want to apprentice at Hotel Adlon.'

'I've heard it is the best hotel in Europe, sir.'

Spangler smiled. 'Quite so. It has also a glorious, although tragic history. Our founder, the late Lorenz Adlon, whose portrait used to hang on the wall behind me, until it was replaced by our leader, was a devoted monarchist. The Brandenburg Gate, which you can see from the windows in our lobby, has a central arch, which was for the Kaiser's use only. When the Kaiser abdicated after the First World War, the centre gate was opened for the motorcar. Herr Adlon never imagined the automobile would use the central arch and he was hit by a car there in 1918. He survived the accident, but three years later, on April 7, 1921 – 13 days before our Führer's birthday – he was hit by a car in the very same spot. This time, he succumbed to his injuries.'

'That's terrible,' said Gretchen.

Direktor Spangler ignored her interjection.

'Hotel Adlon has had many famous people staying here over the years, as you can see.'

He waved a hand towards the photo gallery on the wall.

'Not only film stars, but American presidents such as Franklin Roosevelt and Herbert Hoover. Our guests stay with us not only for the elegance and comfort of our rooms and dining facilities, but because of our discretion. If you are found to be passing information about any of our guests to the newspapers you will be immediately fired. Do I make myself clear, Fraulein?'

'Yes, sir.'

'So, if you are ready to start, I will have Joachim escort you to the kitchens and introduce you to the Chef.'

Gretchen rose from her seat and mumbled her thanks. 'May I ask that you to call your secretary and have her tell my father not to wait for me,' she added.

'Yes, I will do that.'

As she headed for the door, Spangler leant back in his chair with his hands behind his head.

'A word to the wise, Fraulein von Bismarck. The kitchen is a hazardous place for a young lady of your disposition.'

Berlin, January 19, 1941

'Hello, Doktor Professor Messerschmitt. Albert Speer here. Good of you to take my call.'

'*Guten Morgen*, Albert, always a pleasure to talk to you.'

'I have in front of me your drawings for the ME 321.'

'Really? Those drawings are top secret. I gave them to the Führer myself.'

'The Führer has given them to me to help you facilitate construction, Willy. I'm aware that you didn't want Goering and the Air Ministry involved.'

'Quite so.'

'So let me understand what we have here. A glider big enough to carry a 21-ton tank.'

'Precisely. I chose the Panzerkampfwagen IV, our heaviest model.'

'It makes a change from concrete trains,' laughed Speer.

31

'I beg your pardon?'

'It's nothing, Willy. Just a private joke. Explain to me in layman's terms how the glider will be propelled.'

'On the last page you'll see drawings of three Messerschmitt 110's, the fatherland's long-range fighter-bomber. These aircraft will pull the glider which will be launched at take-off by eight rockets, four under each wing.'

'I see.'

'I designed the ME 321 specifically for 'Operation Sea Lion,' the invasion of England. But the Führer postponed the operation. Pity. We just didn't have the air power after the Battle of Britain. But now he's thinking the ME 321 will be perfect for the Russian campaign. To carry men and materiel to the front.'

'How soon can you begin the production?'

'As soon as I have the requisite amount of steel and fabrics. The Führer wants 200 gliders produced by June. I will need more labour, Albert. The figures are all there.'

'You're building them in the Augsburg factory, am I right?'

'No. In the underground tunnel system in Sankt Georgen an der Gusen. That way, we can get workers from KZ Gusen I and Gusen II camps as well as Maunthausen.'

'Very well, Willy. You shall have your workers – and all the steel and fabrics you need. Give my best to Anna Maria.'

'And mine to Margarete. You should drop by sometime, Albert.'

Berlin, March 27, 1941

After two weeks of sinking her arms into hot greasy washing-up water and polishing endless stemware, Gretchen graduated to the 'prep' table. She was happy not to see another dirty dish, but she missed the company of the cross-eyed young Swabian who taught her into the best way to scrape food from a plate.

One of the sous chefs gave her a bundle of knives in a cloth holder and showed her how to sharpen them on a steel. For the next two months, she would be peeling potatoes and dicing vegetables. She would return to the family apartment at night and immediately soak her fingers in milk to get rid of the smell of onions.

As her knife skills improved, she could take her eyes off the vegetables on the chopping board in front of her and watch the chefs preparing the dishes. She got used to the heat, the sudden flashes of fire as they tossed the contents of their frying pans, and the good-natured banter among the line cooks.

Her ready smile and Aryan good looks won over the male kitchen staff, who were not used to having a female in their presence. They tempered their language and would glance sideways at her if someone swore after having burnt himself on a hot pan.

The only moment of alarm in the girl's daily routine was running the gamut of the elf-like elevator boy's leering remarks whenever she found herself near him in the staff canteen.

As the weeks passed, Gretchen was given more responsibilities. She had proven herself to be a quick learner, and was always ready to volunteer for new tasks. One day, the Chef himself approached her as she was filling a stockpot with veal bones.

'Gretchen, there is a waitress uniform in the changing room at your locker. You're to put it on.'

'But why, Chef?'

'There's a special party in the private dining room and the stupid girl slipped on some grease in the pantry and broke her arm. Now hurry along. Their food is almost ready. Come back when you've changed.'

Gretchen wiped her hands on a cloth and took off her apron. She crossed to the changing room and headed for her locker. Hung from the door handle was a wide, long skirt with a bodice, a white blouse and a multi-coloured apron. She quickly changed into the outfit and returned to the kitchen.

Gretchen had never worn a Dirndl before. Immediately, the entire male line began to whistle.

'Silence!' ordered the Chef. Turning to Gretchen he said. 'You look like a little Bavarian in that *Tracht*. Now take the soup tureen up and remember, ladle it on the sideboard and carry it one plate at a time, first to the host who will be seated at the head of the table.'

'Shouldn't the ladies be served first?' asked Gretchen.

'There are no ladies.'

Gretchen climbed the stairs to the private room that was situated to the left of the main dining room. She felt self-conscious wearing the traditional outfit, added to which was her concern about waiting on a table of men for the first time. She paused at the door and listened for a moment. She waited for the sound of laughter to die down and tried to step unobtrusively into the room.

All eyes turned towards her. Gretchen could feel the blood rush to her cheeks. With eyes downcast, she made her way to the dumb waiter and opened the hatch. But she had caught sight of the host who sat at the head of the table: Hermann Goering, resplendent in his slate grey uniform, his chest heavy with medals. At his throat hung the black Grand Cross of the Iron Cross. He smiled indulgently at her.

The chair next to Goering was empty. Seated on both sides of the table were other uniformed Nazi officers. She recognised Heinrich Himmler and Joseph Goebbels from photos she had seen in the newspapers.

A photographer stood discreetly in the corner. His camera would flash intermittently as he took shots of Goering and the other officers.

'Gentlemen, pray silence,' announced Goering, holding up his wine glass. 'We have a vision of Aryan youth in our midst.... A toast to the young people of Germany who will fulfill our Führer's destiny!'

Heads swivelled and glasses were raised.

'What is your name, child?' asked Goering.

'Gretchen, sir, Gretchen von Bismarck.'

'Capital! You hear that, a von Bismarck. Come and stand by me.'

Reluctantly, Gretchen made her way to the table, her fingers interlaced.

'Horst, a photo,' Goering called out to the photographer. '*Prost, Alle!*'

The assembled officers echoed the toast and knocked back their wine as the camera's light bulb flashed.

Beet red, Gretchen backed to the dumb waiter, praying that the bell would ring signalling the arrival of the soup tureen. She saw Himmler lean across to Goering and whisper something. She thought she heard him mention the name Geli Raubal.

Goering was staring at her, his eyes half closed as if he was trying to fix the image of her face in his mind. She didn't know where to look; her hands were shaking and the lacing of her bodice felt like a vice tightening across her chest. Gretchen steeled herself. 'Please don't let me faint.' She turned away and gripped the ledge of the dumb waiter, pressing her forehead against the wood panelling.

The corpulent commander-in-chief of the Luftwaffe turned back to the table and announced: 'Gentlemen, I have some news that is worthy of another toast. Vienna is almost cleared of Jews, and now it is the turn of Berlin.'

A spontaneous cheer went up from the other officers.

At that moment the door burst open and the late guest entered the room. Approaching the table to take the empty chair, he said: 'Apologies for my late arrival, Reichsmarshall, and to all of you. Office business.'

Then, Albert Speer took his seat next to Hermann Goering.

Berlin, March 28, 1941

Each of the kitchen staff at the Hotel Adlon had their own pigeon-hole by the tradesmen's entrance for personal messages. Here, they picked up their wage envelopes, circular memos from management detailing their shifts and protocols regarding evacuation procedures. There was also news of a luxurious bomb shelter currently under construction in the basement; but this, as was underlined in the memo, would be for the hotel guests only. Next time the air raid sirens sounded, the staff would have to make their own arrangements.

The morning after Gretchen had waited on Hermann Goering and his entourage of Nazi officers, she found an envelope in her slot.

It was a handwritten letter from Albert Speer. In the top left hand corner of the cream-coloured paper was the emblem of the Nazi party – an eagle with its wings spread wide; in its claws it held a wreath with a giant swastika in the centre.

'My dear Fraulein von Bismarck, I cannot tell you how surprised and delighted I was to see you at Reich Marshal Goering's luncheon party. If I didn't acknowledge your presence – as someone who knows you well from my visits to your home – I must apologise. Please don't think me rude. I was only thinking of your safety.'

'After you left, you were the subject of much conversation around the table, in the most flattering terms. So much so that the Reich Marshal suggested there may be a more significant role you can play in the advancement of the aims of the Third Reich.'

'Since your father is a colleague in my firm, I volunteered to approach you on behalf of the Reich Marshal to see if you would agree to meet with me at on April 1 at 11 a.m. to discuss a certain matter. I have been in touch with your employer, Herr Spangler, to alert him that you will need time off work. If you call my secretary Frau Kempf at the number below, she will have a car collect you from the hotel and transport you to my office. The driver will escort you back later.'

'I think you will be excited by the remunerative project the Reich Marshal has in mind and I look forward to seeing you.'

'Warmest regards and my best to your father and mother. They would be very proud of you to have been chosen like this.'

'Albert Speer.'

Rüdesheim am Rhein, March 29, 1941

A tall woman with frizzy blonde hair and dark roots sat on the edge of her bed in the topmost room of the Schwann Gasthaus in Rüdesheim am Rhein.

She unpinned her maid's cap and placed it on the night table along with her brass nameplate: Krista Becker, *Kammerzofe*.

She took up a copy of *Das Reich*, the weekly newspaper founded by Joseph Goebbels, and studied the photo on the front page. It showed Reich Marshal Hermann Goering seated at a table in full uniform smiling up at a beautiful blonde girl dressed in a dirndl. The photographer caught her frowning in concentration as she placed a bowl of soup in front of him.

The caption under the photo read: 'Reich Marshal Hermann Goering awes young Berlin Hotel Adlon waitress at a party celebrating the Führer's signature on Directive 27 ordering the assault on Yugoslavia.'

She reached for a pair of scissors and carefully cut out the photo. Taking a scrapbook from her suitcase under the bed and a pot of glue from the windowsill, she opened to a blank page and stuck the photo in. In pen, she noted the date: March 28, 1941.

Berlin, April 1, 1941

Gretchen stood with her back to the bomb-blast wall at the entrance to Hotel Adlon. The wall was now completed and stood a good two feet taller than her. Frau Kempf had said the car would arrive at 10.30 that Tuesday morning. It was 10.15. Each car that passed with a Nazi pennant flying from its right mudguard she thought might be for her.

Her mind was full of questions. What was it that the Reich Marshal had in mind for her? Would it mean leaving the Aldon kitchen just as she was to be moved to the line to do some real cooking? Would her parents be proud of her, as Herr Speer had written? And who was Geli Raubal, the woman whose name Herr Himmler had whispered to the Reich Marshal?

A black 1939 Horch Type 930 V8 without any markings pulled up in front of her. The driver leaned across to the passenger door and opened it from his seat, beckoning her inside.

Gretchen stooped to look at the driver.

'Are you from Herr Speer?'

The young man in a grey suit and open-neck white shirt nodded.

'Get in, Fraulein. I'm not allowed to park here.'

Gretchen slid into the passenger seat and studied the man's profile. He couldn't have been more than twenty, and she wondered why he wasn't in uniform. According to the radio broadcasts, the Reich had mobilised all young men in preparation for a new offensive.

As he was about to pull away from the curb, the car stalled.

'*Scheiss*,' muttered the driver.

Gretchen stifled her giggles.

'I'm not used to this car,' protested the young man.

'You mean you're not Herr Speer's driver?'

'I'm his nephew. He asked me to pick you up and take you to his office. I don't know why.'

So this is not official, thought Gretchen. They want to keep it a secret.

'Are you an architect too?'

'Not yet. I'm a student.'

He kept his eyes on the road as he drove.

'What's your name?'

'Kurt. Kurt Arndorfer.'

'Are you a Berliner?'

'Now, yes. My family is from Bremen.'

'Are you in the army?'

'I am the Berlin leader of the Hitler Youth,' he replied proudly.

There was silence between them until Kurt said: 'And you? What are you doing for the war effort?"

'I – I have a mission chosen for me by Reichs Marshal Goering.'

She wondered what made her say that. Was she trying to impress the young man?

Kurt whistled. 'Mission? What mission?'

'*Feind hört mit*,' said Gretchen, repeating a phrase she had heard on the radio.

'I'm listening, but I'm not the enemy,' replied Kurt, laughing. 'You know what the English say, "Loose lips sink ships."'

He began to flap his lower lip with his forefinger.

Gretchen laughed. 'I can't tell you because I don't know yet. This is what the meeting with Herr Speer is about.'

Kurt pulled the car up on Lindenallee outside Albert Speer's office in the Berlin's West End.

'I will wait for you here, Fraulein,' said Kurt.

'Gretchen, call me Gretchen, Kurt. You make me laugh.'

'Good luck with your mission, Gretchen. I'll take you back to the hotel.'

He flapped his lower lip with his forefinger again.

Gretchen studied the façade of the three-storey building. She had visited the office where her father worked many times, waiting patiently for him to roll up his drawings and secure them with elastic bands before slipping them into a container that looked like an umbrella stand next to his desk.

His office was on the second floor. Albert Speer's was above. Its huge atelier-like windows provided the maximum natural light and from them you could see the river.

She glanced back at Kurt and gave him a wave, moving slowly to the door so as not to reveal the excitement she felt. Shivers of exhilaration vibrated in her stomach as she speculated on what this meeting would hold for her future.

Discreetly, she checked that the seams of her stockings were straight. She patted her hair before ascending the narrow staircase to where the receptionist sat behind a glass-topped desk. She was a blonde girl with rosy cheeks and a ready smile, not much older than Gretchen.

'Hello, Birgit.'

'*Guten tag*, Gretchen, what brings you here?'

'I have an appointment with Herr Speer,' Gretchen announced, feeling very grown-up and business-like. 'Is my father in today?'

'I believe he's with Herr Speer now. I'll let them know you're here.'

The receptionist pressed a key on the intercom next to her typewriter.

'Frau Kempf, Gretchen von Bismarck is in reception. Shall I send her up?'

The disembodied voice of Albert Speer's secretary answered in the affirmative.

Gretchen nodded her thanks and climbed the wrought-iron spiral staircase that led up to the architect's office.

The entire top floor of the building was an open plan-drafting room. The two men were leaning over the largest of the drawing boards. Speer's secretary sat in an office at one corner.

'Ah Gretchen, thank you for coming,' said Speer.

She crossed to her father, kissed him on the cheek and then shook hands with Speer.

'I have told your father what I am about to tell you in general terms, so you might want to discuss it later in private between the two of you.'

He turned to his secretary. 'Frau Kempf, would you mind getting us some coffee. You do take coffee don't, you or would you prefer some fruit juice?'

'Coffee would be lovely,' said Gretchen. She glanced at her father, as she was not allowed coffee at home.

'Please come and sit.'

Gretchen settled herself on a straight-backed leather chair. The coffee table was strewn with architectural magazines.

'Herr von Bismarck, if you'll excuse us.'

Gretchen glanced at her father, trying to read his expression. Why was he not to be a party to their conversation? Herr Speer had said he had discussed the matter with him, but she would have liked to have her father's reassuring presence.

'Of course,' said her father. 'Gretchen, I'm staying in Berlin tonight. We can have dinner together. They have the blood sausage you like at Zur Letzten Instanz on Waisenstrasse. You finish at six, I believe. I'll come by the hotel and we can walk there together.'

'That would be lovely, Papa.'

Gretchen could read nothing in her father's face, but there was a note of sadness in his smile as he walked ramrod-straight towards the staircase.

Speer waited for his assistant to be out of earshot. Turing to Gretchen, he said: 'My dear, you made quite an impression on the Reich Marshal and his staff.'

'Thank you,' said Gretchen, lowering her eyes.

'Goering was talking about having you work with Goebbels. He wants to have you photographed for the cover of a new booklet to be distributed to every member of the League of German Girls.'

He paused and waited for her reaction.

'I don't know what to say.'

Speer nodded.

'That is all very well and no doubt very flattering,' he continued, 'but your talents go beyond being a mere poster girl. I have observed you and the way you taste food. I suspect you have an uncommon ability when it comes to flavours and sensory perception. Am I right?'

'I do smell things other people don't seem to smell.'

'Quite. The question is, would you be willing to put your nose and palate at the service of the Führer?'

Gretchen frowned. 'I don't understand.'

Speer leaned forward. He was about to speak when Frau Kempf arrived with a tray.

'Gretchen, would you mind, moving those magazines,' asked the secretary.

'Don't worry,' snapped Speer. 'Just put the tray on top.'

Frau Kempf gave a cough of displeasure and placed the tray with exaggerated care on top of the magazines. 'There's sugar and milk.'

'Yes, yes,' said Speer impatiently and dismissed her with a wave of his hand.

He made no move to pick up his cup, so Gretchen waited for his cue. Her parents never served her coffee at home and she was looking forward to tasting it for the first time.

'What I have to tell you is in the strictest confidence. You will treat the information as a state secret. This means you cannot, under pain of imprisonment, divulge what I am about to tell you to another living soul. Do I make myself clear, Gretchen?'

The girl nodded, her eyes widening in alarm.

'As I said, I have discussed this with your father only in the broadest terms. He knows nothing of the specifics of what I am about to tell you. All he knows is that you have been chosen for a special assignment, one that is of the utmost consequence to our country. You cannot even tell him the nature of this assignment. Do I have your word on that?'

Gretchen nodded her head vigorously, desperate to hear what could be so important that even her father was not permitted to know.

'There will, of course, be an assessment of your abilities, and if you pass that test there will be more training. But first there will be a thorough background check on you by the Gestapo. Is there anything in your past that might come up that could be viewed as unfavourable? Any skeletons in the closet, so to speak?'

Gretchen bit her bottom lip. 'I was asked to leave my finishing school in Switzerland. But it wasn't my fault. They thought I was spying for Germany just because I took some photographs.'

Speer laughed.

'Yes, your father told me about that. Anything else? For instance, do you have any Jewish friends?'

She was about to say she shared a room with a Jewish girl at Lyceum Bern, but this might compromise the possibility of an exciting new job, maybe being a private chef, cooking for Herr Goering. So she merely shook her head, rationalising to herself that Shona Rosenberg couldn't really be called a friend. She hadn't chosen to room with her. The decision to have her as a roommate was made for her.

'Will you tell me what it is, Herr Speer? Please don't keep me on tenterhooks.'

The architect sighed and nodded his head.

'As you know, if Germany is to lead the fight against bolshevism and create a new world order, we must protect the Führer whose vision it is. There are forces in England and America who plot against our leader's welfare. There have been attempts on his life, assassination attempts. His bodyguards can protect him from bullets, but where do you think he is most vulnerable?'

Gretchen shrugged her shoulders.

'At the dinner table, young lady. They have tried to poison his food. So a team of tasters with extraordinary sensitivities – like yours – has been assembled to taste everything that is put on the table for him. You understand what I'm saying?'

'Yes, Herr Speer.'

'As you know the Führer is vegetarian and he does not take wine. So you will only taste meatless dishes. His tastes are simple. For instance, he has the same breakfast every morning. Coffee, bread and marmalade.'

How boring, Gretchen thought.

'And he only eats vegetables. Piles of vegetables, either raw or pulped to a puree.'

Oh my God. It sounded like baby food. She tried to keep a straight face.

'You will be part of a team, Gretchen,' continued Speer. 'You will work in rotation, but you will never divulge what the Führer eats, where he eats, when he eats, with whom he eats and what his favourite foods are.... Well, what do you say?'

Gretchen shook her head in bewilderment.

'You mean, I will be near the Führer?'

'Yes, child. If you pass the test. And if you say 'yes,' contracts will be drawn up governing your remuneration, your hours of service, and your obligations. And I repeat. There will be no word of our conversation here to anyone. Not even your parents. Do you have any questions?'

'When is the test?'

'You will hear from me in due course. It may take some time, so be patient. Congratulations, Gretchen. Your life will never be the same.'

She left the office in a daze. As she descended the stairs she realised that she never did get to taste the coffee.

Kurt held the passenger door open for her.

'Well?'

'Well what?'

'What did Herr Speer want? You know my uncle is probably the second most powerful man in Germany after the Führer.'

'Is that how you got to be the Berlin leader of the Hitler Youth?'

Kurt looked genuinely hurt.

'I'm sorry,' said Gretchen. 'I was only teasing…they want me to pose for some magazine.'

'Without your clothes?'

Gretchen gave him a playful slap on the arm.

'No, silly.'

It was then she recalled she had not asked the question that was uppermost in her mind: who is Geli Raubal?

As the day wore on, Gretchen could not concentrate on the potatoes she was peeling. Her mind kept replaying the conversation she had had with Speer. She longed to discuss it with her father and have him advise her. But she had given her word that she would not divulge the proposition he had put to her.

After work, she waited on the sidewalk outside the hotel for her father to arrive. How would she express her concern about not being totally honest with him regarding her conversation with Albert Speer?

As these thoughts crossed her mind, Gretchen became aware of a tall blonde woman in a shabby coat on the other side of the road. The woman was staring at her and seemed uncertain as to whether she should step into the traffic.

Just then her father arrived. He raised his hat, a courtesy that always amused her, and he kissed her on the cheek. Gretchen looked back to where the woman had been standing. But she had disappeared.

'I hope you're hungry,' said her father, taking her arm and leading her in the direction of Zur Letzten Instanz.

'It's the oldest restaurant in Berlin, Gretchen. It dates back to 1621. Napoleon ate here and so did Beethoven.'

'You told me that the last time we came, Papa.'

Gretchen realised her father was as nervous as she was.

'Yes, I probably did. Your mother says I'm beginning to repeat myself.'

She squeezed her father's hand.

'I still love your stories.'

They walked the remainder of the way in silence until they arrived at the cobbled street that ran along the facade to the restaurant. The maître-d welcomed Herr von Bismarck by name and was about to usher them to a table when her father said, 'I think we'd like to sit at the *Stammtisch*. Where Napoleon dined.'

He winked at his daughter, who laughed. The maître-d led them to the circular table around a tiled stove where the restaurant's regulars would meet.

'So, how did the meeting go?' asked her father, once they had ordered.

'Fine. Papa, I'm not at liberty to discuss the details, but maybe as Herr Speer is a friend he'll tell you more than I'm allowed to.'

'And what are you allowed to say?'

'Only that it involves working closely with Herr Hitler.'

Von Bismarck nodded and took a sip of wine.

'Even in these difficult times, we still have the wonderful wines of the Mosel,' he said.

'Papa, you know I would love to be able to tell you, but I have given my solemn word.'

'Quite right. Herr Speer is one of the most powerful men in Germany. It would be unwise to go against his wishes. But I am only thinking of your well-being, my child. And how grown-up you have become in these last few months. It must be the war that has changed everything and made things go so much faster.'

'You've always looked after me, Papa,' said Gretchen, placing her hand over his. 'I will be careful.'

The waiter brought their plates of meatballs, blood sausage, and pig's knuckle with pickled red cabbage and potatoes.

'And when do you start this new assignment?'

'I'm waiting to hear from Herr Speer.'

They lapsed into silence again.

Gretchen put down her knife and fork and leaned towards her father.

'Papa, who is Geli Raubel?'

Von Bismarck sat bolt upright and looked around, holding the palm of his left hand towards her. He scanned the faces of the diners around them so as to see if any of them had heard his daughter's question.

'Gretchen, you must not mention that name in public,' he whispered.

'But why?'

'We cannot discuss it here. The walls have ears. We will talk outside.'

Gretchen slunk down in her seat. Why was her father so agitated? She couldn't wait for the meal to be finished. She pushed her plate away and refused dessert, even though she was looking forward to the restaurant's signature *Apfelstrudel mit Schlagsahne*.

Out in the cold evening air, von Bismarck took out a silver cigarette case and lit one. Gretchen had only seen him smoke when he was upset. He seemed to be searching for words, and when they were well away from the restaurant and there was no one within earshot, he said: 'It's important that you tell me where you heard that name?'

'Geli Raubel?'

'For heaven's sake, keep your voice down, child.'

'I'm sorry…when I was waiting on table at Herr Goering's lunch party, I heard Herr Himmler mention it.'

'He mentioned it!'

'Not to everybody. He whispered it to Herr Goering. Who is she?'

Her father sighed.

'Well, I suppose it's best if you hear it from me…. Her real name was Angela Raubel, Geli for short. She was born in Linz in Austria. She was the Führer's half niece.'

'Was?' Gretchen interrupted.

'Let me finish. Geli's mother became Hitler's housekeeper in 1925. Geli and her sister Elfriede moved into Hitler's apartment in Munich in 1929. She was enrolled in medical school, but never finished her studies. While she was living under his roof, Geli had an affair with Hitler's chauffeur, a man named Emil Maurice. Maurice had been arrested and jailed with Hitler after the Beer Hall Putsch in 1923, when Hitler tried to overthrow the Weimar government. While in prison, Hitler dictated part of *Mein Kampf* to him. Maurice was in the SS, but he had Jewish blood. His great grandfather was Jewish, which meant he isn't pure Aryan. All SS officers had to prove their racial purity back to 1750.'

He lifted the palm of his hand in a mocking salute.

'Himmler wanted him expelled from the SS, but Hitler stood by him and made him an Honorary Aryan.'

'Yes, but what about Geli Raubel?'

'I'm coming to that. Because of the affair, Maurice was dismissed as Hitler's chauffeur. And Hitler kept a close watch on Geli from then on, only allowing her out of his sight with people he trusted. She became his prisoner.'

'Poor thing.'

'She took singing lessons and began secretly seeing a man from Linz. She wanted to go there to marry him, but Hitler refused to allow her to marry and forced her to stay with him. In 1931, when he was at a meeting in Nuremberg, Geli got hold of his Walther pistol in the apartment and shot herself in the lung. She was twenty-three.'

'That's horrible,' said Gretchen.

'This is why I'm concerned for you, *liebchen.*

Berlin, June 22nd, 1941

Gretchen's eyes were watering as she chopped onions at the prep table in the Hotel Adlon kitchen. She wished Cook could see her now even though it seemed her life had been reduced to massacring vegetables.

The muscle memory of hand and wrist allowed her mind to wander while she diced the onions in even squares.

She was thinking about Kurt Andorfer and wondering if he would call. And about his uncle, Albert Speer, and why she had not heard any further word from him about the mission he had proposed to her.

And without realising why, thoughts of Geli Raubel kept coming to her mind.

What a romantic and tragic story her father had told her. It reminded her of the bedtime story he used to read to her when she was a child. It was her favourite story from a book of fairy tales by the Brothers Grimm, called *'Kinder- und Hausmärchen.'* About a beautiful blonde girl named Rapunzel who was locked high up in a tower without stairs or a door by Dame Gothel. One day, a handsome prince riding through the forest hears her singing. Falling in love with her voice, he searches for her only to find that he cannot reach her. The only access is to use her hair as a rope; so he calls out to her, Rapunzel, Rapunzel, let down your hair, so that I may climb your golden stair.

At this point in the story, Karl von Bismarck would lean over her and shake his head, so that his thinning hair would fall forward and tickle her nose. She would giggle and beg him to read that passage again and again.

As she chopped mechanically, she wondered if Kurt Andorfer was the prince who would rescue her.

Rüdesheim am Rhein, September 1, 1941

K rista Becker took off her hat and threw it on the bed. She picked up the copy of *Reichsgestzblatt* she had just purchased and read the story on the front page.

The headline proclaimed: 'Police Regulation on the Labelling of Jews.' In smaller type: 'Jewish people of six years and older are forbidden to show themselves in public without a Jewish star.'

The story went on to state the size, shape and colour required, that the star must contain the word 'Jew' and where it must be worn. 'He who violates articles 1 & 2 willingly or carelessly shall be punished with a fine up to 150 Reichsmark or with imprisonment not to exceed 6 weeks. Further protective measures on the part of the police as well as rules according to which a more severe punishment is permitted remain unaffected.'

The picture showed the six-pointed Star of David with the word 'Jew' in the centre spelled out in mock-Hebraic type and circled in black.

The final paragraph stated that the problem of the Berlin Jews was to await the conclusion of the Russian campaign at which time it would be solved in a 'generous fashion.'

Berlin, October 30, 1941

A lbert Speer was conflicted about Hitler's decision to launch Operation Typhoon to advance on Moscow.

The operation was initiated on October 2nd following some early successes. The 3rd and 4th Panzer armies captured Odessa after a 73-day siege. Four days later, German troops took Kharkov and on October 30th reached the strategic Crimea Peninsula port city of Sevastopol.

As a student of history, Speer had read about Napoleon's Russian campaign that ended in an ignominious retreat. The country was just too big for Operation Barbarossa. Supply lines and communications were stretched to the limit. And then there was Russia's natural ally – winter.

Earlier that year, Speer heard from an army adjutant that the Führer had taken the globe in the living room of his Berghof residence and drawn a pencil line from north to south along the Ural Mountains. This, he announced, was to be the border between Germany's sphere of influence and that of Japan. The Soviet Union would crumble before his Panzer armies, and Bolshevism would be defeated.

Speer complained in private to his wife that the resources earmarked for the invasion of Russia would mean that his plans to build monuments to the Third Reich would be put on hold. But he kept his own counsel and concentrated on his drawings.

Berlin: November 2, 1941

Kurt Andorfer tried to block out thoughts of Gretchen von Bismarck. His role in the Hitler Youth had changed dramatically since Hitler had ordered that children of school age in Berlin and Hamburg, and other cities subjected to nightly air raids, be relocated to safer areas in Bavaria, Saxony and Prussia.

Those who did not have relatives with whom they could stay were accommodated in childrens' camps run by the National Socialist Teachers' league. Or they would be temporarily fostered out to ethic or pro-German families in Denmark, Latvia, Croatia, Hungary, Bulgaria, Slokavakia and Poland.

The task of settling these children in the countryside or abroad was given to the National Socialist People's Welfare agency. They, in turn, contacted the leaders of the Hitler Youth Movement to assist in the relocation of children between the ages of 10 and 14.

Not only were there logistical problems of finding adequate accommodation, but also the task of assembling thousands of frightened children at consolidation points around the city for transportation to the train stations. And then marshalling them aboard.

All of this while dealing with tearful parents.

Kurt's special task was to identify children of 'proper attitude and performance' who would be sent to Hungary, Czechoslovakia and Denmark to act as junior ambassadors for the Third Reich.

His orders were to draw up lists of children of German blood for evacuation – as long as they were not suffering from infectious diseases or epilepsy. 'Maladjusted antisocial youths' were to be rejected, as were children of Jewish parents.

Kurt realized that any thought of being reunited with Gretchen von Bismarck would have to be put on hold for the moment. Especially since he had been ordered to the children's camp in Reichsgau Wartheland (annexed Poland) to help the director with the children's leisure activities.

Berlin: December 7, 1941

Albert Speer was about to take his place at the family dinner table, when the front door bell rang.

'I'll get it,' said his wife. 'You eat. It'll get cold.'

Speer pushed the pork schnitzel away. The morning's briefing paper informed him that the Soviet army had started a major counter-offensive around Moscow. German supply lines were extended beyond their ability to cope. The snow had turned the roads to mud and made it impossible for a consistent delivery of fuel for the Panzer divisions and the troop carriers.

'It's the adjutant with more papers,' said Margarete. 'He needs you to sign for them.... Why must they come at dinner time?'

Speer said nothing. He went to the door, signed for the brief case, gave the adjutant a half-hearted salute and returned to the table.

'Must you read it at dinner?'

Speer did not hear his wife's complaint. His eyes widened as he read the opening paragraph.

At 7.48 am this morning Hawaiian time, a Japanese attack force took off from six aircraft carriers 370 kilometres north of Oahu and bombed and torpedoed the United States Pacific Fleet at Pearl Harbour. There was no communication alerting the Führer before the attack. Four US battleships were sunk and another four badly damaged. Three cruisers, three destroyers, an anti-aircraft training ship and one minelayer were either sunk or damaged. 188 US aircraft were destroyed and the loss of life was heavy, although it is too soon give an accurate estimate. Japanese losses were light: 29 aircraft and five midget submarines were lost.

Immediately, Speer's quick mind grasped the political implications of this surprise strike. For Hitler, it could not have come at a better time. Operation Barbarossa had stalled in the snows of winter and the determined defence by the Russian armies. Now Hitler's ally in the East would preoccupy the United States in the Pacific and British troops would be committed to defend Britain's Asian possessions.

But it would mean that the United States, with all its vast resources, would no longer be a spectator and would become a full combatant in the Second World War.

Potsdam, December 24, 1941

'Today is a time for peace,' said Graf von Bismarck as his wife Greta and his daughter Gretchen took their places for their Christmas dinner. 'There will be no mention of the Japanese bombing of Pearl Harbour or of our offensive in Russia. We are here to celebrate our family and the blessings we have. Now let us say grace.'

Gretchen bowed her head and while her father uttered the prayer she allowed her mind to wander. The Christmas tree that had been brought into the house was fully decorated with hand-blown glass ornaments by her mother and the gifts laid underneath. The traditional fruited yeast bread, Stollen, had its prize place at the centre of the table.

They had sung the carols she loved, *O Tannenbaum, Ihr Kinderlein Kommet* and *Stille Nacht*. But something was wrong. She wondered why the excitement she usually experienced on this festive night was missing.

She had not heard from Kurt in weeks. Could he have found another girl-friend?

Cook arrived with a large platter of a goose sitting on a bed of vegetables and placed it with satisfaction in front of the master of the house. He smiled appreciatively up at her.

'How amazing you are, Cook, to have secured a goose for our dinner in these times of want.'

Greta, his wife frowned.

'The gardener shot it on my instructions, my dear.'

'Ah,' said von Bismarck, taking up the carving set. 'And perhaps we should allow Gretchen to have a glass of wine. After all, she is a working woman now.'

Linz: January 13, 1942

Dear Gretchen,
I have given this letter to a friend of mine who is returning to Berlin to hand it to you personally, so that it won't go through the censors.

You may have wondered why I haven't been in touch. Believe me I tried but these few last weeks have been very difficult. You are aware, I'm sure, of the relocation of German children from the major cities to the countryside, to get them away from the bombing. Well, Hitler Youth leaders have been ordered to accompany them to the camps where they are staying for at least six months till the war is over. Thank goodness, I will be relieved after a two-month stay, and I'm counting the days.

The camp where I am is near a city called Linz in Austria. It's almost 600 kilometres from Berlin. There are some 200 boys here aged between ten and fourteen. I work with the camp director who is a teacher. I have a 61-page manual that sets out my duties and responsibilities. It reads like a military training manual.

We wake the kids up at 6.30 and they wash and get into their uniforms. Before breakfast there is the flag-raising ceremony, and then there are classes from 8 am till noon. Lunch and a one-hour rest period before the outdoor activities, mainly sports and games. In the evening, there are sing-songs and propaganda newsreels before bed at 9 pm. Some of the older boys are trained to march and shoot. The SS is training them to become members of the Waffen-SS. As you can imagine, many of the boys are homesick and miss their mothers. At night, I can hear some of the younger boys crying into their pillows.

I miss you and hope you are well, and that it won't be long before I can see you again. In the meantime, don't forget me.

Your friend,
Kurt.

Berlin, March 13th, 1942

On that day, the coldest in Berlin since 1888, an order came directly from Hitler that a series of military camps were to be set up throughout Germany to provide three weeks of mandatory training for all boys aged 16 to 18

Kurt Andorfer had only been back in Berlin for three days.

As the Berlin leader of the Hitler Youth, he was in charge of setting up a training facility in the Grosser Tiergarten, the capital's central park.

While Kurt was happy not having to send out his young charges as mailmen delivering draft notices along with the new monthly ration cards or collecting scrap metals for the war effort, he felt there was a void in his own life. Something that even this testing, new organisational role would not satisfy.

Also, he was concerned that the boys under his command were being recruited by the home guard to operate anti-aircraft batteries. Positioned at the top of towers and tall buildings with only helmets and sandbags to protect them, they were exposed nightly to enemy fire from the sky.

Every time this feeling of emptiness came on him, the image of the girl he had driven to his uncle's office kept surfacing in his mind. Lying awake at night as reflections of the searchlights outside played across the ceiling, he conjured up her face and realised that what he was missing was female companionship. He had kept her father's telephone number and had almost dialled it on several occasions, but somehow he got distracted or lost courage at the last moment.

But hearing the air raid sirens wailing in the night, he realised that life in Berlin had become a lottery. He might be next. Or worse, she might. He should make the call. But would she be interested? Kurt had never tried to date a woman before. Maybe she was too young for him, he rationalised. Sleep was a long time coming.

Berlin, August 30, 1942

D r. Theodore Morell, Hitler's personal physician, rubbed his hands with glee. He had just heard on *Reichs-Rundfunk-Gesellschaft*, Germany's national broadcasting service, that the Third Reich had officially annexed Luxembourg.

Morell had been considering opening a factory in Luxembourg to produce his own patented drug, Vitamultin. He already had pharmaceutical manufacturing plants in Hamburg, Czechoslovakia, Romania and Russia – thanks to his wealthy clientele and, most importantly, the patronage of Germany's leader.

Heinrich Hoffmann, Hitler's photographer, had not only introduced the Führer to Geli Raubel, but also to the doctor whose unorthodox medical procedures, he was convinced, had saved his life. Such was Dr. Morell's international reputation that he was approached by both the Shah of Persia and the King of Romania to be their personal physician – invitations he had turned down.

Having successfully treated Hitler in 1936 for severe stomach cramps and a persistent leg rash with a course of complex vitamins and hydrolyzed *E. coli* bacteria, Hitler had hailed him as a medical genius and instated him within his social circle.

Obese and ugly, with a body odour as bad as Hitler's and halitosis that could drop a cat at three paces, Morell was viewed with both suspicion and envy by the medical fraternity, who considered his outlandish drug treatments to be detrimental to the Führer's health.

But as long as he kept the Nazi leader healthy, or at least functioning, his star was in the ascendancy.

The trick was to convince Hitler that the daily injections and pill regimen worked, and that he was the man to administer them.

Potsdam, December 31, 1942

K arl von Bismarck raised his glass of Sekt and clinked glasses with his wife Greta and his daughter Gretchen.

'Prosit!' they said in unison.

They had eaten the traditional New Year's cheese fondue and were strangely silent at the table, each wrapped in their own thoughts.

Gretchen was wishing she could have seen in the new year with Kurt. Greta wondered how she could keep the household running with the dwindling food supplies available in the local stores; and the head of the family worried about the safety of his wife and daughter.

Before the war, they would have set off fireworks in the grounds of the estate and invited the neighbouring families to witness the spectacle. But with bombing of Berlin, von Bismarck thought it would have been disrespectful to indulge in the customary pyrotechnics.

Besides, there was nothing to celebrate. Certainly not, when it came to the conduct of the war. Rommel's Afrika Korps was trapped in Tunisia and over 230,000 German and Italian troops were taken prisoners. A quarter of a million German troops of General Friedrich Paulus' army were surrounded at Stalingrad. And the governor of pro-Vichy French Somaliland had surrendered to British and Free French forces.

Greta had earlier performed their annual New Year's Eve ritual of melting a small piece of lead in a spoon held over a candle. She dropped the molten lead into a glass of water and the solidified shapes would reveal what the year ahead would hold in store for the family.

'It looks like butterflies!' exclaimed Gretchen.

To Karl von Bismarck, the pieces spread out on a white napkin looked like dead soldiers lying in the snows of Stalingrad.

Villa Speer, Schloss–Wolfsbrunnenweg, Heidelberg, March 7th, 1943

Margarete Speer sat on the floor of the spacious living room of the family's summer home. Spread out on the carpet were photo albums of her six children. Four of them were sitting cross-legged around her, listening to her stories as she pointed to each picture.

Speer had had his family evacuated there – 630 kilometres south-west of Berlin – when the Allied bombing of the capital became a nightly occurrence.

Albert the eldest, born in 1934, Hilde (1936), Fritz (1937), Margret (1938); the two youngest, Arnold (1940) and Ernst (1942), named for his father's brother were upstairs in the day nursery with the nanny.

Margarete was in constant contact with her husband by a secured landline, although she relied on him calling her; when she tried to dial him, she could hardly ever find him at his desk.

How she wished he was there with the children to walk along the banks of the River Neckar and not have to see bomb craters in the streets and charred buildings.

Their conversations were short and impersonal, though her husband sounded exhausted most of the time. She reminded him to take his pills and to stop for proper meals. She worried about his laundry and gave strict instuctions to his secretary Frau Kempf to make sure that he had clean shirts to wear.

She sprang up at the sound of the phone and rushed to the instrument on the hall table, fearful that any call might be the message that she dreaded to hear.

'Hallo…oh, thank goodness it's you. I shake whenever the phone rings. Are you all right?'

'I'm fine, Margarete. How are the children?'

'They're all well. Margaret lost a front tooth this morning. I told her if she put it under her pillow the *Zahnfee* would come and leave a little present. She's very excited.'

'Is she there?'

'No, she's upstairs having a nap. How are things in Berlin?'

'Much the same. I have to go to the Rhur tomorrow to inspect the damage to a ball-bearing factory.'

'Is there any chance you could come here? For a weekend? For a day even?'

'You know I'd love to, Margarete, but I have to be in constant touch with the Führer. Soon, I promise. Give the children my love.... Goodbye.'

She replaced the receiver and sighed deeply. Since their physical separation he had taken to calling her Margarete, instead of his pet name for her.

She wondered if there was another woman.

Berlin, May 22, 1943

Saturday night and Gretchen had drawn the short straw. She was on the line for the evening shift preparing the salads, her least favorite kitchen task. Chef had placed her there out of some lingering spite, she was sure, because of the publicity she had received by being photographed with Goering.

Someone had clipped the picture out of the newspaper and pinned it up on the staff noticeboard in the communal dining room. Chef had angrily torn it down.

Mechanically, she went about cutting the tails off the radishes and deseeding the tomatoes. She wondered whatever happened to the highly secretive job that Herr Speer had spoken to her about two years before. There had been no follow-up call, nothing. But she was working her way up in the Adlon's kitchen, and that was her main concern right now.

Berlin, May 30, 1943

Albert Speer reread the letter that Frau Kempf had placed in front of him for his signature.

From THE REICH MINISTER FOR ARMAMENTS AND MUNITIONS

Berlin-Charlottenburg 2

To the Reichs Führer SS and Chief of German Police, Himmler

Re: Iron and steel quota for SS, especially Auschwitz concentraion camp

Dear Party Comrade Himmler!

On the basis of the reports in front of me and the inspection of the Auschwitz concentration camp by my Messrs. Desch and Sander, I am prepared, over and above the iron and steel quantities allocated to you for the third quarter of 1943 (in the amounts of 450 tons per month to cover requirements within the Reich territory, and 180 tons per month for requirements in the adjacent and occupied territories) to make a once-only allowance of the following quantities :

1000 tons of iron and steel acquisition rights

1000 tons of cast steel tubes, for which the SS is to make available 300 tons of iron and steel acquisition rights from its overall allotment

Approximately 100 tons of half-inch water piping from the disposition stocks of the Plenipotentiary-General for Construction in Hamm

The requisite quantity of 8–20 mm hardened steel rods

These quantities of iron and steel are to be used only for the expansion (or construction) of the concentration camps, particularly Auschwitz. Unfortunately, I cannot allocate further iron and steel quotas for temporary construction requirements incurred by raising the new Waffen SS divisions. The requirement will have to be drawn from the overall iron and steel quota quantities allocated to the SS by the Plenipotentiary-General for Construction. Individual allocation issues are to be determined between your authorities and my own raw materials office. The requisition of acquisition certificates for one thousand tons of cast steel pipes and the dispatch of the water piping have already been set in motion.

Heil Hitler

Yours truly,

Speer.

He pondered for a moment and then took up a pen and added at the bottom: 'I was pleased that the inspection of the other concentration camps yielded a completely positive picture.'

Speer had sent his advisors, Friedreich Desch and Armin Sander, to investigate a number of concentration camps around Germany and Poland, including Auschwitz. On the day they visited Auschwitz, 900 Polish Jews died in the gas chamber.

For Speer the gas chambers were troubling. He would rather the inmates of the camp be put to work to help build the new Germany. After the Russian debacle and the reversals in the desert campaign, he needed manpower to support the war machine.

He sighed as he put his signature to the letter. That steel could have been more usefully used in building tanks for the Russian offensive.

He leant back in his chair and closed his eyes thinking about the Soviet T-34 tank captured by Germany's 3rd and 4th Panzer armies during 'Operation Typhoon,' the attack on Moscow. The tank had been shipped back to Berlin for study as it was judged to be far superior to the Panzer IV's machines in terms of firepower, mobility and ruggedness. In his accompanying report from the Russian front, General Heinz Guderian had written: 'Our Panzer IV tanks with their short 75 mm guns could only explode a T-34 by hitting the engine from behind.'

Field Marshal Paul Ludwig Ewald von Kleist had added a note in his own hand: 'This is the finest tank in the world, vastly superior to our German armour.'

Intrigued, Speer had insisted on inspecting it himself and had driven it around for hours, marvelling at its design.

Fraulein Kampf put her head around the door.

'Herr, Speer, excuse me but you asked me to remind you about the von Bismarck girl.'

Speer frowned. It had been more than two years since he had spoken to Gretchen about the food tasting position. Nothing had happened, but the Führer had a lot to deal with. A new food taster would be at the bottom of his list. Then, surprisingly, the call had come through – send her for the test.

'Ah yes. Send a note to her employer…, what's his name?'

Speer snapped his fingers in an attempt to jog his memory; but the sudden realisation that he was mimicking Hitler drew him up short and he gave an involuntary shiver.

'His name is Herr Direktor Spangler,' replied his secretary. 'Are you all right, Herr Speer?'

'Yes, yes. Just a sudden draft.'

'I hope you're not coming down with a cold. There's a lot of it going around. My aunt has been coughing for –'

'I'm sorry to hear that,' interjected Speer. 'Tell Herr Spangler that Fraulein von Bismarck is to report to Arthur Kannenberg at the Reich Ministry of Public Enlightenment and Propaganda at the Ordenspalais on Wilhelmplatz on Tuesday. He probably knows the building, but remind him it's right across from the Reich Chancellery. Fraulein von Bismarck is to present herself at 10 a.m. Spangler can expect her to be absent for the rest of the day.'

Potsdam, May 10, 1943

Carl von Bismarck climbed the stairs to the attic of his house, ensured the blackout curtains covered the single window and turned on the light bulb.

From a trunk he took out a small short wave receiver and plugged it in. He put on a pair of headphones, and while he waited for the tubes to glow he thought about his wife's warning: he should not be listening to the BBC. The home guard was monitoring the area, picking up radio signals and arresting anyone caught tuning in to enemy broadcasts.

But von Bismarck wanted to learn what was happening in the war. He had the ideal source for information close to him but he didn't trust his employer, Albert Speer, to feed him anything but the party line. And all he heard on German radio were the propaganda speeches from the Nazi high command designed to boost civilian morale.

As the set crackled to life, he turned down the volume and pressed the headphones against his ears. He heard the familiar station identification: the opening bars of Beethoven's Fifth Symphony played on the timpani – the letter V in Morse code, three dots and a dash – da-da-da DAHH. Churchill had adopted the V for Victory sign. How devilishly clever of the British to use our own Beethoven against us, he thought.

'Good evening, this is the BBC World Service broadcasting to you from London. Tonight we are retransmitting information that has come to us from the Polish underground radio station Swit. On Monday, April 19, the Jewish feast of Passover, over 2000 Waffen SS soldiers under the command of SS General Jürgen Stroop attacked with tanks, artillery and flame throwers. A fierce battle erupted between the heavily armed Germans and 1200 Jews armed with smuggled in pistols, rifles, a few machine guns, grenades and Molotov cocktails.'

'The first attack by the SS was repulsed by the Jews, leaving 12 Germans dead. The Germans renewed the attack, but found it difficult to kill or capture the small battle groups of Jews, who would fight, then retreat through a maze of cellars, sewers and other hidden passageways to escape capture.'

'On the fifth day of the battle, an infuriated Himmler ordered the SS to comb out the ghetto "with the greatest severity and relentless tenacity." SS General Stroop decided to burn down the entire ghetto, block by block.

'A report filed by Stroop described the scene: "The Jews stayed in the burning buildings until, because of the fear of being burned alive, they jumped down from the upper stories.... With their bones broken, they still tried to crawl across the street into buildings which had not yet been set on fire.... Despite the danger of being burned alive the Jews and bandits often preferred to return into the flames rather than risk being caught by us."'

'The burnings and renewed German attacks continued, but the Jews in Warsaw resisted for a total of 28 days.'

'On May 16th, amid the relentless German assault, the Jewish resistance finally ended. Stroop sent a battle report stating, "The former Jewish quarter of Warsaw is no longer in existence. The large-scale action was terminated at 2015 hours by blowing up the Warsaw synagogue.... Total number of Jews dealt with: 56,065, including both Jews caught and Jews whose extermination can be proved."'

'Polish sources estimated 300 Germans were killed and 1000 wounded. The result of the Battle was: several thousand Jews were killed, burnt alive, suffocated by gas and about twenty-five thousand were deported to the concentration camps of Trawniki, Poniatow, Majdanek and Lublin. Only the ruins of buildings, destroyed by mines, cannons and fires remain where the Ghetto once stood. The Warsaw Ghetto is now one big cemetery.'

Carl von Bismarck took the headphones off.

He shook his head and said to himself, 'May God have mercy on them.'

Berlin, June 1, 1943

Arthur Kannenberg, as round as a beach ball and as bouncy, danced around the dining room of the Ministry of Public Enlightenment and Propaganda on the tips of his toes. Strapped to his chest was a large accordion on which he was playing a Bavarian polka.

His wife Freda watched indulgently, while three spectators sat in glum silence – a middle-aged woman wearing a feathered hat, a slender young woman dressed in a dark blue skirt to her knees, a white short-sleeved blouse and a black neckerchief held in place by a plaited leather toggle (the uniform of the Bund Deutscher Mädel, the girls' unit of the Hitler Youth), and a muscular blonde girl in her mid-twenties with closely cropped hair and a swastika tattoo on the nape of her neck.

When Gretchen was ushered into the room by a uniformed aide, Hitler's major domo stopped playing in mid-tune and set the wheezing accordion on a chair next to his wife.

'Ah, Fraulein von Bismarck. Finally. We in the Führer's employ expect punctuality. The appointment was for 10 a.m. It is now seven minutes past ten.'

The man's jocular tone was belied by the anger in his protuberant eyes.

'I'm terribly sorry, but the tram was held up. A military vehicle broke down on the tracks.'

'Well, remove your hat and take a place at the table.'

Gretchen took off her hat and shook her blonde hair free. She was unaware that Freda Kannenberg was staring at her as she moved to sit next to the middle-aged woman who, Gretchen noted, was still wearing her hat.

Freda leaned over to her husband and whispered in his ear. As she spoke, his eyes widened, which made them all the more prominent. He nodded to his wife, raised his eyebrows and then approached the table.

'My name is Arthur Kannenberg and this, ladies, is my wife, Freda Kannenberg.'

All eyes turned in Freda's direction. The object of attention gave a regal wave then folded her hands across her ample stomach.

'My wife and I have the privilege of overseeing our beloved Führer's household and making sure everything runs smoothly. We recruit all personnel for the household as well as the kitchen staff. We purchase and control all the food and beverages that appear on the Führer's table. We prepare the daily menus and we are also in charge of state receptions. Any questions?'

Gretchen looked down the line of the other candidates and was about to ask if she was expected to wait on table; but as no one else volunteered a question, she decided to remain silent.

'The purpose of today's exercise is to select a successor to a young lady whom we had to dismiss for reasons I will not go into here. Let us just say they were of a sexual nature.'

The girl in the BDM uniform giggled nervously, which caused Kannenberg to frown at her and open his eyes wide like a goldfish.

'As you have been told, today you will be put through a test. The Führer has a team of fifteen women who taste, on a rotating basis, all the dishes that are prepared for him. Naturally, there is some danger involved, but you will have the honour of being in the front line for the protection of our leader.'

The girl with the swastika tattoo began to clap. Kannenberg raised an arm in a half salute to silence her.

'After scrupulous background checks by the SS, you four have been selected to take this final test. Only one of you will prevail,' Kannenberg continued. 'You have pencils and paper and you will make notes on what you will taste. Deconstruct the dishes and write down the ingredients so far as you are able.'

He took a small hand bell from his pocket and rang it three times. The doors at the other end of the room opened. Four waitresses bearing trays entered and took up positions behind the four contestants. At a signal from Kannenberg, they placed three bowls covered with stainless steel lids in front of the four women, along with a soup spoon, a glass of water and a paper napkin.

'Our Führer, as you know, is vegetarian. His tastes are simple. He eats no animal flesh, only vegetables. His breakfast is bread and marmalade. Keep that in mind when you taste the dishes in front of you. You may proceed.'

The waitresses lifted the lids from each of the bowls and then retreated with their trays to the wall at the far end of the room where they had entered.

Arthur Kannenberg stood up and moved to take up his accordion again.

'A little Viennese music to help you concentrate,' he said, strapping on the instrument.

While the other women picked up their spoons and dipped into the golden-coloured broth flecked with parsley in the first bowl, Gretchen leaned down, closed her eyes and inhaled the aroma. She took tiny little sniffs at first, drawing the scent up to the back of her nose and allowing the olfactory nerve to carry the information to her brain.

The soup smelled to her like Cook's chicken stock at home in Potsdam; but saturated into the chicken flavour were notes of clove and nutmeg. There was also a hint of carrot and celery – or was that celery root? And definitely leek, as well as onion. She recalled how Cook would stud an onion with cloves and immerse it in the stockpot for a few minutes. But what was the final fragrance? Was it bay leaf?

She picked up her pencil, wrote down 'Bowl No. 1,' and began to make notes. Then, it occurred to her: if Hitler was vegetarian, he would not eat chicken soup and she wrote that if such a dish was put in front of him he would surely be offended.

Gretchen lowered her head over the second bowl. It was a clear broth, light brown in colour. She detected the scent of tomatoes, celery and potatoes and a grassy-herbal note of green pepper and cabbage, although there was no evidence of any vegetables immersed in the soup. And peas, there were definitely peas, as well as a note of sweetness there. Could that be corn?

She inhaled deeply just to confirm her analysis and then wrote down her findings under the heading, 'Bowl No. 2.'

As she concentrated, she could hear the slurping sounds of the other candidates as they tasted the soups.

Arthur Kannenberg, who has been studying their progress while riffing on the accordion, stopped playing.

'Fraulein von Bismarck, I see you are not tasting the dishes.'

'With respect, Herr Kannenberg. I am tasting them. I'm smelling them.'

The tattooed blonde next to her smirked. Kannenberg shrugged his shoulders.

'If that is how you wish to proceed, so be it. Your notes will decide whether you are competent to hold a position that all the women of Germany would fight for.'

'I understand,' said Gretchen.

Moving to the third bowl, which appeared to be the same clear broth as in the previous sample, she detected an odour that she couldn't place. The range of vegetables she had smelled in the second bowl was evident, but there was a base note of something else – something that smelled like garlic and bitter almond.

As she was writing her notes, the woman in the feathered hat suddenly leant back in her chair and clutched her throat. She began to cough and tears streamed from her eyes. She appeared to be gasping for breath.

Freda Kannenberg rushed to the table and handed her a glass of water. The woman gagged at the first swallow.

'It's like sea water!'

'Salt. You need salt. You'll be fine,' said Freda. 'The dose was very low.'

Her husband watched the scene with clinical detachment, still fingering the keys of his accordion.

Poison, thought Gretchen. The third soup was poisoned, but only enough to cause distress and not death.

Concern for the afflicted woman was short-lived as Kannenberg instructed his wife to collect the applicants' notes. As she was doing so, there was a commotion at the far end of the room. The doors opened and the waitresses snapped to attention. They raised their right arms in salute as Adolf Hitler strode into the room.

He was dressed in a brown military uniform with a swastika armband. Behind him came a man in civilian clothes carrying a Leica 111c camera and finally a fair-haired woman in a tweed skirt and flat shoes, also carrying a camera.

Arthur Kannenberg struggled to release himself from his accordion straps, hissing at his wife for assistance as the leader of Germany walked towards him.

'Get up, get up,' he mouthed to the women who were momentarily stunned by Hitler's sudden appearance. The accordion made a sound of a dying bagpipe as the major domo deposited it hastily on a chair.

'Mein Führer,' he exclaimed, extending his arm in a full Nazi salute. 'You do honour us with your presence.'

'Sit, sit,' Hitler ordered, smiling at the women. 'Carry on with what you're doing. We are not here to disturb you. I want Hoffman and his assistant to document the exercise.'

Kannenberg scurried to drag a chair so that Hitler could be seated and witness the procedure.

Heinrich Hoffman, Hitler's personal photographer, studied the tableau, assessing the light and the angles, while his assistant held a light metre near the faces of female contestants.

Hitler's gaze rested on Gretchen's face. He stared at her without blinking, making the girl uncomfortable. She fiddled with her pencil and pretended to be making notes as the woman with the light metre approached her. Holding the metre close to Gretchen's face, the female photographer looked back at Hitler and noted his unwavering gaze on the young girl.

She turned back to Hoffman and said in a voice that was louder than necessary, 'Heinrich, F/4 at 1/20 should do it.'

'Thank you, Eva,' said Hoffman, altering the lens setting and timing on his Leica. He began to take candid shots of the four women in quick succession.

Hitler rose from his chair and walked slowly behind the seated contestants, hands folded behind his back. He stopped at Gretchen's chair and leaned forward, close enough for her to smell his body odour and acrid breath.

'And what is your name, *fraulein*?'

She could feel his breath on her ear and she started to tremble.

'Gretchen, Gretchen von Bismarck.'

'A von Bismarck! An illustrious family. Did you know that one of your ancestors, Chancellor Otto von Bismarck, founded the Second Reich? Thanks to him, I have created the Third.'

Gretchen said nothing.

Hitler continued: 'In 1862 Bismarck said, 'The great questions of the day will not be settled by resolutions or speeches…but by blood and iron.' Blood and iron, Gretchen von Bismarck.'

'Yes, Herr Hitler,' she mumbled.

'Now tell me, child, what exactly have you been doing here?'

The room was very quiet apart from the clicking of Hoffman's camera. Gretchen looked imploringly at Kannenberg who nodded his head in encouragement, his eyes bulging out of their sockets.

She kept her head straight in front trying not to breathe through her nose. The odour coming off the man was offensive.

'Tasting these soups and trying to break down their components.'

Hitler picked up the spoon she had been using. He dipped it into the third bowl and held it up to his lips.

Gretchen whirled around and knocked his hand before he could put it in his mouth.

'No! You mustn't!' she cried.

The contents of the spoon splashed over Hitler's trousers and jacket. A communal gasp of horror rose from the witnesses.

Slowly, carefully, Hitler replaced the spoon on the table. Very deliberately he reached for the paper napkin and began to wipe the spreading wet stain on his uniform.

The Kannenbergs, husband and wife, rushed forward with more paper napkins, but Hitler waved them away. The creator of the Third Reich signalled to the photographers to follow him and he stomped out.

The room was silent as the three of them moved to the door, but once they were out of earshot everyone started talking at once. Except for Gretchen who sat shaking with embarrassment and fear.

'Gretchen, come here,' said Arthur Kannenberg. 'The rest of you can go.'

'But what about the results? Who is the winner?' whined the tattooed girl.

'You will all be notified in due course,' said Kannenberg.

Gretchen moved towards the seat that Kannenberg was patting beside him. Tears of mortification stung her eyes.

'Sit down. Don't be upset. That last bowl was doctored with tiny amounts of arsenic. By smelling you knew there was something wrong.'

'But he could have swallowed it.'

'My dear, nothing is left to chance when it comes to the preservation of the Führer. It was a test. He knew which bowl contained the poison. He had no intention of putting it in his mouth. He was seeing how you would react.'

Gretchen's shoulders relaxed and she took a deep breath.

'Congratulations, Gretchen. You've got the job.'

****

Gretchen walked out of the room in a daze. As she moved slowly down the marble staircase of the Ministry of Public Enlightenment and Propaganda, feelings of exaltation were mixed with panic. What had she let herself in for? She could hear the strains of Arthur Kannenberg's accordion as her footsteps echoed down to the stairs and across the spacious hallway.

Kannenberg had told her that she was to report on the following Monday for training. She would be paid 300 Reichsmarks a month – 'a princely salary,' added Kanneberg, 'when you realise the average SS officer earns 100 Reichsmark a month and that our Führer pays himself only 1500 Reichmark a month…. But then he also has the royalties from 'Mein Kampf.'

'So much money,' said Gretchen. 'But when do I start?'

'The training will begin immediately. You must inform your current employer that you will be in the Führer's service. But you are never, ever, to disclose the nature of your work. Is that understood?'

'Of course. Where do I go for the training?'

'Here at the Reichs Ministry. You will receive written instructions in a day or two.'

'And how many days a week will I be working?'

'That depends. You will be on call whenever the Führer is in Berlin and maybe when he is at his retreat. He spends much of his time at a secret location directing the war.'

'And what do I wear?

'You will dress modestly. Skirts six centimetres below the knee. Blouse buttoned to the neck. Flat shoes, no high heels. And no perfume.'

Berlin, June 4, 1943

'Herr Speer, Saukel is sending me skeletons, not men and women. Skeletons!'

The angry voice at the end of the phone was Carl Krauch, Chairman of the Supervisory Board of I.G. Farben.

'We're paying good money to the SS for skilled workers. Three Reichmark a day, five for electricians and welders. How can they be productive living on only 1200 calories a day?'

Speer doodled on a scrap of paper as Krauch ranted on. Half-listening to the monologue on the other end of the line, the image of SS ObergruppenFührer Fritz Saukel sprang to his mind. Saukel – the only son of a postman and a seamstress who had risen in the ranks of the party to become Reich Regent of Thüringia. Now the father of twelve children, Saukel was the man responsible for rounding up slave labour from the eastern territories occupied by the Nazis. They would be sent to work in Germany's armament factories.

Speer recognised he was beholden to Saukel for the workforce he press-ganged into service for the Reich. Although he had no love for the stocky, shaven-headed Gauleiter, he appreciated the man's commitment to meeting his target figures for enforced labour; although he shut his mind to the methods Saukel used to satisfy his escalating demands for more workers.

'My dear Krauch,' said Speer, interrupting his caller, 'As Minister of Armaments and War Production, it is my duty to ensure we have a workforce capable of turning out the tanks and planes, our soldiers and airmen need to protect the Fatherland. While I sympathise with your situation, there are other priorities.'

'But Herr Speer, there are workers dropping dead from starvation over our production lines.'

'My Labour Allocation Department has made representations to Goering and to the Führer himself to improve the feeding and living conditions of the workers. There is only so much I can do. I have a letter on my desk ready to be signed demanding a supplementary meal in addition to the existing ration for factory workers employed in France.'

'And what about our workers in Auschwitz III? No other company is more committed to the war effort than I.G. Farben. As you well know, we produce nearly all the explosives for the German army.'

Speer was surprised that Krauch did not also add that a subsidiary of I.G. Farben also produced the Zyklon-B used in the gas chambers.

He opened a file in front of him and ran a finger down a list of figures.

'According to my records, your Buna Werke factory is 10 kilometres from Auschwitz. The SS established the camp in October 1942 at the express request of your executives in order to provide a labour force for your plant.'

'And we appreciate that.'

'Buna Werke has so far received just shy of 80,000 workers.'

'But they are dying like flies due to malnutrition.'

Speer closed the file.

'Herr Krauch, I do everything I can to facilitate a German victory, but I must admit that German policy makes heavier demands on me nearly every day and these demands do not conform to a definite policy. Gauleiter Sauckel can tell the German workers that they are working for Germany. I cannot say that Frenchmen are working for France. Nor can I say the Jews, the gypsies and homosexuals of Auschwitz are working for the benefit of I.G. Farben.'

'Is that your final word?'

Speer sighed.

'Nothing is final, Herr Krauch. I hear what you're saying and I will make another representation to Goering.'

'Let us hope, Herr Speer, we are not faced in the meantime with another Stalingrad.'

Speer hesitated before speaking, thought better of it and said a curt, *'Guten Tag.'*

He replaced the receiver and buried his face in his hands. The last comment by Carl Krauch had stirred up a memory he was trying to forget. The memory of his younger brother, Ernst.

Ernst had served as an infantryman in the Battle of Stalingrad. A Soviet pincer attack encircled 2,30,000 German and Romanian troops and trapped them in a pocket. The Red Army then formed two defensive fronts, one to contain the Sixth German Army and one facing back to defend against any enemy relief attempt.

In a public speech in the Berlin's Sportpalast, Hitler said that the German army would never leave Stalingrad. Goering promised an 'air bridge' to relieve the encircled troops. But the relief never came. Ernst Speer, who, with foot soldiers of his unit, had been sleeping in a freezing stable without walls, became dangerously ill with jaundice. He was immediately hospitalised, but there was no way to cure him at the front so he returned to his unit. Ernst wrote letters to his mother begging his brother to use his influence to bring him home.

Speer was torn between loyalty to his family and loyalty to the Führer. Hitler had ordered his senior officers not to use their position to do favours for relatives.

Speer's mother had turned up at his office sobbing, waving a letter from Ernst in which he wrote he could no longer stand watching his fellow patients die in the field hospital. She begged him to intercede on behalf of her son. Speer told her he had promised Ernst he would have him transferred to France when the Russian campaign was over.

In January 1943, racked by guilt, Speer contacted Field Marshall Erhard Milch at the Luftwaffe and asked him to find his brother and fly him home. Milch had officers in the field make enquiries about Ernst's unit. But they couldn't locate him. He was listed as missing in action and presumed to be one the 2,50,000 Wehrmacht and Romanian troops who lost their lives in the Battle of Stalingrad.

Berlin, June 7, 1943

Krista Becker stood at the bottom of the steps leading up to the colonnaded entrance to the Ministry of Public Enlightenment and Propaganda. Under her arm she held a large package wrapped in brown paper. In spite of the warm weather she was shivering. She checked her wristwatch; she had stood there watching the doors for three hours.

When Gretchen von Bismarck emerged, Krista turned away, hiding her face. She waited for the girl to descend the curved stone steps to the sidewalk.

'Fraulein von Bismarck,' she called softly to attract the girl's attention.

Gretchen turned and stared quizzically at the blonde woman in the shabby spring coat.

'Do I know you?'

Before Krista could reply, Gretchen said: 'I've seen you before. You're the woman who's been following me. I saw you across the road from the Adlon Hotel.'

'I'm sorry. I didn't mean to alarm you, Gretchen.'

'How do you know my name?'

'Is there somewhere we can go and talk?'

'Who are you?'

'My name is Krista Becker, and I work as a chambermaid at the Schwann Gasthaus in Rüdesheim am Rhein.'

'What do you want with me?'

'I have to talk to you. There is something very important you have to know.'

Gretchen backed away.

'Gretchen, please, you have to listen to me. Your life depends on it.'

'I don't know who you are, but you're frightening me.'

'I'm sorry. There was no other way. Just give me five minutes, that's all I'm asking. Please.'

Gretchen was about to speak when a loud siren sounded.

'It's an air raid,' said Krista, flatly. 'We must find an air-raid shelter.'

Galvanised by the noise, pedestrians began running towards the subway station. Tramcars ground to a noisy halt in their tracks, opened their doors and the passengers piled out.

'Come, follow me,' said Krista, taking Gretchen by the arm.

They moved swiftly, following the crowd towards the U-Bahn station next to the Kaiserhof Hotel as the sirens wailed above the city.

Once they made the entrance they slowed down and descended into the station. Krista led Gretchen to the far end of the platform. There was nowhere to sit so they stood leaning against the wall.

A young couple within earshot was saying, 'Why sirens during the day? They usually bomb us at night, the cowards.'

'It's probably only a practice,' said her companion.

Krista bent her head close to Gretchen and began to whisper.

'What I have to tell you will come as a shock, but you have to know for your own safety.'

'What are you talking about?'

Krista unwrapped the package she had been carrying, rolled the string in a ball and put it in her pocket. Then she folded the brown paper and pocketed that too. She held out a scrapbook and nodded to Gretchen to take it.

The cardboard cover bore the name, 'Gretchen.'

She looked at Krista and frowned.

'Open it.'

On the first page was yellowing newspaper clipping announcing the birth of a daughter to Carl and Greta von Bismarck of Potsdam. Below it was a lock of blonde hair in a cellophane envelope.

There were photos of Gretchen as a toddler and a kindergarten report written in a shaky hand as if someone had reproduced it. There were more photos, each dated underneath, showing Gretchen growing up. The final image was the newspaper photo of her standing next to Hermann Goering who was raising a glass of wine to toast her.

'Is this my hair?'

'Yes.'

'Where did you get these pictures, my hair?'

'Your cook, Hanna, at the house in Potsdam, she sent them to me.... She's my sister..., I asked her to send me anything about you.'

'But why?'

Tears welled up in Krista's eyes.

'Because I'm your mother.'

There was silence for a moment and then Gretchen extended her palms in front of her as if she wanted to push the woman away.

'No, I don't believe you. I have a mother.'

'Gretchen, I bore you. I know everything about you. You have a strawberry birthmark on your right hip.'

'No, it's not possible. Someone must have told you.'

She shrank away from Krista and put her hands over her ears.

'You must hear me out.'

Gretchen turned and began running blindly for the exit. Krista tried to follow, but more civilians had crowded onto the platform and she could not reach the girl.

Gretchen dashed up the stairs and into the deserted street. The sirens had stopped and city was silent. Nothing moved, cars stood abandoned, bicycles lay on the sidewalk.

'Cook,' said Gretchen to herself. 'I must find Cook.'

Berlin, June 8, 1943

G retchen did not sleep well that night. The strange woman who knew so much about her scared her. She lay awake in her parents' Berlin apartment reaching back for her earliest childhood memories.

Her mother had always been there. It was her mother she went to when she scraped her knee or had a stomachache. It was her mother who explained the mysteries of her first period, who had stayed up all night by her bedside when she had the flu.

In her rebellious, early teenage years she had turned to Cook for comfort when her parents scolded her for not tidying up her room or for spending too much time on the telephone. And how angry her mother had been the time Gretchen called her 'Greta' in an attempt to feel grown-up. But her mother was a constant in her life, the mother who loved her and protected her. And now this woman appeared from nowhere and claimed that she was her mother and Cook's sister.

Gretchen made a decision. She would go home and find out the truth from Cook.

Potsdam, June 9, 1943

T he next morning she phoned the Adlon Hotel and told the kitchen that she could not come to work that day because she had a fever.

Without bothering to make herself breakfast, she walked over to the Alexanderplatz station. She was oblivious to the bomb damage around her or the broken pipe that gushed water across the pavement.

At the railway station, she bought a day return ticket to Potsdam. In the carriage, a young soldier with a bandage on one eye tried to engage her in conversation but she just stared out of the window, seeing nothing, hearing nothing.

She walked the kilometre from Potsdam station to her father's estate. She stopped outside its wrought-iron gates decorated with the family crest at eye level – a three-leaf clover and three oak leaves on a shield of red and white bands. Underneath, the motto spelled out in Gothic script: *In Trinitate Robur* ('The Strength of the Holy Trinity').

The hinges of the great iron gate still creaked when she swung it open, the high-pitched squeal that announced the arrival of guests she could hear from her bedroom.

The crunch of the gravel under her feet was another reassuring childhood sound. She looked up at the façade of the three-storey house and tears welled in her eyes at the sight of its solemn grey stones covered with ivy.

Gretchen made her way around to the kitchen door, hoping she would not run into her parents before she had a chance to speak to Cook.

'Gretchen! And what are you doing here,' exclaimed Cook, dusting her hands on her apron. 'Your parents didn't say you were coming.'

'I came to speak to you, Cook.'

'Will you be staying the night? If so, I'll have to have your room aired out.'

'I won't be staying.'

'What is it, child? You look as if you've been crying.'

The tenderness in the older woman's voice unleashed the emotions she had not allowed herself to express. She ran to Cook and hugged her, tears streaming down her cheeks.

'There, there, *liebchen*. Sit down and have a nice cup of tea and you can tell Cook all about it.'

Gretchen allowed herself to be led to the kitchen table. She watched Cook take a second cup and saucer from the cupboard and pour the tea.

'I must have known you'd be coming because I baked your favourite cookies – *Pfeffernüssen*. Would you like some?

Gretchen shook her head.

'Are my parents here?'

'Your father's at his office and your mother is having her hair done. I can't imagine why she'd want to go all the way into Berlin with all the trouble that's going on when there's a perfectly good hairdresser in the town.'

Gretchen took a sip of tea, wondering how to start the conversation.

'I often wondered why I didn't have any brothers and sisters. Lots of cousins but no brothers or sisters,' she began.

Cook shrugged her shoulders.

'Is that's what's bothering you? After all these years?'

'I don't really know much about *you* although I've grown up with you. I don't even know your name. You've just been 'Cook' to me all these years.'

'Bless you, child. Young people are always wrapped in their own lives. My name's Hanna.'

'Hanna..., do you have any brothers or sisters?'

Cook took a sip of tea before replying.

'I have a half-sister. My mother died of tuberculosis when I was ten. My father remarried and they had another child.'

'A boy or a girl.'

'A girl.'

'What was her name?

'Krista.'

Gretchen felt the blood knocking in the veins of her temple.

'Do you ever see her?'

'Why are you asking me these questions, child?'

Gretchen could see that Cook was becoming agitated and was unwilling to look her in the eye.

'Yesterday, I was approached by a woman in Berlin –'

'In Berlin!'

'Yes. She had a scrapbook. It was full of pictures of me from when I was a baby. And there was a lock of my hair in an envelope.'

Cook's hands flew up to her throat. She sat down heavily on a chair opposite Gretchen.

'Krista, oh Krista,' she said, as if speaking to herself.

'We had to run into an air-raid shelter because the sirens were going. She showed me the scrapbook. It had my birth notice from the newspaper.'

Cook's chest was palpitating as if she was having trouble breathing.

'She knew about my birthmark. She knew everything about me.... She said her name was Krista and that she was your sister.'

'What else did she say?'

'She said there was something I had to know, that my life depended on it.'

Cook emitted a sob.

Gretchen lowered her head and hoped that she would not cry again.

'She told me she was my mother.'

Cook buried her face in her hands.

'Oh, dear Lord!'

'Is it true, Cook? Is she my mother?'

'I knew this would happen. One day, I knew it. God would find a way,' replied Cook, wringing her hands.

'Please, I must know.'

'It is not for me to say. It's not right. You must speak to your parents, child.'

'But what can you tell me? If she's my mother, I have a right to know.'

'Please, Gretchen. It's not my place to say anything. You must speak to your parents.'

Gretchen stared at the floor. Tears welled in her eyes and her face was ashen.

'What will you do, child?' Cook asked.

'I'll speak to my parents...as you suggest.'

Potsdam, July 9, 1943

Gretchen waited in her bedroom until she heard the creak of the iron gates. At the sound she jumped up and crossed to the window. She watched her mother stride up the gravel drive way. How confidently she moved, thought Gretchen, her hair newly permed, dressed in a two-piece suit, wearing her habitual strand of pearls, her hand bag slung across her shoulder.

Then the thought passed through her mind: Is this my mother or has my whole life been one long lie?

She waited until she heard the front door close and then walked slowly to the door and out onto the landing.

Greta von Bismarck studied her face in the mirror by the front door, touching her hair. She caught sight of Gretchen looking down at her.

'Gretchen! You gave me such a start. What are you doing here? Aren't you meant to be working?'

'I called in sick today,' replied the girl, moving down the staircase.

'What is it? Have you got a fever? Should you be in bed?'

'No, Mama. I'm OK. It's just that something strange happened and I needed to talk to you about it.'

'Something at work? You weren't molested were you?'

'No, can we sit down in the living room?'

'Of course, darling. Would you like Cook to bring us some tea?'

'I've had tea. I just need to talk.'

Greta frowned. She had never seen her child act like this.

'Is this a woman-to-woman talk or would you like your father to be here? He should be back soon.'

'I don't know if I could talk to Papa about this.'

Gretchen clasped her arms across her chest and began to shake.

'You do have a fever, Gretchen,' said her mother placing her open palm on the girl's forehead.

'No, it's not that. I don't know how to begin.'

Greta sat down on the sofa and patted the cushion next to her.

'Come, sit next to me. You know you can tell me anything.'

Nodding, Gretchen lowered herself onto the sofa.

'Yesterday,' she began, 'I was coming out to the Ministry of Propaganda and Enlightenment –'

Greta's eyes widened.

'What on earth were you doing there? Does your father know about this?'

'I'll tell you about that later. It's fine. As I was saying, I was coming out of the Ministry and a woman came up to me and called me by my name.'

'A woman? Someone from your work?'

'No, a woman I've never met before. She knew my name.'

'An old teacher maybe. A group leader from the League of German Girls. Someone you may have forgotten.'

'Please, let me finish, Mama…. She had a scrapbook with my pictures, this woman even had a clipping of the photo of me with Herr Goering they published in the newspaper…. And she had a lock of my hair.'

Greta von Bismarck began to finger her pearls in agitation. She glanced towards the door hoping her husband would arrive.

Gretchen, aware of her mother's discomfiture, but aching to know the truth, kept talking.

'The sirens were going off. We went down to the air raid shelter together. Someone said it was just a practice, because they never bomb in daylight. She showed me the pictures. It was like the books you and Daddy keep. Photos of me growing up.'

Her mother's face had grown ashen.

'She said she was Cook's sister.'

'Krista,' whispered the older woman.

'Then she told me she was my mother.'

Greta's shoulders sank and she covered her face with her hands.

'Oh, Gretchen, Gretchen. You are my child,' she cried in anguish.

'You must tell me the truth, Mama.'

Greta took a handkerchief from her sleeve and dabbed at her nostrils.

'Yes. I owe you that. I know. I'm so sorry that it had to come out this way…Your father and I couldn't conceive. He desperately wanted a boy to keep the line of our family going. And I wanted a girl above everything….'

Greta kicked off her shoes and pulled her legs up under her.

'Go on, Mama.'

'About a month after we were married I had a riding accident. A spirited horse. A jump too high for me. I fell off and injured myself. An abdominal puncture. I had to have surgery. As a result of the operation, I developed an infection and when it healed the doctors said there was scarring of my fallopian tubes. The result was I could never have children.'

'I'm so sorry.'

Greta drew a deep breath. 'That was the worst news I could have.'

'And Krista?'

'Krista was working here as a maid. Your father hired her the same day as Cook.'

'You mean Papa and Krista –'

'It was my idea. I wished it.'

She paused and in a barely audible voice, said: 'I asked Krista if she would carry our child.'

Gretchen gasped.

'I was desperate, Gretchen. We didn't want to adopt a baby. We wanted a child with your father's blood line.'

Gretchen rose to her feet and began backing away, shaking her head.

'I don't believe this. All these years, I've been living a lie.'

Greta bowed her head.

'You don't understand. We love you. You are our child. Our only child.'

Gretchen backed towards the stairwell, turned and ran up the stairs to her room.

She locked the door of her bedroom and crossed to her closet. She stood on a chair to reach a lacquered red box and took it to her bed.

It was what she called her 'memory box' and it contained the knick-knacks and souvenirs that reminded her of special times in her life.

The box, a gift her father had brought back from Japan, could only be opened if you knew how to slide secret panels back to reveal a hidden compartment with the key to unlock the top.

She opened it and spread the objects out on her duvet.

There was a lace embroidered button from the dress she had worn at her first communion; a pressed flower in a cellophane envelope from the corsage her cousin had given her when she attended her first dance. A shell she had found on the beach when her parents had taken her to Biarritz. A rosette she had won for coming second in a dressage competition. A mood ring from a cereal box. A photo of Shona Rosenberg and herself at Lyceum Bern, dressed in gymslips, their arms around each other, mugging for the camera. And the most recent addition to the memory box – the newspaper clipping showing her with Hermann Goering.

All of these memories were tied to the parents she had grown up with, the parents who had nurtured her and provided a privileged life for her. But the woman Krista – she could not think of her as her mother – had never forgotten her. From a distance she had watched her grow, thanks to Cook. But why had she waited so long to make contact?

The creaking of the front gate announced the return of her father. From her window, she watched him drive the Mercedes

Stromlinien-Limousine inside the property, alight and close the gate again.

How proud he was of that car, purchased a mere month before the war had broken out. Looking at him as he lowered himself into the driver's seat, Gretchen realised how tired he appeared. His face was lined with worry. The war had taken its toll on him as if he alone bore the responsibility for the safety of the Fatherland and all itsinhabitants.

She knew the first thing her mother would say to him when he crossed the threshold and she expected his knock on her door. She tiptoed across the room and unlocked it before returning to the bed to gather up her memorabilia and return the items to her memory box.

She sat down on the edge of the bed and waited.

The knock on the door was so faint at first that she didn't hear it.

'Gretchen. May I come in?'

'Of course, Papa.'

Carl von Bismarck, in his habitual tweed suit, drew up a chair and sat down. He stared at the floor, gathering his thoughts.

Gretchen waited for him to speak.

'I just had my hair cut this afternoon,' he began.

'It looks nice, Papa.'

There was a pause before he spoke again.

'Your mother tells me that you met Krista Becker.'

He looked at Gretchen, waiting for affirmation.

She nodded, fighting back the rising tears.

'And she told you that she was your mother.'

'Yes.'

'There is more to being a mother, Gretchen, than conceiving a child. A mother nurtures her baby and protects her. You remember how your mother would comfort you when you had bad dreams. Or when you were afraid of thunder. She sat by your bedside all night when you were sick.'

'I know, Papa.'

'Krista broke an oath when she made herself known to you.'

'What do you mean?'

'We had a…an arrangement. Your mother, as she has told you, could not have children. So we asked Krista to be a surrogate mother, that she would carry a child for us. No one was to know. We paid her handsomely for her trouble and had the best doctors attend to her welfare. Before it became obvious that she was pregnant, we sent her to a private clinic in the Schwartzwald, where she stayed for the remaining months until she delivered you. Your mother had to pretend that she was pregnant.'

'How did she do that?'

'She ate a lot and put on weight and wore loose clothing. Then when Krista was due your mother went to the clinic and brought you home as our baby. Which is what you are, Gretchen, and will always be.'

Carl fell silent and neither spoke for some time.

'Our agreement,' her father continued, 'was that as soon as you were born Krista would be given a monthly allowance for the rest of her life, on the understanding that she would have no contact with you or any member of the von Bismarck household. That she would move out of the area and start a new life somewhere else.'

'But she kept in contact with Cook.'

'Yes, Cook, it seems, was sending her information about you. I can understand Krista's need to have news of you. It must be very hard to give up a child.'

'But why did she wait all this time?'

'Did she say anything to you, apart from showing you her scrapbook?'

Gretchen tried to remember their conversation.

'She said there was something I had to know for my own safety.'

Her father sighed.

'I understand it now. It was that photo in the newspaper. You with Goering.'

'What do you mean?'

'She was afraid for you being so close to the Nazi leadership.'

'Why?'

'Krista Becker is Jewish. And under Germany's new law that means you too are technically Jewish.'

'Jewish? Like my friend Shona Rosenberg?'

'Yes…and in these times it puts you in great danger.'

'How Papa?'

'The Nazis are rounding up Jews from all over Europe and sending them to concentration camps.'

'Even if you're my father?'

Carl von Bismarck lowered his head and breathed heavily through his nose so Gretchen would not see the tears form in his eyes.

'I'm afraid so.'

Potsdam, August 8, 1943

'Hanna, it's me, Krista.'
'Krista!'
Cook lowered her voice to a whisper.
'You shouldn't be phoning here.'
'I know, I know, but I have to speak to her.'
'She's not here.'
'Where is she?'
Cook was silent.
'Hanna, it's important. You know what's happening to the Jews.'
'I've heard the stories.'
'They're not stories, Hanna. I've seen the trains. Where is she?'
'If they knew I've been talking to you, they'd fire me. What would I do then?'
'If you have any feeling for the child, or for me, you'd tell me where she is. I have to talk to her.'
'You're putting me in a terrible position.'
'For the love of God, just tell me where I can reach her.'
'She's living in the apartment. Ever since she went to work at the Adlon. But she's got some new job. I don't know what it is.'
'Are they there too – in Berlin?'
'The von Bismarcks?'
'Of course, the von Bismarcks.'
'No, they're here. In the house.'
And as if the conversation between the two sisters had conjured up Cook's employers, the couple walked into the kitchen.
Aware of their presence, Cook spoke loudly into the phone.
'No, Mr. Schultz, we are not interested in your black market butter, so kindly do not call us again.'
She slammed down the receiver.
Carl von Bismarck nodded appreciatively.
'Well said, Cook. Germany is suffering enough without some wretched individuals trying to profit from our deprivations.'
Greta von Bismarck said nothing, but merely raised a sceptical eyebrow.

Berlin, August 24, 1943

W henever he did not want his assigned driver reporting his movements to the SS, Albert Speer called his nephew Kurt Arndorfer. He instructed the young man to pick up his personal 1939 BMW 326 Cabriolet and park it in a side street behind the office with the top up.

He wanted to see for himself the damage to the city caused by the latest British bombing raid.

Special bulletins on the radio had announced that German fighters had downed 290 Stirling and Halifax bombers during the month of August, claiming the lives of 143 RAF pilots. Only three Messerschmitts had been lost in the engagements.

Hitler had gleefully shown him the report from Goering, slapping his leather boot with a crop as he read out the figures. So effective were the flak barrages in conjunction with fighter interceptions that German intelligence estimated that British pilots had a one-in-six chance of returning to their bases alive after their bombing missions.

But Speer was leery of anything he heard on the radio or from Hermann Goering for that matter.

It was the mandate of Joseph Goebbels, the Reichs Minister of Propaganda, to bolster the morale of the German people as the Allied bombing raids became more frequent and more devastating.

Reports coming back to Speer's office showed that bomb damage to the industrial plants in the Ruhr Valley, Ravensbrück, Essen and elsewhere had caused a nine per cent drop in production. The incendiary bombing of Hamburg on July 28th created such a firestorm that the city was destroyed, killing between 40,000 and 50,000 inhabitants – news that did not make the radio.

Four days later, Speer experienced one of Hitler's volcanic, finger-clicking rages when he suggested that if six more German cities were to suffer the same fate as Hamburg, Germany would lose the war.

In retaliation for the bombing of Coventry and London, Churchill had ordered the RAF to bomb Berlin. Speer recalled the night it happened: August 25th, 1940. He was home with Margarete having a late dinner when he heard crumping, thudding sounds followed by sirens and crack of anti-aircraft fire. At first it sounded like New Year's Eve fireworks, but one look at the sky told Speer that the British had brought the war to the inhabitants of Berlin.

He calculated that the bombs were exploding in the Kreuzberg district. Probably they're after the Görlitzer train station on Skalitzer Strasse, he guessed.

'We must take the boy and go down to the cellar,' he had said to his wife. 'And bring the case you've prepared for emergencies.'

Speer recalled that on October 3rd, 1940, Germany's Unity Day ('they would pick our national holiday') the bombers were back. This time the targets were the Henschel locomotive assembly plant in Kassel and munitions' depots west of Iringshausen.

So it begins, he had said to himself. We bomb their civilian population and they bomb ours. There is no chivalry in war.

The appearance of Frau Kempf at his desk broke into his reverie.

'Herr Speer, your nephew Kurt is outside. Do you want him to come up?'

'No, I'll join him downstairs.'

'Will you be gone long? You have a meeting with Reichsleiter Bormann at 2 o'clock.'

'I haven't seen the agenda.'

'It's about the churches again. He wants to have them appropriated by the Reich,' replied Frau Kempf, casting her eyes to the ceiling.

'Fine. I'll be on time, unless the Almighty has other plans for me this afternoon.'

Kurt was leaning against the BMW, smoking a cigarette and reading a copy of the *Hitlerjungen* monthly magazine, *Wille und Macht*. When he saw his uncle he hastily tamped the coal from the cigarette and slipped the butt into the breast pocket of his uniform before opening the passenger door.

'I want to see the Steglitz district.' said Speer, after they had exchanged greetings. 'They were bombed last night.'

'Steglitz?' asked the young man.

'How long have you been living in Berlin, Kurt?' said Speer, laughing. 'It's on the way to Potsdam. Drive to the Friedenau station. That must have been their target.'

They drove in silence before Kurt, who had been drumming his fingers on the steering wheel, glanced over at Speer.

'Uncle, that girl you asked me to bring to your office a while ago, remember? Gretchen von Bismarck...

'Yes? Pretty, wasn't she.'

'Yes...well...I was thinking...'

'What were you thinking?'

Speer knew exactly what his nephew was thinking, but he decided to tease the information out of him. He could see the colour rising on the young man's cheeks.

'Well, she seemed a little young for me then, but now...well, I thought I might ask her out. A movie or maybe dinner. Only I don't know how to get in touch with her. Can you help me?'

'Kurt, the young lady has a very important assignment from the government. Highly confidential. Top secret.'

'Is she a spy? Is she being sent to England?'

'You've been watching too many movies, my boy. But I doubt if she'll have time to go out on dates.'

'But I can try. I think she liked me.'

'I'll tell you what I'll do. In the interests of young love, I'll give you her parents' phone number. If they agree to put you in touch with their daughter, so be it. But you'll have to use all your powers of persuasion. They are a very respected, noble family.'

'Here, you didn't get this from me. You could have found it in the telephone directory.'

'Thank you,' said Kurt, grinning broadly as he pocketed the piece of paper.

They lapsed into silence again, Kurt staring straight ahead, Speer looking out of the passenger window at the buildings as they passed.

'Uncle, can I ask your advice?' said Kurt, finally.

'Of course.'

'I've been told that I'm to be promoted as a section head of the 12th SS-Panzer Division *Hitlerjugend*.'

'Congratulations, my boy.'

'Yes, but I don't know if I should accept.... They told us if we see our parents listening to enemy broadcasts, we have to report them to the SS. And the same thing if we find out that a neighbour is harbouring Jews.'

'Pull over to the curb.'

Kurt eased the car to the curb, put the gear in neutral and applied the hand brake.

'When you entered the *Hitlerjungen* you swore an oath, did you not?'

'Yes, sir.'

'And what was that oath?'

'You want me to say it?'

'If you would.'

Kurt cleared his throat and paused to recall the oath he had memorised as a 12-year-old boy.

'I swear, in the Hitler Youth, always to do my duty with love and loyalty, for the Führer and our flag, so help me God. In the presence of this blood banner, which represents our Führer, I swear to devote all my energies and strength to the saviour of our country, Adolf Hitler. I am willing and ready to give up my life for him, so help me God.'

'And there's your answer. You made a military oath – an oath based on the same promise that the medieval Knights Templar made to their Emperor.'

'But if I had to denounce my parents – '

'Are you telling me that Margarete's brother is listening to enemy broadcasts?'

'No, uncle. He doesn't. I'm just asking what should come first, loyalty to my family or obeying the rules of the party?'

Speer said nothing. The memory of his brother's death returned and he closed his eyes. Suddenly, he felt very tired and he wished the war would go away, just evaporate, so that he could get back to creating buildings.

Kurt glanced at him expectantly.

'You must be guided by your conscience, Kurt,' he said. 'Sometimes we make mistakes when we follow our heads rather than our hearts. Do what is right for you…. Now let's drive on.'

As they approached the Friedenau railway station, Speer could see the effects on the RAF bombing raid. Crews with bulldozers were clearing rubble from the streets. Whole city blocks had been gutted by the fires started by the incendiary bombs. Buildings had collapsed inwards, their blackened facades standing like rotten teeth above piles of bricks and smoldering timber. Fire hoses played over the debris. There were no cars on the road. Pedestrians moved about in a daze, scrambling across the mountains of brick and slabs of concrete.

'Oh, my God,' murmured Kurt.

Speer shook his head in sorrow.

A policeman wearing a swastika armband ordered the BMW to stop. Speer wound down his window and handed the cop his identification card. The man clicked his heels and extended his right arm in salute. '*Heil Hitler*,' he shouted and waved the car through.

Berlin, August 26, 1943

'Albert.'

Margarete Speer called from the kitchen.

'Help me dry the dishes, and then you can read a story to Albert Junior.'

Speer sighed, put down the newspaper he had been reading, and moved reluctantly to the kitchen.

'Here's an apron. You don't want to get water on your uniform. I can't understand why you wear it around the house.'

Speer put the apron on. She held out a pair of rubber gloves to him.

'I don't need those,' he said. 'Bormann should only see me now.'

'Maybe I should take a photograph,' she smiled. 'The Führer would be amused.... I see our nephew took the car today. Did you tell him he could?'

'I needed him to drive me somewhere.'

'Isn't it dangerous for you to be driving around the city without a military escort?

Speer picked up a plate and began to polish it with a tea towel. He did not wish to justify to his wife his need to travel without the inevitable detail of SS troops. He decided to change the subject.

'How is Albert Junior's stutter? Is it getting any better?'

'The speech therapist says he's traumatised by the bombing. It's the war, Albert. When it's over they say he should be fine.'

'He's nine years old. I have no idea how long this war will last. It's painful to listen to him.'

'Well, he's in good company,' said Margarete, trying to make light of the subject. 'The King of England has a worse stammer.'

Speer turned furiously on his wife.

'How do you know that? Have you been secretly listening to BBC broadcasts?'

'No, of course not. Everybody knows the stupid man stutters. The kids made fun of him at school. K-k-k-king G-g-g-george. What are you so upset about?'

Speer put the plate down, grasped the edge of the sink and breathed heavily through his nose.

'Kurt tells me he's been asked to report any family members who listen to enemy broadcasts. Tell your brother to be careful. I know Kurt wouldn't denounce his father, but we need to be cautious. As I told you, there are ears everywhere.'

Margarete put her arms around her husband's neck.

'We need a holiday, Albert. More important, you need to get away from all this. Even for a few days. We can take the children out of school and go to the mountains.'

'I can't, Margarete. At the beginning of the war the Führer said, "Give me six hundred tanks and we will abolish every enemy in the world." That was the magic figure, six hundred tanks. By the end of this year, I will have Germany producing 1,000 tanks a month.'

'And what good is it doing us? Tanks don't stop bombs, Albert. I don't want to go to bed at night wondering if our children will see the morning. There has to be an end.'

'Much as I would like to get away, my dear, I have to tour a ball-bearing factory in Poland.'

'How long will you be away?'

'A few days. Two only. Maybe three. It depends on how much damage there's been.'

'And what other trips have you planned? Frau Kempf guards your diary like it's Wagner's handwritten score for *Lohengrin*.'

Speer smiled. He enjoyed his wife's sense of hyperbole.

'If memory serves, I know I have to be in Posen in October.'

'Posen? Where's Posen?'

' In the east, about three hours by car.'

'Why do you have to go there?'

'Himmler is delivering a speech to SS Group leaders. The Führer wants us all to be there. October 4th, about the Jewish question.'

Berlin, August 27, 1943

A lbert Speer opened the file marked 'Top Secret' and read through the Luftwaffe's report with growing concern.

July 28: The last raid totally shut down production at Krupps' Essen plant. See accompanying aerial photographs that show an area of 148 acres of Krupp's factories and 20 square kilometres in the city, from the main station to Altenessen, completely destroyed. Our statisticians estimated that some 125 high explosive bombs and twenty thousand incendiaries were dropped in the attack. The fuse factory took a direct hit and production had to be moved to Auschwitz.

Panzer construction shop No. 3 (responsible for crankshaft manufacture) was also destroyed which has put back production of both the Panzer and Tiger models by at least two months.

The good news is that British Bomber Command lost five per cent of their Wellington Bombers, thanks to the accuracy of our flak artillery and the harrying tactics of our Focke-Wulf fighters.

August 2: A night time raid on Hamburg by 791 aircrafts. Bomber Command lost 30 aircrafts (4.1% of the force). The hottest day in ten years amplified the effects of the incendiary sticks. 900,000 people were displaced by the fires that raged. 40,000 civilians are estimated to have been killed.

August 17–18: Peenemuende was subjected to a devastating attack by 517 bombers that, according to Werner Von Braun, has forced production of the A-4 long-distance rocket underground at Nordhausen.

August 17: A second wave of 230 USAAF 8th Air Force B-17s attacked Schweinfurt-Regensburg – the location of most of the Reich's ball-bearing production. 300 of our defending fighter aircrafts and intense anti-aircraft artillery managed to beat off the attack. As a result, only 184 aircrafts were able to actually strike their targets while 36 bombers were downed.

Speer closed the file and pinched the bridge of his nose. If only we had not lost access to wolframite from Portugal, he mused. Wolframite is the main source of the metal tungsten, and Germany's minimum warfare requirements were 3,500 tons per year. The loss of this metal, 1.7 times heavier than lead with a high melting point, had created a critical situation for the production of solid core ammunition.

As a substitute for wolframite, Speer had immediately ordered the release of 1200 metric tons of uranium ore – ore that had been seized in Belgium in 1940 and was destined to be used to create Germany's atom bomb.

'Frau Kempf, can you get Herr Saur on the phone,' he said into the intercom.

Speer had always been uneasy about his deputy, Kurt Saur. Hitler had called his Minister of Armaments at the beginning of every month to ask for production figures. But on August 1st Hitler had not called him. He had phoned Saur instead.

Saur was friendly with Bormann and his pal Dorsch whom Speer had superseded when Hitler had appointed him Minister for Armaments and Munitions. He recognized the hand of Hitler's personal secretary in these attempts to undermine his authority.

The telephone jangled.

'Speer here. Kurt, I've just been reading Goering's report on the latest raids…you've seen the report too!... Ah yes, Private Secretary Bormann. Well, then, you are aware of the damage to our production facilities in Essen and Peenemunde. We have to get these plants operational as soon as possible.... You're correct. To do this we need more labour. The Führer has ordered Himmler to use the workers in the camps for A-4 production at Nordhausen…yes, the A-4 is an improvement on the V-1 and V-2s… So you need to take a contingent of prisoners from Buchenwald to Nordhausen…. You will contact the camp commandant Oberführer Hermann Pister and have his physicians select the healthiest specimens…. As many as you can get, 100, 200…By truck, man, by truck. Requisition the number of trucks you need and I will sign the order.'

He slammed down the receiver.

'Do I have to win this goddamned war by myself!' he muttered.

Berlin, September 1, 1943

'Welcome to the team, Gretchen. My name is Marlene von Exner and I am the Führer's dietician and cook. You will report to me each time you are in the rotation.'

Gretchen sat nervously in the kitchen of Reich Chancellery on the first day of her new job.

Von Exner was dressed in an immaculate white jacket buttoned to the throat, her name embroidered on the left breast. Her dark hair escaped from under the white cap she wore. A pretty woman of twenty-four with a prominent nose, she paced up and down the kitchen as she talked.

'Like our leader, I am Austrian,' she continued, 'from Vienna. You may ask how does a woman of my age gets to cook for the Chancellor of Germany?'

Gretchen nodded, not responding verbally to what was obviously a rhetorical question.

'A year last May, the Führer had a meeting with Marshal Antonescu. You know, the Prime Minister of Romania. It turned out that both of them had the same stomach condition. I was working as a dietician at the Vienna University Hospital at the time and I had treated Antonescu. He was so pleased he offered me a position in Bucharest to cook for him. You know where Bucharest is, right?'

Again, Gretchen nodded although she had no idea.

'Anyway, he told Herr Hitler about me. And the Führer's own doctor made a special trip to Bucharest to persuade me to come to Berlin, and – voilà – here I am.'

She crossed to the stove on which a large pot was warming over a low light. She reached for a bowl and ladled out a serving of soup.

'Come and sit at the table. They tell me you have an extraordinary sense of smell. I want you tell me what I put into this soup.'

Gretchen did as she was ordered. She picked up a spoon, dipped it into the liquid and raised it to her nose.

'I get garlic, bay leaf, tomato juice, celery, carrots, cabbage…'

She tasted a mouthful.

'… and green pepper and maybe potatoes…and there's something else. It tastes like bone marrow. It's delicious.'

'Excellent! You have a remarkable palate, young lady.'

'Is this for Herr Hitler?'

'Yes,' replied von Exner. 'But it's our little secret. Just between us girls. It drives me nuts that he's a vegetarian. I hate his diet. You know he exists on oatmeal with linseed oil, cauliflower, cottage cheese, artichoke hearts, and asparagus tips in white sauce.'

'Sounds like hospital food,' said Gretchen.

'And you know what. It gives him terrible gas. He farts like a walrus.'
The two young women dissolved into laughter.

Berlin, September 2, 1943

Kurt Arndorfer lay on his bed in his parents' flat near the Branden-burg Gate. Lost in thoughts, he was oblivious to the sound of the air-raid sirens that had become almost a nightly occurrence.

He tried to block out the angry voice of his father who was com-plaining to his mother that the Jewish tailor across the street had been taken away. The suit that he had been measured for would never be made.

Kurt was replaying in his mind last week's phone conversation with Gretchen's father. At first von Bismarck had been aloof and distant as if he was not listening; but as soon as he had identified himself as Albert Speer's nephew the man's tone became much warmer.

Kurt asked his permission to call on his daughter. Von Bismarck had laughed and said it was really up to Gretchen, but he appreciated the boy's old world courtesy – something, he said, that had been lost in the war.

Now that he had Gretchen's father's qualified approval, the ques-tion was how to approach the girl herself – and what sort of meeting he should propose?

The bombing raids made a nocturnal tryst in Humboldthain Park a proposition fraught with danger. He couldn't afford to take her to dinner. There was always the cinema, but the last time he went to the Admiralspalast to see 'The Big Game' there was a power cut in the middle of the movie and he never did get to see which of the rival foot-ballers won the hand of Grete and if their team went on to win the cup. So movies were out even though they would be in the dark.

They could go for a glass of Hefeweitzen beer and pretzels, but the beer halls weren't much fun in the blackout even though that would make for a romantic atmosphere.

Then he had an idea.

A week earlier a bomb had destroyed a record store two blocks from his parents' apartment. Dressed in his Hitler Youth uniform he decided to see the damage for himself. Mindful of the number of pedestrians who had been hit by motorists during the blackout, he worked his way carefully through the streets.

As he approached the ruined building he thought he heard the sound of a muted trumpet and a guitar.

He picked his way through the piles of bricks and charred timbers until he came to a flight of stone steps that led down to a metal door.

The music got louder as he descended the steps. He put his ear to the door and he could hear the syncopated beat of New Orleans jazz. He listened to a guitar solo, which ended in muffled applause before a trumpet took up the melody, backed by a bass and drums.

He eased the door open. At the creak of the hinges the musicians stopped playing. The audience of a dozen people sitting at candle-lit tables with shot glasses in front of them turned their gaze on the intruder.

'*Entschuldigen*,' murmured Kurt, embarrassed.

The guitarist rose from his chair on the tiny stage. He looks like he's my age, thought Kurt.

'Come on in. You like jazz, kid?'

'Yes, I do,' stammered Kurt.

'Well, don't just stand there. Take seat. Have a drink. I'm Heinz Schumann. They call me Coco. And this here's Charlie on trumpet.'

He pointed to a gigantic black man whose hands dwarfed the instrument he held.

'Helmut on drums and that handsome fellow at the back on bass is Ziggy.'

Helmut the drummer punctuated each introduction with a brush riff on his cymbals.

Kurt, mortified at being the centre of attention, slithered into the nearest chair.

For the next ninety minutes he sat mesmerized as Coco Schumann and his quartet jammed, their music filling the smoky cellar with sounds that obliterated the images of war outside.

Recalling that night, as the sirens wailed above the rooftops. Kurt knew where he would take Gretchen.

He sat down at his desk and wrote a letter asking her if she would like to meet him on Saturday night. He would hand deliver it to the von Bismarck's apartment the next morning.

Berlin, September 4, 1943

G retchen sat down at the roll-top desk in the study of her parents' Berlin apartment. She took out a sheet of paper embossed with the family crest, unscrewed the top of her fountain pen, and began to write.

Dear Shoshie,

I've been meaning to reply to your last letter for so long, but so many things have happened I just haven't had time to sit down. Life seemed to be so much easier at Lyceum Bern. But I'm not complaining, really it's quite exciting here in a weird kind of way.

I told you about getting that job at the Hotel Adlon in spite of my parents' objections. It took a lot of persuading to let me work in the kitchen, but you know how much I love cooking.

Well, that led to me meeting Herr Goering and several other Nazi officers. I had to serve them lunch in a private room. I was so nervous trying not to spill anything. But guess what! It ended with my picture in the newspaper! Me and Herr Goering! Can you image what Frau Seigert and Jorg would say about that?

Anyway, it's a long story, but as a result I was invited to be part of a very special assignment, which I am not allowed to divulge under oath. I wish I could tell you, but this is one secret I cannot share with you.

But something I can tell you – I think I have a boyfriend! His name is Kurt and he's very handsome. I wish I had a photo of him to send you. He is the nephew of Herr Albert Speer, the architect, the man my father works for. I say I think he's going to be my boyfriend because I haven't actually gone out on a date with him yet. But he telephoned my father apparently and asked if he could contact me! And he did!! I received a note from him this very morning. We're going to meet on Saturday. I wrote back and asked him where we're going so I'd know what to wear. He said it's a surprise, but he hopes I like music. I can't imagine where as there are no concerts in Berlin because of the bombing raids. Anyway, I don't really mind because I just want to see him again.

I'll let you know what happens, and in the meantime please write and tell me how life is in Zurich. How I wish I were there with you.

Love, Gretty.

When Shona Rosenberg opened the envelope a week later, this is what she read:

Dear Shoshie,
I've been meaning to reply to your last letter for so long, but so many things have happened I just haven't had time to sit down. Life seemed to be so much easier at Lyceum Bern. But I'm not complaining, really it's

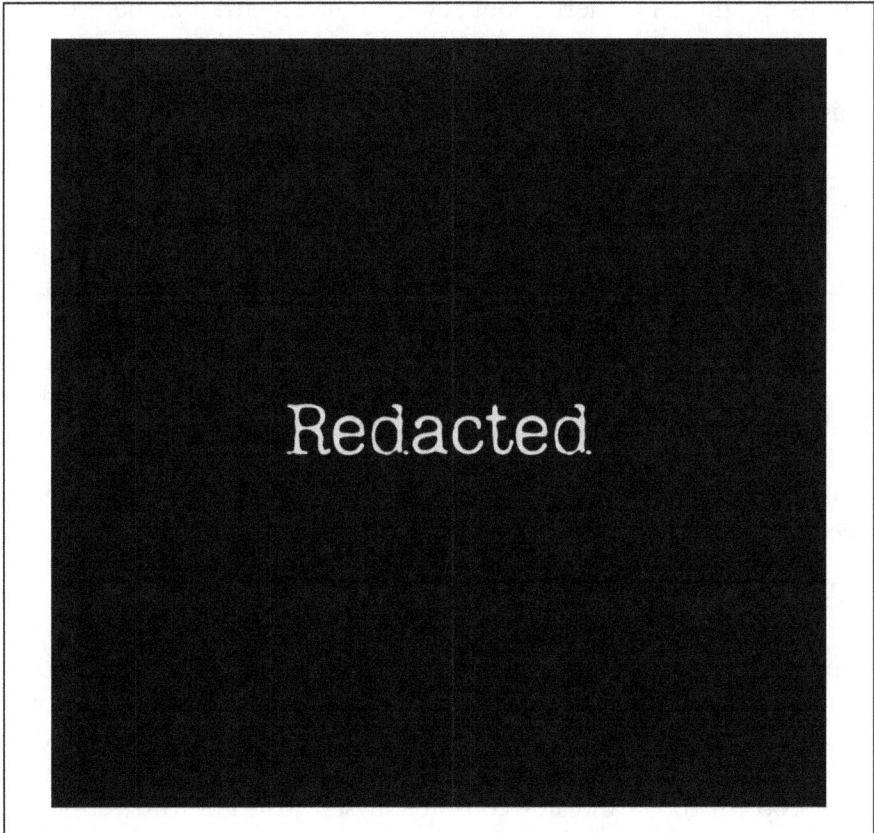

Love, Gretty.

Posen, Poland, October 4, 1943

On the long drive from Berlin through occupied Poland to Posen, Albert Speer felt a growing pain in his left knee.

The dizzy spells and fainting episodes he had experienced as a young boy had been diagnosed by the family doctor as 'weakness of the vascular nerves.' He wondered if the pain he was now suffering was somehow connected to this condition or was it caused by the daily stress of his position.

He had no interest in hearing Reichsführer Heinrich Himmler addressing the SS leaders about Jews. He had heard it all before. But the Führer had ordered all senior SS officers to be there.

The pain was intense as he climbed the stairs of the town hall. He found a chair at the back that would enable him to stretch out his leg. He looked at his watch. He counted the heads in front of him; there were ninety-one. It would be a long afternoon.

Himmler would be carried away by his own rhetoric and although he only used handwritten notes, the speech he was about to deliver would be endless. But the message must be important, he thought, to bring so many ranking officers together in this Godforsaken neck of the woods.

The Reichsführer took the stage and surveyed the audience. Satisfied with the attendance, he took off his glasses and cleaned the lenses with a handkerchief. Pausing for dramatic effect before speaking, he looked up at the raftered ceiling as if invoking the Nordic Gods whose mysticism infused his worldview.

The oppressive heat in the room made Speer sleepy. He closed his eyes and could feel himself drifting off.

When he heard Himmler shout the term, *Jüden,* his eyes snapped open and he began to concentrate on what the man was saying.

'I ask of you that that which I say to you in this circle be really only heard and not ever discussed. We were faced with the question: what about the women and children? I decided to find a clear solution to this problem too. I did not consider myself justified to exterminate the men – in other words, to kill them or have them killed and allow the avengers of our sons and grandsons in the form of their children to grow up. The difficult decision had to be made to have this people disappear from the earth. For the organisation which had to execute this task, it was the most difficult which we had ever had ....'

Speer tried to make sense of what he was hearing. Was Himmler actually articulating the need to kill all the women and children in case future generations of Jews would take revenge on Germans for the slaughter of their ancestors?

And still Himmler droned on.

'...I felt obliged to you, as the most superior dignitary, as the most superior dignitary of the party, this political order, this political instrument of the Führer, to also speak about this question quite openly and to say how it has been. The Jewish question in the countries that we occupy will be solved by the end of this year. Only remainders of odd Jews that managed to find hiding places will be left over....'

As unobtrusively as he could, Speer got to his feet and left the hall by the back door.

Berlin, October 5, 1943

Krista Becker turned up the collar of her shabby coat against the wind as she waited outside the von Bismarck's apartment block on Petersburger Strasse. Searchlights scanned the heavens eradicating the stars.

She was determined to see Gretchen and make her understand the danger she was in. Krista had quit her job at the Schwann Gasthaus in Rüdesheim am Rhein, withdrawn all her savings and rented a small room three blocks away from her daughter. Now that Gretchen knew the truth there was no need for pretence anymore; no need to hide. If the father of her child cut off her monthly annuity because she had reneged on their contract, so be it. Her daughter's safety was her first concern.

Posing as a maid from the von Bismarck household who had an urgent message for Gretchen, she had learned from the concierge that the girl had left the building earlier in the evening in the company of a young man. She settled herself in a coffee house across the road. She waited, watching the entrance to the building until the manager made it obvious that she should order food or move on.

****

'So what's the big mystery, Kurt?' asked Gretchen as they walked the ruined streets of Berlin, hand in hand.

'You'll see. We're nearly there…. So how's the new job?'

'Oh, it's fine,' she replied, lapsing into silence.

'Fine? Is that it?'

'That's all I can tell you, Kurt. I took an oath.'

'Yeah, I know what you mean. I took an oath when I joined the Hitler Youth. But give me a clue, and then I'll tell you where we're going.'

Gretchen stopped and pulled him close to her. Then she kissed him on the lips.

'There. Does that answer your question?'

'No, but I like the result. Maybe I should keep asking questions.'

'Maybe you should.'

They walked along in silence, both of them smiling, feeling the warmth of their clasped hands.

When they arrived at the bombed out building, Gretchen hesitated, seeing the piles of brick and charred beams.

'We're going in there?'

'Don't worry,' said Kurt. 'Trust me.'

'It's going to ruin my shoes.'

'Do you want me to carry you?'

'No thanks,' she said laughing, and she followed him to the stone stairs that led down to the cellar.

'Listen,' said Kurt.

Gretchen could hear the faint sound of a muted trumpet. It seemed to emanate from the bowels of the earth, a brittle plangent sound of mourning. She felt a thrill of excitement as she descended the stairs, not knowing what to expect.

Kurt knocked on the steel door and pushed it open.

'Hi,' he said to the assembled musicians. 'I said I'd be back, and this is my friend Gretchen.'

'I remember you. Come on in,' said the trumpeter Charlie.

As they took seats at a table next to the tiny bandstand, Kurt asked: 'So where's Coco, the guy on the guitar?'

The band members looked at each other before Charlie answered.

'Coco, he got taken away two days ago.'

'Taken away?' enquired Kurt. 'Taken where?'

'He's Jewish, man. They took him to the camps they got for Jews. Ziggy knows someone in the party. They told him Coco's gone to Theresienstadt or somewhere in Sudeten.'

'At least he got to take his guitar with him,' added Ziggy, the bass player.

There were three other couples at tables around the stage. Kurt led Getchen to an unoccupied table. Leaning towards her, he whispered: 'Theresienstadt is a transit camp. They take the Jews and other prisoners by rail from there to <u>Treblinka</u> and <u>Auschwitz</u> where they gas them and burn the bodies.'

'How do you know all this?' asked Gretchen, incredulous.

'I was driving my uncle and he was with Anton Burger, the Commandant of Theresienstadt, in the back seat. I overheard him asking for timber to build more housing. Burger was saying that he had 40,000 prisoners standing out in freezing weather for the camp census. He said three hundred people died of hypothermia.'

'What did your uncle say?'

'I don't know. He closed the glass partition between us.'

****

'I'm sorry about your friend Coco,' said Gretchen as they walked back to her parents' apartment.

'He wasn't my friend,' said Kurt. 'I only met him once.'

'Still, it's sad.'

'Yeah.'

They walked in silence, picking their way carefully through the cobblestone-strewn streets, passing strangers who nodded their greetings. Inspectors with Nazi armbands scanned the windows for chinks of light.

When they approached Gretchen's parents' apartment building, she turned to Kurt and impulsively kissed him.

'I don't know what's going to happen,' she said, 'but I'd like to fall in love in spite of the war.'

'Or maybe because of it,' replied Kurt, holding her to him.

Over her shoulder Kurt could see a woman standing on the corner, staring at them. As he caught her eye, the woman began beckoning him to approach her.

Kurt half-turned Gretchen so that she could see the woman.

'Do you know her?

Gretchen drew in her breath in a sob.

'Ignore her. Let's go.'

'But she might be in trouble. She's coming over.'

'I don't want to talk to her.'

'Something's wrong. She's crying.'

Gretchen's shoulders slumped.

'Wait here, Kurt. Please.'

She moved toward Krista, placing a finger to her lips, willing her mother not to speak in earshot of Kurt.

As she approached Krista, she looked back and made a hand gesture at Kurt to signify that everything was fine and he should wait where he was.

'Gretchen,' said Krista. 'I have to talk to you.'

'It's not a good time.'

'You have to understand why I'm worried for you. My mother was Jewish. That means you are Jewish. They are killing Jews, Gretchen. There are camps they take us to and nobody gets out alive.'

'My father told me everything. I'm a von Bismarck. They wouldn't do anything to me.'

She began to back away.

'Please, Gretchen. I've given up my job to warn you. I've taken a small room on Eldenaer Strasse so I can protect you.'

'I don't need to be protected. I have important...'

She was about to tell her mother that she was working for the Führer now, but the memory of the oath she had taken prevented her from revealing this information.

Krista, with a mother's instinct, understood what she was about to say.

'Yes, you have your picture in the papers with Herr Goering, but what if he finds out your mother is Jewish, your grandmother is Jewish?'

'I'm blonde and blue-eyed. I'm German,' snapped Gretchen. 'Is that why you dyed your hair blonde?'

Krista touched her hair and sighed.

'Oh Gretchen, Gretchen, if you only knew....'

'I'm sorry. I shouldn't have said that.... I don't know what to call you.'

'If you can't call me Mother then let it be Krista – as long as you call me something. Here, I've written down my address. There's a public phone in the hall if you have to contact me. I know how to reach you.'

Gretchen looked back at Kurt. He was leaning against an unlit lamppost, hands in his pockets.

'I have to get back to my friend,' said Gretchen.

'He looks like a nice boy,' said Krista, leaning forward, hoping her daughter would embrace her.

But Gretchen just accepted the proffered note and slipped it into her pocket.

'Tell me you'll call me,' said Krista, plaintively.

'OK, I'll call you, but please stop following me.'

Krista nodded and then turned away to hide the tears that had begun to fall.

Gretchen crossed the street and joined Kurt.

'Hold me, please,' she said.

'Who was that?' asked Kurt as he drew her to him.

Gretchen buried her face in his neck.

'Her name is Krista. She's my old teacher from the Gymnasium. She...she wants me to try out for a university scholarship.'

'She must be very conscientious to track you down like that.'

'Yes...I was one of her favourites. But can we talk about something else?'

Berlin, October 10, 1943

A lbert Speer studied the framed photo of the Führer that hung on the wall in his office. It was a shot of Hitler putting his signature on the Munich Agreement on September 29, 1938.

Hitler was standing bent over a desk, looking down at the document, penned poised. In the background were Benito Mussolini and Hermann Goering. This was the document that permitted Nazi Germany's annexation of Sudentenland – the document that the British Prime Minister Neville Chamberlain would wave in front of the assembled journalists when his plane touched down at Heston Airport a day after the signing. A piece of paper promising Britons, 'Peace for our time.'

Hitler had autographed the photo in black ink: 'To Albert Speer, whose buildings will project the grandeur of the 1,000 Year Reich. A. Hitler.'

He had presented it to Speer a few days after they had visited Paris on June 28th, 1940. How proud he had been to receive it and to hang it on his wall where every visitor could see it.

Hitler's spiky handwriting sloped downwards and Speer recalled an article he had read about this phenomenon by an expert analyst: it was one of the signs of a depressed individual with suicidal tendencies, a person who was running out of mental stamina. And so much had happened since those glory days in Paris when every day brought more victories. But how circumstances had changed: the disastrous Russian campaign, the destruction of factories producing war materiel, the Allied bombing of German cities…. All he wanted was to build while all about him he only saw demolition.

Then there was that troubling speech by Himmler in Posen. He had no doubt in his mind that Himmler was merely giving voice to Hitler's inner thoughts. He had actually articulated that the children of Jews and their mothers had to be killed in case they would rise up and take vengeance on future generations of the German people.

And yet, there were Jews who now served as senior officers in Hitler's army.

Speer took the photo off its hook and placed it carefully on his desk. Behind it was a wall safe in which he kept documents too sensitive to be seen even by the faithful Frau Kempf.

He dialled in the combination, opened the steel door and took out a file marked 'Jews.'

He had been given the documents in the file by a high-ranking member of the SS for a favour Speer had performed – getting the officer's dull-witted son into architecture school in Switzerland. 'You might need this one day,' said the grateful father.

Sitting down at his desk he opened the file. On the top of was a photograph taken at a Nuremberg rally on September 12th, 1938. It showed a group of senior officers in conversation – his friend Field Marshall Erhard Milch of the Luftwaffe, the man who had tried in vain to rescue his brother Eric from Stalingrad, Wilhelm Keitl, chief of the Oberkommando der Wehrmacht, Walther von Brauchitsch, Commander-in-Chief of the German Army. Erich Raeder, Grand Admiral of the Navy and Maximilian von Weichs, Field Marshall General.

All of them were defined under the Law of the Restoration of the Professional Civil Service (April 7, 1933) and the Nuremberg Laws (September 15, 1935) as Jews.

Reading the file, Speer came across terms he had not heard before: Mischling First Degree and Mischling Second Degree. He knew in racial terms it meant 'mixed' but was unaware of the distinctions.

'Mischling First Degree: a person with two Jewish grandparents and two non-Jewish grandparents, who was either baptized and brought up Christian or practiced no religion.

Mischling Second Degree: A person with one Jewish grandparent and three non-Jewish grandparents, who was baptized and raised Christian or with no religion.'

A Jew was defined under the Civil Service Act as a person who had at least one Jewish parent or grandparent. Under the Nuremberg Decrees the concept was further refined: German citizens with only one Jewish grandparent were defined as Mischling of the second degree.

Speer flipped through the thick wad of documents noting that there were two field marshals and fifteen generals who had been categorised as Jewish. Their profiles were neatly sequenced by rank in alphabetical order.

He noted that Wilhelm Keitel had five children: Kurt-Heinz, Nona, Hans-George, Ernst-Wilhelm and Erika, whose names could not be more German. Von Brauchitsch had three. If anything happened to their fathers – if the Führer turned against them – would they grow up bent on revenge?

Speer unclipped the profile headed 'Field Marshal and State Secretary of Aviation Erhard Alfred Richard Oskar Milch.'

Under Milch's photograph in full military dress with a chest full of medals, the file read: 'In 1933, Frau Krista Milch swore an affidavit in the presence of her son-in-law Fritz Heinrich Hermann at that time President of Police in Hagen, Northern-Rhine-Westphalia (subsequently an SS General) that she did not have her six children born of a union between herself and her Jewish husband Anton Milch, but as a result of an on-going affair with her deceased uncle, Kurt Brauer. The case was investigated by the Gestapo but Hermann Goering in his capacity as President of the Reichstag interceded on Milch's behalf and showed the affidavit to the Führer. In 1935, the Führer granted Milch a German Blood Certificate.'

Someone had added a pencilled notation: 'I decide who is a Jew.'

Goering, thought Speer. Funny, in these days incest is more socially acceptable than being Jewish.

Berlin, October 12, 1943

When Gretchen clocked in for work at the Reichstag, she went straight to Marlene von Exner's office. It was her first official day at work and she wondered how she would be assigned. Would there be other women she worked with, tasting the Führer's lunch? What was the protocol? Once she had tasted the dish, what then? Did she have to sign a logbook or what? Would she alert Marlene or did she have to take the food to be reheated before it was put on the Führer's table?

And what if her sense of smell let her down, and she actually ingested some poison? Were there antidotes at hand in the kitchen? Would there be a doctor available?

She knocked on the door of the chef's tiny office. An unfamiliar voice invited her in.

Seated at Marlene von Exner's desk was a tall, large-boned woman with a broad, open face and a ready smile.

'Oh, sorry,' said Gretchen. 'I was looking for Frau von Exner.'

'You must be Gretchen. Come in if you would. It's a bit cramped in here, you must excuse me.'

Gretchen settled herself in the only chair and waited for her to speak. The woman seemed to be struggling to find the right words.

'My name is Constanze Manziarly. My father was Greek and my mother came from the Tyrol. I was born in Innsbruck. I am to be the Führer's new dietician and cook. From now on you will be reporting to me. Are you prepared to travel?'

'Yes, Frau Manzi- uh…' Gretchen stumbled over her name.

'It's a difficult name to pronounce,' laughed the woman. 'The Führer calls me Mozart and you can too if you like.'

'Frau Mozart?'

'Good. I will be cooking for the Führer wherever he is. When he is not in Berlin he stays mainly at his home in Obersalzberg in the Bavarian Alps. Near Berchtesgaden.'

Gretchen had no idea where that was.

'Is it far from Berlin?'

'It's about an eight-hour drive,' laughed the woman.

Her smile lit up her face and Gretchen did not feel the least embarrassed by her ignorance. 'Of course, by plane to Salzburg it's less than two hours.'

'I've never been in a plane,' said Gretchen. 'May I ask you what happened to Frau von Exner?'

The woman rose from her seat and closed the office door.

'Marlene became engaged to an SS adjutant, Gretchen. Naturally, they would do a thorough background check. They discovered that her great grandmother was Jewish. The Führer had no option but to fire her immediately. He made the rule, you see. He was sorry to see her go, he loved her Austrian cooking, but he told me, "I can't make one rule for myself and one for everyone else."'

Gretchen nodded but she was thinking of Kurt's friend, the Jewish guitarist. And her own mother.

Berlin, November 22, 1943

It was 7.30 pm when the sirens sounded.

Albert Speer was in the middle of a conference in his private office at the Ministry of Armaments and Munitions. He immediately ordered the meeting adjourned and had his driver take him to a nearby flak tower so that he could witness the attack.

He could hear the drone of the approaching aircraft. Even before the sound of the detonations reached him he could see the black flowers of the 22 millimetre anti-aircraft shells beginning to bloom in the beams of the searchlights.

He was on the final flight of steps to the top of the tower when the first bomb burst nearby causing the tower to shake. The rush of air from the blast threw the gunners against the concrete walls. Holding their ears, they rushed down the stairs past Speer amid a shower of dust that congealed the blood on their faces.

Speer waited until the explosions had stopped and the artillery fell silent. He climbed out onto the platform, ignoring the throbbing pain in his leg. Whenever he climbed stairs now he felt the pain. The searchlights were still raking the sky, but all was ominously quiet. The barrel of the flak gun was still hot and smoking.

He looked over at the building he had vacated a mere twenty minutes before. It was engulfed in flames. The fire lit up the night sky, and the space where his private office had been was now a deep crater.

He ordered his driver to take him back to what remained of the building. 'We must save what we can,' he said.

He saw secretaries in steel helmets carrying armfuls of files out of the burning building. But the fire was so fierce, whipped by the wind that it was now too dangerous to enter. The eight-storey Army Ordnance Office nearby was threatened by the flames.

Ordering the bystanders to follow him he rushed inside.

'At least we can save the special telephones,' he shouted. 'Rip them out of the walls and store them in the basement.'

Berlin, November 23, 1943

The next morning Speer was visited by General Emil Leeb, the chief of the Army Ordnance Office, to assess the damage.

'The fires in my building were extinguished in the morning hours,' Leeb told him. 'But unfortunately, we can't do any work now. Last night somebody ripped out all the telephones from the walls.'

Berchtesgaden, November 24, 1943

'They bombed the <u>Deutsche Opernhaus</u> on Bismarckstrasse last night,' said Constanze Manziarly, 'and I was so looking forward to going to the opera when the war is over.'

Gretchen did not want to talk about war and bombings. She was excited by the thought of her first flight in a plane and the prospect of being in the countryside away from smoldering buildings of Berlin.

They were en route to the Berghof, Hitler's mountain retreat in the Bavarian Alps. They had flown in a military plan to Salzburg and would be picked up by the Führer's personal chauffeur for the twenty-minute drive into the mountains.

From her window seat Gretchen looked down on the lush green valleys sloping steeply to the snow-capped mountains.

'I have copied out a list of menus for you – breakfast, lunch and dinner. Please look them over and memorise their ingredients. Once you have memorised them, you will give the file back to me.'

She handed Gretchen three-ring binder, which Gretchen began to study, although she would have preferred to enjoy the scenery.

Erich Kempka, Hitler's personal chauffeur, was waiting on the airstrip in a black Mercedes as the plane taxied to the single storey building. He took their luggage from them and placed the bags in the trunk.

'How are things at the Berghof?' asked Constanze by way of opening a conversation.

Kempka did not take his eyes off the road.

'Fine,' he replied.

They drove in silence up a dusty road pitted with potholes.

'It's like driving in Berlin now,' laughed Constanze, as they bumped along.

But still there was no reaction from Kempka.

'That's the Untersberg,' she said, pointing out the peak of a mountain range to Gretchen. 'It's 1,972 metres high. We'll get a really nice view of it from the Berghof.'

Ahead of them, Gretchen could see a high wire fence with barbed wire across the top. At the gate was a guardhouse manned by two soldiers armed with Sturmgewehr 44 assault rifles.

The chauffeur took out his pass and a letter of authorisation for Constanze and Gretchen. The soldier nodded to his partner who raised the bar allowing them through, then cranked a telephone.

A moment later, they arrived at another high fence with its command post and the same procedure was followed.

'There, Gretchen, you can see the Berghof now,' said Constanze. Lowering her voice, she added: 'Between us girls, I'm told he bought it with the royalties he made from the sales of *Mein Kampf*.'

Kempka parked the car at the front of the house.

'Are we sleeping here tonight?' whispered Gretchen as the chauffeur retrieved the bags.

'No, we have reservations at a pension in town. They'll drive us there.'

Gretchen breathed in the air. It seemed so pure and fresh in the mountains. Constanze beckoned her to follow. There was an elevator that had been blasted out of the rock that took them to a flag-stoned patio furnished with a couple of round tables, wooden chairs and canvas umbrellas.

Suddenly, a door next to the gigantic picture window opened and a German shepherd bounded out.

'Blondi, heel!'

The command came from inside the room, but it was soon followed by the presence on the patio of Hitler himself. He was dressed in lederhosen, knee-high socks and a cap. He carried a walking stick. The dog slunk to his side and eyed the two women suspiciously, then lowered herself to the flagstones on all fours.

'Ah, Frau Mozart. Welcome again to the Berghof. And who do we have here?'

Constanze gave the slightest of curtsies and replied: 'Mein Führer, this is Gretchen von Bismarck. She will be helping me in the kitchen for the next couple of days.'

Hitler stooped to pat the dog's ears.

'Yes, I remember you now. A little mishap with the soup if memory serves.'

Eva Braun appeared at his side.

'You should know we could never get it properly clean, Fraulein. The Führer could not wear it again.... Come Adolf, we should start our walk before it gets chilly.'

Hitler ignored her.

'Do you see that peak?' he said, pointing with his stick and looking straight at Gretchen. 'That's the Untersberg. There's a legend that the Emperor Frederick Barbarossa is sleeping inside the mountain. He's waiting for the day when he'll be reborn. He has a round table and his beard is growing longer and longer every year. It's curled twice around the table. After all, we're talking about the eleventh century, young lady. The legend says that when Barbarossa's beard has grown three times around the table...the end of the world will come.'

Hitler laughed and Eva Braun glowered at Gretchen. She took Hitler by the arm and began to lead him to the stairs that descended to the parking pad and the meadow beyond.

Hitler tipped his hat and touched Blondi with his stick. The dog leapt to her feet and followed her master, her tail wagging.

Gretchen watched them as Hitler and Eva Braun walked arm-in-arm across the meadow.

'We should go inside and prepare for dinner tonight,' said Constanze.

Gretchen followed her into the entrance hall. There were cactus plants in majolica pots around the walls. Beyond, Gretchen found herself in the great hall, a room that was full of heavy Teutonic furniture. A huge globe of the world stood in one corner. Three marble steps, the colour of dried blood, lead up to a huge fireplace. To the right of the fireplace was an oil painting of a naked woman. She was reclining on a pink taffeta sheet in a pastoral setting as a curly-haired angel, also naked, took an arrow from the quiver on his back.

She leant forward to read the plaque: 'Venus and Amor by Paris Bordone (1500–1571).'

'We'd better get set up in the kitchen,' said Constanze. 'He's having guests tonight.'

'Guests? Do you know who's coming?'

'Herr Goering and Martin Bormann.'

****

Carl von Bismarck checked the blackout curtains in his study and then hunched over the radio. He turned the volume down low and tuned into the frequency for the BBC Overseas Service.

He placed his ear against the speaker. In the distance, he could hear explosions like rolling thunder as the British and Americans continued to bomb Berlin.

So intent was he on hearing what the BBC announcer had to say, that he was unaware of his wife Greta's approach.

He started at the sound of her voice.

'You shouldn't be listening to that, Carl. They're driving around with equipment monitoring houses, as I've told you.'

'With all the bombing I don't think they're worrying about who's listening to the BBC at the moment, my darling. At least Gretchen is away from Berlin.'

Greta took a seat next to her husband.

'That's what I wanted to talk to you about. I know she can't tell us what she is doing, but maybe Herr Speer could give us an idea as a family friend.'

Von Bismarck switched off the radio.

'If he were able to tell me, I'm sure he would. From the little I know, I suspect that she is working with the Nazi leadership. That photo in the paper, remember it? She called me this morning to say she's going to the country for a couple of days.'

'The country?'

'Something to do with a new chef taking her to prepare meals in Berchtesgaden.'

'Berchtesgaden? Where's that?"

'Hitler has a mountain retreat there. She'll be cooking for the Führer I presume.'

'Oh Lord preserve us. Surely they'll be bombing there.'

'She's safer there than in Berlin.'

'Can't we send her away somewhere? Now that that woman has resurfaced...' Greta did not finish the statement.

'If Gretchen were to leave now they'd be suspicious. The Gestapo would follow her. It would only be a matter of time before they discovered a link to Frau Becker.'

Greta wrung her hands. 'I wish Krista were dead and her secret with her.'

'Greta, my love. It's our secret too.'

'But I'm only thinking of Gretchen, Carl. Maybe we can get Krista out of the country. To Switzerland or to Spain. She can start a new life there. Surely there must be a way. Cook will know where she is now.'

'It's not that simple, Greta. The moment we contact her we are compromising Gretchen's safety. We must protect the woman at all costs. If the SS finds out she's Jewish they will come after us for having hired a Jew.'

'But we are von Bismarcks!'

'In these times, *meine liebchen*, nobody is above Hitler's laws.'

****

Gretchen tied an apron around her waist and studied the printed menu that Constanze had placed on the kitchen table.

Asparagus with hollandaise sauce
Vegetable broth with semolina dumplings
Roasted red peppers
Rice
Salad
Vegetable stew
Chocolate eclairs
Tea

'The guests will be having Wienerschnitzel with boiled potatoes and sauerkraut,' said Constanze, 'and he will tease them about their meat-eating habits.'

She opened a cardboard box. 'Have a look at these.'

Inside the box were a dozen chocolate eclairs each decorated with little marzipan swastikas.

'They're his favourite, 'said Constanze. 'His pastry chef Gerhardt Shtammer makes them and we have to have them on hand all the time. How he loves his desserts. You know, he puts seven teaspoons of sugar in each cup and on those rare occasions he takes a glass of wine, he puts sugar in that too. Can you imagine?'

'So once we've prepared the food what do I do?'

'You will go into the room adjacent to the kitchen and sit down at the table. An SS officer will bring in each dish with a copy of the menu and a pencil. You taste each dish and check them off one by one, writing any notes you think necessary and then you sign and date the menu.'

'What happens then?'

'The officer reads what you have written, and when he's satisfied he will have the meal served at the Führer's table. The menu is then filed for future reference…. At least you get to eat well.'

Gretchen looked longingly at the eclairs. 'Those look great. I'm not a great fan of marzipan though,' she said.

'You just have to taste a bit,' said Constanze.

It wasn't the marzipan that Gretchen objected to but the idea of ingesting a swastika.

'Why is he so worried about being poisoned?' asked Gretchen, lowering her voice. 'With all that security and the SS around nobody can get in here.'

* * * *

Gretchen could hear the conversation coming from the Great Hall. Hitler was holding forth in an unbroken monologue. He sounded as if he was on the radio.

'Christianity is the prototype of Bolshevism,' Hitler droned on. 'The mobilisation by the Jew of the masses of slaves with the object of undermining society. Science cannot lie, for it's always striving, according to the momentary state of knowledge, to deduce what is true. When it makes a mistake, it does so in good faith. It's Christianity that's the liar….'

Constanze shook her head and smiled. 'Imagine having to listen to that all night. Poor Eva, she isn't even allowed to wear make-up.'

There was movement in the Great Hall, suggesting that Hitler was inviting his guests to the table.

A tall, gaunt SS officer appeared in the kitchen.

'The Führer is at the table, Frau Manziarly. You will begin service.'

He turned to leave and then stopped.

'I have your report,' he said to Gretchen, then to Constanze, 'The Führer has asked that the young fraulein serve him and his guests.'

He waited for Constanze to acknowledge the command, then clicked his heels and disappeared.

'My goodness,' said Constanze. 'You *did* make an impression.'

When the first course of asparagus and hollandaise sauce had been plated, Gretchen placed the four dishes on a tray. She lifted the tray, took a deep breath, and pushed open the door to the dining room.

With lowered eyes she took it in the room. Hitler was seated at the head of the table, the furthest from her. On his left sat Eva Braun and adjacent on Hitler's right sat Martin Bormann, almost obscured from her vision by the corpulent figure of Hermann Goering whose back was to Gretchen. Bormann had an open notebook on the table and appeared to be writing down everything Hitler said.

Barely visible in the shadowed corner of the room sat two SS guards.

Goering, who had not noticed Gretchen's entrance, was saying, '...and according to Lieutenant Colonel Eichmann, when we invade Hungary he will need more trains to move the Jews to –'

Hitler waved a finger at him.

'Hermann, no doubt you will recognise the young lady behind you as you both graced the front page of Das Reich. When was it, Martin?'

'March 24, 1941, mein Führer.'

'What a memory. You should be in cabaret,' smirked Hitler. 'Blind-folded, reciting the Berlin phone directory.'

Bormann smiled thinly. Goering shifted his bulk for a better look at Gretchen, who had placed the tray on the sideboard behind him.

'Ah yes,' said Goering. 'The Hotel Adlon. I do remember. Maybe I should be in cabaret too.'

The assembled company laughed as Gretchen carefully placed the plates of asparagus in front of Hitler and his mistress. Eva Braun's eyes never left her. Bormann was staring at her breasts.

'The flower of German youth,' said Hitler, smiling up at Gretchen. 'The quintessential Aryan.'

'You're making the child blush,' scolded Eva. 'Do you want more hollandaise? You know how much you like it.... Fraulein, bring more sauce for the Führer.'

'Perhaps later,' said Hitler, leaning back in his chair. 'Please give my compliments to Frau Mozart, Gretchen von Bismarck.'

Gretchen, relieved to be dismissed, retreated back to the kitchen. She waited behind the closed door for the conversation to start again.

Goering was speaking, loud enough for her to hear through the stout oak door. 'Eichmann has estimated that there are 500,000 Jews living outside Budapest. He's suggesting for ease of transport so they can be rounded up and dispatched to the cities....'

'Gretchen,' called Constanze, 'can you give me a hand with the dumplings.'

Reluctantly, she made her way back to the kitchen.

Eva Braun followed her in.

'Frau Manziarly, may I see the menu,' she asked.

Constanze wiped her hands on her apron and took down the menu she had pinned to a corkboard.

Eva scanned it quickly.

'Please ensure the soup is hot. I will take it in. There is no need for this young lady to wait on the table. I imagine you have other chores for her.'

'As you wish, Frau Braun.'

'But she can clear the dishes now.'

Constanze nodded to Gretchen, who moved towards the dining room.

When Gretchen returned with the dishes, Constanze was ladling out portions of piping hot soup over the semolina dumplings.

Eva bent over and lifted the tray when the four bowls had been filled. As she began to move towards the dining room, Constanze called, 'Wait!'

Hitler's mistress stopped and frowned. Constanze came up behind her. She was carrying a small plastic container. Dipping her fingers into it, she withdrew a pinch of chopped parsley, which she sprinkled over each bowl.

The cook, waiting until Eva was out of the room, beckoned Gretchen closer. In a low whisper, she said: 'You have to forgive her. It can't be easy. She's not allowed to be seen in public with him and whenever she travels with him there are always two secretaries with her. I don't understand why he keeps up the pretence. Everybody knows.'

'Maybe he wants us to believe he's married to the German people,' said Gretchen.

They both put their hands to their mouths to stifle their giggles.

Suddenly, there was a roar of anger from the dining room.

'Oh Lord,' said Constanze. 'You'd better go and see what happened.'

Hitler was sitting bolt upright in his chair, his arms fully extended, his hands in tight fists. He glared at Gretchen as she entered.

'Come here!'

Gretchen approached the table.

'Here! Beside me.'

She looked nervously around the room hoping she could get some clue as to the reason for Hitler's angry outburst. The others were staring at their plates.

'You tasted the food?'

His eyes were blazing and the blood vessels stood out on his neck.

'Yes.'

'Yes, what?'

'Yes, mein Führer.'

'And what did you think?'

'The broth was delicious.'

'The broth was delicious. Well, taste it again.'

Hitler pushed the bowl roughly towards her, spilling some of the soup on the tablecloth.

All eyes were on her as she picked up the spoon Hitler had used and dipped it into the bowl. Carefully, she lifted the spoon to her lips and took a sip.

The broth tasted like seawater.

'Take it away and send in Frau Manziarly,' ordered Hitler.

Gretchen, shaking, tears glistening in her eyes, picked up the offending bowl, mumbled her apologies and backed away to the kitchen.

Constanze eyed her quizzically.

'He wants to see you.'

The cook took in a deep breath and raised her eyebrows.

Alone in the kitchen, Gretchen sat down at the table and rested her head on her arms. She willed herself not to cry. Would it be like this all the time? She wished she had never taken the job.

'I don't think I can take more of this,' she said to herself.

She could hear Hitler's angry voice and Constanze trying to mollify him. When she came back to the kitchen, the cook was ashen-faced.

'Where is it?'

Gretchen indicated the bowl that she had left by the sink. Constanze took a clean spoon from the drawer and took a taste of the broth.

Immediately she spat it out into the sink.

'Oh, sweet Jesus…that bitch!'

'What happened?'

Constanze struggled to control herself, gritting her teeth and pressing her interlocked fingers together.

'When she came in here, I saw her put a salt shaker in her pocket.'

Berlin, January 12, 1944

'Do we really have to go to his birthday party?'

Margarete glanced at her husband's reflection in the mirror. She saw him wince as he pulled on the trousers of his dress uniform.

'If we don't go, he'll take it as a personal insult. I need him as an ally, with Sauckel and Bormann conspiring against me.'

Margarete drew a brush through her hair.

'How old is he now?'

'Goering? He must be sixty. No, sixty-one. He expects everyone to bring him expensive presents. You know what he wanted from me?'

'No.'

Speer laughed.

'A marble bust of Hitler by Arno Breker. You remember the statue Breker did – the one just as you come into the carriage entrance of the Reich Chancellery?'

'You mean the naked man with the torch?'

'Yes. It's meant to represent the spirit of the Nazi Party. Goering wants Breker to do Hitler's bust, only larger than life size.'

Margarete saw him wince again.

'You're going to have to do something about that knee, Albert. You can't go on ignoring it.'

'I wish I had the time. If you're out of the Führer's circle you're out of his mind, and you might as well just fade away.'

'But you're killing yourself with work. And for what? We're losing this war.'

'Don't ever say that!' flared Speer. 'Don't let anyone ever hear you say that. There could be consequences.'

'But it's true. It's never been the same after Russia. Now they're bombing us all the time…. What will life be for us, Albert? The British and the Americans will put you on trial with the rest of them.'

'You must not talk like that, Margarete. There are things you don't know. Things I can't tell you.'

'Then promise me at least you'll have your knee looked at.'

'I will,' he said. 'But do get ready. Kurt will be downstairs with the car in fifteen minutes.'

Carinhall, January 12, 1944

C arinhall, Herman Goering's country residence, was a large hunting estate an hour's drive from Berlin. Goering named the house after his first wife, Carin Fock, the daughter of a Swedish baron. Carin Fock died of a heart attack in Stockholm while attending her mother's funeral in 1931, and in 1935 Carinhall became the venue for the wedding to his second wife, Emmy Sonnenmann.

All this Speer recounted to Margarete as Kurt drove them through the blacked-out city and north to the Schorfheide forest. He was determined to distract his wife from her mood of pessimism.

Margarete wondered how Emmy Sonnenmann must have felt, living in a house named after her husband's first wife. At least I don't have an ex-wife to contend with, she thought. Only a mother-in-law who disapproved of her son marrying me. It took seven years, seven years, after our marriage before she invited me to stay in their house. And then only after I gave them a grandson.

'So, Kurt,' said Albert, turning his attentions to the driver, trying to keep the conversation light. 'How are things with you and the von Bismarck girl?'

'Pretty good,' replied the young man. 'I haven't seen her much lately. She's been travelling. She's coming back next weekend, so perhaps we'll get together.'

How casually the young took these things, thought Speer. Maybe it's the war that's changed everything, the uncertainty of the future. Living for the moment. It was all so different from those bygone days when I was courting Margarete.

The party was well underway when the Speers entered Carinhall. Uniformed SS guards took their coats and handed them a glass of champagne.

'Nothing but the best for Hermann,' whispered Speer to his wife. 'Apparently, his old pilot buddy Bruno Loerzer flies in planeloads of stuff from the Italian black market, nylon stockings, soap and other luxury goods that Goering gets his people to sell. Look around the walls and you can see where all the money goes.'

Just then their beaming host approached them with open arms.

'Herr Speer and the beautiful Margarete! Welcome to Carinhall.'

'Thank you, a pleasure to be here to celebrate your birthday, Reichsmarschall.'

'And how is Herr Brecker's bust coming along?'

'I was hoping to have it ready so that I could deliver it to you on your birthday, but you know how artists are. Any day now, he promised.'

'Ah yes, the artistic temperament, not so dramatically manifest in architects though, eh, Herr Speer? Not for someone who manages war production like you.'

Speer did not know whether to take this as a compliment or a sly dig at someone who had not risen within the party ranks from the days of the Beer Hall Putsch. He merely smiled and nodded.

'Come, I want to show you the tributes I've received. And I have something else I'd like you to see.'

Tributes, thought Speer, you mean bribes. He allowed himself to be led into the library where a large oak table was laden with oil paintings and sculptures and cigars from Holland.

Spread out on an adjacent table were architectural drawings weighted down with gold bars.

'These are plans for the extension to my private residence,' said Goering with pride. 'I'd like your professional opinion.'

Speer glanced at the plans. With a practised eye he could tell this was no mere extension. It would double the size of Goering's home to the dimensions of a palace.

'Very impressive,' said Magarete, without enthusiasm.

'Ah, I think I see Field Marshal Milch. You must excuse me,' said Goering, walking quickly away towards the hall, leaving behind him a gossamer net of his perfume that hung in the air with the odour of rotting lilies.

Speer leant over the table. He could feel himself beginning to sweat. He began to tremble.

'Maragrete,' he whispered. 'I don't feel well. Please get my coat. I have to leave. But quietly, without a fuss. Get Kurt. We're going home. I don't want these vultures to smell carrion.'

Berlin, January 13, 1944

Krista Becker's eyes constantly flicked to the windows of the coffee shop as she methodically dried the cups. Across the street she could see the entrance to the apartment block where the von Bismarcks lived when they were in Berlin.

She had inveigled herself a job there, accepting a lower wage than Heidi, the sullen, truculent girl who read Prinzess Baccara romance magazines instead of tending to the needs of the clientele.

Krista had hoped that she would catch sight of her daughter, but the days had passed with no sign of the girl. She had ingratiated herself with the doorman by bringing him coffee and had learned that Gretchen would be back today. No, he didn't know where she had travelled to, only that she had a suitcase with her.

She caught sight of an official-looking black Mercedes drawing up to the curb in front of the apartment block. The driver, in Nazi uniform, opened the rear door and Gretchen stepped out. She waited on the sidewalk as the driver went to the trunk to retrieve her suitcase.

'Heidi,' Krista whispered to her co-worker seated behind the bar, engrossed in her magazine. 'I have to go out for one moment. Will you cover for me, please?'

The girl sighed. 'OK, but don't be long. The lunchtime rush will start soon.'

Krista took off her apron and reached for her coat. She waited until the car had pulled away and ran across the street, calling to Gretchen.

The girl stopped as she was about to enter the building.

'Krista, what is it?'

'I have to talk to you.'

'How long have you been waiting here?'

'I took a job across the road,' she said, pointing to the coffee shop.

'Are you spying on me?'

'No, child, but there are things you have to know.'

Tears coursed down Krista's cheeks.

'You're crying. What's the matter?'

'It's my mother...your grandmother. A neighbour reported her because of the noise of her radio. My mother is going deaf, so she always had the volume turned up. The police came and they found a Hebrew prayer book. They took her away, Gretchen. They took my mother to a concentration camp.'

Gretchen gasped.

'That's awful. I'm so sorry.'

'Gretchen, you must speak to your father. He must help her. I can't leave her to die in a concentration camp.'

'I don't know what my father could do.'

'But you know these people. Your photo in the newspaper with Goering. Herr Speer. You must save her. She's your grandmother.'

'Where did they take her?'

'I'm not sure, but I think it's Ravensbrück.'

'Ravensbrück?'

'It's a concentration camp for women north of Berlin. They have gas chambers there, Gretchen. They're going to kill my mother...Your grandmother.'

Gretchen had never met either of her von Bismarck grandmothers. They had both died before she was born. As a child, playing with her dolls, she had often wondered what it would be like to have a grandmother. She had only read about them in books. White-haired old ladies with glasses who smiled and dandled their grandchildren on their knees and hugged them a lot.

Hearing Krista's news, she felt a sudden pang of loss as if a memory of what might have been had been snatched away from her. A grandmother she never knew she had and might never get to know.

Berlin, January 14, 1944

They made love for the first time in Gretchen's bedroom. Kurt had laughed when she turned her teddy bear to face the wall.

Wrapped in each other's arms they were oblivious to the air raid sirens and the crump, crump sound of exploding ordinance.

For Gretchen it was the first time and she thought if she were to die that night at least it would be with a heart full of love.

They lay quietly for a while afterward, each with their own thoughts.

'When this war is over,' Kurt began, but Gretchen placed a finger on his lips to kill the thought.

'Let's not talk about the war. Let's just enjoy this. I'm so tired of it all.'

'I know,' said Kurt. 'But it's all around us. Listen to the bombs.'

'If only we could run away to somewhere safe, where people aren't crying in the streets, where there's no need for bomb shelters.'

'I thought you were excited about your new job…whatever it is.'

'Oh Kurt, I wish I could tell you about it. There are so many things I wish I could tell you. So many secrets, sometimes I think my head is going to explode.'

Kurt propped himself up on one elbow and studied her face.

'You're very beautiful, Gretchen.'

She smiled, 'Thank you.'

'Today, while I was walking over here,' said Kurt, 'I saw an old man being beaten by two SS types. He had a Star of David sewn to his coat. He had a white beard that was turning red with blood. I tried to intervene, but one of them pulled a pistol on me.'

'What happened to him?'

'They took him to a car and drove off.'

'What would you have done if you could?'

'I don't know. Stopped them hurting him, I guess.'

'You know what will happen to him, don't you?' said Gretchen.

Kurt nodded.

'I've heard about the camps. The father of one of my troop leaders is the commandant at Buchenwald. He told me about the gas chambers. And the black smoke from the chimneys that hang over Weimar when they burn the corpses. He told me the maids complain because they have to dust twice that day because of the ash…. He actually laughed.'

'That's horrible. How can people be so cruel?'

Kurt traced the line of her cheek with his fingertips.

'In the Hitler Youth they taught us to hate Jews. It was all their fault, the treaty from the first World War, the economic situation, the reasons for this war. They blame everything on the Jews…. I know I shouldn't say this, Gretchen, but I'm ashamed of being German.'

'You have a good heart, Kurt.'

Kurt smiled.

'I think my uncle is losing faith in Hitler. In our ability to win the war.'

'How do you know?'

'It's just a feeling. Nothing he's said. But when I'm driving him he seems to be spending a lot of time brooding. He has papers on his lap but he's not reading them. He stares out of the window at the destruction of Berlin.'

Gretchen wondered if she could confide in him, but once he knew what was in her mind there could be no turning back – because, at that moment, with the wail of the sirens, the distant explosions, and the flashes of the searchlights playing across the ceiling – she knew she had to do something.

Hohenlychen Hospital, January 19, 1944

Albert Speer lay back in his hospital bed, his inflamed left knee in a cast supported by a sling attached to the ceiling.

He had been admitted the day before to Hohenlychen Hospital, situated in a pastoral, wooded setting by a lake 100 kilometres north of Berlin. But for the work-driven Speer, it might well have been the dark side of the moon, so removed was he from the daily flood of communications. A bank of telephones had been installed to keep him in touch with his office, but there had been few calls.

SS Gruppenführer Dr. Kurt Gebhardt had performed his operation the previous day. He was Heinrich Himmler's personal physician and the doctor who had been consulted on a knee injury to the Belgian King Leopold III. Gebhardt was also the coordinator of surgical experiments conducted on inmates at Ravensbrück and Auschwitz.

When Speer had awakened at his customary hour of 5am he found a brown paper envelope had been slid under the door.

He rang for a nurse and asked her to bring him the envelope.

'Do you know you left this?' he asked.

'No, Herr Speer,' replied the nurse.

He turned it over and inspected both sides. The envelope had been fastened with a wax seal. There was no indication as to who had sent it or how it had arrived.

'Will you find out if anyone approached my room last night?'

'I was the only one on duty, sir. No one passed my station.'

'Thank you. That will be all.'

When the nurse had left the room, he broke the seal and pulled out a file. There was a note clipped to the cover: 'For Your Eyes Only. Read And Destroy.'

Inside were 17 typewritten pages. From the format it appeared to be an official SS document. It was headed, 'A Timeline of Attempts to Assassinate the Führer.'

The door opened and Speer slid the file under the blankets.

'Your breakfast, Herr Speer,' said an orderly as he placed a tray on the bedside table. 'Will you have coffee this morning or would you prefer tea with lemon as the doctor prescribed?'

'Coffee. Later. And you will kindly knock before entering.'

'*Jawohl*, Herr Speer.'

Alone again, he pulled out the file and began to read its contents with a growing sense of alarm.

Each page had columns headed 'Date,' 'Place,' 'Type,' 'Assassin' and 'Details.'

The first entry was dated Munich, November 1921; an unknown shooter fired shots at Hitler from a crowd he was addressing. In 1923 in Thuringia, the same thing. In that year shots were fired at Hitler's car in Leipzig. In January 1932, an attempt was made to poison him and his staff as they dined at the Hotel Kaiserhof. Within an hour of eating, most of his guests had fallen ill. In 1934, there were four attempts on his life, two bombings and two shootings; from 1935 till the outbreak of the war, there were a further nine attempts on Hitler's life.

On July 27th, 1940, Count Fritz-Dietlof von der Schulenberg had planned to shoot the Führer as he watched the victory parade in Paris; but Hitler had cancelled the parade.

The most recent attempt was engineered by Major General Henning von Tresckow, Field Marshal Günther von Kluge and other sympathisers. Tresckow asked a colleague if he would take a bomb disguised as two bottles of Cognac on Hitler's plane, which would detonate in midair. The bottles were placed in an unheated overhead locker. The cold interfered with the detonation mechanism and the bomb failed to go off.

The final page described the last recorded effort to dispatch Hitler. A group of U.S. airmen planned to overfly the Berghof and drop huge quantities of pornographic films and magazines. The rationale was that Hitler would go mad with lust and kill himself. The Gestapo had gotten wind of the plan, but the U.S. military had already dismissed the idea as 'silly.'

Speer counted up the number of documented plots and attempts on the life of Adolph Hitler: there had to date been thirty-two.

The man leads a charmed life, he said to himself.

A knock at the door startled Speer. He quickly gathered up the papers and stuffed them back into the envelope, hiding it under his pillow.

'Come in.'

Dr. Kurt Gebhardt entered. He wore a white coat with a stethoscope hooked around his neck.

'*Guten Morgen*, Herr Speer. And how's my patient this fine morning? Any pain? Did you sleep well?'

'As well as I could, hoist up here like a trapeze artist.'

The doctor laughed.

'Let me have a look at it.'

As Gebhardt lowered his head for a closer inspection of his patient's cast, Speer slid out the envelope for him to notice.

Was Gebhardt the messenger?

There was no reaction from the doctor when Speer casually tapped the envelope with his fingertips.

'Once you're out of the plaster cast, we'll start you on a course of physiotherapy,' said the doctor. 'No skiing for you this season, I'm afraid.'

If it was not Gebhardt who had put the file at his bedside, who had?

Was it the same anonymous SS officer who had provided him with the secret list of Jewish officers in the Wehrmacht? And if so, what was the purpose?

Was it a warning or a threat?

Or was it a call to action?

Berlin, January 19, 1944

G retchen clasped the cup of tea in both hands. It was freezing in the apartment. The radiators were cold. She had called down to the concierge desk and asked if this was the only apartment without heat.

'No, Fraulein. The fuel truck with the oil for the furnace hasn't arrived yet. Our ration has been cut and the road at the back where they deliver is impassable.'

The cold had added to Gretchen's sense of depression. She had awoken that morning drenched with perspiration from a nightmare. She had dreamt that a gang of Hitler Youth dressed in their brown shirts was dragging Krista down a street to a railway station. A woman with white hair and glasses was standing at an open cattle car, beckoning to her and smiling. Behind her was a man seated on a chair bent over a guitar in the attitude of a lover. There was black smoke in the air and ashes were falling like grey snowflakes.

She kept going over the conversation she had had with Kurt, the night they made love. His words came back to her about the death camps and the old Jewish man he had witnessed being beaten.

The time had come, she decided, that she had to do something. She had to be brave. She could not sit back and close her eyes to what was happening around her.

But what could she do?

Hohenlychen Hospital, January 20, 1944

T he drugs that Dr. Gebhardt had prescribed for Albert Speer not only eased the architect's post-operative pain, but caused him to hallucinate. The thoughts that had preoccupied him in his lucid moments – of being undermined by his subordinates as he lay helpless in his hospital bed – developed into a drug-induced state of paranoia.

He was convinced that the SS guard posted outside his door to protect him was a member of the Gestapo who had been eavesdropping on his telephone conversations; and what if he had been talking in his sleep?

He sent a message to his nephew Kurt asking him to come to the hospital and to bring him his Luger. He would find it in a holster hanging on a hook inside the wardrobe in his bedroom. Kurt was to put the gun in a box, cover it with parchment paper and a layer of cookies that Margarete had baked for him.

Speer lay back on the pillows determined to do without the pills the nurse brought to him in a tiny paper cup twice a day.

He fell into a much-needed sleep, but sprang up two hours later at the sound of a knock on the door.

'Come in.'

The door opened and Kurt stepped inside the room holding a cardboard box with both hands.

'Ah, excellent, Kurt. You've brought my favourite cookies,' he said loud enough for the guard outside to hear. 'Come, sit down by me.'

Kurt shut the door with his elbow and placed the box on the table next to the bed.

'How are you feeling, uncle?'

'As if I've been hit with a Howitzer. Thank you for coming.'

'How long will you be in here?'

'The doctor says at least two weeks, and then there will be physiotherapy.'

He reached for the box and began to untie the string.

Kurt felt uncomfortable seeing his uncle wince in pain.

'You heard that the Luftwaffe sank a British destroyer off the Italian coast last week, uncle.'

'Yes, they keep me briefed. Goering must be thinking there's another medal in it for him…. Cookie?'

'No, thank you.'

Speer lifted the parchment paper and took out the Luger. He felt its weight and then slipped it under his pillow.

'You can't be too careful these days…. So, how goes your romance with the von Bismarck girl?'

'That's what I wanted to talk to you about, uncle. A friend of mine, a pilot, said he'd been looking at the log books for flights to Obersalzberg. And he noticed Gretchen's name, several times, for periods of a week. Why would she be flying to Obersalzberg?'

Speer bit into a cookie and chewed as if he hadn't heard the question.

'Are you sure you don't want a cookie? Your aunt is a wizard in the kitchen.'

'No, really. I've never heard of Obersalzberg. I looked it up on the map. It's in the Bavarian Alps. What would she be doing there?'

'Have you asked her?'

'She won't talk about it.'

Speer nodded.

'Are you in love with her?'

'Yes…, I think I am.'

'Then you must trust her.'

'But how can I be sure? I tell her everything, uncle. I have no secrets from her.'

The sadness in the young man's eyes evoked a memory of his courtship of Margarete. He recalled meeting the woman who would become his wife in June 1922. She was the daughter of a successful craftsman living in Heidelberg; but she was not socially acceptable to Speer's class-conscious mother. The couple married six years later against her wishes.

'Come a little closer,' said Speer. 'Lean in. I will tell you something that will put your mind at rest.'

Kurt pulled his chair closer to the bed.

'Your young lady is in the service of the Führer. Obersalzberg is where he is staying. I cannot tell you more than that.'

Far from putting Kurt's mind at rest, his uncle's revelation had caused the blood to rush to his face.

The girl he was in love with, the girl he would ask to marry him, he now understood was Hitler's mistress.

Hohenlychen Hospital, January 28, 1944

Every day as he lay in his hospital bed, fretting about his staff undermining his authority, Albert Speer received reports on the conduct of the war on all fronts. These were not the anodyne, morale-boosting

bulletins issued by Joseph Goebbels' Ministry of Public Enlightenment and Propaganda designed to reassure the German people that
their army was invincible and that they were winning the war.

Nor were they the encoded messages sent by the front-line generals who tempered their reports so as not to incur the carpet-biting
wrath of the Führer.

They came from officers Speer had befriended over the course of
his dealings with the military. They arrived, secretly and unadorned,
and they spoke of the reality of the situation as it was on the ground.

They made depressing reading for the Minister of Armaments and
War Production.

He read that Soviet troops had advanced into Poland. That the
American 697th Field Artillery Battalion was using 240 mm Howitzers
to bombard German-held territory near Cassino, Italy. He learned
that on January 22nd, the Allies had landed at Anzio on the Lazio
coast, a mere 50 kilometres from Rome. Five days later, the siege of
Leningrad was relieved by a Soviet Leningrad-Novgorod Strategic
Offensive, which expelled German forces from the southern outskirts
of the city.

As his informant noted, the siege of Leningrad was one of the lon-
gest and most destructive sieges in history and the most expensive in
terms of casualties. Nearly two million soldiers and civilians perished
during the 900-day siege. One in three of the city's population died of
starvation in the streets.

Speer lowered the paper to his chest, thinking of his brother dying
of jaundice in Stalingrad. He could have saved Ernst if he had acted
sooner, and not put his loyalty to Hitler above his own family.

He smiled ruefully, remembering how Hitler was so confident in
the beginning that his forces would take Leningrad that he had the
invitations for the victory celebrations already printed. The event was
to be held in Leningrad's Hotel Astoria, where it would be announced
that the city would be renamed Adolfsburg.

The final sheet contained a single paragraph, which was the most
disquieting news of all. 'One of our agents in Madrid has picked up
information that the British, Americans and Canadians are planning
to invade France in the summer, landing somewhere along the north
coast. The invasion goes under the codename, 'Operation Overlord.'

It was this revelation that made Albert Speer realise then and
there that Germany had lost the war. That all his plans for the future

– rebuilding the cities, creating a Thousand-Year Reich, the glory that might have been – would come to nothing.

And one man was responsible for the ultimate catastrophe – Adolph Hitler.

As a minister, he had sworn an oath of allegiance to his leader. And as the Führer's protégé, he had risen to be one of the most powerful men in Germany without having to climb within the ranks of the Nazi Party. Hitler had treated him like a son and applauded all his triumphs, shown him special favours and brought him into his inner circle. He recalled the hours they had spent alone together poring over the plans for the Nuremberg Stadium, the Chancellery, the Great Hall and Hitler's new palace and all the other buildings that would celebrate the New Germany in stone and concrete.

How could he turn against the man who had provided him the means to reshape his Fatherland?

And yet, the same man was bringing the country to its knees. The Russian disaster was bad enough. Had Hitler, a self-proclaimed student of history, learned nothing from Napoleon? Then there was Himmler's Posen decree that Jewish women and children should be exterminated along with their men – an order from the Führer that would come back to haunt the German people.

The conclusion was shocking yet inevitable: Hitler had to be gotten rid of before Germany imploded.

Berlin, January 29, 1944

The order came from Himmler himself. Squads of Hitler Youth were to take to the streets of Berlin. They were to assist the civil authority by removing debris from the major thorough fares, so that ambulances and fire engines could move freely around the city.

As the Berlin leader of the Hitler Youth, Kurt Andorfer was tasked with allocating areas of the metropolis to fifty squads comprised of ten boys each. He chose for his section a five-block area around Petersburger Strasse – the street where Gretchen lived.

The previous evening's bombing raid had caused multiple fires. Mercifully, there had been no wind so the conflagration created by the incendiary bombs had been contained; but the streets were littered with upturned cobble stones, bricks, charred timbers and the personal effects of the civilian population.

Kurt stationed his section outside Gretchen's apartment building as he briefed them on their assignment. Any object larger than a pebble had to be removed from the street and placed at the outer edge of the sidewalk. Cobble stones should be replaced and any damage to water mains or electrical wires be reported to him and he would mark them on his map and radio the locations to the local fire department.

He handed out workman's gloves to each of the boys and ordered them to start the clean-up.

'Be careful of any traffic. If you see a car, drop what you're doing and raise your hand like a traffic policeman. I don't want anyone to be hit. Is that clear?'

The boys nodded their assent.

'Then off you go.'

'Aren't you forgetting something, Herr Andorfer?' said the eldest boy. 'Our salute.'

'Oh yes. Very good, Stephan…. Heil Hitler!'

'Heil Hitler!' piped the section in unison, their left arms raised.

Across the street, Krista Becker observed the scene through the window of the coffee bar. She saw the uniformed boys fan out and begin to collect the debris from the street.

She recognised Kurt as the young man she had seen with Gretchen. She watched him as he entered the apartment block. A minute later he reappeared and began to assist his section in replacing cobblestones.

Krista turned away to serve a coffee to a customer.

Suddenly, there was a loud explosion that shattered the window of the coffee bar.

One of the boys working a few metres away from Kurt had unearthed an unexploded cluster bomb wedged between the cobblestones. He was trying to extract it.

The blast had killed the boy instantly and knocked Kurt off his feet. He lay dazed and disoriented in the road, blood trickling from his ears.

Krista grabbed a towel and rushed into the street. The boys had gathered around Kurt in a circle. Some were crying. All of them were trembling.

Krista pushed her way through and knelt down beside Kurt. She cradled his head and felt his neck for a pulse.

'Go into that apartment building and get the doorman to call an ambulance,' she ordered. 'Now!'

As the boys rushed en masse to the apartment building, she shouted after them,' And bring a blanket to cover that poor boy.'

She wiped the blood from Kurt's face and spoke softly to him.

'Stay calm. You'll be all right. The ambulance is on its way. Just think of Gretchen.'

At the sound of her name, Kurt's eyes flickered. He frowned and stared up at the woman who held his head so tenderly.

'Gretchen,' he murmured.

And then he lost consciousness.

****

When the ambulance arrived, Krista Becker insisted on accompanying Kurt to the hospital.

'Where are you taking him?' she asked the medic who was monitoring Kurt's heart rate.

'Are you his mother?'

'No, his aunt,' she replied, hoping that this would be enough to allow her to accompany the wounded man.

'Most of the hospitals in Berlin are full,' replied the medic. 'People are being treated in the corridors. Mostly eye injuries from the bombing. We have to go to the Beelitz Sanatorium, southwest of Berlin.'

Kurt had regained consciousness, but his eyes were closed and he was trying to speak. Krista took his hand and pressed it reassuringly.

'Just be still. You're going to be fine. They'll take good care of you.'

'Your nephew is lucky,' said the medic. 'The Beelitz is where the Führer was treated for a thigh injury during the Battle of the Somme in the First World War.'

When news of Kurt's injury reached Albert Speer later that day, he immediately phoned the Sanatorium and asked to speak to the chief medical officer.

'This is Albert Speer, Minister of Armaments and War Production. Who am I speaking to?'

'Dr. Helmut Burger, Herr Minister. To what do I owe the pleasure?'

'You have a newly admitted patient, Kurt Arndorfer. I want him to have the best possible care. He is very important to the war effort. Can you tell me his status?'

'Arndorfer, you say. Let me consult the records and get back to you. You must appreciate our staff is under a great deal of pressure due to the bombing.'

'Yes, yes. I understand. He is to have a private room and I want updated bulletins on his progress. I will give you my private number. You will call me as soon as you have word.'

'Of course, Herr Minister.'

'Heil Hitler.'

****

That evening when Gretchen returned to the von Bismarck apartment, the doorman waylaid her and recounted the scene he had witnessed earlier in the day.

'A group of Hitler Youth were clearing the street of debris and suddenly there was an explosion. One boy was killed and a lady from the coffee bar came out to help. They took the leader away in an ambulance,' he said, breathlessly.

Gretchen experienced a sudden sense of dread. She headed straight for the coffee bar looking for Krista, but her mother was nowhere to be seen.

'Excuse me,' she said to the girl who was reading a romance magazine behind the counter, 'is Krista Becker here?'

'No, she just took off with an ambulance leaving me to do everything,' she said, clearly annoyed.

Gretchen ran back to the apartment building to get more information from the doorman.

'The woman who left in the ambulance, did she say which hospital they were going to?'

'I heard the driver speaking into his radio. He said the Beelitz Sanatorium.'

Gretchen remembered the town of Beelitz. It was about 18 kilometres from the family home in Potsdam. She used to go there with her father to buy white asparagus.

'I need to get a car to take me there,' she said.

'Now?'

'Yes, now.'

'It'll be expensive.'

'Please, just order a car.'

She knew it was Kurt. That intuition of a girl in love told her that the injured Hitler Youth leader was her boyfriend.

Beelitz, January 29, 1944

When they arrived at the sanatorium, she gave the driver a fistful of Reichmarks and told him to wait. She ran up the stairs past the colonnaded portico to the reception desk.

'I'm looking for Kurt Arndorfer,' she said. 'He was hurt in Berlin and the ambulance brought him here.'

The uniformed nurse ran her finger down an entry logbook.

'Arndofer...Arndorfer...yes, he was admitted at 12.21 pm. You are a relative?'

'We're engaged,' lied Gretchen.

'Congratulations,' said the nurse. Adding through pursed lips, 'He must have some influential friends because he was moved to a private room.'

'What room is he in?'

'West Wing, first floor, room 102. You must check in at the nursing station.'

'Thank you.'

Gretchen followed the signs to the West Wing and climbed the carpeted cement steps to the first floor. The duty nurse took down her name and pointed the way to room 102.

Her heart was pounding. How injured was he? Was he in a coma? Would he recognise her?

She peered through the small glass window in the door. He was lying on his back; his head was bandaged, asleep. Sitting in a chair furthest from the window was Krista who appeared to be dozing.

At the sound of the door, Krista opened her eyes.

'Gretchen,' she whispered. 'He's going to be fine, but might lose the hearing in one ear. The doctor says he needs rest.'

'Did he ask for me?'

'He said your name before he lost consciousness.'

'Why did you do this? What are you doing here?'

'The time I saw you two together I knew that there was something between you. I could tell by the way you looked at each other. I couldn't have just left him lying on the road.'

'Thank you.'

'Do his parents know?'

'I'm sure they do. The nurse downstairs said he must have influential friends to get a private room. I imagine his uncle, Herr Speer, must have called.'

Kurt began to stir.

'How are you getting back to Berlin, Krista?'

'I hadn't thought.'

'I have a car waiting downstairs. I'll give you a lift. But will you give me a few moments alone with Kurt?'

'I'll be downstairs.'

Gretchen waited until her mother had left the room and then she approached the bedside.

'Kurt. It's me, Gretchen.'

Kurt bent his head in the direction of her voice. His eyes slowly opened. He focused on her for a moment and then turned his head away.

'What's the matter, Kurt?'

'What are you doing here?'

'They told me you'd been injured. A bomb or something. I came as fast as I could.'

'Did Hitler give you permission?'

'What are you talking about?'

'You've been flying to his personal retreat. I know. I've been told about the flight logs. You're Hitler's mistress.'

'Kurt, you don't understand.'

'I thought we loved each other. I had plans for us after the war.'

'Please, Kurt. Listen to me.'

'Go back to Hitler.'

Tears welled up in her eyes.

'You wanted me to tell you what I'm doing. I'm going to tell you. Can you hear me all right?'

'I can hear you.'

'OK. I'm going to whisper this to you.'

Gretchen knelt down at the side of the bed. Cupping her hand around her mouth, she lowered her head until her lips almost touched his left ear. She began to speak.

Kurt shook his head.

'Come the other side. My right ear.'

Gretchen moved to the other side of the bed.

'Can I trust you, Kurt?'

'Let me hear what you have to say.'

'I am putting my life in your hands.'

'You can trust me.'

'I have a gift. Or maybe it's a curse. My senses of smell and taste are way above normal. Maybe I'm a freak, but I can smell and taste things that other people can't.'

'Like a dog.'

'Yes, maybe like a dog,' laughed Gretchen. 'Anyway your uncle recruited me to be one of Hitler's tasters. There's fourteen of us, all women, and we taste everything before it's put on the table in front of him.'

'In case it's poisoned?'

'Exactly. So that's why I've been flying so often to the Berghof. I'm not his mistress, Kurt. He's repulsive. I can't stand to be near him. Besides, he already has a mistress. Her name is Eva Braun. She's with him all the time, but they're never together in public…. I think she hates me.'

It took Kurt some time to digest what Gretchen was telling him.

'Why do you still do it if you can't stand to be near him?'

'You said I could trust you. I'm going to tell you two things, either of which could get me killed.'

Her lips were brushing his ear as she whispered.

'Please don't react. Just listen. First, the woman who brought you here in the ambulance is my mother. And she is Jewish.'

Kurt tried to lever himself up on his elbows, but Gretchen gently pressed him back to a prone position.

'That means I'm Jewish too. Her mother, my grandmother, has been arrested and taken to Ravensbrück, where she most certainly will die in the gas chambers. And where I could too if anyone heard this conversation.'

Kurt closed his eyes and reached for Gretchen's hand.

'I promise,' he began. 'I love you. If anything happened to you, I wouldn't want to go on living.'

'I love you too, Kurt.'

The tears that had been threatening began to course down her cheeks.

"We are meant to be together. I will find a way.'

She kissed him on the forehead.

****

Krista Becker waited patiently in the grounds of the Beelitz Sanatorium. She sat on a bench under a linden tree. She kept an eye on the entrance and the taxi that was parked on the gravel driveway nearby.

She began to cry. Every time she thought of her mother tears came.

She wiped her eyes as soon as she saw Gretchen emerge from the building.

'I spoke to the nurse and she says he should be out in a day or two,' said Gretchen. 'Let's get back to Berlin.'

'Can we talk here for a moment?' said Krista, patting the seat beside her. 'I'm worried sick about your grandmother.'

The tears began again. Gretchen sat down and took her mother's hand. Krista smiled at her in appreciation.

'Your family knows Herr Speer. He's a very influential man, Gretchen. They say he is Hitler's favourite.'

Krista hesitated, but Gretchen knew what she was about to say.

'You want me to speak to Herr Speer and try to get her released.'

Krista's face beamed.

'Would you! That would make me so happy. We have to try everything to get her out. I don't have much money, but if it's a question of money....'

'I don't think he needs money,' said Gretchen. 'I'll talk to him. My father says he's in hospital for an operation on his knee. They don't know when he'll be back in the office.'

'It has to be soon, my dear. I'm so afraid they'll....' Krista let the unspoken thought hang in the air.

'I'll do what I can,' said Gretchen. 'Let's get into the car. By the way, what is her name?'

'Ruth, Ruth Rosenberg. But ever since 1939, all Jewish women have to be called Sarah in their official documents to identify them to the authorities as Jews. And all men must be called Israel.'

Seated in the back of the taxi, Krista reached for her daughter's hand. They drove in silence back to the city, each wrapped in their own thoughts.

Gretchen pondered on what would be the best way to approach Albert Speer without revealing her own Jewish roots. She would say that her grandmother and not her mother was a maid in the von Bismarck house. But first she had to talk to her father.

Hohenlychen Hospital, January 30, 1944

Albert Speer had not slept well for a week. He had asked Dr. Gebhardt to prescribe some sleeping pills for him; but the physician, sensing evidence of depression in his patient, and fearing he might overdose, had given him placebos which had no effect whatsoever.

Speer had lain awake night after night in his hospital bed rehearsing a variety of scenarios. He had read through the file of attempts on Hitler's life so many times, he could almost recite it verbatim.

Did he have the will to see the deed through? Did he have the courage? The man seemed to have more lives than a cat. And what if he succeeded in assassinating his leader? Would Goering have him and his family arrested and he himself shot for high treason?

But what was the alternative? To allow the man to destroy the country that he loved?

In the rare moments when he drifted into a shallow sleep, he had a recurring nightmare. He was in Paris with Hitler. They were looking up at the Eiffel Tower. It was festooned with bodies, thousands of bodies, that hung by their necks from wires attached to the ironwork. It looked like the Christmas tree from hell, a Christmas tree designed by Bruegel. Hitler was laughing. 'See Speer, our enemies are now decorations. We rule the world.'

He awoke drenched in sweat and called for the nurse, who would immediately take his temperature.

But as the news from the battlefield became bleaker and bleaker, his resolve hardened. He called his office and asked Frau Kempf to send over drawings of the Führerbunker in the garden of the Reich Chancellery. And to find the telephone number of Carl Krauch, Chairman of the Supervisory Board of I. G. Farben.

Hohenlychen Hospital, January 31, 1944

Albert Speer had had a special telephone line installed in his hospital room by his own technicians to ensure that his private conversations would not be monitored.

On this line, he dialled the number Frau Kempf had given him. He waited for the secretary to connect him to Carl Krauch.

'Good morning, Herr Krauch, Speer here. I trust you're happy with the work force that Goering and I have provided for your company.'

'Ah, Herr Minster. Yes indeed, very satisfactory. And what can I do for you?'

'As you know, the Führer's birthday is coming up on April 20th. I was thinking of getting him something special this year. He'd been complaining about the camps...how can I put this delicately... that the camps are not operating as efficiently as they might. I was thinking that the problem might be with the gas. I thought if you were to send a sample to my office, I might have our chemical engineers have a look at it. To speed up the procedures, you understand.'

'I assure you Herr Speer that Dr. Gerhardt Schrader and our laboratory technicians have produced the most effective product.'

'I understand, but I've found in all spheres of human activity there is always room for improvement, Herr Krauch. And in my note of congratulations to the Führer, I will mention that you made the gift possible.'

The disgruntled tone of the business executive on the other end of the line changed immediately to one of abject compliance.

'Well, of course, Herr Minister. The question is whether you would prefer a sample of Zyklon B or Tabun? They are both organophosphate nerve agents produced from hydrogen cyanide.'

'Which is the most commonly used?'

'We are shipping more Tabun these days.'

'Then that will be fine. I take it you have printed material on the safe handling of the product.'

'Yes, of course. That will be included with the sample. You would like to have it sent to your Ministry?'

'Unfortunately, my Ministry sustained a great deal of damage in the last bombing raid. I'll give you the address of the place I am currently working out of. And I'm sure I can rely on you to keep this confidential between us. I wouldn't like to have the surprise spoiled.'

'My lips are sealed.'

'Splendid. Good day, Herr Krauch.'

Potsdam, February 1, 1944

Carl and Greta von Bismarck had eaten the same breakfast every morning since the day they were married: assorted cold cuts, a slice of *butterkaese*, rolls and butter, apricot jam, and a boiled egg. Although Cook was finding it increasingly difficult now to buy jam, even on the black market.

The couple sat in the dining room across from each other, reading their newspapers.

'Worse and worse,' muttered Carl, shaking his newspaper in annoyance. 'They'd have us believe we're winning the war. Do they take us for fools?'

'Perhaps what you hear on the BBC is just propaganda too, Carl.'

'Herr Speer has his own sources of information. He tells me things that you don't read in the newspapers. When I went to see him in the hospital yesterday, he told me a Red Army offensive in the Ukraine has forced us into a major retreat. I don't see that in the newspaper.'

'How is Herr Speer?' asked his wife in an attempt to change the subject.

'He can't wait to get back to the office, but frankly he spends so much time at his ministerial position he has no time for our architectural work. Not that we're building anything. Mostly propping up damaged buildings or demolishing them.'

Cook brought in a fresh pot of ersatz coffee and placed it on the table.

'I thought you'd like to know that Fraulein Gretchen is in the kitchen. She said she would join you momentarily.'

'Gretchen!' exclaimed Greta. 'This is a surprise. I didn't think she was coming back from wherever she goes until the weekend.'

'Now don't go hounding her with questions, my dear. You know that she's not allowed to tell us her business…whatever it is.'

A few moments later Gretchen entered the dining room. She greeted her parents with a kiss and took a seat at the table.

'Will you have breakfast?' asked Greta. 'You look so thin.'

'I've already eaten, thanks, Mama. I can't stay, but I wanted to have a word with you, Papa,' she said, turning towards him. 'May I ask you something?'

'Of course, my dear.'

'The young man I'm seeing, the nephew of Herr Speer, was injured outside our apartment.'

'How terrible,' exclaimed Greta.

'He was taken to the Beelitz Sanatorium. I went to see him.'

'How is he?' asked her father.

'He's going to be all right. But he may lose the hearing in one ear. There was an explosion. One of the boys in his section was killed in the blast.'

'I'm so sorry,' said Greta.

'The woman who found Kurt and took him to the hospital in an ambulance, was Krista Becker.'

Her parents exchanged glances.

'She was in Kurt's room when I went to see him. Before I gave her a lift back to Berlin, we sat in the garden and talked.'

'She's living in Berlin?' exclaimed Greta.

'Yes. Anyway, she told me that her mother was arrested by the SS and taken to Ravensbrück.'

'Ravensbrück,' repeated Greta, looking enquiringly at her husband.

'It's a concentration camp for Jewish women, Mama.'

'Where did you hear such stories, Gretchen?'

'It's what's happening, Mama. They're arresting Jews and sending them to camps. There are gas chambers. They're being killed.'

'This couldn't happen in Germany. Carl, tell her,' said Greta.

Carl von Bismarck took a deep breath.

'This is what they're saying on the BBC too, Greta.'

'But...it can't be true. I know they were sending Jews away, but not to gas chambers.'

'The point is, Papa, that Krista's mother was taken to Ravensbrück. And she could die there. Krista asked me if you would speak to Herr Speer and see if he could use his influence to get her released.'

Carl von Bismarck stared at his plate.

'Would you do that, Papa?'

'If only it were that simple, my dear. If Herr Speer made enquiries the SS might investigate and trace her mother back to Krista and then to us. Which could mean –'

'You're saying you won't help her?'

'I'm not saying that, Gretchen. I just want to protect you.'

'Then I'll ask him myself,' said Gretchen.

Greta stood up causing the plate in front of her to rattle on the table.

'Gretchen, I forbid you to contact Herr Speer, do you understand?'

'Mama, I will do what I have to do.'

'Speak to her, Carl, Tell her she's putting the whole family in danger. If they find out about Gretchen they could take her too.'

'Greta, please, sit down.'

'And what if they find we've been hiring Jews all this time when it's against the law?'

'Nobody's going to find out anything, Greta. Herr Speer is an honourable man. He would not let any harm come to us. Gretchen, you must not speak to Herr Speer about this matter. I will speak to him.'

'Thank you, Papa. I really appreciate it. But, please, do it soon.'

Berlin, February 3, 1944

O nce released from hospital, Albert Speer was issued with a pair of crutches, so that he would not put pressure on the stitches around his kneecap.

On his first day back at work, he found his office festooned with flowers. He read the cards, wondering if the well-wishers would have preferred to be sending him a funeral wreath instead of floral offerings. There was, he noted, no card from Hitler.

His secretary, Frau Kempf, had placed a file on his desk containing messages welcoming him back to work. A separate file held letters that needed his signature and assorted phone messages. One of these was from his colleague, Carl von Bismarck requesting an urgent meeting.

He hoped the old boy was not going to tell him that he was retiring. He relied on his subordinate to run his architecture practice in his absence.

'Frau Kempf,' he said, speaking into the intercom. 'Will you get von Bismarck on the phone.'

The conversation was short. His employee gave no indication as to what he wanted to say, only that he requested a face-to-face meeting to discuss a very delicate matter.

Speer suggested he come to the Ministry, but von Bismarck had demurred, asking if they could meet privately somewhere. Perhaps in the Reichstag garden. In spite of the inconvenience of having to hobble a couple of hundred metres and it being a cold February day, Speer reluctantly agreed.

As he made his way to the Reichstag, placing his crutches carefully along the cracked sidewalks, he wondered what was on the old boy's mind. Had Hitler made a pass at his daughter? Was she in some kind of trouble?

Carl von Bismarck was seated on a bench in the Reichstag garden. He rose to greet Speer and apologised.

'Had I known you were on crutches, Herr Speer, I would have made alternative arrangements. I'm so sorry.'

'Don't worry. The doctor says I should take exercise. The muscles atrophy when you spend a long time in bed with your leg in the air. Now what's this all about?'

'You and I have known each other a long time, Herr Speer.'

'Albert. Call me Albert. Yes, we have been friends a long time.'

'I knew your father before I knew you. We were at university together.'

'Yes, it was he who suggested I contact you when I started the firm.'

'And we have dined together many times.'

'Yes, of course.'

Speer was willing him mentally to get to the point.

'Our family are true German patriots, going back many generations, even before my great grandfather Otto von Bismarck.'

'Carl, please, you don't have to remind me. I have the utmost respect for your family name.'

'Then I will tell you what's on my mind.'

Von Bismarck cleared his throat and lifted his head, concentrating his gaze on the ruined dome of the Reichstag, still blackened from the fire that destroyed it in 1933.

'For some years, we had in our employ at our estate in Potsdam a woman named Ruth Rosenberg. We knew she was Jewish, but this was before the laws about hiring Jews were enacted. She was a good worker, very fond of our daughter but because of the Nuremberg Laws we had to let her go. Reluctantly, I have to tell you. We made sure she was settled financially, but over the years we lost touch. Then we heard that she had been arrested and sent to Ravensbrück.'

'How do you know that?'

'She had a daughter. She called me asking if I could help.'

'And what happened to the daughter?'

'I don't know. I think she's in hiding.'

Speer sighed.

'You know, when I look at this magnificent building, I wish I had designed it. Maybe after the war I'll have the opportunity.'

He turned to the older man, wincing in pain from the movement.

'What exactly are you asking of me, Carl?'

Von Bismarck lowered his gaze to the ground.

'Could you find it in your heart to intercede for this poor woman and have her released?'

Speer looked away.

'There are protocols, Carl.'

'I respect that, but a word from you, the Minister of Armaments and War Production. I know I shouldn't ask, but what will I tell her daughter if she were to die there?'

Speer raised himself onto his crutches.

'Herr von Bismarck, this conversation has not taken place. You will not mention it to anyone. Even to your wife. Do I make myself clear? Now I must get back to the office. Good day to you.'

Zurich, February 4, 1944

*D*ear Gretty,
Your letter took weeks and weeks to arrive, but it was so good to hear from you.

I am helping out at my father's clinic as we have many wounded American pilots sent to us. When they fly into Swiss airspace, they get shot down because we're a neutral county and we can't favour one side or the other. We, that is my father and the staff at the clinic, look after them until they're well enough to be interned. You won't believe it, but they are put up in ski resorts that are empty because there are no tourists in Switzerland now.

This is all to tell you that one of the American pilots I'm looking after is from Wisconsin. His name is Steve and he's absolutely gorgeous. I wish I could send you a photograph of him. He reminds me a bit of Jorg, but much taller and blonder. I can't really understand his accent, but he makes me laugh. He's always joking even though he's in pain (a bullet wound in the shoulder). He gives me chewing gum and I'm learning English much better.

I'll be sorry when he's well enough to leave the clinic, but he said he'd write although I don't know if prisoners of war or whatever he is are allowed to write letters.

Otherwise, life here is rather boring. I have heard about the bombing in Berlin and I hope you and your family are safe. Do write soon and tell me all your news (especially about Kurt!!).

I miss you. When the war is over you must come and visit.

Love, Shoshy XXX

Painting by Adolf Hitler

Adolf Hitler at Kransburg Castle

Hitler & Albert Speer at the Castle.

The Fûhrer and Eva Braun

A photo of one of Hitler's Tasters , Margot Wolk

Hitler Youth

Hitler Youth

Hitler's Inner Circle

Hitler's Inner Circle at the Wolf's Lair

Hitler at the destruction of the Wolf's Lair

Reichstag, June 1945

Hitler's Bunker, 1945

Berlin, February 4, 1944

'Frau Kempf, find out who the Commandant of the Ravensbrück camp is and look up his number for me…. And get rid of these flowers. They smell like death.'

Albert Speer was feeling slightly nauseous from the sweet, peppery scent of the tiger lilies in vases around his office.

He was curious as to why the aristocratic Carl von Bismarck had asked him to intercede on behalf of a Jewess. Had they been lovers in the past? Was she blackmailing him?

Albert Speer was working out of his private office because of the disruption caused by the bomb damage to his ministry. He had spread out on his desk the drawings for the Chancellery he had built for Hitler in 1938.

Bismarck's old Chancellery, Hitler had said, was fit only for a soap factory and not the grandiose headquarters of the Greater German Reich.

Speer regarded the building as his greatest achievement. He had the new Chancellery built within a year at a cost of 900 million Reichmarks. Hitler had said that money was no object. Four thousand workmen laboured in shifts around the clock to meet Hitler's deadline for its completion.

Speer had the building finished 48 hours before the target date. He smiled as he remembered how delighted the Führer had been with the 145-metre long gallery and his personal office that measured 400 square metres. Hitler had called him 'a genius.'

He was tracing his finger along the venting system into Hitler's office, when Frau Kempf entered and handed him a sheet of paper.

'As you requested, Herr Speer.'

'Thank you.'

He glanced at the information his secretary had typed out. 'Sturmbannführer Fritz Suhren…! I don't know him.'

'I took the liberty of examining his file, Herr Speer. He joined the party in 1928 and became a Stormtrooper before moving over to the SS in 1931. He was trained by the Wehrmacht, but was stationed at the Sachsenhausen camp in 1941.'

'No battlefield experience?'

'Apparently not. The next year he was promoted to Lagerführer of the camp and –'

'Yes, yes. Thank you, Frau Kempf. That will be all.'

She turned on her heel and stomped out of the room.

Speer waited until she had closed the door behind her before picking up the phone and dialling.

'Sturmbannführer, I hope I haven't caught you at an inconvenient time,' he began.

Once the pleasantries had been exchanged, Speer laid out his request – that the prisoner, Ruth Rosenberg, newly admitted to Ravensbrück, be released into his custody for interrogation.

'Herr Minister, we are happy to interrogate the prisoner here, if you would send us the questions you would like answered.'

'I'm well aware of your competency in these matters, Fritz – may I call you Fritz? – but there are some delicate matters regarding a highly placed person and discretion is required. The less people know about this the better. We would not like to have one of the most highly regarded citizens of the Reich open to public scandal. I'm sure you would understand that.'

'But this is most unusual, Herr Minister.'

'Normally, I would agree with you. But time is of essence in this matter. I've been looking over your record and I see you have risen quickly in the ranks of the party. You've seen the war so far from an office desk, while most of your colleagues in the Wehrmacht are serving at the front.'

Speer paused to allow the implications of his remark to sink in before continuing.

'I would esteem it a personal favour if you would grant me my wish. And I will make sure it is noted on your record.'

'Very well, Herr Minister. But I will need the necessary documentation.'

'I will have it forwarded to you. In the meantime, if you could have the prisoner Rosenberg ready to be transported to me in Berlin by tomorrow afternoon, I will send a car for her. With the necessary security, of course.'

'I will see to it, Herr Minister.'

'And Fritz, make sure she is bathed and has civilian clothes. We don't want her appearing in Berlin in striped pyjamas, do we?'

Ravensbrück, February 5, 1944

Albert Speer had given his nephew Kurt specific instructions. He was to take Speer's car, rather than an official vehicle, drive to the Ravensbrück concentration camp and report directly to the commandant, Sturmbannführer Fritz Suhren.

'The commandant will release to you a woman named Ruth Rosenberg. I will give you the necessary papers, but you are to sign nothing. If he asks you to put your signature to anything tell him to call me. Do you understand?…Oh, and make sure you get her file. I want you to bring her here to my office, not to the ministry. Park at the back of the building and use that entrance. I will ensure the door is left unlocked.'

Kurt had recovered from the explosion, but his hearing was not as acute as it had been and his vision was somewhat blurred at times. He had to squint to concentrate on the road, working his way through the deeply pot-holed streets until he was clear of Berlin.

During the 90-kilometre drive north of the city, he thought of what Gretchen had told him. He guessed that the woman he was about to pick up was Gretchen's grandmother.

As he approached the village of Ravensbrück, he saw single train tracks leading to a long low building with a tower in the middle. The train tracks ran directly through an opening under the tower.

A guard ordered him to stop and present his papers. Having seen the order from the Minister of Armaments he waved Kurt through, indicating the way to the Commandant's office.

Kurt took in the barbed wire fences and the emaciated women in striped pyjamas and white cotton headscarves who stared out with unseeing eyes.

He parked the car and made his way to Sturmbannführer Fritz Suhren's office. He noted the long parallel rows of wooden barracks stretching as far as he could see. Columns of women, six abreast, were shuffling back towards them.

'Ah. You are here at the request of our illustrious Minister of Armaments and War Production,' smiled Suhren. 'May I see your papers?'

Kurt handed him the document Speer had prepared for him. Suhren looked over it and then cranked a telephone on his desk.

'Have Frau Elfriede Muller escort prisoner Rosenberg from Stalag 24 to my office immediately.'

They sat in silence as Suhren busied himself with paperwork.

From outside the office Kurt could hear a woman shouting. A moment later Elfriede Muller, dressed in uniform, entered dragging a reluctant and confused Ruth Rosenberg into the office.

'As ordered Sturmbannführer, here is the prisoner Rosenberg. Heil Hitler.'

Addressing her prisoner, she said: 'Stand up straight.'

She poked the old woman with a baton she was carrying. Ruth Rosenberg gave a little sob and closed her eyes.

'I see you've dressed her for a party,' smirked Suhren.

The guard made no reply, but gave her prisoner another jab with her baton.

Kurt studied the woman. Unlike the other prisoners he had seen, she was dressed in civilian clothes, ill fitting though they were. Her hat barely covered the fact that her head had been shaved. She seemed to be tottering on the shoes that were too big for her. Lipstick had been applied, a red gash across her mouth, and her sunken cheeks had been daubed with rouge, giving her the appearance of a circus clown. She could hardly stand up and she gazed around the office in bewilderment.

'Thank you, Frau Muller. You may return to your duties.'

The guard gave a stiff-arm salute and made for the door.

'Now, *mein Herr*,' said Suhren, turning to Kurt, 'I respect that you are a ranking member in the Hitler Youth and an emissary of our Minister of Armaments, but I am curious as to why this partic-ular Jewess should be of interest to the Minister. As you see she is hardly the keeper of secrets that might threaten the security of Third Reich.'

Ruth Rosenberg stood trembling in front of the commandant's desk. Her lips were moving, but no sound came out.

'My orders,' replied Kurt, 'are to deliver this woman to the Minis-ter. I am not party to any information other than that.'

'Very well, then if I am to release her in your custody, I need you to sign a release form.'

'I think Minister Speer was quite explicit in his order that there was to be no paper work. This is an unusual case, but there are rami-fications that both you and I do not understand. The minister will see to it that you have acquitted yourself with the highest expression of professional service as a German officer.'

Suhren raised an eyebrow and shook his head.

'So. Take the woman.'

'The Minister has asked for her file.'

'Ah yes,' said Suhren, opening the drawer of his desk. 'Her file. She must be very important for the Reich for such attention.'

Slowly, deliberately, he withdrew the file from the drawer and slid it across his desk.

Kurt retrieved it and raised his arm in salute. Without another word he took the confused woman by the elbow and led her out of the building to the parked car.

He opened the back door and helped Ruth Rosenberg into the seat. He could feel the bird-like bones in her arms. She winced in pain as she settled herself in the seat.

He drove through the archway, past the guard, keeping his eyes on the rear-view mirror. The woman was mumbling to herself. He strained to hear what she was saying.

'The Beast of Ravensbrück, the Beast of Ravensbrück.' She repeated the phrase over and over like a mantra.

He watched her lick the two middle fingers of her right hand and rub at a number that had been tattooed on her left forearm. It looked as if she was trying to wash it off.

Back in Berlin, Kurt parked the car as he had been instructed and half-carried the woman to the back door. He could feel her resistance as he moved inside the building to the cement staircase but he tried to reassure her that she would not be harmed.

Frau Kempf, Speer's secretary, clutched her throat in alarm when Kurt led the woman into her office. She had been briefed to receive the Rosenberg woman and to show her into Speer's office as soon as she arrived. But Frau Kempf was not prepared for the sight of this old woman who looked like a wizened child who had found her way into her mother's make-up kit.

'Would you care for a cup of tea?' she asked. 'Would you like to sit down?'

'The Beast of Ravensbrück, the Beast of Ravensbrück,' murmured Ruth Rosenberg, glancing nervously around the room.

'What does that mean?' Frau Kempf asked Kurt.

'That's all she's been saying since I collected her.'

'Herr Speer is expecting you in his office. Please go through.'

Kurt ushered the woman forward. She was trembling. He gripped her firmly by the elbow to ensure that she would not fall.

'Come in,' commanded Speer at his knock.

Speer's reaction when he saw Ruth Rosenberg was even more extreme than his secretary's.

'You poor woman. Kurt, bring the lady a chair.'

'I think she might fall if I don't support her, uncle.'

'All right,' he replied, and he fetched the chair himself. 'Please, Frau Rosenberg, sit down.'

The woman gave a half smile, a memory response perhaps to courtesies shown in her past life.

'You brought the file, Kurt?'

'It's in the car.'

'Go down and get it, please.'

Kurt left the office as Frau Kempf entered holding a small tray with a cup of tea, a small jug of milk and a sugar bowl. She placed the tray on a table next to the woman.

'Milk? Sugar?' asked the secretary.

Ruth Rosenberg's eyes darted from one to the other. She pressed herself against the back of the chair, shying away from them as if she expected to be beaten.

'Give her both,' said Speer.

While Frau Kempf prepared the tea, Speer sat down at his desk, feeling uncomfortable whenever the woman's eyes rested on him. Her pupils seemed to quiver and for a brief moment he thought he could see the skull beneath her skin.

'Have your tea,' coaxed Frau Kempf, handing the cup out to her.

The woman took the proffered cup in both hands, but she was shaking so violently that the liquid slashed into her lap.

'It's all right. I'll get a cloth. Please, just sit back.'

Kurt re-entered carrying the file. He handed it to Speer who was relieved to be able to concentrate on something other than the fragile, trembling woman in front of him.

While his secretary wiped Ruth Rosenberg's skirt with a towel, Speer opened the file. With a practiced eye he scanned the document. There was a photo of her and underneath her name and her prison number.

Against the item, 'Next of kin,' there was a notation in ink: 'Daughter – Krista, single, whereabouts unknown. SS to open file. Contact Kriminal-Oberassistent Othmar Veigl, Berlin HQ.'

Speer leant back in his chair and gazed at the ceiling. Von Bismarck had mentioned that Ruth Rosenberg had a daughter though he added he did not know where she was.

Someone in that household must know, he thought.

He recalled the conversation he had with von Bismarck.

'*She had a daughter,*' his assistant architect had said. '*She called me asking if I could help.*'

'*And what happened to the daughter?*' he had asked.

'*I don't know. I think she's in hiding.*'

Von Bismarck remarked that she was very fond of their daughter, Gretchen. Maybe they had kept in touch. Maybe Gretchen knew where Ruth Rosenberg's daughter was.

'Frau Rosenberg,' said Speer. 'I have gone to great lengths to have you removed from Ravensbrück.'

'Ravensbrück. The Beast of Ravensbrück!' cried the woman.

Startled, Speer looked enquiringly at Kurt.

'That's all she's been saying. Nothing else.'

'What does she mean?'

'I think she's referring to one of the female guards who brought her in. She kept poking her with her baton to make her stand up straight in front of the Sturmbannführer.'

'You witnessed this?'

'Yes.'

'Do you know her name, her rank?'

'The Sturmbannführer referred to her on the phone as Frau Elfriede Muller.'

Speer made a notation in the margin of the document.

'Now, Frau Rosenberg. We have to think about your future. Where will you go? Where will you live? It says here you have a daughter name Krista. No doubt she is worried about you. Would like to live with her? Perhaps you can tell me how we can contact her.'

The woman sat in silence and began to rub her fingers over the tattooed number on her forearm.

'We are trying to help you, Frau Rosenberg. How can we communicate with your daughter Krista?' Speer repeated a little louder.

Kurt watched the interrogation with growing alarm. If this was indeed Gretchen's grandmother then finding her daughter would eventually lead to Gretchen and the revelation that Gretchen was born of a Jewish mother.

He could see Speer's growing irritation with the woman's silence. He approached his uncle and whispered in his ear.

'I think she's a little odd in the head. I couldn't get any information out of her either. The treatment she got there probably affected her mind.'

Speer sighed and closed the file.

'I have no time to waste on this. I want you to drive her to von Bismarck's house in Potsdam. She'll be his problem now.'

Kurt went to assist the woman to rise.

'Oh and Kurt,' said Speer. 'Are you still seeing the von Bismarck girl?'

Kurt thought fast. The less his uncle knew about his involvement with Gretchen the better.

'I haven't seen her for a while. I guess it must be over.'

'Pity,' said Speer. 'But there are other fish in the sea.'

He made a mental note to contact Kriminal-Oberassistent Othmar Veigl and to find out what he knew. If any of this got out…well, it would not be good for him or his family. And Kurt? Maybe he should find out more about how close he was to the von Bismarck girl.

Potsdam, February 5, 1944

Kurt pulled into the driveway of the von Bismarck estate. Ruth Rosenberg had fallen asleep in the back seat.

He knew that Gretchen was the daughter of an aristocrat, but he had not realised that the family lived in such palatial surroundings.

He drew up to the front door of the mansion, alighted and opened the passenger door.

'Frau Rosenberg,' he said, softly. 'Time to wake up.'

The woman sat bolt upright, eyes wide open.

'Roll call? Is it roll call?'

'No, we're here at the von Bismarck residence. They will take care of you. Come, I'll help you out.'

Kurt eased the woman out of the back seat and supported her as they moved to the door. He lifted the knocker and heard its dull thud echo through the house.

Presently, the door was opened by a stout woman in an apron.

Kurt clicked his heels and bowed slightly at the waist, wondering if this was Gretchen's mother.

'I am Kurt Arndorfer. Is Graf von Bismarck at home?'

'I am the von Bismarck's cook. The master is not at home at the moment, but I will call the lady of the house.'

Although she addressed Kurt's question, her eyes were fixed on Ruth Rosenberg who seemed to be about to buckle at the knees.

'Come inside,' said Cook. 'There's a chair in the hallway for the lady.'

Kurt held Ruth Rosenberg by the elbow and escorted her to a chair by the coat stand that was hung with a variety of hats, its base bristling with walking sticks.

'Would you like a glass of water?' she asked the woman, who looked as if she might pass out at any moment.

'The Beast of Ravensbrück,' shouted the woman, her eyes darting around the unfamiliar surroundings.

Cook backed away, unsure as to whether to leave them alone in the foyer. Two minutes later she was back with Greta von Bismarck.

'Can I help you?'

'Frau von Bismarck. My name is Kurt Andorfer. I'm the nephew of Herr Albert Speer.'

'Ah, yes. You are a friend of my daughter. And who is this lady?'

'She has recently been confined in a women's detention centre at Ravensbrück, but through the good offices of your husband she has been released into his custody.'

'My husband?'

'Yes. She is the mother of a woman who used to work for you. Krista Becker.'

Greta von Bismarck and Cook exchanged glances.

'And why have you brought her here?'

'Herr Speer gained her release as a favour to your husband. There is nowhere else for her to go, Frau von Bismarck,' said Kurt. 'We've not been able to locate her daughter.'

'Let me take her down to the kitchen, ma'am, and I'll make her a nice cup of tea. We'll wait for the master to come back.'

'Very well,' said Greta, agitated. Krista Becker's mother. A concentration camp victim. In her house! What was her husband thinking?

'Please say hello to Gretchen for me,' said Kurt, as Cook led the confused woman down the hall to the stairs that led to the kitchen.

'Yes, and our regards to Herr Speer,' said Greta, her eyes on Cook until the pair had disappeared from view.

Kurt was relieved to have discharged his obligation to his uncle. As he drove out of the gate he did not note the black Mercedes parked under the trees on the other side of the road. Nor was he aware of it pulling out into the road and following him at a discreet distance all the way to Berlin.

Potsdam, February 24, 1944

Graf von Bismarck was bent over his radio listening to a BBC World Service transmission when his wife Greta entered his study.

'Please, Carl. Turn that off. I have to talk to you.'

Reluctantly, von Bismarck switched the radio off.

'What is it, my dear?'

'Something has to be done with that woman. She's been in the guest room for nearly three weeks now. Cook has to bathe her. If she screams 'the Beast of Ravensbrück' one more time I think *I'll* go mad.'

'What would you have us do? Throw her out into the street?'

'Why can't she go back to where she lived before?'

'Before what? Before the Nazis put her in a concentration camp? They confiscate the property of incarcerated Jews, Greta.'

'Well, her daughter then. She could move in with her daughter. Maybe Herr Speer can help us locate Krista.'

'Greta, we have an obligation here.'

'You have an obligation to your family, Carl. We are harbouring a Jewess.'

Carl von Bismarck stood up.

'As long as she is in this house, under my roof, she has my protection, Greta. That is the von Bismarck code. You will continue to treat her as a guest until we find alternative accommodation for her. Do I make myself clear?'

Greta von Bismarck turned and left the room, slamming the door behind her.

Potsdam, March 1, 1944

'Hanna, It's me Krista.'

'Krista! You know you shouldn't be phoning here.'

'How's my mother?'

'How did you know she was here?'

'Gretchen's boyfriend drove her to Potsdam. How is she?'

'She's driving madam crazy.'

'Is she eating?'

'That's all she's doing. She hasn't left her room in days. It's your old room at the top of the house. Herself wants her out of the house. I heard them arguing about it. She wants her to come and live with you.'

'But I have this tiny room. I can stretch out both arms and touch the walls.'

'I don't know what arrangement you made with the master, but maybe he could find you a bigger place. They own properties in Berlin, you know.'

Cook had her back to the kitchen door when Greta von Bismarck walked into the room.

'Who is that on the phone?' she demanded, imperiously.

'Ma'am, it's only...,' stammered Cook.

'Give it to me.'

Greta snatched the handset from Cook.

'Krista? I thought it would be you. Now you listen to me. We had an agreement. And you have broken it. Not only that, but you have placed us in a very risky position. The presence of your mother in this

155

house exposes the von Bismarck family to great danger. If you have any respect for us, you will assume the responsibility of looking after your own mother.'

'I will do what I can,' Krista replied, sighing deeply to stop from crying.

'I expect to hear from you in one week, otherwise I shall be forced to contact the necessary authorities.'

Before Krista could reply the phone went dead.

Berlin, March 2, 1944

G retchen went to the grocery store to shop. She was confused by the colour coding of the food stamps Greta von Bismarck had left for her: white for sugar, blue for meat, purple for fruit, yellow for dairy products and green for eggs. Above all she yearned for coffee, but the Kaffee-erstaz they sold in the shops was a mixture of roasted barley, oats and chicory bound together by chemicals extracted from coal oil tar.

She realised she had become used to the fresh food and real coffee served at Hitler's table. Watching the housewives clutching their stamps as if they were gold coins and scanning the shelves for bargains made her feel ashamed. She had heard that anyone caught stealing food stamps could be sent to a forced labour camp.

When Gretchen returned to the apartment, the doorman handed her an envelope with her name written on it. The handwriting was unfamiliar to her.

She tore it open in the elevator and read the short note:

'Dear Gretchen, I have to speak with you urgently. Please come to the coffee house across the road when you get this.'

It was simply signed 'Krista.'

Gretchen left her shopping bag at the doorman's desk and hurried across the street.

Krista was serving a customer when she entered the coffee shop. She inclined her head to indicate a vacant table in the corner.

Gretchen nodded and took a seat. How pale and tired the woman looked, she thought. A moment later Krista approached, note book in hand, her back to the other customers who were busy reading newspapers or chatting to each other.

'Are you OK?' asked Gretchen.

Krista moved a lock of hair from her cheek.

'A little tired. And you, how are you?'

'Fine. What's all the urgency?'

Krista leant down and lowered her voice.

'It's your grandmother. They're going to evict her by the end of the week.'

'Surely my father wouldn't do that. Not after he –.' She stopped herself in mid-sentence when Krista raised a finger to her lips.

'I have to find her a place to live. My room is just too small. For a day or two, but it would just be impossible in the long term. Do you think you could speak to your father? Or Herr Speer.'

'I understand, but –'

'Frau von Bismarck has given me an ultimatum. If my mother is not out of the house within a week she'll call the authorities.'

Gretchen realised the implications. Her grandmother would be returned to Ravensbrück.

'I'll see what I can do,' she said. 'I might have an idea.'

Berlin, March 3, 1944

If Gretchen was to help her grandmother, she decided it was time to visit Doctor Bidermann.

Isaac Bidermann had been the von Bismarck's family physician for thirty years although he, like other Jewish doctors, had been banned from practicing his profession when the Nazis came to power.

He worked out of his rambling, old house in the Schöneberg district that backed on to the Südgelände park, making house calls to his Jewish patients and seeing them clandestinely in his basement surgery.

He augmented his dwindling income by performing ritual circumcisions when there were no rabbis left to officiate.

But Carl von Bismarck had taken a principled stand and continued to remain on Dr. Bidermann's panel.

As she was growing up, it had never occurred to Gretchen that Dr. Bidermann was Jewish. He was just Dr. Bidermann, the kindly old gentleman who always had lollipops in his medical bag and hummed while he took her pulse.

Had he been rounded up with the rest of the Jews who lived in Schöneberg? Her father had told her about the laws enacted by the Nazis in 1937 and 1938, forbidding Jewish doctors from treating non-Jews, and revoking the licences of Jewish lawyers to practise law.

Gretchen approached the front door with trepidation. There was no shingle outside. But then he would not want to draw attention to himself, she told herself.

She pressed the bell and waited. She could hear footsteps and the turning of locks and the unchaining of the door.

'Gretchen! What a pleasant surprise. Come in, child. It's cold out there.'

Dr. Bidermann seemed smaller than the man she remembered, stooped and diminished somehow. He wore a waistcoat over a collarless shirt, creased trousers and bedroom slippers.

'Dr. Bidermann, I hope it's okay my just turning up like this. I didn't know if – I mean, it's been such a long time.'

'It's always a pleasure to see you, Gretchen. Would you like a cup of tea? Since my wife passed I've learned the most elementary of the culinary arts, having mastered the boiling of water. I hope you don't mind if we sit in the kitchen. It's the warmest room in the house and they've stopped delivering coal.'

He took Gretchen's coat, hung it in the hallstand and ushered her along the corridor past the living and dining rooms to the kitchen.

'I'm so pleased to see you, Dr. Bidermann.'

'Yes, you never know these days, do you? But I will let you into a little secret. There is no need to worry about me, my dear. You see, I'm an honorary Aryan.'

The old man laughed and his eyes twinkled as he placed a kettle on the gas stove.

'Confusing, no? Isaac Moses ben Avrum Bidermann, an honorary Aryan. My late father, *olev hasholem*, would be spinning in his grave.

But shall I tell you how Isaac Moses ben Avrum Bidermann became an honorary Aryan?'

Gretchen nodded in answer to the rhetorical question.

'My speciality before it became impossible for me to work in hospitals was, you should pardon the expression, sexually transmitted diseases. One day I got a call from Heinz Goering, the adoptive son of Hermann Goering. I probably shouldn't be telling you this, but what does it matter now? Not to speak ill of the dead, but Heinz's mother had syphilis. They called me in to treat her. I did what I could, but she was in the final stages of the disease. Her pupils could not move. But I made her passing pain free and for that Hermann Goering interceded with Hitler on my behalf. And now, my dear, you see before you an honorary Aryan who is tolerated to practise medicine in Berlin.'

The kettle began to whistle and Dr. Bidermann levered himself out of his chair to attend to the preparation of the tea.

'Did you know that one of the laws passed against the Jews by the administration – I have it somewhere, let me recall. November 29th, 1937. The Reich Interior Ministry forbids Jews to keep carrier pigeons. What did they think? We were going to train a battalion of pigeons to carry us to New York?'

Gretchen laughed with him.

'So tell me, my dear. What can I do for you and I hope you haven't come to me because of my specialty.'

'No, Dr. Bidermann, nothing like that.'

She paused, wondering how to approach the subject that had been keeping her awake at night.

'Is talking to a doctor like talking to a priest? I mean, like the confessional.'

'Are you asking if I can keep a confidence?'

'It's more than that. What I'm about to ask you could put us all in danger.'

'Gretchen, knowledge is only dangerous when it's put to evil ends. I am an old man. There is nothing I fear now. I see you're struggling with a dilemma. Let me help you resolve it. Think of your dilemma as a disease. I am a doctor and I can cure your disease.'

He took two mugs from a cabinet and poured the tea.

'Milk? Sugar?'

'Just a splash of milk, please.'

He opened the fridge and took out a bottle of milk. He removed the cardboard cap, sniffed it and shrugged.

'Not so bad. Please pour it yourself. My hand is not so steady these days. Good thing I'm not a surgeon, eh?'

Gretchen poured the milk and took a sip of tea.

'Dr. Bidermann, can I ask you something. If you don't want to do it, I'll understand. What I'm asking is an enormous favour. Not for me but for people…for people dear to me.

The old man could see tears brimming in her eyes. He took her hand in his.

'Tell me what you want.'

'You live all alone in this big house and I can see you have no one to look after you.'

'True, but I'm used to it since my wife passed on.'

'There is a woman. Her name is Ruth Rosenberg. She was sent to Ravensbrück.'

'The concentration camp for women, yes I know of it.'

'Well, Herr Speer interceded for her and got her released.'

'You know Albert Speer, the Minister of Armaments? A very powerful man.'

'Yes, my father works in his architectural firm. It was my father who spoke to him. Ruth Rosenberg was released a few weeks ago thanks to him.'

'And how do you come to this Frau Rosenberg?'

Gretchen hesitated. Should she tell him the whole story?

'She is the mother of a maid who used to work for my parents.'

'And how is she now?'

'I don't know. I haven't seen her. She's staying at the Potsdam estate at the moment, but Greta wants her out of the house. She's threatening to call the authorities if she's not out in a few days. I was just wondering…. Her daughter Krista is living in a one-room apartment in Berlin. She could cook and clean for you and look after the house. And her mother would have a safe place to stay. She wouldn't be any trouble. What do you think?'

Dr. Bidermann sat back in his chair, momentarily speechless.

This girl was asking him if he would shelter two women. What would this mean to his solitude? The routine he had established for himself since his wife Sarah had died fifteen years ago had kept loneliness at bay. He had his occasional patients, his books and his prayers. Certainly, there was room enough for the two women, but how would they react to his nocturnal wanderings and his friend Asher who dropped in unannounced at all hours for a game of chess.

Gretchen waited wide-eyed for him to respond.

'There hasn't been a woman in this house since my wife Sarah died. I am an old man with fixed habits. I tend to fall asleep listening to concerts on the radio. I'm not a very good housekeeper as you can see. Perhaps a female hand might be a good thing.'

Gretchen sprang from her chair and hugged him.

'So you're saying they can come here and live with you in your house. And take care of you?'

'I suppose I am saying that but first I must meet the ladies. They may not approve of living under the same roof as a crusty old bachelor.'

'I'll tell my – Krista right away. Thank you, thank you, thank you.'

'It's a *mitzvah*,' Dr. Bidermann said to himself as he watched Gretchen fairly skip from the room. 'I need all the points with the Almighty I can get.'

Berlin, March 10, 1944

Gretchen and Kurt had spent the evening together listening to jazz. On their way back to the von Bismarck's apartment, Gretchen glanced over at the blacked-out windows of the coffee house, wondering about Krista and her grandmother. Two days before, Kurt had driven to Potsdam, picked up the old lady, and delivered her to Dr. Bidermann's rambling home. 'Your mother was waiting for her,' he told Krista. 'I don't know what happened after I left.'

Were they all right, Gretchen wondered? Thank heavens for Dr. Bidermann, she thought, but now they were all at risk. And it was all because of her, she realized.

When she unlocked the apartment door she saw a letter propped up on the hall table. Next to it was a hand-written note.

'Gretchen, this arrived for you at the house. I thought I would deliver it as I was in town to have my hair done and a manicure. I was hoping you would be here so that we could chat.

Your Mother.'

Gretchen took a deep breath. Ever since she had learned that Krista was her natural mother, she had begun to have ambivalent feelings towards Greta von Bismarck. Yes, Greta had always been there for her; but ever since she was a little girl she had sensed that Greta never treated her as other mothers treated their daughters. She never held her hand, and if she kissed her it was always on the forehead. And it was always Cook who cuddled her.

Even Greta's written communications, like the one she was holding, were without warmth and merely a means of imparting information. She loved Greta as a child is meant to love a mother, but on reflection – since Krista had come into her life – she came to understand that affection had not been reciprocated.

She picked up the envelope and studied it. Her name and address were typewritten. The blue stamp had a stylised image of a dove in flight with the words PAX HOMINIBUS BONAE VOLUNTATIS ('Peace to men of goodwill'). At the bottom, the name Helvetia, and the denomination, 1 Franc.

Shoshie!

Excited, she slit the envelope with the jade-handled opener her mother kept on a tray where the mail was customarily placed.

Dear Gretty,

Your letter took forever to arrive! You dated it October 12th, 1943 and I only got it today (March 2nd)!! So I'm replying right away and hope that it won't take that long to reach you.

Did you know a lot of it was blacked out with crayon? My Dad says the military censors must have read it, so I shouldn't say anything that might get you into trouble.

Are you surprised that I'm typing this letter? My parents made me take this stupid typing course, so that if I fail my exams (they want me to follow in my father's footsteps and become a doctor! Can you imagine me a doctor!!), I'll have something to fall back on. Like being a secretary. Ugh! Anyway, maybe I'll meet somebody rich who wants to marry me. I can always live in hopes.

I'll keep this letter short because my fingers are sore already, and the teacher says I have to cut my nails. You know how I love long nails and that purple nail polish I wore once at school, and Frau Seigert made me take it off. Remember that? How I hated her, the witch.

Well, Gretty, I hope you and your family are keeping yourselves safe. I read in our newspapers what is happening in Berlin. You are all very brave. I really miss you and would love to see you here. You have my address so maybe when the war is over...

Love always, Shoshie.

Gretchen showed the letter to Kurt.

'We were best friends at school. It was a finishing school in Bern. My parents thought I'd be safe there.'

'I've never been to Switzerland,' said Kurt.

'When the war is over, we'll go there together. You'll like Shoshie. She's a real rebel.'

Wednesday, June 7th, 1944

When Albert Speer arrived at his office at 7.30am, there was an urgent typewritten message on his desk. It had been sent to him by Generaloberst Friedrich Dollmann, commander of the Werhmacht's Seventh Army in Northern France.

Frau Kempf had deciphered and transcribed the transmission in a state of agitated excitement.

'Herr Minister, shortly after midnight yesterday morning American, British and Canadian forces landed on five beachheads along an 80-kilometre stretch of the Atlantic Wall fortifications. The Führer had anticipated the invasion to be at Pas de Calais, the shortest distance across the Channel from England. This landing point had been confirmed by our intelligence agents, but was obviously a bluff as an estimated 130,000 troops and 20,000 tanks stormed the beaches of Normandy.'

'In preparation for these landings, French terrorists destroyed 52 locomotives and cut railway lines in more than 500 places. We are virtually isolated here. I ordered an immediate counter-attack with the 21st Panzer Division, but the enemy, with their unchallenged air superiority, dropped flares to illuminate our men and armour. The 21st division has lost 5 tanks, 40 tank trucks, and 84 other vehicles.'

'Rommel is currently planning a counter attack, but without air support and the inability of the High Command to understand the gravity of the situation I am not confident we can turn back the invasion. My sixteen division and five corps commands are fighting as best they can, but without logistical support we cannot sustain resistance for long. Reports of our casualties come in at an alarming rate. There could be as many as 9,000 fatalities.'

'I urge you to intervene with the Führer and have him release the five Luftwaffe divisions, two Panzer divisions, and 24 infantry divisions, who are awaiting orders should the British and the Russians launch a further attack along the coast of Norway. Otherwise we will lose France. Heil Hitler.'

France is already lost, Speer thought to himself. The real question now is whether we can save Germany.

Wolf's Lair, July 20, 1944

On that fateful day, Gretchen and the other tasters had been ordered to present themselves at the kitchen in Wolf's Lair earlier than usual. The fortress had been built in Prussia as the eastern front headquarters for Operation Barbarossa – the invasion of the Soviet Union – in 1941.

The Führer had called a strategy meeting for 12.30 pm and wished to have an early lunch.

Hitler usually held such briefings in the bowels of the concrete bunker, but as it was a hot summer day the location had been changed to a light and airy wooden hut in the grounds.

It was so hot in the kitchen that Gretchen was relieved when a couple of soldiers walked in and invited them all to the screening of a black and white movie in a tent that had been set up in the grounds as a make-shift cinema.

One of the soldiers made a point of insinuating himself into a seat next to Gretchen. As the movie started, he brushed his leg against hers. She pulled away from him. A few moments later, she felt his arm slide along the back of her folding chair. She leaned forward to avoid contact. Then she felt his hand on her thigh.

Gretchen stood up suddenly and as she did so there was an ear-slitting explosion that threw her sideways and deafened her for a moment.

Pandemonium broke out on the grounds. The soldiers rushed out of the tent, reaching for their side arms. An air-raid siren wailed. An ambulance revved up its engine. The *Reichssicherheitsdienst* – Hitler's bodyguards in steel helmets, carrying machine guns – poured out of a building not 300 metres from the cinema tent.

Gretchen watched them encircle the hut where Hitler's meeting had been taking place. The roof had fallen in from the blast and smoke billowed from a gaping hole.

Someone has tried to kill Hitler, she said to herself. Please God, make him dead. All the horror would end, the war, the bombing, the extermination of the Jews....

But her shoulders dropped when she saw a dazed Führer being supported away from the smouldering wreckage of the hut by two officers. His pant legs were in tatters; his face blackened and streaked with blood, his hair singed.

Officers mustered their infantry, and ordered them to fall back to a safe distance from the point of the explosion in case there was a secondary device.

Gretchen could see an officer with a black eye patch commandeer a Horch 108 off-road passenger car with a driver and speed towards the gates of the compound.

Her ears still ringing from the blast, she realised that Adolph Hitler had survived, but there were people who wanted him dead.

Berlin, July 20, 1944

At 1 pm that same day, Albert Speer was in Berlin addressing some two hundred ministers, state secretaries and officials of the Reich. The meeting was held in the Ministry of Propaganda. Speer was appealing to them to dedicate their efforts to reinvigorate the home front's commitment to the war.

At the end of the meeting, which Goebbels himself chaired and made the final remarks, the Minister of Propaganda invited Speer back to his office to continue the conversation on how to mobilise the home front.

They had just settled in their chairs when a voice crackled over the loud speaker. There was an urgent phone message from headquarters; Otto Dietrich, the chief press officer of Nazi Germany, was on the line.

Goebbels flipped a switch and had the call put through to his private phone.

Speer watched the man's face turn ashen as he received the news that an attempt had been made on the Führer's life. A bomb concealed in a briefcase had exploded in the meeting room. Only the thick oak leg of the map table had saved Hitler's life.

Goebbels slumped in his chair. 'The Führer thinks it may have been one of the Todt Organisations. Probably a Jew.'

He looked directly at Speer as he said it.

And Speer knew exactly what Goebbels was thinking. The Todt Organisation was Germany's civil and military engineering group, notorious for using slave labour recruited from concentration camps. Among a vast number of other projects, the Todt Organisation was tasked with constructing the Wolf's Lair and was currently expanding its fortifications.

The Minister to whom the Todt Organisation workers reported was Albert Speer.

The thought flashed through Speer's mind that, if it was true that a worker on the site had tried to blow up Hitler, then he himself was in danger. Bormann would use this speculation to further undermine his position.

'Where was the security? Where were the precautions?' shouted Goebbels.

He mimics Hitler when he rages, thought Speer.

'I'd better get back to my office. I'll find out how this could have happened. I'm sure it's not the Todt workers. They're carefully screened and there are three checkpoints before they can enter the grounds.'

'Wait one minute,' said Goebbels, as he began writing furiously on the pad in front of him.

'Before the rumours start I'll have to go on the radio and tell the German people that the Führer has survived another assassination attempt,' he said as he wrote. 'Then he will have to address the people himself to prove he is still alive. Here's what I have written for the Führer.'

He slid the pad across the desk for Speer to read.

The claim by these usurpers that I am no longer alive, is at this very moment proven false, for here I am talking to you, my dear fellow countrymen. The circle that these usurpers represent is very small. It has nothing to do with the German armed forces, and above all nothing to do with the German army. It is a very small clique composed of criminal elements, which will now be mercilessly exterminated...

Having read it, Speer passed the sheet of paper back and stood up.

'Was anyone else injured?'

'Of course,' stormed Goebbels. 'It was a bomb in a packed meeting room. Luftwaffe General Korten, Colonel Brandt, Luftwaffe General Bodenschatz, General Schnunt, Lt. Colonel Borgman – they were all severely wounded...and some stenographer named Berger was killed on the spot.'

Speer nodded glumly. He then stood up, clicked his heels and saluted.

'Heil Hitler!'

****

Albert Speer left Goebbels' office, but he did not head for his ministry. Instead, he walked over to his private office. Checking to see that he was alone, he locked the door and took the framed photo of Hitler off the wall, to reveal the wall safe. Turning the dial to the numbers of his wife's birthday, he opened the door and took out the file that enumerated the previous attempts on Hitler's life.

Sitting at his desk, he read through it carefully, trying to see if there was a clue in the seventeen pages of the file as to who could have planned and executed this latest assassination attempt.

Speer sensed the motivation behind the plot: whoever it was – and it must have been a high-ranking officer with many sympathetic contacts in the Wehrmacht – was determined to effect a coup and sue for peace with the Western allies as soon as possible; and to show them that not all Germans were like Hitler, the SS and the Nazi party.

How ironic, he thought: the weather – the one thing Hitler could not control – had saved his life. Had the day not been so hot the meeting would have been convened, as was the custom, inside a concrete bunker; where the concussion blast would certainly have ended the Führer's life.

Instead, the meeting had been moved to an airy hut on the grounds, a hut that Speer himself had designed.

He didn't know then that his name was on a list of ministers – the only one from the Nazi regime – to head up a post-Hitler government. That incriminating document would be found later in a safe belonging to one of the conspirators.

Berlin, July 23, 1944

Constanze Manziarly was concerned for the physical and mental health of those women tasters who had been on duty when the bomb exploded at the Wolf's Lair. With the permission of the ranking SS officer, she gave them a week's holiday.

Gretchen was delighted. The break would allow her to see her parents, spend time with Kurt, and to catch up on news of her grandmother and Krista.

The first thing she did when she arrived at the Berlin apartment was to phone Kurt.

'It's me, Gretchen. They've given me time off. Do you want to go to the cinema this evening? But no films about war.'

They chose the Admiralspalast cinema in Berlin's Mitte district on Friedrichstraße. There was an anti-aircraft battery on the roof. They held hands throughout the screening of 'The Woman of My Dreams,' a musical comedy film starring the beautiful Egyptian-born star Marika Rökk.

Following the movie, there was a black and white documentary entitled 'Der Führer schenkt den Juden eine Stadt' (The Führer Gives the Jews a City).' It was shot by Kurt Gerron, a Jewish actor-director, who was promised that *he* would not be shot.

The film showed a beautified Theresienstadt concentration camp and how happy the inmates were, treated to musical entertainments such as a children's opera, *Brundibár*, and two musical performances on a wooden pavilion in the town square – Karel Ančerl conducting a work by Pavel Haas, and a jazz concert by Martin Roman and his Ghetto Swingers.

The propaganda film had been inspired by a hoax that the Nazi government had perpetrated on the Danish Red Cross. They had cleaned up the camp and sent numerous inmates to Auschwitz before the arrival of the delegation. After the completion of the film, its director was sent to Auschwitz where he died in the gas chamber along with the other members of the cast, including the children who performed in the opera.

Kurt squirmed in his seat as he watched the documentary. His mind went back to his visit to Ravensbrück and the haunted looks of the women prisoners as they clutched the barbed wire fences. Gretchen could feel his palm sweating.

'Let's get out of here,' he whispered to her.

As they left the theatre, a man in civilian clothes rose from a bench across the street. He marked the time of their departure in a small notebook and nodded to a second man who stood smoking outside the theatre. The second man crossed the road and began to follow the young couple.

****

They sat in silence in the dark, drinking a glass of Riesling, listening to the far-off *crump, crump* sound of bombs exploding on the city suburbs. They had heard the sirens, but had made no move to seek the safety of the nearby shelters. As if by an unspoken agreement they would wait out the air raid, and if it was their night to die, then so be it.

It was Kurt who broke the silence. 'Sounds like Kreuzberg is getting it tonight,' he said, glumly.

Gretchen nodded.

'Ever since I went to Ravensbrück to collect your grandmother,' he continued, 'I've had these nightmares. It's their eyes. The eyes of those women in rags, staring out at you. Like walking skeletons. Why are they doing this to women? It has to be stopped.'

'There is only one way to stop it,' said Gretchen.

Kurt waited for her to continue. Instead, she walked over to the window, pulled back the curtain, and gazed out in the direction where the bombs were dropping. She could see the glow of countless fires as searchlights raked the night sky. It would be beautiful if it weren't so terrible.

'That day in the Wolf's Lair when the bomb exploded, I thought that would be the end of it,' said Gretchen. 'If Hitler had died then.... Now he's taking his revenge, especially against the Jews.'

'But at least your grandmother's safe,' said Kurt. 'I don't think your mother was too pleased to see her.'

When he said the word 'mother' out loud the image that first sprang to Gretchen's mind was the face of Krista. She wondered how they were faring with Dr. Bidermann. She would stop by tomorrow.

Had she looked down instead of out at the distant pyrotechnics, she would have seen a man dressed in a black leather coat who lingered in the shadows of a doorway across the road from her vantage point.

Potsdam, August 8, 1944:

G raf von Bismarck was bent over his radio listening to a BBC World Service transmission, when his wife Greta entered his study.

She was about to speak when he held up his hand, pressing his ear closer to the speaker.

'...*Colonel Claus Count von Stauffenberg, who placed the bomb in Hitler's ward room, was tracked down and shot by firing squad. The trials of the other conspirators, according to our sources in Berlin, resulted in guilty verdicts. Within two hours of Judge Roland Freilser reading his verdict the accused were hanged. Their bodies were then hung on meat hooks. The grisly proceedings were recorded on film with the intention of having them shown in cinema newsreels for the German public. Seven thousand people were arrested for allegedly being implicated in the assassination attempt and 4,980 were executed....*'

Berlin, August 28, 1944

Margarete Speer had set the dinner table with the best plates and prepared her husband's favourite meal: seasoned beef rolls stuffed with bacon and caramelised onions, covered with pan gravy and served with spaetzle.

She had chilled a bottle of Riesling Kabinett and placed candles on the table beside a centrepiece of flowers. She wore a new dress.

'Dinner's ready,' she called.

Margarete was pleased to see that her husband was no longer wearing his uniform around the house; but she had not commented on the fact as he had become moody and preoccupied of late. Where once he would confide his problems to her and listen to her suggestions, since his operation he had become withdrawn and taciturn, only responding to direct questions.

When Speer entered the dining room, he was surprised by the festive table.

'What are we celebrating?'

'Don't you know?' said Margarete, tears welling in her eyes. 'Sixteen years ago today we were married. You didn't remember?'

'I'm so sorry, *liebchen*. I've had so much on my mind.'

He crossed the room and took her in his arms.

'I'm truly sorry. When this war is over, we'll go away. A second honeymoon, wherever you want.'

She leant her head on her husband's shoulder.

'I'm so tired of it all,' she said.

'It will soon be over.'

'I wish I could believe that.'

Speer sighed.

'Today, our forces in southern France surrendered at Toulon and Marseilles. The American General Patton's Seventh Army tanks have crossed the Marne.'

'Then it will be over soon.'

'Maybe sooner than we think.'

Their intimate moment, one of the few in the last several months, was interrupted by the doorbell.

'Who can be calling at this hour, Albert?'

'I'll get it.'

Margarete watched her husband open the door. She saw a man in a black leather coat give her husband the Nazi salute.

Speer stepped out into the corridor and closed the door behind him.

Margarete edged towards the door, but she could not hear their conversation. Looking through the spy hole she saw the man handing her husband a file.

She heard her husband say, 'So, they are still together.'

The other man nodded.

She returned quickly to the dining room and pretended to be rearranging the flowers. She saw her husband place the file on the table in the hall.

'Who was that?' she called to him.

'Nothing important. Just some papers from the office.'

'Do you mind fetching the corkscrew, Albert? You'll find it in the drawer next to the stove.'

While her husband went in search of the corkscrew, Margarete moved to the hall table. She picked up the file. It was marked '*Streng Geheim*: *Kurt Andorfer.*'

She frowned, wondering why there should be a Top Scret file on her newphew.

'Found it!' Speer called from the kitchen. When he joined his wife in the dining room, she was holding the file.

'And what's this? A dossier on my brother's son? You had our nephew followed?'

'It's a matter of state, Margarete. There is information –'

'You're spying on our nephew, Albert. Has it come to this?'

Potsdam, August 28, 1944

As always at this time, Carl von Bismarck was tuned in to the BBC World Service. An unusually excited newsreader was broadcasting the news that the Allies had liberated Verdun, Dieppe, Artois, Rouen, Abbeville, Antwerp and Brussels. And this a mere eight days after the liberation of Paris.

'It won't be long now,' he said, shaking his head.

Berlin, August 29, 1944

Albert Speer locked the file on his nephew back in his wall safe and crossed to a bookshelf. He took down a well-thumbed copy of '*Mein Kampf*' and opened it at the bookmark.

He had been alerted to two passages in Hitler's tome by Dr. Friedrich Lüschen, head of the German electric industry. Speer had drawn a pencil line in the margin against a passage on page 693. Although he almost knew the lines by heart, he read them out loud:

'The task of diplomacy is to ensure that a nation does not go heroically to its destruction but is practically preserved. Every way that leads to this end is expedient, and a failure to follow it must be called criminal neglect of duty.'

A second bookmark guided him to another pencil-marked passage on page 104:

'State authority as an end in itself cannot exist, since every tyranny on this earth would be sacred and unassailable. If a racial entity is being led towards its doom by means of governmental power, then the rebellion of every single member of such a Volk *is not only a right, but a duty.'*

Hitler's own words from 1926.

Speer went back to his desk and took up the plain brown envelope that his secretary had placed on the blotting pad. He read the note she had pinned to it.

Herr Speer, I found this envelope when I opened the office this morning. As you see it is addressed to you and there is no indication as to who sent it or who delivered it. I did not open it as there is a seal on the back so I imagine it is for you only to read.

He took up the ceremonial dagger he used as a letter opener and slit open the top flap. The blade was engraved with the legend, *Alles für Deutschland.*

Inside the envelope was a single typewritten sheet. He scanned it, but could find no date or indication as to who had typed it.

'Herr Minister, I am sending you this information as I think you should be aware of the situation and will know how to act upon it.

As you are aware, the Führer is being treated by his personal physician, Dr. Theodor Morell. Morell is half-Jewish.

Professor Ernst-Günther Schenk, the nutrition inspector for the Waffen SS, was concerned about the tablets Morell was prescribing for our leader and managed to get hold of a few of them. He crushed them in a mortar and pestle so that they would not be identifiable by their shape and sent them for analysis to the laboratories in the Nutrition Inspector's office.

The report confirmed that the tablets did contain vitamins as Dr. Morell had prescribed, but also caffeine and an extremely strong stimulant, Methamphetamine. As you may know amphetamines are dangerously addictive.

These tablets are produced in one of the pharmacies owned by Dr. Morell.

Dr. Schenk showed the report to Reich Health Leader Dr. Leonardi Conti who immediately informed Reichsführer Himmler who instructed him to tell Dr. Schenk to destroy the report.

I became aware of this only recently, although the analysis was performed last year. I am confident, Herr Speer, that you will know best how to proceed in the best interests of the German people.

A loyal Nazi.

Speer had heard Goering joke with Himmler that he called Dr. Morell, 'Herr Reich Injektion Minister' for all the times Hitler called for him to administer the needle. Himmler had been keeping a medical file on Hitler since 1938.

Had Himmler been told by Hitler not to interfere? If Hitler was on the way to becoming a drug addict, he could not be relied upon to make decisions in the best interests of the German people as Speer's anonymous informant would wish.

Or was Dr. Morell trying to poison the Führer?

He tore the letter into little pieces, set fire to it in an ashtray.

Berlin, September 5, 1944

Albert Speer studied Hitler's decree. The Führer had ordered the destruction of all coal and iron production, power plants and industrial installations in Luxembourg, Holland and Belgium to prevent them falling into the Allies' hands.

'This is sheer madness,' he said to himself.

He pressed the key of the intercom.

'Frau Kempf, I need you here, please.'

His secretary took a seat with her stenographer's pad at the ready.

'Send an urgent message to Field Marshall Günther von Kluge, commander of the Western front.'

Frau Kempf coughed.

'Is something wrong?'

'Herr Speer, did you not hear? Von Kluge was called back for a meeting with the Führer after the failed coup. He committed suicide. Poison.'

Speer sighed. So many of his colleagues had been hanged, guillotined or shot following the assassination attempt. He had forgotten about Günther.

'And who was assigned in his place?'

'Field Marshall Model, Herr Speer.'

'Ah yes, the one with the monocle…. Send him this message: You will have received a communication from Headquarters that in case of occupation by the Allies, the Führer has ordered a far-reaching system of destruction of war industries in Luxembourg, Holland and Belgium. According to planned preparations, coal and mineral mines, power plants, and industrial premises are to be destroyed.

'This destruction makes no sense and has no purpose and I, in my capacity of Armaments Minister, do not consider this destruction necessary. Thereupon no order to destroy these resources is to be given.'

Frau Kempf put down her pad.

'Herr Speer, you are countermanding a direct order from the Führer.'

'I am aware of that, Frau Kempf. I am the person responsible for supplying electric current to the undertakings on the other side of the front. If we destroy the pump stations in the coal mines, they'd be flooded. So, please see to it that the message is dispatched immediately.'

Annamarie Kempf, torn between her loyalty to her employer and her love and admiration for her leader, debated whether to alert her contact in the SS.

Berlin, October 11, 1944

The *Geheime Staatspolizei*, better known as the Gestapo, was housed in a massive five-storey building on Berlin's Prinz-Albrecht-Strasse (a block away from what would become Checkpoint Charlie).

As the official secret police of Nazi Germany and German-occupied Europe, their ranks were tasked, along with other duties, with spying on the local population for signs of disaffection and possible insurrection. They closely monitored church organisations and citizens who had access to Hitler but were not Nazi party members.

Following the July 20th plot, Heinrich Müller, chief of the Gestapo, ordered his agents to keep a close watch on the civilians who worked at the Wolf's Lair.

And this is how a file labelled 'Gretchen von Bismarck' came to land on the desk of Kriminal-Oberassistent Othmar Veigl.

Veigl had opted to join the SS – the organisation whose officers operated the Gestapo – rather than be sent to the Russian front. A man who feasted on gossip, he relished his job, spending hours reading the files to learn of the indiscretions and personal habits of those under surveillance.

His brief, like all other members of the Gestapo in Germany and in territories occupied by the Reich, was to flush out anyone suspected of treachery to the Führer. If someone even told a joke about Hitler or celebrated January 27th – the birthday of Kaiser Wilhelm II, which suggested implied sympathy for monarchism and an affront to the Nazi party – they would find themselves in the cellars at Prinz-Albrecht-strasse.

Veigl had a penchant for pastries and other sweetmeats, in addition to a well-concealed predilection for pretty young blond boys.

He took another bite of his favourite pastry, a Bethmännchen, which he baked himself from marzipan, powdered sugar, rose water, flour and eggs.

He wiped the confectioner's sugar delicately from the corners of his mouth with a silk handkerchief and dusted down the front of his uniform before opening the file.

He studied the photograph of Gretchen – the one taken with Goering that had appeared on the front page of *Das Reich*. He placed his fingers around her face to block out her long blonde hair, trying to imagine her as a boy.

He read the report written by his commanding officer investigating Gretchen's background when she applied to be a taster for Hitler. 'Impeccable credentials,' someone had scribbled in the margin. The handwriting looked like Goering's.

He noted that the girl's father was employed in the architectural firm owned by Albert Speer and that she was currently 'in the company of a very attractive young man, named Kurt Andorfer, who happened to be Speer's nephew. The boy was a prominent figure in the Hitler Youth who had recently survived an explosion. Just like the Führer, he thought.

Veigl looked for a photo of Kurt Andorfer and was disappointed not to find one.

It all seemed too perfect, but there was something that worried Othmar Veigl.

The girl had spent time at a finishing school in Switzerland. An agent in Bern who worked as a janitor at the school had reported back that Gretchen von Bismarck had roomed with a Jewess. Strange, thought Veigl, that this had not barred her from a position so close to the Führer.

Othmar Veigl would make it his business to take over the file personally, especially as the request had come from the Minister of Armaments and War Production himself.

Berlin, October 14, 1944

'Herr Speer, I have a call from a Captain Aldinger. He seems distraught. Shall I put it through on your private line?'

'Yes, of course, Frau Kempf, put him through.'

Speer wondered what Field Marshall Rommel's aide had on his mind. He picked up the receiver.

'Speer here. And how is my old friend Erwin, Captain?'

'Herr Minister, I regret to inform you that the Field Marshall is dead.'

'Dead? Why? How?'

Speer knew the answers already. Rommel's name was on the same list of senior officers and ministers who would take over the reins of government following a successful assassination of Adolf Hitler. Rommel's chief of staff and commanding officer had already been executed.

'They forced him to commit suicide, Herr Minister. Generals Burgdorf and Maisel. They came to the house. His son Manfred was here with me. They asked to speak to him alone. When they'd finished he went up to see his wife. Then they took him away. He was wearing his Afrika Korps tunic and carrying his marshal's baton. They gave him a choice, either a public trial which would certainly end with the death sentence or suicide and –'

'Slow down, man. A gunshot or cyanide pill?'

'We've been sworn to secrecy, but it was cyanide. Manfred wanted to defend his father but he said 'no.' the place was crawling with SS and the boy is only fifteen. They've issued a statement from the Wagnerschule Reserve Hospital in Ulm to say Rommel had a brain seizure on the way to a conference, that he died of the wounds he got in Normandy in July when his staff car was strafed by the British. They're giving him a state funeral,' he added, bitterly. 'The hypocrites.'

Speer knew exactly why Hitler wanted no word to leak out about how Rommel met his end. The Desert Fox was a national hero and for the Führer to order his death would have caused riots throughout Germany.

'Where did it happen?'

'They drove up the hill from the house and parked at an open space by the woods. There were Gestapo everywhere ready to shoot him if he offered any resistance.'

He could hear the Captain sobbing on the other end of the line.

'When is the funeral?'

'October 18th in Ulm.'

'I'll be there. Thank you for calling,' said Speer. 'My deepest condolences.'

Although he rarely saw Rommel, Speer counted him as a friend for whom he was willing to do favours. In his capacity as Inspector General of Buildings for the Reich Capital – an appointment bestowed on him by Hitler in 1937 – it was in Speer's power to dispose of the houses and apartments of Jews whose properties had been appropriated by the regime.

Rommel had asked him if he could find an apartment for his newly wed adjutant Baron Melchior von Schlippenbach. When the bridegroom had learned that the accommodations he was being offered belonged to a Jewish family who were about to be evicted, he angrily turned it down and complained to Rommel.

Now Rommel, like many of the officers Speer knew and liked, was dead. Some five thousand military personnel and civilians had been executed and thousands more sent to concentration camps on Hitler's orders following the July 20th bomb plot.

Albert Speer felt the Gestapo's shadow falling on him. He would have to act, but he had to choose his time carefully to protect his family.

Berlin, October 16, 1944

Kriminal-Oberassistent Othmar Veigl was not a field operative, but he desperately wanted to be one. If only to be able to wear street clothes rather than his scratchy uniform. The collar on his tunic was giving him a rash around his neck.

With the Gretchen von Bismarck file, he thought he had found a way to impress his Gestapo boss, Heinrich Müller, with his commitment to rooting out possible dissidents and, better still, fifth columnists.

Having located the address of the von Bismarck apartment he decided that he, rather than one of his subordinates, would personally inspect the property and through a casual conversation with the doorman learn about the girl's comings and goings when she was not on duty at the Wolf's Lair.

Veigl had discovered that the best way to ingratiate oneself with a prospective informant was to travel with a bag of pastries and offer to share one with the unsuspecting individual. As such delicacies were hard to come by in war-torn Berlin, he found it a most effective way of gathering intelligence.

The ploy had worked on the doorman at the Petersburger Strasse apartment block – or rather on the son of the doorman who had been deputised by his father to watch the front desk, while he went in search of some potatoes his wife required for a stew.

Between mouthfuls of Berliner Pfannkuchen, a jam-filled donut that Veigl favoured, the boy had told him that Gretchen von Bismarck indeed did live there – when she wasn't away – and that she sometimes received letters from Switzerland. As he collected stamps, he was going to ask her if he could have the envelopes.

'What's your name, young man?'

'Horst, mein Herr.'

'You have a big collection of stamps, Horst?' asked Veigl, feigning interest.

'Oh, yes. A big book full of them. Maybe a hundred and fifty from all over the world.'

'That's wonderful. And the envelopes from Switzerland. Did you ask the young lady for them?'

'No, not yet.'

'When you do, I'd really like to see one. I too collect stamps. If I were to give you my phone number would you call me when you have it? I have a particular fondness for Swiss stamps.'

'I'm not sure I should....'

'Take it anyway, just in case,' said Veigl, tearing some paper from the donut bag and scribbling a phone number on it.

The boy put it in his pocket and took another bite of the donut. With his mouth full, he said: 'But if you want to see her you can ask her yourself.'

He pointed at the door.

'She's across the road in that café. I saw her go in a few minutes ago.'

Veigl couldn't believe his luck.

'Here,' he said, handing the boy the bag containing the remaining donut. 'You're a good boy. Enjoy it.'

And as fast as his legs could carry him, Othmar Veigl scurried across the road and entered the café.

He looked around for Gretchen. She was seated at a table in the corner. A tall woman with blonde hair and dark roots was standing over her.

The table next to them was empty. Veigl insinuated himself into a seat with his back to the women. He took a newspaper from his jacket pocket and pretended to be reading, straining his ears to try and catch their conversation.

The woman standing seemed to be excited as if she had just received good news. From their body language it appeared that they knew each other and were not just waitress and a customer. And the way they spoke was not just the casual exchange of ordering a drink or a meal. There was something conspiratorial about the way their heads were so close.

It was hard for Kriminal-Oberassistent Othmar Veigl to eavesdrop above the noise of people moving around him and the girl at the counter shouting orders through a hatch to the kitchen. But some words filtered through to him: 'Doctor…a big house…cleaning…bedrooms–and something about food stamps.'

But what caught his attention was the mention of 'Ravensbrück.'

'I'm sorry, sir, I didn't see you come in. Can I take your order?'

The blonde woman was standing over him now, order pad in hand.

'A coffee,' he said. 'And show me what pastries you have.'

Berlin, October 18th, 1944

Margarete Speer had set the table in the kitchen for dinner. To make it a little more festive, she placed a bowl of poppies as a centrepiece. She had traded the florist two pork loins for the flowers.

'You're unusually quiet tonight,' she said as she watched her husband toy with his schnitzel.

'I'm sorry,' replied her husband, 'I'm preoccupied.'

'Maybe if you told me what it is that's keeping you tossing and turning at night and pushing your food around the plate, I could help.'

Speer sighed.

'They buried Erwin Rommel today. Earlier Speer says he would attend the funeral'

'I know. I saw a photo in the papers of the wreath the Führer sent. It was taller than you.'

Speer had said nothing about the suicide. He desperately wanted to attend the funeral of his old friend but a worried call from his secretary prevented him from going. A bomb that had exploded close to his office had weakened the structure of the building and there were fears that it might collapse. Frau Kempf had pleaded with him to inspect the damage.

Speer raised his head and studied his wife. He realised he had neglected her of late and it wasn't only because of the constant travelling to factories in the occupied territories, but when he was at home he had become distant.

They had argued about his surveillance of their nephew Kurt, but Margarete sensed that there was something deeper troubling her husband.

Speer pushed his plate away.

'A few days ago I received an anonymous letter. It was signed 'a loyal Nazi.' It was about the Führer and the amount of drugs that his personal physician has been prescribing him. The writer said that analysis showed in addition to vitamins the pills contained amphetamines, which are highly addictive. Doctor Morell produces them in his own factory.'

'Dr. Morell! Theodor Morell? That quack.'

'You know him?'

'No, but my friend Sonja, you know Sonja, she's married to one of the Krupp cousins. She heard he was Hitler's personal doctor and it's just like her to brag that she's treated by the same doctor as the Führer. Anyway, she went to him because she had a case of pink eye. Morell said he was going to give her the same eye drops that he had prescribed for Hitler. It turns out the solution contained 10 per cent cocaine. The first time she took them she nearly drove their Mercedes into a tree.... He should have his licence taken away.'

'The point is, if Morell is pumping the Führer full of addictive drugs, how can he make intelligent battlefield decisions?' he said, more to himself than to his wife.

'Maybe that's why they tried to blow him up.'

In earlier days, if Margarete had made such a statement he would have rounded on her, accusing her of disloyalty and defeatism. But the accumulation of recent events – the decimation of the officer class following the July plot, Hitler's sudden indifference to his efforts to protect his position and the morale-sapping news from the Western front – all this had forced him to re-evaluate his loyalty to his leader.

Why am I procrastinating, he had asked himself. Was it cowardice or fear of what might happen to his family if he acted? Or was the love and admiration he had felt for the Führer too deep in his soul for him to raise a hand against the leader who was responsible for what he had become?

Albert Speer neither shared this insight with his wife, nor did he tell her that the agent assigned to follow Kurt had reported back that his nephew had driven Speer's car to Potsdam a few months ago. He had picked up the Rosenberg woman and driven her to the Berlin home of a Jewish doctor named Bidderman.

Berlin, October 18, 1944

When the call arrived, it took Othmar Veigel a moment to realise it was from the boy Horst, whom he had met in the vestibule of the von Bismarck's apartment block.

'Horst, my young friend, just a moment while I close my office door.'

He did not want anyone to hear his end of the conversation.

'So, what can I do for you?'

'I have the stamp.'

'Why are you whispering?'

'You said it was our secret.'

'Very well, I'll whisper too. Did she give it to you?'

'Yes, she gave me the whole envelope. I have it here. Do you want to see it?'

'I would like very much to see it.'

'Do you want me to bring it to you?'

'No, no.'

The thought of the boy walking into the Gestapo headquarters alarmed him. This was his investigation and his colleagues were not to know of it until he had reached a triumphal conclusion.

'I will meet you across the road from where we talked. That coffee place you directed me to. Remember?'

'Yes.'

'How about this afternoon at 3 o'clock?'

'OK.'

'Do you have a watch?'

'Yes.'

'Good. I will see you at 3 o'clock in the coffee place.'

'Will you bring along your collection so I can see it?' asked Horst.

'Oh, it's locked away safely at home. But another time perhaps. Goodbye.'

Veigl put the phone down and shook his clenched fists.

'Yes!'

He was sure the envelope would lead to a Swiss Jewess.

One thing concerned him though. The Gestapo in their security check on the Gretchen von Bismarck had discovered that she had roomed with a Jewess in Bern – it was all in the file; and yet, she had been cleared to be near to the Führer as his taster. Somebody must have intervened.

He opened the file and studied the newspaper photo of the girl with Goering. He took out a magnifying glass from the drawer and studied her features closely.

'I see it now,' he said to himself. 'She looks like a younger version of Geli Raubel.'

He locked the file away in his desk and whistled as he walked out of his office.

As he entered the stenographers' room he asked if anyone had any foreign stamps.

One of the women put up her hand.

'I just got a letter from my husband who's serving in Hungary. Will that do?'

'Perfect,' said Veigl. 'Do you mind if I have the envelope? You will be proud to know that it'll be in the service of the Reich.'

The woman took out the letter and handed him the envelope, which Veigl slid into his jacket pocket.

He whistled all the way out of the building.

Horst was waiting for him outside the coffee shop. He was holding a book close to his chest.

'Ah, young man, what a pleasure it is to see you again. Let's go inside and have a pastry.'

A creature of habit, Veigel chose the same seat he had occupied on his previous visit.

'Now, let me see it,' he said when Horst had taken the chair opposite him.

The boy opened the book and leafed through a few pages until he arrived at one headed in block capitals, 'Switzerland.'

A single stamp had been affixed with a tab.

'There it is,' said the boy, proudly.

'And the envelope? Where's the envelope?'

'I soaked the stamp off. I threw it away.'

Othmar Veigel stood up, his face purple with fury.

'You stupid, stupid boy!'

The anger in his voice attracted the attention of the other customers – as well as Krista Becker, who approached the table.

'Is everything all right here?' she asked.

Veigel turned to her. He was about to say something and then stopped. He nodded menacingly at the boy and reached into his jacket pocket. He took out the envelope and scrunched it into a tight ball and tossed it onto the table.

'Here,' he said. 'Add this to your collection.'

Berlin, November 2, 1944

'Gretchen! I was wondering when you'd be calling,' said Dr. Bidermann as he responded to the doorbell. 'Come in, child.'

'How is my – Frau Rosenberg?' asked Gretchen as she entered, taking off her coat.

'She is progressing nicely. She sleeps a lot, which is a good thing. She's put on weight, which she has to do slowly, and she likes to sit in the garden and talk to the flowers. But it's a little too cold for her now.'

'Can I see her?'

'She's sleeping now. Can you come tomorrow morning?'

'I'll try…. And you, how are you getting on with two women in the house?'

'I enjoy their company. Look around. The place has never been so clean. No dishes in the sink, no dust in the corners. Krista is a wonderful cook although she works too hard. She has her job at the coffee house as you know and then she comes home to cook and clean the house and look after her mother.'

'Has she said anything about me?'

'You? No. She's a very private person. I suspect there are events in her life that she would rather not talk about. Perhaps when she grows to trust me more. Let's go into the kitchen. I can still make a pot of tea.

Gretchen was relieved that her relationship with Krista was still a secret and it would be she who would ultimately reveal it.

Dr. Bidermann talked as he pottered about preparing the tea.

'According to the BBC the Luftwaffe is sending V-2 rockets over London, eight a day. You know, I visited London as a medical student at the turn of the century. It is a wonderful city. The museums, the parks, the concert halls…. I fell in love with an English girl. She was a teacher. But I had to return to Berlin and then I met my Sarah. I have a photograph of her on our wedding day somewhere.'

Gretchen waited for an opportunity to break into his reminiscence. 'Dr. Biddermann, I have a new job….'

'*Mazeltov.*'

He waited for her to continue, nodding his encouragement.

Gretchen took a deep breath.

'OK. Here goes…I am one of the women who tastes the food that's put in front of the Führer.'

The mug was halfway to Dr. Bidermann's lips when it stopped and quivered, spilling some tea on the tablecloth and down his front.

'I'm part of a rotation of women who live near his compound in Rastenberg. We taste every plate before it's delivered to the table.'

Dr. Bidermann, eyes wide open, absent-mindedly brushed the droplets of tea from his waistcoat.

'I'm worried if a dish I've got to taste is poisoned, what should I do? What precautions should I take?'

The old man sat back in his chair and was silent for a moment.

'Let me tell you a story,' he said finally. There was an emperor in India whose name was Chandragupta Maurya. He ruled India for 27 years. I'm talking some 300 years before the Christian era. His court-iers would select the most beautiful girls and feed them poison in tiny amounts. This would make them immune to poison. The girls were called *vishakanyas*, 'poison maidens.' It was believed that those who lay down with *vishakanyas* would die instantly. So they were employed to kill the emperor's enemies.'

'Do you mean if I swallowed one tiny bite from a dish that had been poisoned I'd be okay?'

'It would depend on the poison. It could remain in your system and accumulate there. It depends on how each poison is metabolized by the body, Gretchen. Certain toxic substances, such as hydrofluoric acid and heavy metals like arsenic, mercury and lead in small doses are either lethal or have little or no effect.'

'But if I were ingesting small amounts of poison over a period of time, is there any way of stopping it from accumulating in my body?'

Dr. Bidermann sat back in his chair.

'Are you being serious?'

Gretchen nodded.

'Well, I suppose the simplest way would be to drink a large glass of salt water after each meal. This would cleanse your entire digestive tract and detoxify your colon.'

'And what if I knew what the poison was? Would I be in a better position to combat it?'

Dr. Bidermann's eyes widened.

'I don't think I should be hearing this, child. What are you not telling me?'

Gretchen leaned forward until she was looking directly into his eyes.

'You were our family doctor. Were you there when my mother gave birth to me?'

'No, your mother delivered you in a Swiss sanatorium.'

'Did you examine her at any point during her pregnancy?'

'She told me she had her own obstetrician.'

'Did you ever attend any of the staff at our house?'

'Why are you asking me all these questions?'

'Please. It's important.'

The old man shut his eyes, searching his memory.

'I recall once your father contacted me. One of your maids. He wanted to know if she was pregnant. A pretty young thing. I probably have a record of the visit on file somewhere.'

'Dr. Bidderman. That maid's name was Krista Becker. She was my mother. Like you, Krista is Jewish.'

The old man seemed to age before her eyes. The full implication of her questions and the unspoken thoughts behind them became clear to him now.

He stood up and placed his hands on her shoulders.

'Gretchen, tell me the truth…. You want me to help you to poison Hitler.'

****

Dr. Bidderman paced up and down the corridor of his house in an attempt to keep warm.

The visit that morning by Gretchen von Bismarck had disturbed him more than he had realised.

The revelation that she was not the daughter of Carl and Greta von Bismarck but the result of a liaison between his aristocratic friend and a maid in his service had taken him by surprise. But on going back over his records he saw that he had been consulted soon after the couple's wedding by Greta with regard to her futile attempts to get pregnant.

Why had he not remembered that? Especially when, a few years later, Greta had returned from Switzerland with a baby girl.

But then, who was he to judge? Desperate couples will take desperate measures to have a child.

And now that child had come to him to ask for his help in ridding the world of a monster – a monster who was systematically exterminating his people.

She wanted him to prepare the instrument that would dispatch the hated Adolf Hitler and to teach her how and when to administer it.

But he was a doctor, trained to heal patients not to kill them. He recalled the oath he had taken as a newly minted physician when he graduated from the Medical University of Vienna in 1904. He had graduated top of his class in both medicine and pharmacology from the oldest German-speaking medical school in the world. The certificate still hung on the wall of his surgery.

The Hippocratic oath was administered to him first in and then in High German. The part that now resonated in his memory was: 'Nor shall any man's entreaty prevail upon me to administer poison to anyone; neither will I counsel any man to do so.'

Yet it isn't a man who is entreating me, he thought; it's a child, a Jewish child whose own life is in danger. I remember my father who escaped the pogrom in Kiev in 1881; he taught me about the Crusades and the destruction of the Temple by the Romans. On Seder night he read to me from the Haggadah: 'In each and every generation they rise up against us to destroy us. And the Holy One, blessed be He, rescues us from their hands.' But where is the Holy One now?

Dr. Isaac Bidderman went down to his dispensary in the basement and began to sort through the glass stoppered bottles.

Berlin, November 3, 1944

K riminal-Oberassistent Othmar Veigl, concealed in the shadow of a doorway opposite the coffee shop where Krista Becker worked, waited until she had finished her shift.

He had not forgotten the conversation he had overheard several weeks earlier between Gretchen von Bismarck and the blonde waitress; but his professional attentions had been directed by his commanding officer to a more pressing matter. He had been ordered to investigate the flood of counterfeit food stamps that had suddenly appeared in the shops of Berlin.

Were the Allied bombers dropping them in mailbags over the city to create havoc in the marketplace? Or was there a gang of disloyal Germans – probably Jews who had evaded arrest – with a printing machine somewhere in the city?

Veigl could not arrest everyone who was found in possession of forged food stamps, as it would mean processing thousands of them through the courts; and their ultimate destination would be the camps. Then there was the question of morale. If the citizens of Berlin were unwittingly duped into using the stamps and then arrested, there could be riots in the streets.

He did not know where to begin his investigations, short of apprehending a bunch of housewives found to be using the bogus stamps, herding them into the cellar below his office and threatening them with torture unless they revealed where and how they had acquired them.

And then he recalled that he had overheard the blonde waitress mentioning food stamps.

He could kill two flies with one swat by interrogating the woman and furthering his understanding of true sympathies of Gretchen von Bismarck.

Veigl saw Krista Becker exit the coffee shop and pulled himself deeper into the shadows. He waited until he could determine in which direction she was walking and then began to follow her. It would be perfect, he thought, if she did some shopping on her way home and he could catch her red-handed passing off counterfeit food stamps.

But the woman did not deviate from the rutted sidewalks and moved at such a pace that he was perspiring in his efforts to keep up with her. When she boarded a yellow tram he hopped aboard at the last moment, concealing himself behind a newspaper, keeping an eye on her back.

Krista Becker got off at the Tempelhof stop and walked in the direction of Südgelände park. Veigl waited until she had crossed Arnulfstrasse. The bombed-out buildings on either side of the wide avenue stood like rotten teeth, blackened and jagged, casting grey shadows in the late afternoon winter sun. The pedestrians, no longer bewildered by the devastation of their city, went purposefully about their business as they hurried home after work.

Veigl saw the woman enter the park. The encircling iron railings that he remembered as a boy were no longer there – hacksawed off as scrap metal to support the war effort. He watched her sit down on a bench and pull a paper bag from her purse. He moved closer.

Krista took out a handful of crumbs and scattered them at her feet. And suddenly from nowhere, as if rising from the earth itself, were a dozen or so green finches pecking hungrily within touching distance of her shoes.

Veigl wondered idly where the birds went during the bombing. If they had any sense they'd fly to the country and stay there. He shifted his weight uncomfortably from one foot to the other, silently willing the woman to get up and finish her journey. He had to find out where she lived and what she had meant when she had referred to a 'big house' and a 'Doctor.'

To pass the time he took out a small black leather notebook and began to write details of his investigation. He would not include this departure from his daily routine in the office logbook. Instead, when his investigation of Gretchen von Bismarck came to its triumphant conclusion, he would submit a fulsome report to Heinrich Müller and receive the recognition he deserved. Possibly a medal in the bargain.

When the woman finally stood up and snapped her purse shut, he waited to see in what direction she would move. It was getting near dinnertime according to the rumblings of his stomach.

He followed her through the park until she came to a row of houses set back behind fences, their gardens surprisingly well cared for in contrast to the bomb-damaged streets beyond the perimeter of the park.

He saw her open the gate to a large, rambling house and climb the stairs to a covered porch. He made a note of the address and the time in his book and watched her as she slid a key into the lock. Why was a woman who worked as a waitress in a coffee shop living in such a magnificent house, he thought to himself. He had not detected a wedding ring on her finger so perhaps she was a maid or a housekeeper.

Veigl waited until she had entered the house and then nonchalantly strolled through the gate and made for the front door. He rang the bell, placed his hands behind his back and began rocking on his toes.

Krista opened the door.

'Yes, can I help you?'

'There have been some complaints from neighbours about your blackout,' he improvised. 'I am here to inspect the premises. I will need to see your papers.'

Krista studied the short, fat man in his ill-fitting suit.

'On whose authority?'

Veigl reached into his breast pocket and took out his wallet and extracted an identity card the colour of dried blood. He held up in both hands for Krista to read:

Dientaus Weis Ne. 223
für
Othmar Veigl,
Kriminal-Oberassistent
Beim Geheim Staatspolizeiamt
Berlin, den 2. Januar 1943
Der Chef der Sicherheitspolizei
Und des SD
(under which was a signature)

In the left-hand corner was a black and white headshot of an unsmiling Veigl, like a passport photo, certified with a stamp of the Chief of German Police. Below it, the signature of the bearer.

Krista nodded and beckoned him inside, holding the door open. Veigl entered and studied the long hallway.

'Oh, Dr. Bidermann,' Krista called in a loud voice. 'We have company. Can you come here please?'

'I will need to see your papers, Frau –?'

'Of course, they're in my purse. I'll get them as soon as Dr. Bidermann comes.'

The object of her attention emerged from the kitchen in his slippers. From her position behind Othmar Veigl's back, she pointed to her left forearm and then half-raised her right hand at the elbow.

Dr. Bidermann got the message. He had a Gestapo agent in his house and he could see that Krista was trembling, fearful the man might discover her mother upstairs.

'Good evening, my name is Bidermann. How can I be of assistance?'

'Othmar Veigl, Kriminal-Oberassistent, Staastpolizei.'

'And you are not in uniform, Herr Veigl. I shall have to see your identification if you please. You know, there are a lot of rascals around these days masquerading as SS officers and up to no good.'

Veigl clicked his tongue in annoyance.

'I have already shown it to the lady.'

'Then I will take you on trust. Please come in, and to what do I owe the pleasure of your company?'

'There have been complaints about your blackout. I have to inspect your rooms to ensure you have the necessary curtains. And I will need to see your papers.'

'I shall be happy to escort you around, but I am an old man and I cannot move very fast. So please bear with me. Krista, I have a patient waiting for me in the garden. Will you please tell her I won't be long. Perhaps you can walk with her while I tour the house.'

Krista understood that her mother was sitting out under a tree, which she did every evening at this time, even when it was cold. And it would not be advisable to their guest to run into her.

'Come along, Herr Veigl,' said Dr. Bidermann. 'I might have to lean on you while we climb the stairs. I hope you don't mind.'

Othmar Veigl left Dr. Bidermann's house no wiser than he had entered it. The woman had disappeared and not shown him her papers. He did not even find out her last name. And his informal interrogation of the doctor had elicited no information other than, though Jewish, he was an honorary Aryan and had been permitted to practice medicine in a limited manner by Hermann Goering himself.

There must be another avenue to explore. And then it came to him. Albert Speer had contacted him personally to have his nephew Kurt Andorfer followed. As he hated driving almost as much as following suspects around, he had passed on the assignment to a deputy in his department. But he recalled reading in the file that Andorfer was seen in the company of Gretchen von Bismarck. And as a leader in the Hitler Youth, Andorfer had an obligation to help him in his investigation.

Berlin, November 5, 1944

'So tell me about his routine?'

Gretchen sat in Dr. Bidermann's kitchen holding a mug of tea.

'I got friendly with his valet, Heinz Linge. He's the one who organises our roster. He told me he wakes Hitler at 11 am every day and gives him the morning newspapers and his messages. When he gets dressed he has Ligne time him with a stopwatch. Weird. He takes a breakfast of tea and an apple. Then a light lunch at 2.30 pm. Dinner is at 8 pm, usually with a few guests.'

'Tell me more about his eating habits.'

'First of all he has awful table manners.'

'Yes, I would have expected that. And I know about his being vegetarian and not drinking alcohol. What kind of life is that?'

'He only drinks water with his meals.'

'Water is not a good medium for poison. The dose would have to be tasteless and odourless like Sodium fluoroacetate. But that's impossible to get nowadays.... I suppose I could synthesize some by treating sodium chloroacetate with potassium fluoride, but that would take time and I'm not sure I could concentrate it to the right strength.'

'He eats a lot of vegetables. Is there any poisonous vegetable?'

'Certain beans contain toxins. So does cassava root and nutmeg, but you'd have to ingest an awful lot.... Then there's hemlock. That's how the philosopher Socrates died. Eating a salad of hemlock leaves would work but where do you get fresh hemlock these days?' laughed Dr. Bidermann. 'In the Old Testament there is a description of the Israelites who ate quail that had consumed hemlock seeds. They contracted a disease called rhabdomyolysis.'

'What's that?'

'The hemlock causes the muscle tissue to break down which releases the muscle fibre content into the blood causing damage to the kidneys. Very unpleasant. Then there's oleander.'

'The flower?'

'Yes, such a pretty flower and so dangerous. If you eat the petals or chew on the leaves or stems it stimulates the heart, causing sweating, vomiting and bloody diarrhoea.'

'There must be something less unpleasant, Doctor.'

'There is arsenic, a classic poison, usually in powder form as arsenic trioxide. It causes severe gastric upset.'

'That's interesting because his dietician told me that he takes these little black pills before he eats. Lots of them a day. They were prescribed by his doctor.'

'Little black pills? Do you remember if they were Dr. Küster's Anti-gas pills?'

'Yes, exactly!'

'Ah-ha, then we have the answer, Gretchen. Those pills contain strychnine. If Hitler, as you say, has been taking them daily he'll have an accumulation in his system. We just add to it. Strychnine is a highly toxic alkaloid that has a bitter taste and is not as fast-acting as arsenic. It comes as a colourless powder. The question is how to administer it to your dish in the right dosage, undetected by his guards or the kitchen staff.'

Berlin, November 20th, 1944: Gestapo Headquarters

Heinrich Müller, the Gestapo Chief, summoned all the senior operatives of his department for a briefing.

Kriminal-Oberassistent Othmar Veigl took a mirror from his desk drawer and looked at his reflection to ensure there was no butter cream on his chin. He closed the file on Gretchen von Bismarck, buttoned his uniform, and made his way to the assembly hall two floors down.

There was a buzz of excitement in the room as such a meeting of the entire senior staff was rare. Veigl took a seat in the last row so that he could see who was attending and who was out of favour.

When Heinrich Müller took the podium on the raised dais, the assembled SS officers fell silent.

'Gentlemen,' he began, 'you are aware that our soldiers have suffered some reversals in the field, but let no one here have any doubt that Germany will win this war!'

Almost instantaneously, the audience erupted in cheers and the thunderous noise of foot stamping that seemed to shake the room.

'I have gathered you here to tell you that our leader, Adolf Hitler, is returning to Berlin to be in the heart of Germany with his people to conduct the war to its victorious conclusion. He will be living and working in the Reich Chancellery, but for his personal safety he will spend the night in the *Führerbunker*, which cannot be harmed by enemy bombs.'

More foot stamping. Müller held up his hand for silence.

'The *Führerbunker* is part of a complex that includes two separate shelters, the *Vorbunker* and *Führerbunker*. They are connected by a stairway and can be closed off from each other by a bulkhead and steel door. The *Führerbunker* is located about 8.5 metres under the garden of the Reich Chancellery. Its roof is made of concrete almost three metres thick. It contains 30 small rooms, which are protected by four metres of concrete; exits lead into the main buildings, as well as an emergency exit that opens up to the garden. So, there is no bomb that can penetrate this space. The Führer will take up residence there on the 16th of January. He will be joined by his senior staff, including Chief of the *Padrteikanzlei*, Martin Bormann. There will be support, medical and administrative staff sheltered there as well. These include the Führer's secretaries, a nurse and telephone switchboard operator, Oberscharführer Rochus Misch. It is our sworn duty to protect the Führer in these difficult times until we have achieved the ultimate victory. In the meantime, you will continue your work to root out enemies of the state. Heil Hitler!'

The audience rose to its feet as one and with arms raised shouted their allegiance to Hitler.

Othmar Veigl was first to leave. He was already late for his appointment with Kurt Andorfer.

Veigl had initiated the meeting on the pretext that he wanted Kurt, in his capacity as Head of the Hitler Youth in Berlin, to instruct his young charges to be on the lookout for anyone trafficking in food stamps.

Rather than summon the young man to his office on Prinz-Albrecht-Strasse, he decided to make the meeting place in the eastern part of the city where the Hitler Youth Headquarters was located at Torstrasse and Prenzlauer Allee.

There would also be the delightful possibility of running into some handsome young boys.

It always amused Veigl that the eight-storey, white monstrosity that housed the Hitler Youth organisation measured 80,000 square metres, which made it larger than Buckingham Palace and fifteen times bigger than Washington's White House. The building had been commissioned in 1928 by two Jewish watchmakers, who wanted to open a department store. As Jews could no longer own business when the Nazis came to power, the owners took in two non-Jewish partners who eventually threw out them out.

In the cemetery across the street, Veigl stopped momentarily at the square concrete block that was placed over the grave of Horst Wessel, the young Nazi activist who was shot dead by Communists in 1930 and would become a martyr for the Nazi cause. There were fresh flowers at the base of the stone.

Veigl entered the building, showed his credentials to the guard at reception and asked directions to Kurt Andorfer's office. He proceeded up the vast marble staircase to a cubbyhole of a room on the second floor.

'Good day, Herr Andorfer. Thank you for taking the time to see me.'

Kurt rose from his chair to acknowledge his visitor. He noted the sheen of perspiration on the man's forehead. There was something about him that put Kurt on his guard – the ingratiating smile and the way he did not look Kurt in the eye when he spoke to him.

'Won't you sit down, please. How can I be of service?'

'There are two matters under investigation by my department. The first requires the cooperation and participation of your fine organisation.'

'We will assist you, of course.'

'Good.'

'There is a meeting of our sections heads in ten minutes.'

'Excellent. Perhaps I could save us all time if I could address them.'

'By all means. And the second matter you're investigating?'

Veigl's chair creaked as he changed position.

'This matter is very delicate, Herr Andorfer, as it concerns you.'

Me?'

'Yes. Let me start by reminding you that you took an oath when you joined the Hitler Youth.'

'I'm aware of that,' responded Kurt, now wary and on the defensive.

'Good. We have reason to believe that the young lady you are seeing may not be as loyal to the Reich as you are.'

A tremor of fear passed through him. He tried to remain nonchalant and show nothing of his concern.

'Which young lady are you referring to?'

'I'm sure a handsome young man like you has many female admirers. But the one we are interested in is a young woman by the name of Gretchen von Bismarck.'

'Gretchen von Bismarck,' repeated Kurt, trying to give himself time to calm his agitation.

'We know that you have been keeping company with her.'

'Ah, yes. *That* Gretchen. I see her now and again.'

'Well, as a good German who is loyal to the Führer, I'm sure you would want to cooperate with us. There is also an older woman named Rosenberg and there seems to be a connection between her and your Gretchen. We would like to know more about both of them. And there is also a Jewess in Switzerland with whom your Gretchen has been corresponding. I'm sure you understand these suspicions would be put to rest if we knew exactly the nature of these associations. So, what do you say?'

Kurt stood up.

'In the interest of the party, I am prepared to end the relationship. Heil Hitler!'

'No, no, dear boy. You don't understand. I admire your conviction, but it would be in the best interests of the party if you'd continue to see her and report back to me anything and everything she talks about. Do I make myself clear?'

'Perfectly, Kriminal-Oberassistent Veigl. At your service.'

'Excellent. I rely on your discretion in this matter. Here is my card with a direct phone line to my office. Now, let's go to your meeting.'

Kurt, his mind reeling, escorted Veigl out of his office and down the stairs to the assembly room on the ground floor.

There were some twenty section heads gathered in the room, all in their brown uniforms. Kurt mounted the three stairs of the dais and invited Veigl to join him. He stood clutching the sides of the podium to steady his nerves.

'Please rise for the salute.'

There was a scraping of chairs as the boys rose.

'Heil Hitler!'

The audience responded, repeating the salute before taking their places again.

'Gentlemen, we are honoured to have with us this afternoon, Kriminal-Oberassistent Veigl of the Staatspolizei who would like to say a few words.'

'Thank you, Kurt. It is a pleasure for me to stand before you shining examples of the new Germany. We must always be vigilant because, my friends and fellow citizens, there are those among us who are working to destroy what we are building. It is not just spies and traitors in our midst who attempt to undermine us, but even innocent people who suffer through the bombing of our city along with patriots like us.'

He looked around at the faces turned up to him to see what effect he was having on them. They gazed back at him without expression.

'I am here today to tell you that some unscrupulous individuals have been printing off counterfeit food stamps and selling them on the black market. What this does is compromise our food supplies. Everyone has an allotment of food stamps. By exchanging these counterfeit stamps you are taking the food out of the mouths of your neighbours and their children. So, if you see or hear of anyone trying to sell these bogus stamps you must report them to your leader here, Kurt Andorfer. It makes no difference if they are your uncles, your cousins, your next door neighbours or even your mothers and fathers, it is your patriotic duty to inform Herr Andorfer.'

He looked intently at a small blond boy in the front row and then scanned the rest of the upturned faces.

'Young soldiers of the German Reich, there is a difference between a patriot and a nationalist. Do you know what the difference is?'

He saw no mark of recognition in the blank faces.

'A nationalist,' he continued, 'is someone who is ready to kill for his country. A patriot is a man who is willing to die for his country. Hands up those of you who are willing to die for your country.'

Spontaneously, without looking at their neighbours, all hands shot up.

'Heil Hitler,' Veigl shouted.

'Heil Hitler!' the boys responded with one voice.

'Sheep,' Othmar Veigl said to himself, 'idiots.' Then he left the stage, glanced back at Kurt and tapped the side of his nose with his left forefinger.

Kurt gave a sigh of relief when Veigl left the building. His final words to Kurt were: 'I expect to hear from you soon.'

Kurt returned to his office in a state of shock. Veigl knew about Gretchen and about Ruth Rosenberg; but did he know of the family connection? If he found out it would mean the Ravensbrück for Gretchen. She must be warned.

In the meantime, he would play along with the SS man and feed him innocuous information.

Berlin, November 27, 1944

D r. Bidermann set out neatly all the equipment he needed on his kitchen table: a tape measure, note pad and pencil, pair of scissors, roll of surgical tape, two pairs of rubber gloves, two cloth face masks, a glass measuring column, jug of water, length of fine latex rubber tubing and rubber bulb.

On a small, covered Petri dish was a white crystalline powder that looked like a tiny hill of salt. Beside it was a metal spatula.

He had spent many hours pondering the most efficient way for Gretchen to introduce poison into Hitler's food without detection.

The answer came to him while he was preparing to pray.

As an observant Jew, every weekday morning when he arose, Avrum Bidermann laid *tefillin*.

He would take the two small black leather boxes that contained Hebrew parchment scrolls from the blue velvet bag embroidered with the Star of David. He would place one of the boxes against his left bicep (close to his heart) and wind the long leather strap attached to it around his forearm down to his fingers.

The straps of the second box were tied together so that it could sit high on his forehead just above the hairline.

When he had placed the both boxes in position he would recite the prayer: 'Blessed are You, Lord our God, King of the universe, who has sanctified us with His commandments, and commanded us to put on *tefillin*.'

It was when he had finished praying one morning, and was unwinding the strap from his arm, that the idea came to him.

But his next thought was, if he used the idea of a *tefillin* strap in his plan would that be sacreligious.

Then he recalled a phrase from his Hebrew studies – *Pikuach Nefesh,* a principle in Jewish law that the preservation of a human life supercedes any other religious consideration.

He wondered what the Talmud had to say about it. If only he could discuss it with his rabbi.

But his rabbi had been taken.

Bidermann put the phylacteries carefully back into the bag and zipped it up. Oddly excited, he waited for Gretchen to arrive.

He jumped at the sound of the doorbell.

'Good morning, Fraulein,' he said.

He helped Gretchen off with her coat, noting with satisfaction that she had followed his instructions and had on a long sleeved blouse buttoned at the wrist.

'Everything is prepared. Please, step into the kitchen.'

Gretchen's eyes widened as she took in all the paraphernalia on the table.

'This morning we are going to practice how you will administer the poison to the dish you will taste before Hitler.'

Gretchen's eyes were drawn to the Petri dish.

'Is that the strychnine?'

'Yes. It looks very innocent, doesn't it, but it's deadly.'

'Where does it come from?'

'Strychnine is an alkaloid that's extracted from the seeds of the Strychnos nux-vomica, a tree that grows in tropical forests in Southern India and Indonesia. The fruit, the size of a large apple, has five very hard seeds. These seeds contain the strychnine.'

'Where do we start?'

'First, I'd like you to remove your blouse.'

'I beg your pardon!'

'Gretchen, I have seen more brassieres than you will ever wear in your lifetime. So please trust me.'

She turned away from him and began to unbutton her blouse, which she draped over the back of a chair. She turned back to him, her arms folded across her chest.

'What now?'

'Which hand do you use for a soup spoon?'

'My right.'

'Good. I need to take a measurement now. Please hold out your left arm. Straight out, like this.'

Dr. Bidermann measured the length of her arm from armpit to wrist and made a notation.

'Now I must measure your arm in several places.'

He applied the tape first around her bicep and then moved it down to the elbow, the forearm and the wrist, nodding as he did so.

'What's that for?' she asked.

'You'll see.'

He mumbled the numbers as he wrote them on the pad. Then he picked up the transparent latex tubing and stretched it out.

'Keep your arm up please, parallel to the floor.'

He drew out of length of tubing that reached from her armpit to her wrist with a few centimetres extra and cut off that section with the scissors.

He picked up the roll of surgical tape and consulting his note pad began to measure off strips which he stuck to the edge of the table and allowed them to dangle. He hummed as he worked.

Then he took up the rubber bulb and poured some water into it before inserting one end of the latex tube to the aperture and secured it in place with a little tape.

'Now, I'm going to attach this under your arm so that the rubber bulb rests just below your armpit. Hold it there like so while I tape the tubing to your armpit and down the inside of your arm.'

Dr. Bidermann cut more tape and began to fix it around Gretchen's outstretched arm.

'Do I need so much tape?' she asked.

'Twelve times around you, twelve for the twelve tribes of Israel. Now lower your arm and be careful not to apply pressure to the bulb until you're ready to dispense the strychnine which will be dissolved in water.'

Gretchen lowered her arm gingerly, conscious of not squeezing the bulb.

'Put your blouse back on please,' he said, handing it to her. 'We'll test it out now. Perhaps you should wear a watch so the end of the tube is covered by the strap…. Please sit down at the table. I'm putting a soup plate in front of you. Position your hand over the plate. Now I'd like you to squeeze the bulb gently.'

Gretchen looked down at the plate as she pressed her bicep against her left breast.

A trickle of water flowed into the soup plate.

'Wonderful!' exclaimed the doctor. 'It works. Now I will show you how to dissolve the powder in water in the right proportions. Please put on this facemask so that you don't accidentally breathe in any of the power. And never touch strychnine with your hands. Always use the tip of a knife.'

Dr. Bidermann began to show Gretchen how to measure the exact amount water and powder to give the desired dose.

'You'll have to make up the solution for each application, Gretchen. And be very careful pouring it into the bulb and fixing in the tubing. When you prepare the dose always wear these rubber gloves I'm giving you.'

'What about the symptoms? What should I be expecting?'

'Well, you may experience some tightness and twitching in your muscles. But the dosage I've devised is so light that you should be okay. As soon as you can after eating take an activated charcoal infusion. I will give you the tablets. This will absorb any strychnine in your digestive tract that hasn't been absorbed into the bloodstream. I'm also giving you phenobarbital tablets in case you experience any minor convulsions – but that shouldn't happen with this dosage.'

Gretchen swallowed to cover her alarm.

'So, would you like to try a dry run? From the beginning.'

Berlin, November 10, 1944

There was a rumour circulating among front line Wehrmacht officers that Germany's scientists and engineers had developed a
secret weapon so powerful that it would bring Britain to its knees and
have Churchill sue for peace.

The V2, short for *Vergeltungswaffe 2* ('vengeance weapon'), was
the world's first guided ballistic missile. It was developed by Werner
von Braun.

Forty-six feet long, weighing over thirteen metric tons and fuelled
by a mixture of liquid oxygen and alcohol, it travelled at twice the
speed of sound. Each V2 rocket cost 40,000 Reichmarks. It was to be
the prototype of the rocket that 25 years later would put an American
on the moon.

The German general staff did nothing to disabuse its soldiers
or the civilian population of the veracity of the rumour as evidence
of the vengeance weapon's destructive power to both property and
morale had been seen in newsreels that showed London in flames.
The 'wonder weapon' was the last hope for Germany to win the war
and knowledge of it would keep the front-line troops fighting and
buoy up the spirits of the German civilians whose cities were being
bombed nightly.

Originally manufactured at Peenemünde on the Baltic coast, the
secret site was heavily bombed by the RAF on August 17, 1943. Hitler
ordered the construction of a new V2 plant to be sheltered from air
attack. Rocket production was moved underground to 13 kilometres
of chalk caves at the southern border of the Harz mountains near Nordhausen – the Mittelwerk rocket factory.

The facility was near the Dora-Mittelbau concentration camp,
whose inmates became the forced labour required to build the rockets; 12,000 forced labourers and concentration camp prisoners died
producing these weapons.

After the launch of the first V2 that targeted London on September 8, 1944, Hitler had ordered 900 rockets a month to be constructed
at Mittelwerk. In the next six months, over 3,000 V2s rained down on
London, Antwerp and Liege.

London was hit at the rate of eight rockets a day. And still there was no capitulation by the British.

Albert Speer had, with reluctance, visited Nordhausen in December the previous year. He had not agreed with Hitler regarding the production of V2 rockets. He had argued instead for the immediate production of a ground-to-air defensive rocket, codenamed Waterfall; but Hitler was bent on revenge for the bombing of German cities and made the V2 his major priority.

Nor did Speer believe that the massive production of V2 rockets would win the war for Germany. Too little, too late, he had commented to Goering.

And now with the Russians approaching from the East and the Americans, British and Canadians advancing towards the Rhine,the war was surely lost. What would become of Germany if Hitler insisted on a scorched earth policy, shattering everything the nation had achieved since the Versailles Treaty? How would the country rebuild when all its industries, natural resources and infrastructure were destroyed?

The idea was insane. Even to suggest it was the final, desperate act of a madman. The German people deserved better than this.

He knew that soon one day the Führer would issue a Nero decree to prevent the country's resources falling into the hands of the Allies – the same as he had already tried to do with Paris, Luxembourg, the Netherlands and Belgium, only this time targeting Germany itself.

He had to be stopped before it was too late.

Berchtesgaden, November 15, 1944

Fraulein Manziarly placed a bowl of steaming vegetable broth in front of Gretchen in the kitchen of the Berghof.

Gretchen was wearing a dark coloured blouse buttoned to the neck that would not show any trace of the tube strapped to her left arm.

'May I have some water, please?'

'Of course, my dear,' said the cook, reaching for a glass.

Gretchen leant over the bowl and waved the vapours towards her nose, conscious of the SS officer seated in front of her, watching her with interest.

She could smell the carrots, onions, celery and mushrooms. There was also the aromas of parsley, thyme, bay leaves and ground peppercorns.

She extended her left hand over the dish and turning her head sideways she gave a cough into her right hand. As she did so, she pressed her left elbow into her side.

She had practised the manoeuvre many times in order to apply the right amount of pressure to the rubber bulb that would release the strychnine solution into the tube.

She could detect no smell of the strychnine that had dribbled into the bowl from the tube at her wrist. Dr. Bidermann was right when he said that strychnine was odourless.

'Are you all right, Gretchen?' asked the cook. 'You look a little pale today. Even the Führer remarked on it when he saw you arriving this morning. I hope you're not coming down with something.'

'I'm fine, thank you very much, Frau Mozart. It's very kind of him to be concerned. It's just, you know, my time of the month.'

The SS officer smirked.

'Ah, then I can assure him that it will pass,' said the cook. 'We are short two tasters who are down with the flu which makes it difficult to keep the roster.'

Gretchen trembled as she dipped the spoon into the steaming broth. It was to be her first taste of the poison that would kill Hitler.

She willed herself to control her shaking hand as she lifted the spoon to her lips. She took a sip, mindful of the officer who was studying her intently.

Having swallowed, she placed the spoon on the table, remembering that she would have to wash it.

'It's very good, Frau Mozart. He will like it.'

'Yes, I'll take it into him while it's still hot.'

Frau Mozart lifted the bowl from the table, placed it on a tray and carried it to the door.

Gretchen took up the glass of water and drained its contents.

The SS officer had lost interest now and having made a notation in his logbook he picked up a newspaper and began to read.

Gretchen took the spoon to the sink and turned on the hot water. She felt a tingling sensation in her jaw muscles. She did not realise the effect would be so immediate. She had hoped to be in the privacy of her hotel room if there were to be any reaction so that she could take the necessary antidotes.

Suddenly the silence in the kitchen was shattered by a roar from the adjacent room. The SS officer rushed to the door and nearly collided with Frau Mozart who was hurrying back carrying the bowl of vegetable broth in both hands.

Hitler was ranting, 'Take it away, take it away and don't ever let this happen again!'

Frau Mozart threw the soup into the sink. Tears clung to her eyelashes.

'What's the matter?' asked Gretchen, terrified that Hitler had sensed what she had done.

'He asked me about you again and I told him why you looked unwell. Then he just started shouting at me. He told me he must never be served food that had been tasted by someone who is menstruating.'

'I'm so sorry,' said Gretchen.

'It's not your fault. I have to sit down. I'm shaking all over.'

'Can I get you a glass of water?'

'Yes,' said the cook, fanning herself with her hand.

'Did he try the soup?' asked Gretchen, as she turned on the tap.

'No, not a mouthful,' said Frau Mozart. 'I thought he was going to throw it at me.'

Berlin, December 5, 1944

G retchen sat at the kitchen table of Dr. Bidermann's house, despondent.

Dr. Bidermann placed a stethoscope on her chest and listened to her heartbeat.

'Take a deep breath,' he said.

Next, he listened to her lungs. He noted that she had lost weight and there was a pallor to her skin.

'Open your mouth and stick out your tongue, please.'

With a wooden tongue depressor he probed her cheeks and palate.

Gretchen had arrived at the house in a state of depression. She had been administering small doses of strychnine to Hitler for several days now, but she could not see any noticeable change in his condition. As Dr. Bidermann had instructed, she had kept mental notes about the number of poisoned plates she had prepared for the Führer. She was never to commit anything to paper.

'And how about this behaviour?' asked the doctor.

'He just seems more irritable all the time, screaming at everyone.'

'Do you notice any bulging of the eye balls?'

'When he gets angry, yes, but he was always like that.'

'Any evidence of cyanosis?'

'Cyanosis?'

'I'm sorry, I'm talking to you as if you were a doctor. It's a habit we fall into. Any discolouration of the skin, a bluish tint? It's caused by a lack of oxygen in the blood.'

'Not that I noted.'

'Any muscular twitching?'

'I don't get that close to him. I only see him when they open the door to take in his plate.'

Dr. Bidermann was concerned for the girl. He saw the lilac grey shadows under her eyes.

'And you. How are you feeling?

Tears began to well up in Gretchen's eyes.

'Oh, Dr. Bidermann, I thought it would be quicker than this. I don't know how much longer I can do it. I get the feeling I'm being watched.'

'Courage, my dear. It will soon be over.'

'But what happens if I get sick before the strychnine works on him?'

'You are a healthy young woman. He is under great stress which will intensify the effects of the dosage.'

'But how long will it take?'

'Given the number of applications you say you've administered, he must have built up some immunity from the pills he's been prescribed. But the angry outbursts you speak of show it is taking effect. I wish I could say a week, but we must be patient.'

The tears that had threatened began to slide down Gretchen's cheeks.

Dr. Bidermann stood up and wrapped his arms around the girl. He was torn between his concern for his patient and the ultimate goal of his strategy. He realised he had put Gretchen in great danger, but the number of lives that could be saved if his plan worked was incalculable.

He gave her a reassuring pat on the back.

'Whatever happens, remember, you are doing God's work, my child.'

'Hitler's moving back to Berlin. I heard Eva Braun making plans with Frau Mozart about packing. They're going to live in a bunker in the garden of the Reich Chancellery.'

'Then maybe we should hold up on our experiment. For the sake of your health. Let's see if the strychnine that Hitler has accumulated will take effect.'

'You mean I am to stop putting it in his food?'

'For a while. My supply is running low. I have to find a source. So continue to dress as you have been doing.'

Gretchen nodded.

'How is my...Frau Rosenberg?'

'She is coming along nicely. She has been eating and slowly putting on weight. Krista is looking after her.'

'Can I see her?'

'Of course. She's upstairs in her room. Why don't you knock at her door? Take the stairs and turn left at the grandfather clock. Her room is at the end of the corridor facing the garden.'

Gretchen climbed the stairs with her heart pounding. She didn't know what she was going to say to her grandmother or even how to explain who she was.

She put her ear to the door and listened for a moment. There was no sound from within. Perhaps the old woman was sleeping.

Gretchen knocked gently. She could hear some movement.

'Yes? Who is it?'

The voice was frail, almost a hoarse whisper.

'My name is Gretchen and I'm...I'm a friend of Krista's. May I come in?'

'A friend of Krista's?...Yes, come in.'

She opened the door and saw a tiny woman sitting on a narrow bench in front of a mirror, a brush in her hand. She was smiling.

'You are a pretty girl. Please, sit on the bed. There is only this chair but I'm comfortable here.'

Ruth Rosenberg glanced around the room.

'I used to be pretty like you, many years ago. You remind me of my Krista.'

Gretchen debated when she should tell the old woman that she was Krista's daughter. But she held back, not knowing whether Krista had told her mother she had a granddaughter. It was not her secret to divulge.

'Would you like me to brush your hair? I used to brush my daughter's hair. But she had long, dark hair.'

Gretchen moved towards her and sat with her back to the woman who began to run the brush through her hair, singing a soft lullaby in time with each stroke.

She recognised the tune and the words. It was a lullaby Greta von Bismarck used to sing to her.

Gretchen turned her head and glanced at the woman's reflection in the mirror. Tears were running down her cheeks.

Berlin, December 15, 1944

'Thank you for seeing me, uncle, I know you're very busy.'

Kurt Andorfer sat opposite Speer in his Ministry office.

'My mother wanted you to have these *Zimtsterne*. She baked them specially for you. She said they're your favourite, especially around Christmas time.'

He handed his uncle a round tin packed with the spicy, star-shaped cookies.

'She said you need something sweet to keep up your strength in these difficult times.'

Speer leant back in his chair and closed his eyes. He had not slept well for several nights. What kept him from falling asleep was the plan he was formulating to save Germany from a leader bent on destroying the country he loved.

'Surely you didn't take time off from your duty to the Fatherland to deliver me cookies.'

'I must confess I have my own reasons to speak to you, uncle.'

'So?'

Kurt hesitated before he began. He turned around to make sure the door behind him was closed.

'Can we speak freely here?'

'Yes, of course. What's on your mind?'

'I'm not sure, but I think I'm being followed.'

'What makes you think that?'

'When I dropped that woman from Ravensbrück at the von Bismarck estate – as you asked me to – there was a car that followed me all the way back to Berlin.'

'What else?'

Kurt was not about to mention his visit to the cinema with Gretchen and the feeling he had that someone was tailing them as they walked home to the von Bismarcks' apartment.

'It's just a feeling I get wherever I go now.'

'You're being paranoid, young man. You have a position of authority in the Hitler Youth, why would you be followed? Unless you have something to hide.'

Kurt evaded the question by bringing up the circumstances of his meeting with Othmar Veigl.

'He wanted me to report back to him on the movements of Gretchen von Bismarck.'

'I thought you said you were no longer seeing her.'

Kurt thought fast.

'I'm not. That's why it seemed so weird. He also wanted my section to be on the look out for forged food stamps.'

'Which is only right and proper given the situation.'

'Yes, of course…maybe you're right. With all the bombing and the sirens I suppose it gets to you like that. But can I ask you something and please don't think I'm being defeatist…. Are we losing this war?'

Speer sighed. He stood up and looked out of the window across the rubble-strewn streets.

'There is a weapon that the Führer believes will bring Britain to its knees.'

Kurt waited for an explanation as to what this miracle weapon might be, but nothing was forthcoming.

'With respect, uncle, you haven't answered my question.'

Speer rubbed his eyes.

'Come and look at this.'

Kurt joined him at the window.

'Do you see the destruction? This tragedy is being repeated all over Germany. My own house has been bombed out. I have sent your aunt and the children to Berchtesgaden and I have to live in a wing of this ministry that's not damaged. There's no heat and I have to work by candle-light. All our cities are being systematically destroyed by fire-bombs, Kurt, but we still have the will to resist. The Fatherland cannot afford to lose. Our people are strong. We must have an honourable peace that will allow us to rebuild.'

'And how can we expect to get an honourable peace when there are places like Ravensbrück?'

Speer put his arm around his nephew's shoulder.

'I was wrong to send you there, Kurt. I'm sorry. But there are things I cannot tell you. Except that there are people high up in the government who want to see an end to the carnage and it may be sooner than you think. Please go now. This conversation was just between you and me, not for repetition. Do I have your word?'

'Of course, uncle.'

'And please give my thanks to your mother for the *Zimtsterne*.'

When Kurt had left the office, Speer took out the rolled-up drawings of the Führerbunker in the garden of the Reich Chancellery and spread them out on his desk. He traced his finger along the ventilation system from the bunker where Hitler would live and conduct the war.

On his walks through the garden Speer had noticed a metal grate at ground level camouflaged by a small shrub. This, he had realised, must be the air intake for the ventilation shaft. And this would be the means by which he would assassinate Hitler, the leader who had committed high treason against his own people.

Potsdam, December 17, 1944

C arl von Bismarck leaned into his radio and adjusted the dial to 94.6 MHz on Long Wave to pick up the signal from the BBC World Service in London. In spite of his failing hearing, he turned the volume down low, more conscious of his wife than the possibility of detection by the SS's electronic triangulation monitors.

He waited for the chimes of Big Ben, signalling the start of the lunchtime news broadcast. The announcer opened with the words, *'Hier ist England, hier ist England.'* This was followed by the first four notes of Beethoven's 5th Symphony, repeated a second time. And then the German-speaking broadcaster delivered the news of the day.

'The Germans have mounted a series of counter-attacks on the Western front allowing them to recross the borders of Luxembourg and Belgium. On the second day of what now appears to be a full-scale counteroffensive, the Germans are attacking with tanks and aircraft along a 70-mile front guarded by American forces in the Ardennes region. The main thrust has been launched from the northern Ardennes near the town of Monschau. Two further attacks have taken place further south. German paratroops have been dropped behind Allied lines. Allied army reports say some of them have been "mopped up," others are still at large. Reports from the U.S. Ninth Army, attacking a line to the north of the Ardennes region, say the German Luftwaffe also launched a concerted bombing campaign in support of its ground forces.

'The United States Army Air Forces claim to have shot down 97 Luftwaffe planes overnight, and 31 of their own aircraft were lost. According to the reports, the Luftwaffe put up "what was probably its greatest tactical air effort since D-Day."

'German aircraft appeared in force over the western front. More than 300 German planes were deployed in the Bonn and Cologne areas last night and a similar number have been active again during the day. During today's action, the USAAF has strafed infantry and tanks from Monschau to Prum, 24 miles to the southeast. Initial reports say 62 armoured vehicles, tanks and horse-drawn wagons were put out of action.

'They say the recent failure of German fighters to interfere with heavy bombing attacks on the Reich in daylight now makes it clear they have been saving their resources for this concerted attack. One U.S. officer told The Times newspaper: "The German pilots showed more aggressiveness than at any time in the last three months."

'The German Commander-in-Chief in the west, Field Marshal Gerd von Rundstedt, has ordered his troops to "give their all in one last effort." The message was broadcast two days ago before this latest offensive began.

He said: "Soldiers of the western front, your great hour has struck. Strong attacking armies are advancing today against the Anglo-Americans. I do not need to say any more to you, you all feel it strongly. Everything is at stake."

Von Bismarck switched off the radio, put on his glasses and reached for an atlas from the shelf above his desk. He opened it to the map of Western Germany and, with the aid of a magnifying glass, located the town of Monschau where the announcer had said the German operation had begun.

Monschau. He had fond memories of the ancient town with its cloth mills, its half-timbered houses and narrow streets and its 13th-century castle perched on the hill. As a student he used to go to the annual open-air music festival held in the castle.

Monschau, he reckoned, must be 180 kilometres from Antwerp. Obviously, the German counter-offensive was aimed at cutting through the Allied armies and recapturing the port of Antwerp, the Allies' most vital supply port. Hitler's strategy, von Bismarck surmised, was to encircle and destroy four Allied armies, force them to sue for peace and then concentrate on the Eastern Front to defeat the Russians.

He shook his head and replaced the atlas on the shelf. The engagement he had listened to on the news would become known as 'The Battle of the Bulge.'

Berlin, December 20, 1944

Othmar Veigl hated Christmas. While his fellow officers joined in the enforced bonhomie of the season by sending greeting cards and exchanging gifts with individuals they had no time for the rest of the year, Veigl felt excluded from their rituals.

His widowed mother, Dagomar Veigl, used the season to badger him about getting married and presenting her with grandchildren; although her feminine intuition had long since informed her that her son had a predilection for young boys rather than the opposite sex.

The tension between mother and son was exacerbated at this time of year by the Nazis' loathing of the Christmas story. As Jesus was a Jew, Nazi propagandists contrived to take the Christ out of Christmas.

The Nazis had renamed the festival *Julfest* and reached back to German mythology to explain it as a celebration of the winter solstice. They claimed that early Christians had superimposed their notion of the birth of Jesus on the older pagan tradition of welcoming the rebirth of the sun. The swastika, they insisted, was an ancient sun symbol and that Santa Claus had been appropriated by Christians and was really the old Norse God, Odin.

To Aryanise the story, Mary and Jesus became blonde and the manger changed to a garden with wooden deer and rabbits.

Christmas carols and hymns were rewritten to purge them of all religious references; for instance, the words to 'Unto us a child is born' were changed by the Nazi poet Paul Hermann to, 'Unto us a time has come.'

Festive-minded parents could shop during the holiday season from catalogues offering chocolate SS soldiers, toy tanks, fighter planes and machine guns. And housewives were encouraged to bake cookies in the shape of birds, suns and swastikas for their children. They could also buy Christmas tree ornaments in the shape of miniature replicas of German World War I soldiers, hand-grenades and bombs.

It was this last pressure to desanctify Christmas that caused the ongoing argument in the Veigl household. The ageing Dagomar, sentimental to the core, had made a collection of Christmas tree ornaments, one for every year after her only child was born. Since Othmar had joined the party in 1933, he had told her not to use them again. He had even smashed one to make his point.

His mother had not talked to him for three months after that incident until he relented with the following compromise. The tree could stand in a corner of the living room and his mother's traditional decorations could be hung on the back where they would not be seen by visiting neighbours.

She had held out for the star on the top of the tree, but Othmar would have none of it.

He had screamed at her: 'Don't you realise a six-pointed star is a Jewish symbol! And a five-pointed star represents Russia!'

Othmar Veigl was sitting in his office, not wanting to go home to listen to his mother's complaints. The weather outside was dull and misty, adding to his sense of dejection. He had not received a Christmas card from Heinrich Himmler as had most of his colleagues. But once he had found the proof to expose the daughter of one of the most illustrious families of the Fatherland, he would be the hero of the hour.

He opened the file marked Gretchen von Bismarck and reviewed what he had learned so far. She was one of fifteen women who tasted the food put in front of the Führer. She had obtained that position by the sponsorship of both Albert Speer and Hermann Goering, two of the most powerful men in Germany. And yet it was Albert Speer who contacted the SS to have his own nephew followed. And this nephew, the handsome Kurt Andorfer, was Gretchen's lover. Why, he asked himself, would Speer have his nephew followed? Could he be jealous of the boy? Was Speer secretly in love with the daughter of the man who worked for him?

Then there was the Swiss connection – the Jewess Gretchen had roomed with in Bern. And what she was writing to her about? And where did Sarah Rosenberg fit into the story? She had been 'liberated' from Ravensbrück at the special request of the Minister of Armaments himself. In the file there was a transmission from Sturmbannführer Fritz Suhren, the camp commandant, dated February 5th, 1944, expressing his concern that the woman was to be set free in the custody of the Minister's nephew. And this same woman was then transported directly to the office of Albert Speer by the boy Andorfer. He subsequently drove her to the house of Carl von Bismarck.

From his records Othmar Veigl noted that she had stayed there for several weeks before taking up residence with this Dr. Bidermann – a Jew who had been permitted to continue practicing medicine by order of Hermann Goering himself. And the bleached blonde woman named Krista he saw at Bidermann's house. He never did get her last name. She worked in a coffee house; so what was she doing there – unless she was a prostitute?

His thoughts went back to Kurt Androfer, the attractive young Hitler Youth leader, who was to report back to him about his girlfriend's movements. Veigl had heard nothing from him yet. The girlfriend's time was probably taken up in the Wolf's Lair. But with the Führer returning to Berlin on January 15th, there would be ample opportunity to keep an eye on her. Perhaps he could bring Kurt into play on that score.

There was something in the back of his mind that troubled him about Kurt Andorfer. He thought back to the conversation he had had with the boy. He seemed to have had difficulty listening because he had turned his head sideways to favour his left ear.

Veigl opened the file on Kurt Andorfer and began to read.

And there it was – the incident report on the explosion that killed one of Andorfer's young charges. It was noted that Kurt had been transported by ambulance to the Beelitz Sanatorium on January 29th and had been hospitalized there for three days.

Veigl pressed a key on his telephone.

'Get me the phone number of the Beelitz Sanatorium.'

Three minutes later, he was dialling the number.

'This is Othmar Veigl, Kriminal-Oberassistent, Staastpolizei. I would like you to consult your records for January 29th of this year. I am looking for information about a patient who was admitted with an ear injury. His name is Kurt Arndorfer…yes, Arndorfer. I would like to speak to the attending nurse. You will find her name and you will call me back at this number. Understood?…Heil Hitler.'

Othmar Veigl reached into his drawer and took out a bag full of cookies his mother had baked for him. They were in the shape of the sun.

****

When the Beelitz Sanatorium called him back, Othmar Veigl asked the receptionist to put him through to the nurse who was on duty in the emergency ward on January 29th. Her name was Anna Schmidt.

'Yes, I received the patient Andorfer, Herr Veigl.'

'How did he arrive?'

'By ambulance. He was bleeding from his left ear.'

'Was he alone?'

'No, he was with a woman who said she was his aunt.'

'Did she give her name?'

'No.'

'You didn't ask her for identification, Frau Schmidt?'

'My first concern was for the patient, Herr Veigl. He was bleeding. He needed immediate attention.'

'Quite so. Would you recognize this woman if you were to see her again?'

'Yes.'

'What makes you so sure?'

'I took special care because the patient must have been very important. Minister Speer himself called to make sure he got a private room and the best medical attention.'

'I see. The Minister himself called?'

'Apparently, I didn't take the call,'

'And what else do you remember?'

'The patient was visited in his room by a young woman. She was very beautiful. I thought she might be the daughter.'

'The daughter?'

'Yes. The daughter of the woman who brought him in.'

'Why do you say that?'

'Because I thought I saw a family resemblance.'

'A family resemblance?'

'Yes. They could have been mother and daughter. They had the same jaw line.'

Othmar Veigl tried to keep his voice level, not to show his mounting excitement.

'The young woman who visited him in his room, did she give her name?'

'No, she told the desk she was his fiancée.'

'Fiancée?'

'Yes..., I must be getting back now, Herr Veigl. My shift is about to start.'

'Just one more thing. Can you describe her to me.'

'The young one?'

'Yes.'

'She was blonde with blue eyes. Her hair was cut short.'

'How tall was she?'

'About 1.7 metres, I'd say.'

'How long did she stay in the patient's room?'

'About an hour.'

'And then?'

'Then she left.'

'That's all. She didn't leave a number where she could be reached?'

'No. She just left and the other woman, the aunt, waited for her in the garden. They drove off in a car together.'

'You saw them leave together.'

'Yes, I was giving the patient Ardorfer his pain medicine and I noticed them from the window.'

'Thank you very much, Frau Schmidt, you have done a great service for the Reich. Good day to you.'

Othmar Veigl slammed the receiver down in triumph. His hunch had proved correct. There was a connection between the woman in the coffee shop and Gretchen von Bismarck. And to the woman who had been a recent inmate of Ravensbrück.

The jigsaw pieces were beginning to fall into place. It was time to talk to the woman who 'resembled' Gretchen.

But first he had to return home and endure the Christmas rituals with his mother.

Berlin, January 3, 1945

Othmar Veigl removed the Der Zeit photograph of Gretchen von Bismarck with Hermann Goering from the file and placed it on his desk. With his index finger he traced the line of her jaw as he played back in his mind the conversation he had had with Nurse Anna Schmidt.

A family resemblance, she had said, to the woman he had first seen in the coffee house speaking with the girl; and then again at Dr. Bidermann's where the Jewess Sarah Rosenberg was currently living.

It was time to test the credibility of the nurse's testimony. A conversation with the woman Krista might give him a better understanding of who these women were.

He placed the newspaper cutting back in the file, put the file in his brief case, and left his office.

With the streets pock-marked with bomb craters and the piles of debris everywhere, it was quicker to walk than to order up a car. As he turned down Petersburger Strasse he saw workers sweeping glass from the sidewalks from last night's bombing raid; but still he could hear it crunching and splintering under his feet. The air was heavy with the smell of charred wood and particles of dust danced in the cold morning air. Some of the beams that stuck out from the ruined houses were still smoldering as the firefighters played their hoses over the devastation.

Veigl entered the coffee bar where the blonde woman worked. He had to confirm the sequence of events of January 29th as recounted to him by Anna Schmidt. He would compare the girl's jawline with that of the woman whom he only knew as Krista. If, indeed, there was a family resemblance between her and the girl, what could that mean?

A coincidence? A Doppelganger? Or was there a blood relationship?

He entered the coffee bar and took a seat at the counter. There was no one else in the place. A girl was seated in the corner behind the counter reading a magazine.

'Fraulein, if you please,' he called to her.

Reluctantly, the girl put down her magazine.

'I would like a cup of coffee and one of those pastries on the tray. If you will be so kind as to bring it here.'

He watched her slouch over to the glass-topped counter and take out the tray from the illuminated shelf.

'What is your name, Fraulein?' he asked, smiling.

'Heidi.'

'Ah, Heidi, that was my grandmother's name. Now, if you were me, which one would you choose?'

'Depends on what you like.'

'That cream one looks delicious. I'll have that one. Would you like to have one too?'

'I'm meant to be working.'

'There's no one here. Go on, choose one for yourself.'

Heidi looked around to confirm they were alone.

'Ok, as long as you're paying I'll have that one.'

'Good. I hate to eat pastries alone.... Now, Heidi, I'm sure you could use a few food stamps.'

He pulled a yellow card from his pocket and slid it across the counter to her.

The girl regarded him suspiciously.

'I'm not that kind of girl.'

'No, no. Nothing like that. Think of it as an early Easter present. You can help me with some information.'

'What kind of information?'

'Your colleague, Krista, who works here. Where is she now?'

'She has the day off. With all the bombing there hasn't been much business,' said Heidi, pocketing the food stamps.

Veigl tried to conceal his disappointment.

'Do you know where she lives?'

'I just see her at work. She walks here though, so it must be near.'

Heidi placed a cup of coffee in front of him.

'Sugar?'

'Yes, please…. Does she have any family?'

'Well, there was a woman here the other day. She came in with Krista. I heard her call her "Mutti."'

'Mutti! That's what I call my mother…. What did she look like, this woman she called Mutti.'

'She was short, very frail. She had white hair. She looked Jewish.'

'Ah. Now, tell me if you've seen this young lady.'

Veigl took out the newspaper clipping from his briefcase and held it up.

Heidi took a bite of her pastry and squinted at the photo. Licking the cream from her lips, she said: 'Yes. I recognize her. She was sitting over there.'

'When was that?'

'It must have been four or five months ago.'

'That's some time ago and yet you say you remember her.'

'You don't forget a face like that. She was so beautiful, I thought she was a movie star.'

'And have you ever seen me before?'

The girl shook her head.

'Very good, Heidi, you have still not seen me. Not a word to Krista. I want to surprise her. Just to keep our little secret, here are some more food stamps…by the way, what's Krista's last name?'

'Becker,' she replied, and the stamps disappeared as if she were a magician.

Veigl nodded and paid the bill for the coffee and two pastries. He left the establishment whistling.

So, he said to himself as he walked back to his office, Krista is the daughter of the Jewess Rosenberg.

Berlin, January 15th, 1945

It was a chance meeting in the Ministry's air-raid shelter that had prompted Albert Speer to proceed with his plan to assassinate Hitler.

As the sirens sounded around the midnight, Speer descended into the small shelter reserved for high-ranking officers of the Reich. He found himself alone with the head of his ministry's munitions division, Dieter Stahl.

The two men were friends. Speer had interceded with the Gestapo when Stahl had been arrested in June for uttering defeatist sentiments (he had been overheard saying that the war was lost – a crime punishable with death). Speer had interceded with Gauleiter Emil Stürtz of Brandenburg to have him released. Their friendship and trust deepened as they spent weekends together at Stahl's cottage at Bad Wilsnack in the Elbe Valley.

As the bombs exploded above them, Stahl grabbed Speer's arm and exclaimed: 'It's going to be frightful, frightful.'

Emboldened by his friend's views on the conduct of the war, and enervated by the noise and falling dust, Speer asked how he might acquire some Tabun gas. He did not reveal that he had made a request to Carl Krauch of I. G. Farben a year ago; but the consignment had never been delivered and he had not followed up.

Stahl showed no surprise at Speer's next statement: 'It's the only way to bring the war to end.... I want to try to conduct the gas into the Chancellery bunker.'

He merely nodded and said he would make some enquiries. A few days later, he came back with the answer after having contacted the head of the munitions department in the Army Ordnance Office, Lieutenant-Colonel Soyka. He had camouflaged his request by saying that his munitions factory was considering redesigning artillery shells to carry a warhead of poison gas. On further research, Speer learned that the gas would only be effective if it were made to explode. But an explosion would have ripped apart the thin sheets of tin that radiated from the air-conditioning plant before the gas could spread around the intended target.

Another gas would have to be found.

Berlin, January 18, 1945

G retchen shivered as she descended the wrought-iron spiral staircase. She was carrying a tea tray and crumpets from the kitchen in the upper bunker down to the *Führerbunker* that housed Hitler's quarters, the conference room and Eva Braun's bedroom/sitting room.

How she missed the clean mountain air and pastoral setting of the Wolf's Lair in Raustenburg. The bunker, 55 feet below the grounds of the Reichstag Chancellery, was like living in a concrete submarine. The tiny rooms were painted battle-ship grey and the unfinished walls of the corridors were stained with the moisture that seeped through. The overhead lights quivered with the vibrations of the exploding bombs outside and water dripped from the ceiling where workers had not finished plastering.

And the worst thing to Gretchen's sensitive nose was the smell; the reek of dank woollen uniforms, sweat and old socks mingled with the acrid aroma of the chlorine used to disinfect the living quarters seemed to emanate from the walls.

A guard leered at her as she brushed past him through the bulkhead and great steel door that sealed off Hitler's quarters from the rest of the maze of tunnels that led to the Chancellery and into the gardens. She had noticed the young SS man watching her as she made her way slowly down the spiral staircase. He was staring up her skirt but with both hands occupied in carrying the tray she could do nothing about it.

Hitler was seated at a table in his office with Eva Braun and his secretaries, Traudl Junge and Gerda Christian, awaiting the arrival of the tea. On the wall hung a large portrait of Hitler's hero, Frederick the Great.

Gretchen placed the tray on the table without making eye contact with Hitler. She noted that his hand trembled as he reached for a crumpet. His grey dress uniform, stained with food, intensified the pallor of his skin. His eyes were glazed and bloodshot. His hair and characteristic moustache had turned as grey as his uniform. The doses of strychnine she had been administering, she now saw, were beginning to take effect.

Hitler nodded his thanks as she backed out of the room and closed the door. The smell of disinfectant, the claustrophobic corridor and the effects of the strychnine she had been ingesting made her feel queasy. She put a hand on the wall to steady herself as she moved towards the steel door.

She saw the SS guard leaning against the bulkhead smiling at her. The heels of her flat shoes echoed along the corridor as she passed through the open steel door. The guard put his arm out to block her passage.

'You have just come from the Führer,' he said, playfully. 'I will have to search you.'

Gretchen began to panic. The plastic tubing and strychnine delivery system were still strapped to her left arm. She tried to move around him but he pinned her to the wall and pressed his body against her. He wrapped his arms around her and tried to kiss her.

She could smell the alcohol on the breath and feel the bristles of his beard rasping against her cheek. She wondered if she should call out, but she realised this might bring other guards and her assailant could claim she had refused to be searched.

She let herself go limp and turned her head away from him. She put her left hand between her legs and squeezed the rubber ball under her armpit. The fluid flowed out and spread across her dress.

'You've made me wet myself,' she hissed at him.

The guard drew back and grimaced at her. He looked down and saw the wet stain spreading around her crotch.

'If you don't let me pass, I'll scream for the Führer,' she whispered.

The SS man pushed her away with a look of disgust on his face.

'If you can't control your bladder, what good are you to the Fatherland,' he said and turned away from her, running his hands over his pants to see if they were wet.

Potsdam, March 17, 1945

'G*ood evening, this is the BBC World Service broadcasting to you from London. Since the capture of the Ludendorff Bridge at*

Remagen by the 9th Armoured Division of the U.S. First Army under General William Hood Simpson, American and British troops have been crossing the Rhine into the German heartland. The German army failed to blow up one of the last bridges over the river in spite of having wired it with 2,800 kilograms of demolition charges. The Nazis have used every weapon at their disposal to demolish this strategic link – howitzers, mortars, floating mines, mined boats, a railroad gun, and even V-2 rockets. But still it stands, in spite of an attempt to send in underwater divers with depth charges. These frogmen were caught in the searchlights mounted on the American tanks before they could set their explosives. All were captured or killed. To counter attacks by the Luftwaffe, the Americans have assembled the largest concentration of anti-aircraft weapons so far in this war. Over the past ten days, 367 German planes have flown sorties against the bridge; 30% of them never returned to their bases. Allied high commander Dwight Eisenhower congratulated his troops on the capture of the bridge, saying that it will enable Allied forces to –.'

Carl von Bismarck raised his head from the speaker, wondering why the broadcast had ended so abruptly.

He turned to see a man wearing a black leather coat with a swastika armband, holding the plug.

****

A tearful Greta von Bismarck called Albert Speer on his private line.

'Herr Speer, forgive me for phoning you so late but I'm frantic. They've arrested my husband.'

'What?'

'They caught him listening to the BBC. I told him it was dangerous.'

'When you say 'they,' who do you mean exactly?'

'I don't know. The Gestapo, I imagine. Two men rang the doorbell. They had a truck outside with an antenna. They asked where Carl was. One of them held me in the hall at gun point. The other went upstairs to find him. They took him away, Herr Speer. He was still wearing his bedroom slippers.'

The old fool, thought Speer, how many more times do I have to bail him out?

'Can you speak to someone, Herr Speer? Please, I beg you.'

'I'll will put things right, Frau von Bismarck. Don't worry. I will speak to the proper authorities personally. I will call you in the morning. You get a good night's sleep now.'

He put the phone down. A night in a Gestapo cell should cure von Bismarck of his stupidity, he thought to himself.

To his wife in the bed next to him, he said: 'Margarete, remind me I have to call Goebbels in the morning.'

****

Word of the von Bismarck arrest spread like a brushfire through Gestapo headquarters on Prinz-Albrecht-Strasse.

When the news reached Othmar Veigl, the overweight Kriminal-Oberassistent closed the door of his office and danced a little jig.

'*Ausgezeichnet, Ausgezeichnet!*' he chortled.

At last he had a legitimate excuse to enter the von Bismarck household. He sensed he would learn more as to why the woman Rosenberg was driven there immediately after a short meeting in the Minister of Armaments' architectural office.

It had puzzled Veigl why that meeting had taken place in the Minister's private office rather than at his ministry – unless Herr Speer did not want his colleagues to be aware of his connection to the Jewess Rosenberg.

He had just received some other good news. *Reichsjugendführung* Artur Axmann, the leader of the Hitler Youth, had agreed to his proposal to have Kurt Andorfer assigned from his duties as section leader in Berlin to be a guard in the Führerbunker.

Veigl had couched the request as a reward to the young man for his exceptional work in the field and the injury he had sustained in performance of his duties. Andorfer would be there to help protect the Führer and what greater gift could there be for a young German hero than to be near Der Chef.

And the fact that Kurt Andorfer was the nephew of the Minister of Armaments was also a factor to be taken into consideration.

What Veigl did not reveal was that he wanted Kurt to be near the girl Gretchen so that Andorfer could report back to him. The Führer had complained to Gruppenführer Johann Rattenhuber, his head of security, that someone in the bunker was leaking information to the British. Promotions of German officers, medals awarded, and gossip about who was sleeping with whom among the Nazi leaders were broadcast by fluent German-speakers on a British 'black' radio program called Soldatensender Calais beamed at Germany.

Hitler suspected that the traitor who was leaking the information was a woman in the bunker. The Gestapo has been called in to identify the woman.

Veigl picked up the phone and pressed a key to communicate with his secretary. When she responded, he said: 'Would you please go to the archives and get me any photographs of a Greta von Bismarck you can. You might find her in her husband's file, Carl von Bismarck. Full-face pictures if possible.'

Berlin, March 18, 1945

When Albert Speer called the Minister of Public Enlightenment and Propaganda Joseph Goebbels was not in a good mood.

He had just received a memorandum that had been typed up by his secretary but delivered by his personal bodyguard. She had been too embarrassed and fearful to hand it to him.

The memorandum referred to the lyrics of a song that was being sung by British soldiers to the tune of the Colonel Bogey March.

> 'Hitler has only got one ball
> Goering has two but very small
> Himmler is rather similar
> And Goebbels has no balls at all.'

Joseph Goebbels, the father of five daughters and a son, was not amused.

He crumpled the paper into a ball and tossed it into the waste paper basket.

'Yes, what is it, Herr Speer?'

'And good morning to you too, Herr Reich Minister. You have heard no doubt that the head of one of Germany's most illustrious families had been arrested for listening to the BBC.'

'Yes, I have heard.'

'First, I would like to compliment you on the efficiency of your radio detection operation, but the arrest of Graf Carl von Bismarck puts me in a rather embarrassing position.'

'How so?'

'As you know, von Bismarck is an associate of mine in my architectural firm. A valued colleague. And it was I who had asked him informally to monitor BBC broadcasts.'

'And why would you do that, Herr Speer, knowing that my ministry has a whole department of linguists and technical experts engaged in monitoring radio signals from around the world?'

'Quite simply, Herr Goebbels, in the interests of the war effort. I need to know if the British and Americans are aware that the Führer is in Berlin.'

'And why is that information important to you?'

'Because, if our enemies know the Führer is here in the city, they will concentrate their bombing raids on Berlin rather than on my ball bearing and munitions factories in the Ruhr.'

'You need only have asked my department for a summary of these broadcasts. I get a copy on my desk first thing every morning.'

'With the utmost respect, Herr Goebbels, your department is not exactly open-handed when it comes to the dissemination of sensitive information.'

'Be that as it may, Herr Speer, the man broke the law.'

'He did so on my orders as Minister of Armaments and War Production!' shouted Speer.

There was silence at the other end of the line.

'I expect you to contact SS-Obergruppenführer Heinrich Müller and instruct him to have von Bismarck released immediately... or I will take the matter up myself with the Führer.'

'Very well, Herr Speer, but I would suggest you and your associate put an end to this game of private detective and come to me directly when you need such information in the future.'

'Thank you. Please have your office contact me when von Bismarck is at liberty. Good day.'

Potsdam, March 19, 1944

O thmar Veigl parked a short distance from the gates to the von Bismarck estate. He took out the file on the girl Gretchen and studied her face.

His secretary had been able to find two press photos of Greta von Bismarck; one was taken on the couple's wedding day: Carl von Bismarck, unsmiling in morning dress like an ambassador, and his bride with just the suggestion of a smile, wearing a soft draping pane velvet white dress gathered over the left hip, with white gloves and a cloche headdress to which was attached a veil that touched the floor. The clipping was dated April 24th, 1924.

The second photo showed the couple at a charity event. Greta was wearing a form-fitting cocktail dress, which emphasised the flatness of her stomach. A tab on the photo stated that it had been taken on March 12th, 1926.

Veigl checked the file on Gretchen, looking for the date of her birth. It was noted as April 17th, 1926. He looked again at the von Bismarcks' photo taken at the charity event. Greta would have been eight months pregnant and yet the dress showed no evidence she would be delivering a baby in less than a month. Unless some librarian had made a mistake with the dates, Greta von Bismarck showed no sign of advanced pregnancy.

Othmar Veigl didn't know much about women's bodies, but he had seen enough women with protruding bellies weeks before they were to give birth.

He put the photo of Gretchen side by side with the von Bismarcks' wedding photo. He studied each of the couple's faces to see if there was any family resemblance to be seen in the photo of Gretchen.

He noted that the girl had her father's chin and fair hair while the woman, from what he could tell from the black and white image, was a brunette and her face was round and not angular like Gretchen's.

As he was putting the papers back in the file, he heard a car approaching.

Instinctively, he ducked down out of sight.

He heard the car draw up at the gate, the opening of a door, and the crunch of footsteps on gravel. Then the creak of an iron gate opening.

As the vehicle moved into the driveway, he raised his head and noticed it was an official car. The license plate bore the two Sig runes, the twin lightning bolt symbol of the SS.

In the back seat, sitting erect and tight-lipped was Graf Carl von Bismarck.

Berlin, March 19, 1945

A lbert Speer sat in his ministry office reading Hitler's newly issued order. It was headed, 'Demolitions on Reich Territory Decree.'

'It is a mistake to think that transport and communication facilities, industrial establishments and supply depots, which have not been destroyed, or have only been temporarily put out of action, can be used again for our own ends when the lost territory has been recovered. The enemy will leave us nothing but scorched earth when he withdraws, without paying the slightest regard to the population. I therefore order:

'1) All military transport and communication facilities, industrial establishments and supply depots, as well as anything else of value within Reich territory, which could in any way be used by the enemy immediately or within the foreseeable future for the prosecution of the war, will be destroyed....'

Speer shook his head and rubbed his eyes. As Minister of Armaments and War Production he had imposed upon Hitler to make him responsible for the implementation of this scorched earth policy.

But he had no intention of following through on the Führer's order. The war was lost. Most of the territories the Wehrmacht had conquered had been recaptured; the Ardennes offensive had failed; Paris, the greatest prize of all, had been liberated; and the allied armies were closing in on Germany from both the east and the west.

When the Red Army had taken control of Silesia in February 1945, Speer knew Germany could no longer win the war. He had sent a memo to Hitler telling him that 60 per cent of the Reich's coal came from the Silesian mines. The loss of these mines would mean German coal production would drop to a quarter of its previous year's total. Production of steel and aluminum for tanks, planes and armaments depended on coal. Without Silesia, he had written to Hitler, at the risk of his own safety, 'the war is lost.'

Hitler had filed the memo in his safe.

Speer recalled his leader's response to the news that General George Patton's U.S. Third Army was advancing on Paris eight months earlier. The Führer had sent orders to the military governor of the city, Dietrich von Choltitz, to blow up the Eiffel Tower and key transportation points.

Von Choltitz, a Francophile with a long-standing affection for the city he occupied, disobeyed his leader and instead surrendered the city unharmed to the Americans and the Free French forces on August 25th, 1944.

Speer determined to emulate his honourable example. At this point in the war Hitler's 'Nero decree' would cause unnecessary suffering and hardships for the German people and destroy the very industries that Germany would need to rebuild when peace prevailed.

He would use all his powers of persuasion with the generals and regional party leaders to avoid having to follow through on a decree he considered 'insane.'

Potsdam, March 19, 1945

Othmar Veigl waited until the car deposited Graf von Bismarck at the doorstep of his house, cruised back down the driveway and turned left in the direction of Berlin.

He would give the man enough time to settle in before he rang the doorbell. As he waited he looked at the photos again to familiarise himself with Greta von Bismarck's face.

She was a handsome woman but he knew her kind. Nose in the air, used to her own way, treating her servants with contempt. But those days were gone for the Prussian aristocracy. There would be a new order coming, whatever happened to Germany.

Yet, for all his left-wing notions, Veigl could not but be impressed by the grandeur of the von Bismarck mansion with its grey stone façade – the same colour as Nazi officers' field uniforms. The apartment he shared with his mother in Kreuzberg, one of the poorest districts of Berlin, would fit in the garage here, he mused.

He rang the doorbell. A moment later, Hanna the cook opened the door.

'I am Kriminal-Oberassistent Othmar Veigl of the Berlin SS,' he announced loudly 'I am here to see Graf von Bismarck.'

Hanna stepped back to allow him to enter.

'He's lying down at the moment,' she said. 'I will get Frau von Bismarck. You can wait in the library.'

Veigl followed her down the marble hallway surreptitiously glancing at the rooms they passed.

'Please make yourself comfortable here.'

Hanna closed the door, crossed herself and hurried up the staircase to alert her mistress.

Veigl ran his fingers along the oxblood leather sofa. The walls of the room were lined with books from floor to the ceiling. He had never seen so many books. A log fire burned in the open hearth. He wondered why they would light a fire when it was almost spring-like outside.

His attention was drawn to a portrait of a balding man with a bushy white moustache, dressed in a double-breasted black frock coat. His arms were crossed in front of him. He held a cane in his right hand and in his left a wide-brimmed, white hat.

The subject seemed to gaze forlornly out of the frame, his head turned slightly to the left, staring far into the distance; he had the look of a man who realised he had little time left and had not accomplished the goal of his life. There was something hypnotic about the way the man commanded his attention.

Lost in his study of the painting as he warmed his hands at the fire, Veigl did not hear Greta von Bismarck enter the room. He whirled around at the sound of her voice like a guilty schoolboy.

'That's Otto Eduard Leopold, Prince of Bismarck and Duke of Lauenburg,' said Greta, 'my husband's great grandfather…. And you are?'

Veigl stepped back from the fire and reached into his breast pocket for his ID card. He was determined to pre-empt the woman's demand to see identification.

Greta lifted the glasses that hung from a gold chain around her neck, settled them on her nose and made a performance of scanning the card.

Irritated, Othmar Veigl, shifted his weight from foot to foot.

'So Herr Veigl, what is the purpose of your visit?'

'It's in the matter of your husband listening to broadcasts from our enemies overseas.'

'Yes, yes. He has already paid the penalty. A night in your jail has given him a rash. We've had to call in our doctor. He should be arriving momentarily, so if you'd be good enough to state your business.'

Othmar Veigl felt that he was losing the initiative. He needed to assert himself and let this woman know that she did not trifle with the SS.

'Your daughter, Frau von Bismarck.'

'What about my daughter?'

'Gretchen von Bismarck, aged eighteen, educated at the Lyceum private school for girls in Bern, Switzerland,' he began, staring at the ceiling as if reminding himself of the contents of a dossier.

'That is so. Do sit down.'

'I prefer to stand. While your daughter was in that school, she shared a room with a Jewess named Shona Rosenberg.'

'You seem to be remarkably well-informed Herr Veigl, but what is the point of all of this?

'Our sources tell us she is still in correspondence with her Jewish friend.'

'She writes to her occasionally, yes. As you say, they are friends.'

'Your daughter is employed by the Third Reich, Frau von Bismarck. She works for the Führer. Very intimately, in fact. She is under an oath not to divulge exactly what she does, so I trust that she has not revealed the nature of her work. Even to you, her mother. Nor to your husband. Her father who listens to enemy propaganda broadcasts…. Am I right?'

Veigl could sense that the haughtiness with which the woman had greeted him had now changed to alarm and a willingness to placate him.

'My daughter has kept her word. She has never mentioned anything about what she does. Never.'

'So you see why we are interested to learn more about your daughter's association with Jews as she is in close contact with our leader.'

'It's an innocent friendship, Herr Veigl. That is all.'

The SS officer now decided to pursue the real reason why he had infiltrated the von Bismarck family home.

'Your daughter was also born in Switzerland, was she not?'

'What makes you say that?'

'Because I could not find any record of her birth in the hospitals in Berlin or in the Potsdam area. Unless of course you gave birth to her here in this house.'

'You really must sit down, Herr Veigl. You're making me uncomfortable standing there like that.'

'If you insist…. You were about to tell me where your daughter was born.'

'I think I hear my husband calling. You'll have to excuse me for a moment. I don't know what he picked up in your jail last night but he's been scratching himself till he bleeds. I'll be right back. In the meantime, I'll get you some tea if you like.'

'Thank you, no tea. I'll just wait here for you.'

He watched the woman back to the door, pleased with himself for his line of questioning that had caused her to leave the room in panic. He had not lost his knack for interrogation.

As he waited for Greta von Bismarck to return, he wandered over to a radio that rested on a table like a miniature cathedral in polished walnut. He checked the dial to see what station it was tuned to – Reichs-Rundfunk-Gesellschaft, Germany's national network. Either von Bismarck was canny enough to change the dial after listening to the BBC, he thought, or the traitor used another radio. He would have to check.

Then he began ambling around the room studying family photos in silver frames that stood on a table draped with an oriental rug. He picked up the couple's wedding shot, which was much clearer than the press slipping in his file. Then he reached for a photo of Gretchen. She was mounted on a horse dressed in jodhpurs and a riding helmet, smiling nervously at the camera.

She had her father's chin, but he could see no facial similarity to her mother.

The ring of the doorbell echoed down the hall interrupting his thoughts. He replaced the photo on the table and moved to the door. He closed it leaving himself just enough space to peer out. He saw the woman who had let him in waddling down the corridor, drying her hands on her apron.

From his angle he could not see the front door, but the sound of the bell had brought Greta von Bismarck hurrying down the staircase.

Veigl heard her say, 'Thank heavens you've come, Doctor. He's in a terrible state. The itching is driving him mad.'

Veigl could not hear the doctor's muffled reply, but as the footsteps approached the staircase he opened the door for a clearer view.

It was then that he recognised Dr. Isaac Bidermann.

Berlin, The Führerbunker, March 20, 1945

For his new duties in the Führerbunker, Kurt Andorfer had been given the field rank of *Unteroffizier*. He had been issued with the enlisted infantryman's M36 uniform with its dark-green collar and shoulder straps and the Wehrmacht's spread-eagle insignia above the right breast pocket.

He also had to sign for a Walther PP semi-automatic pistol in a black leather holster.

Kurt had not seen Gretchen in several weeks, during which time he had supplied Othmar Veigl with innocuous pieces of information about his girlfriend that he had fabricated.

Neither he nor Gretchen was prepared for their accidental meeting on the lower level of the bunker as Kurt was being briefed on his role as a guard outside Hitler's private quarters.

Gretchen was following Constanze Manziarly down the spiral staircase, carrying a tray of vegetables from the storeroom in the upper level when she saw him.

Kurt's back was to the staircase and only when she stopped short on the last step at the sight of him and gave a little gasp that he turned. She looked so drawn and exhausted he thought that she was going to fall over.

Gretchen's eyes widened and her face lit up in a smile. For a split second she hesitated, as if she was about to speak to him. Instead, she winked and moved quickly past, following Constanze Manziarly into Hitler's private dining room.

The guard who was briefing Kurt caught the silent exchange between the two young lovers. He was the same man who had accosted Gretchen a month earlier.

He made a point of reporting what he had just seen to Gruppen-führer Johann Rattenhuber, the bunker's head of security.

'The Führer has ordered that we don't use the full salute down here,' said the guard, continuing to instruct Kurt in bunker protocol. 'The space is too confined. So, just the half salute. From the right elbow. Understand?'

'Perfectly,' replied Kurt.

And as if conjured up by the uttering of his name, Hitler suddenly emerged from his private suite into the corridor.

It was the first time Kurt has seen the Führer so close. He had always seen this isolated figure standing up in a car at rallies or review-ing troops as they marched past below him.

Kurt was so taken aback by the sight of this dishevelled, stooping individual with his stained uniform and shuffling gait that he almost forgot to salute. More alarming were the man's unnaturally bright eyes that blazed bloodshot above his sunken cheeks.

'I will see you tomorrow, Morell, the same time,' Hitler called over his shoulder.

Emerging from Hitler's private quarters, carrying his medical bag, was the bull-necked Dr. Theodor Morell.

Schöneberg district, Berlin, March 20, 1945

Isaac Bidermann was not surprised when two Gestapo agents turned up at his doorstep that morning. He had been expecting them in light of what Greta von Bismarck had confided in him.

To be on the safe side, he had warned Krista and her mother to be out of the house.

As soon as he had arrived at the von Bismarck mansion, Greta had explained the circumstances of her husband's arrest and overnight incarceration. She also warned him that a Gestapo officer was waiting to speak to her in the library.

Bidermann asked his patient to sit up in bed and to remove his pyjama jacket. There were rows of angry red spots up his arms and across his shoulders. He inspected the spots and the surrounding rash at close quarters.

'Bed bugs,' he announced, turning to Greta who shuddered with disgust at the thought.

'I want you to wash the affected areas well with soap and water. I'm going to prescribe a topical corticosteroid cream such as Hydrocortisone. That will relieve the itching. And half an hour before bed give him 50 milligrams of diphenhydramine.'

'Diphenhydramine?' queried Carl von Bismarck.

'It's an antihistamine. You don't need a prescription. You can get it over the counter in any pharmacy. That's if there's any left in Germany. But I may have some in my bag.'

Dr. Bidermann accepted no payment for his consultation or the pills and wished them both well in these difficult times.

Greta von Bismarck escorted him to the front door in silence.

From the window in the library Othmar Veigl watched the doctor step into his car and drive away. He jotted down the license number in his notebook and the time and duration of the visit.

As soon as he got home, Isaac Bidermann went to the basement and opened a filing cabinet that contained the medical records of his patients. He made a note on Carl von Bismarck's file of his prognosis and the treatment he had prescribed.

On a hunch he read through the whole of von Bismarck's medical history in case there was anything that the Gestapo could use against his old friend.

Satisfied that there was nothing that could be incriminating, he locked the file away again.

When the Gestapo agents demanded to see his medical files he demurred at first, saying that they were in storage as he no longer practised. But they put a pistol to his head and forced him to tell them where he kept the records of patients he was currently seeing.

They took him down to the basement and searched him for the key to the filing cabinet. When they opened it, they riffled through the files and extracted one.

Isaac Bidermann was surprised that the file they were after was not Carl von Bismarck's – but the medical record of his wife, Greta.

Berlin, March 21, 1945

O thmar Veigl took a bite of a Spritzkuchen and wiped the sugar from his lips. He dusted his fingers with his handkerchief before he opened the file containing Greta von Bismarck's medical records.

Why do doctors have such terrible writing, he said to himself.

He looked for Greta's birth date – 'March 28th, 1899,' he said aloud. 'She looks older than forty-six, but I suppose the war has done that to us all.'

Veigl checked his own von Bismarck file for the date of the couple's wedding; then he cross-checked the medical record for any mention of a blood test for pregnancy later that year. There was nothing for the following year either.

Nor were there any entries of visits by Dr. Bidermann to the mansion in Potsdam or her visits to him at his practice in Berlin for the following three years. The girl Gretchen would be eighteen by now.

He scanned down the pages looking for any reference to a baby. There were none.

Curious, he went back to the woman's medical history before her marriage. Could she have become pregnant before the wedding?

What a scandal that would be.

Then he happened on an entry that noted a hospital stay for the treatment of an abdominal injury sustained when Greta von Bismarck was thrown from a horse.

Dr. Bidermann's notation read: 'The prognosis following a lengthy surgery – confirmed by my colleague Dr. Schultz, the head gynaecologist at the Potsdam Clinic – is that the patient will be unable to conceive.'

Othmar Veigl pounded the desk with his fist in triumph.

Berlin, March 22, 1945

A lbert Speer sat dejectedly in the dark in his bombed out office, not even bothering to light a candle for a pinprick of light or a modicum of heat.

Several days had passed since his surreptitious tour of the gardens above the bunker. There was no possible way he could carry out his attempt to assassinate Hitler – now that the chimney had been built above the air shaft and a twenty-four hour guard mounted around the perimeter of the gardens.

Thoughts of suicide, flashed through his mind but he could not do that to Margarete and the children. He wished he could see her and the children now, but they were safe from the bombing, sequestered in his friend Erhard Milch's hunting cottage in Stechlin Lake.

But Hitler must die. Germany was defeated and the only course was to surrender unconditionally. But Hitler would never surrender and he would bring down the country with him.

And if I was the instrument of Hitler's death, he said to himself, this would sit well with the Allies when I surrender myself to the Americans. I would have a bargaining chip to escape the gallows.

There must be a way to end Hitler's life; even in a prison like the bunker, surrounded by his bodyguards.

His bodyguards…

Speer reached for the telephone, cranked it up, and dialled the home of his sister-in-law.

'Anni, Albert Speer here. How are you and Gunther?'

'Albert, how nice to hear from you. Gunther is on duty, spotting for the flack guns. How are Margarete and the children?'

'They are fine, Anni, but I was looking for Kurt.'

'He's not here, Albert. He too is on duty.'

'Yes, I know. I hear he has been transferred for special duties.'

'And I'm so worried. I know it's all secret but I'm afraid for him.'

'I will personally make sure he is in no danger, Anni. Do you know his schedule? When he will be home?'

'He doesn't tell us a thing. Not even whether he'll be home for dinner.'

'If you see him before I do, please tell him that I need to talk to him. I'm in my office for the rest of the day.'

'Thank you, Albert. I know you'll look after him. And take care of yourself.'

Speer put the receiver down and tapped his fingertips together, lost in thought.

His nephew Kurt could be the answer.

Berlin, March 23, 1945

At 11.30 am, Othmar Veigl, accompanied by two Gestapo agents, entered the coffee shop where Krista Becker worked.

There were three customers seated at separate tables. Krista was wiping down the counter and her indolent assistant was lolling by the serving hatch, filing her nails.

'*Jeder heraus!*' shouted Veigl, flashing his Gestapo identity card as if it were necessary given the presence of two men in black leather coats and swastika armbands who accompanied him.

The customers rose obediently and filed out, leaving their coffee cups on the tables.

'You, go,' ordered Veigl, nodding at Heidi.

'You will remain, fraulein,' he said to Krista.

Krista recognised Veigl immediately and waited until the shop was empty before she spoke.

'What is this about, Herr Veigl?'

'You have a good memory for faces, Frau Becker. But it is I who will be asking the questions.'

He pulled a chair from a table and indicated for her to sit. He nodded to his agents who locked the front door, turned the 'Open' sign around and pulled the blackout curtains over the windows.

From his coat pocket Veigl withdrew a pair of handcuffs.

'Hands behind your back if you please.'

Krista experienced the coldness of the steel as it clamped around her wrists. She could feel her heart pounding against her ribs, sounding unnaturally loud.

'Now, Frau Becker, I am going to ask you a simple question. How you answer it will determine how long we will remain here. Do you understand?'

Krista nodded, bile rising in her throat.

'My colleagues here are quite skilled in eliciting information, so it is up to you as to how we will proceed.'

He could see that the woman was trembling with fear.

'Now...although you call yourself Krista Becker, you are, in fact, the daughter of Ruth Rosenberg. Am I correct?'

Krista stared directly ahead of her, not looking at her inquisitor.

'Hmmm. I was hoping you would be more cooperative...for your own sake.... Claus, fetch a towel from the kitchen and fill that jug with water.... Now again, I'm asking you if you are the daughter of Ruth Rosenberg who currently resides at the house of a Dr. Bidermann?'

Krista gritted her teeth and said nothing.

Veigl nodded to his agents who approached Krista from behind. One of them placed the towel over her head so that it hung down over her face. He then held her shoulders back against the chair as the other agent began to dribble water onto the towel.

Krista convulsed in a fit of coughing, shaking her head violently to dislodge the towel that now stuck to her face.

After a few seconds, Veigl nodded for the towel to be removed.

Krista gasped for air.

'I will ask you again, Frau Becker. Are you the daughter of Ruth Rosenberg?'

Krista hung her head and nodded.

'I take it that that is a 'yes.' Now, I'm going to ask you another question and if you don't respond my colleagues will apply the towel again.'

Krista tried to work her hands free of the cuffs to no avail.

'Am I correct in saying that you have a daughter named Gretchen who goes by the name of Gretchen von Bismarck.'

Krista said nothing.

Veigl nodded to the agents who repeated the procedure. It took both men to hold her down as she struggled to breathe.

After a minute, Veigl raised his hand and the towel was withdrawn.

Krista retched and coughed, her whole body shaking; she felt as if she was drowning.

'Now, again. Are you the mother of Gretchen von Bismarck?'

Krista looked defiantly at him, saying nothing.

Veigl nodded to the agents who put the towel over her face again and began pouring more water on it.

Krista tried to scream, but this only caused the fabric to be drawn into her open mouth causing her to gag.

Veigl gave a signal to remove the towel. Krista's face was red. Her lungs burning, she fought for breath.

Veigl put his face close to her and murmured, 'All you have to do is answer the question and all this will stop. Like magic. Frau Becker, is Gretchen von Bismarck your daughter? If you can't speak just nod your head.'

Krista turned her face to his and drew her head back. Then she spat at him.

Furious, Veigl shouted, 'Continue!'

Once again the soaking towel was placed over her face and water applied. Krista's body began to spasm.

'Hold it tight across her face. More water,' he ordered as he wiped the spittle from his chin with a handkerchief.

Krista lashed out with her feet and Veigl moved out of range. The agents watched him, waiting for his signal to remove the towel.

But Krista was suddenly still. Her body sagged and her head lolled to on side.

The agents looked at each other.

'I think she's dead,' said Claus.

Othmar Veigl pulled the towel from Krista's face. Her eyes, open wide, stared back at him accusingly. He felt for a pulse in her neck, but there was none.

'You fools!' he screamed. 'Why did you leave it so long?'

'We were waiting for your order Herr Kriminal-Oberassistent,' said Claus, snapping to attention.

Veigl turned away from him in disgust.

'Bring the car around to the back and get rid of her,' he ordered.

As the two agents lifted the lifeless body of Krista Becker from the chair and carried her towards the kitchen, Othmar Veigl sat down in the vacated chair and considered his situation.

A Jewess had died under interrogation, yes. But he would not be blamed. The information he had gained was of supreme importance to the Reich. The end justified the means.

By refusing to answer his question, Krista Becker had confirmed his suspicion.

Gretchen von Bismarck must be her daughter.

Only a mother would sacrifice herself to save her child.

The question now, he asked himself, was how and when to use this information to his best advantage?

Potsdam, March 24st, 1945

I t was remorse rather than guilt that impelled Albert Speer to pay a visit to his senior architect, Carl von Bismarck, at his ancestral home.

Greta met him at the door, thanked him for coming and escorted him up the stairs to her husband's bedroom. She paused on the half landing and said: 'After my husband was arrested, we had a visit from a detestable little man from the Gestapo.'

'That wouldn't be Kriminal-Oberassistent Othmar Veigl by any chance?'

'The very same.'

'What did he want?'

'He was snooping around here, asking questions about my – about our daughter Gretchen.'

'What sort of questions?'

'Where she was born. Why would the Gestapo be interested in where she was born?'

'Frau von Bismarck, your daughter works in close proximity to the Führer. It's a matter of security.'

'But I'm worried about her safety. They say the Russians have crossed into Germany. They are raping women, grandmothers even....'

'Your daughter couldn't be safer than where she is, believe me. Now, if you'll take me to your husband.'

Graf von Bismarck was sitting up in his bed reading a book as his wife knocked on the door.

'You have a visitor,' she said.

'Herr Speer, what a delightful surprise! Come in, come in. I'm sorry to greet you like this, but as you know I was a guest of the Gestapo for a night and I caught some wretched bug or other.'

'Don't get up. I'll just pull up a chair,' said Speer.

'Greta, please leave us. There are matters I have to discuss with Herr Speer.'

His wife hovered at the doorway, wishing to be part of the conversation but she could see that her presence was not wanted.

'I'm sorry for what you've been put through. I did what I could to make sure you were released as soon as possible,' said Speer.

'I appreciate that…. As an old family friend, I'd like you to be honest with me. There are rumours that Germany is under attack from all sides. They are saying that the war is lost. That Hitler is in Berlin to make a last stand. The Russians are pushing forward from the east, but the Western allies are holding back. Why do you think that is?'

Speer sighed.

'I don't know what's in the minds of Churchill and Roosevelt, but I'd say that they made some sort of deal with Stalin to let the Russians be first into Berlin. Revenge for Stalingrad.'

'God help us all…. What about you?'

'Me? I will see my family safe and if it comes to it, and if I can't break out, I'll make sure I'm captured by the Americans.'

'But what about my daughter? We haven't heard from her in days. I know she's back in Berlin. The concierge at our apartment keeps us informed. But if the Russians overrun the city….'

'Your daughter,' Speer began, wondering if he should confide in his old colleague, 'Your daughter is working in a bunker under the Reichstag. The Führer is conducting the war from there.'

'Oh my God.'

'From the point of view of the bombing, it's probably the safest place in Berlin. Remember, we designed it ourselves. There's enough concrete in there to build a three-metre wall around the city.'

Von Bismarck lay back on the pillows.

'As non-combatants with no affiliation to the Nazi party you and your wife will be safe,' Speer continued.

'And what of the German people?'

'The German people are resilient. They will rebuild and it is architects like you who will be needed then.'

'And you?'

'I am the Minister of Armaments and War Production. In the eyes of the victors I am a war criminal. If I'm captured I'll be put on trial along with the other leaders of the Reich. What happens then is in the lap of the Gods. But, old friend, we've had a good run, you and I. We've built some magnificent buildings. Let the memory of them be our legacy. And, the fates be willing, we'll meet again in quieter times.'

Albert Speer rose, shook von Bismarck's hand and left the room.

Greta was waiting for him in the hall.

'Herr Speer, before you go, there is something you must know. Please, sit down with me for a moment.'

She led him into the drawing room and sat down beside him on the sofa.

'That awful little man Veigl, I think he's discovered something about our daughter Gretchen.'

'What do you mean?'

Greta sighed and rubbed her hands together.

'The truth is Gretchen is not *my* daughter.'

'Not your daughter?'

'She is my husband's daughter...just after we were married, I had a riding accident. My horse shied as we were about to jump a stone wall on the property. I was thrown and landed heavily on the wall, rupturing something in my abdomen. I was rushed to hospital and operated on immediately. I took a long time to recover and when I finally did, the doctors found that I could no longer have children. Scarring of the fallopian tubes, they said. Carl was desperate to have a heir and we didn't want to adopt. I would have given anything to bear his child, but it wasn't to be. So we chose a surrogate mother.'

'A surrogate mother?'

'Yes. We had to be discreet. Nobody should know. So, with my blessing, my husband impregnated our maid who carried the child to term for us.... Please don't judge me.'

Speer shook his head sadly and remained silent.

'The maid's name is Krista Becker. Her mother is the woman you got released from Ravensbrück. Jewish, which means our daughter is part Jewish.'

'Does Veigl know this?

'I think he suspects something from the questions he was asking me.'

'What did you tell him?'

'I told him nothing.'

'Good. I will make sure Gretchen knows what the situation is.'

Berlin, March 25, 1945

Isaac Bidermann was worried. Krista had not returned from work the previous evening and her mother was agitated.

He knocked on the door of Krista's room to see if she had returned late; but there was no response.

It was her custom to lay out the breakfast dishes for him the night before; but the kitchen table was bare when he rose at his customary 6 am.

Bidermann decided to visit the coffee shop where she worked.

There were no trams running so he had to walk. It was a depressing journey, climbing over rubble, passing buildings once familiar to him, now skeletal wrecks, bearing witness to the devastation from the previous night's air raid.

He passed a group of three women by a damaged fire hydrant that was gushing water. They were bent over buckets and pails washing their clothes. Beside them was a burnt-out shell of a scout car that had taken a direct hit from an incendiary bomb. And everywhere the pervasive, acrid smell of sulphur.

It took him almost an hour to reach the coffee bar on Petersburger Strasse. He noticed that it was opposite the building where the von Bismarcks had an apartment. He had visited it many years ago, he recalled, when Gretchen had whooping cough.

The coffee bar was empty when he entered. There was no one behind the counter.

'Hello,' he called.

A head poked through the serving hatch from the kitchen.

'We're closed,' said a young woman.

'There was no sign on the door.'

'It must have fallen off.'

'Please, I haven't come for coffee. My name is Bidermann and I'm looking for a Frau Becker who works here. I am her doctor.'

'Oh Lord!' sobbed the girl. 'I'm coming out.'

Bidermann leaned against the counter. The walk through the streets of Berlin had exhausted him, physically and emotionally. The city of his birth looked like the first circle of Hell.

'Frau Becker is not only my patient,' he said, when the girl appeared, 'she is also my housekeeper. I am concerned because she did not come home last night.'

The girl stood in front of him, her elbows pressed into her sides. She was shaking visibly.

'Are you all right?'

The girl burst into tears.

'They came in here yesterday. Three of them.'

'Sit down, my dear. Please be calm. Tell me.'

'Gestapo. Three of them.'

Gulping and sobbing, she recounted what she had witnessed.

'They ordered everyone out. I went two doors down to the tobacco shop and hid in the doorway waiting for them to leave.'

'And Krista. What happened to Krista?'

'They told her to stay.'

'Then what?'

'I looked at my watch because my shift was coming to an end and I had to punch the clock. They must have been in there for twenty minutes. I saw one of them come out and drive his car around the back. There's a door that leads to the alley.'

'Did you see them taking Krista?'

'No, but when they'd gone I went back and she wasn't there.'

'Did you see anything else?'

'There was a towel on the floor. It was wringing wet. And jug of water. And that chair, it was in the middle of the room and it was all wet too.'

Isaac Bidermann groaned.

'And another thing. The shower curtain in the bathroom back there. It was missing.'

Gestapo Headquarters, Berlin, March 26, 1945

O thmar Veigl signed the letter with a flourish. It was addressed to his Gestapo boss, Heinrich Müller.

Before attaching the letter to a sheaf of papers, neatly stapled into a file folder and annotated by date, he re-read what he had written.

SS-Gruppenführer und Generalleutnant der Polizei Heinrich Müller,

In my official capacity as Kriminal-Oberassistent, I have undertaken an investigation on my own initiative (and on my own time) of one Gretchen von Bismarck of Potsdam and Berlin, aged eighteen.

Although she bears an illustrious name that speaks of the noble history of the German people, through intensive research, both by interrogation and archival records (documented here under subsection 2a - 1), I have determined conclusively that – as defined by the Nuremberg Laws of 1935 – she has Jewish blood.

You will see from these documents that Gretchen von Bismarck is the natural offspring resulting from a sexual liaison between Graf Carl von Bismarck and a woman named Krista Becker (now deceased) who was employed by the von Bismarck household as a maid in the late 1920s.

You will note that Graf Carl von Bismarck was arrested on March 17th of this year for listening to enemy radio transmission (page 17, paragraph 3) and spent a night as our guest.

The mother of Krista Becker, a Jewess named Rosenberg, was detained in Ravensbrück until recently, but was released by the personal intervention of the Minister of Armaments and War Production, Albert Speer (pages 23–24). The woman Rosenberg currently resides in the house of a Dr. Isaac Bidermann, a Jew who was granted honorary Aryan status by Reischmarshall Hermann Goering in 1937.

Since September 1ˢᵗ, 1943, Gretchen von Bismarck has been employed as one of the Führer's food tasters. She is currently on a roster of women who ensure that the food put in front of our leader in the Führerbunker has not been contaminated in any way. She was, coincidentally, on duty on July 20th when traitor von Stauffenberg tried to assassinate the Führer.

Given the girl's bloodline, I would strongly recommend – with your approval, of course – that she be relieved of her duties and dispatched to Ravensbrück immediately to ensure the protection of the Führer.
Heil Hitler,
Kriminal-Oberassistent Othmar Veigl.

He smiled with satisfaction as he slipped the letter and accompanying file into an internal envelope. Then he pressed the key on his telephone to connect with his secretary.

'Get me Gruppenführer Müller.'

'The Gruppenführer is in the file room supervising the removal of documents, Herr Veigl.'

'Never mind. I'll see him later.'

Veigl put the receiver down and drummed his fingers on the desk. 'Why give the file to Müller?' he said to himself. He'll only take the credit for all my hard work. There's no pay-off in that.

I'm going to give it directly to the Führer.

Berlin, April 2nd, 1945

'Let's take a walk, Herr Speer,' said Dieter Stahl, the head of his ministry's munitions division. 'What I have to tell you my friend is for your ears only.'

The two men left the partly demolished ministry building and picked their way through the rubble-strewn street.

'I think I have found what you were looking for,' said Stahl, glancing around to ensure no one was within earshot. 'It's a gas called Sarin. According to my contact at I. G. Farben, in its purest form, Sarin is 26 times more deadly than cyanide.'

'Does Farben manufacture it?'

'Yes. Apparently, it was discovered in 1938 after they made Tabun. My source tells me that Sarin is highly volatile and the slightest inhalation can be very dangerous. If it touches your skin it can penetrate. A lethal dose can kill a man in a minute.'

'Can we get some? A test sample?'

'Yes. I believe I can.'

'How does it come?'

'In a glass vial inside a protective metal canister.'

'So once it's out of the metal canister, it could be dropped into the air shaft which would shatter on impact?'

'I imagine so, but it would be best to get an empty vial and test it first. What I saw looked like a small light bulb.'

'Can you get me a couple of empty vials and a sample of the gas?'

'Where do you want it to be picked up?'

'I'll let you know…. I'll send my nephew, Kurt Andorfer.'

****

Albert Speer realised that his nephew was integral to his plan. The boy had firsthand knowledge of Hitler's movements in the bunker, when he dined, when he was in conference and who would be visiting him. But first he had to make Kurt aware that if he agreed to be part of an assassination attempt, his life would be in danger: he would be party to the ultimate act of treason. And rumours of the fate of those implicated in the July plot were still current in the minds of the members of the Hitler youth.

Having lectured Kurt on the sanctity of the oath he had sworn to Adolph Hitler when he joined the movement, he now had to play Devil's Advocate, reverse himself and convince the boy that he could play a major role in history.

From his sister-in-law, Speer learned the timing of Kurt's daily guard duties in the bunker.

He made a point of arriving there as Kurt was finishing his morning watch. When the guards at the gates of the Reich Chancellery challenged him as he drove in, he flashed his pass. They saluted and lifted the barrier to allow him to pass through.

On the passenger seat was a book-marked copy of '*Mein Kampf.*'

Speer waited at the entrance to the Führer bunker until his nephew appeared. He tooted the horn and leaned across to open the passenger door.

'Why are you here, uncle?'

'Get in, Kurt. Don't say a word until I have parked the car. Understood? Just put that book on your lap for the time being.'

Kurt nodded and sat down, concerned now that perhaps Gretchen's plan had been discovered.

'Am I in trouble, uncle?'

'I said not a word. I'll tell you in a moment.'

They drove in silence through the ruins of the city until they came to the Tiergarten, a mile away from the Reichstag. Speer pulled to the curb and turned to Kurt.

'Kurt, do you know what a lemming is?'

'A lemming?'

'Yes.'

Kurt shrugged.

'A lemming,' said Speer, 'is a small rodent, the same family as rats, mice, hamsters and gerbils.'

Kurt looked at his uncle wondering whether he had lost his mind.

'Only lemmings have this particular trait. A subconscious need to follow a leader even if it means to their own destruction.'

'I don't understand, uncle.'

'If their leader runs to the edge of a precipice and throws himself off, the rest of the lemmings will follow blindly and perish with him.'

Kurt studied his hands, wondering where this would lead.

'You will recall a conversation we had many months ago about the oath you swore when you joined the *Hitlerjungen.*'

'Yes.'

'Well, there comes a time when one must re-evaluate an oath if the individual to whom you swore it has betrayed the ideals that he set for you – and for himself.'

'I don't understand.'

'The leader you swore an oath to is like that lemming. He is racing towards a precipice and he expects the German people to follow him.'

'What are you saying, uncle?'

'Open that book where it's marked and read me the underlined passage.'

Kurt opened the book and ran his finger down the page.

'*State authority as an end in itself cannot exist, as every tyranny on this earth would be sacred and unassailable. If a racial entity is being led towards its doom by means of governmental power, then the rebellion of every single member of such a* Volk *is not only a right, but a duty.*'

'Do you understand what that means, Kurt?'

'I guess it means the lemmings should fight back, right?'

'Exactly. "Not only a right, but a duty." Those were the Führer's own words when he founded the Nazi party. Now *we* must fight back, otherwise the German people – our civilisation – will be destroyed by the insane actions of one man.'

'What are you saying?'

'Can I trust you, Kurt?'

'Of course, uncle.'

'There are many officers of the Wehrmacht who want this war to end, to seek an honourable peace with our enemies. They know the war is lost. Too many people have died already. But the Führer is determined to fight till the last drop of German blood. He must be stopped now.'

'Stopped?'

'To put it bluntly. Killed.'

Kurt sat back and stared through the windscreen. The young leaves of the trees were thick with plaster dust from the bombing raids.

'But how?'

'I have the means,' said Speer. 'But I need your help. If you are willing, I'll explain it all to you. If you don't want to hear, I will understand and we will forget that this conversation ever took place.'

'You're putting yourself in great danger, uncle.'

'Yes, and you would be too. But the cause is bigger than both of us.'

Kurt closed the book and placed it on the back seat.

'You don't have to answer me this minute, Kurt, but I need to know very soon. Another thing I should tell you. Your girlfriend Gretchen –'

'What about Gretchen?'

'A Gestapo agent went to the von Bismarck house and questioned her mother.'

'Othmar Veigl.'

'You know him?'

Kurt nodded.

'He's the one who asked me to spy on Gretchen. I fed him some little bits of no importance. What did he want to know?'

'About who her mother was. I think he found out that her mother was Jewish.'

Kurt sat bolt upright. So his uncle knew. Who else knew? He had to warn Gretchen. If Veigl had this information, why had she not been arrested already?

His mind was reeling with different scenarios. Should he escape with Gretchen, maybe get to Switzerland? If Hitler was killed, would that stop the internment of Jews? Should he confide in his uncle that Gretchen was trying to kill Hitler, which was exactly what his uncle was proposing? Should he kill Veigl before the Gestapo had Gretchen arrested?

Kurt turned to Speer.

'Tell me what your plan is. But if I agree, you have to protect Gretchen.'

Berlin, April 3, 1945

I t had been a week since Krista Becker's disappearance and each day Ruth Rosenberg had asked Dr. Bidermann where she was.

He had not told her he suspected that she had been murdered and after long deliberation he decided to visit Gestapo headquarters and file a 'missing person' report.

He would do it directly to Kriminal-Oberassistent Othmar Veigl.

When he arrived at the immense Gestapo headquarters on Prinz-Albrecht-strasse, he was asked to wait while a receptionist called Veigl's office.

Bidermann chose a seat so he did not have to look at the life-size portrait of Hitler on the wall.

'Let him wait for twenty minutes and then have him sent up,' said Veigl, when his secretary informed him that a Dr. Bidermann had arrived without an appointment.

'Ah, Herr Doktor,' this is a surprise,' exclaimed Veigl, indicating a chair for him to sit on the other side of his desk. 'What brings you here?'

'Good day, Herr Kriminal-Oberassistent. My housekeeper, Frau Becker, the woman you met when you paid a visit to my house. She has gone missing. At the risk of trespassing on our social relationship, I am asking whether you might make some enquiries as to where she might be.'

'You say she's gone missing.'

'Yes, she has not returned home in a week.'

'Many people in Berlin are on the move, Dr. Bidermann. They are concerned about the advancing Red Army. It is no secret the Russians are attacking Vienna as we speak. People are afraid. Especially women and they have good reason. May I offer you a Streuselkuchen?'

Veigl slid a plate of pastries towards him.

'No, thank you. And I have reason to believe that you may know where Frau Becker is.'

'And why would that be?'

'You are a very able detective, Herr Veigl. You have been asking questions about her. Not only of me but of Frau von Bismarck.'

'I have no knowledge of the woman, Herr Doktor.'

'Just tell me. Has she been taken to Ravensbrück?'

Othmar Veigl stood up, turned around and gazed out of the window.

'And why would she be taken to Ravensbrück?'

'Come, Herr Veigl, let's not play games. I said you are a good detective. All your questions lead me to suspect you think Frau Becker is Jewish.'

Veigl whirled around and planted his fists on his desk. His eyes bulged and the colour rose in his neck.

'Dr. Bidermann,' he shouted, 'be very careful. You are skating on thin ice. Even if you are an honorary Aryan.'

Berlin, April 9, 1945

D ieter Stahl was as good as his word. As soon as he had taken possession of the Sarin gas sample with the extra glass vials, he called Albert Speer.

'Albert, finally, I have the Easter cake you ordered, the *Bienenstich.* I'm sorry it's late for Easter, but it took a little time to assemble.'

'Easter cake, Dieter? Oh, of course, *Bienenstich.* The Bee Sting Cake. How very appropriate.'

'How would you like it delivered?'

'Thank you, Dieter. I will have it picked up by my nephew. Please give me the address. And Dieter, my profound thanks. I'm sure it will be most appreciated by the family. Goodbye, my friend.'

Berlin, April 10, 1945

T he next day, following instructions from Speer, Kurt drove to an abandoned warehouse on the western edge of the city. Stahl himself handed him a canvas bag that contained a metal box and two carefully wrapped glass vials.

'Be very careful, young man,' said Stahl. 'Avoid the potholes. I wish you good luck. My respects to the Minister. He is doing the right thing.'

Kurt drove with infinite care through streets pitted with shell holes, the tarmac corrugated by tank tracks and littered with obstructions. Mindful that any sudden jarring motion might dislodge the vial of gas from its bed of cotton batting, Kurt steered slowly through an obstacle course of bricks, girders, stones and wooden window frames. He tried to avoid the eyes of destitute victims of the nightly bombings as they picked through the rubble of destroyed houses searching for treasured memories.

'Come directly to my office at the Ministry,' Speer had told Kurt. 'I will leave a word with the guard to let you in without a search. If they ask you, tell them it's a thermos of coffee for me.'

'Your coffee, uncle,' said Kurt as he placed the canvas bag carefully on the desk.

For a moment they both stared at the limp canvas bag without saying a word.

'And the glass vials?' asked Speer.

'They're in there too.'

Speer nodded.

'We must test them out.'

He spread out his architectural drawings for the bunker on a drawing board.

'You see this main airshaft? It leads from ground level in the Reich Chancellery garden down into the lower bunker,' said Speer, tracing its length with his finger. 'The shaft intersects with ventilation pipes that pass through the Führer's private quarters and out into the corridors. At intervals along these pipes, there are vents which allow the fresh air to be pumped into the rooms. You see that vent? It's above the desk in his sitting room where he works. That's why I have to know exactly when he's in there.'

'His routine is the same, uncle. Never varies. He has tea with his secretaries at around 5 o'clock then he sits at his desk, working.'

'How long for?'

'An hour, two maybe. How will it be done?'

'You see this small circle here. This is where the airshaft opening is – here at this point at ground level. An iron grate, concealed under a shrub, covers it. We'll need something to lever it open and drop the vial of gas down. An object falls at the rate of 9.81 metres per second. The Vorbunker is 1.5 metres below ground. The Führerbunker is 2.5 metres below the Vorbunker, which means the vial will drop five metres. We will have half a second from dropping the vial until there is impact and the glass is shattered.'

'That doesn't give us much time.'

''Well, the gas is heavier than air which means it will drop down. But the warm air rising in the shaft could cause some esters to rise so we'll carry wet handkerchiefs to put over our noses and mouths as soon as the vial is dropped.'

When do you want to do it, uncle?'

'Tomorrow evening.... Pity we can't wait ten days. For his birthday.'

****

Graf von Bismarck lay in bed. The cough he had picked up during his night of incarceration had not cleared up.

He had given up all pretence of listening in secret to the BBC broadcasts. Over her strenuous objections, he had Greta move the radio into his bedroom and placed close to his head.

He listened grimly to the news that American soldiers of the Ninth Army had captured the city of Hanover – a mere 215 kilometres west of where he lay.

He turned off the radio and lay back on the pillows.

He recalled his university days in Hanover, studying mathematics. He met his wife Greta there, at the Hanover Schützenfest, the largest marksmen's funfair in the world. How they both had enjoyed the 12-kilometre-long 'Parade of the Marksmen' with participants from all over Germany and the world – the marching bands, the wagons, carriages and floats. He had taken Greta on the 60-metre Steiger Ferris wheel and she had clung to him in fear.

All those memories that even this bitter war could not erase. He wondered if there would ever be a 'Parade of Marksmen' again. One day, perhaps, he would return to Hanover with Gretchen and show her where he had been happy.

His thoughts were interrupted by a gentle knock on the door.

'Come in.'

'I hope I'm not disturbing you if you were sleeping,' said Greta, 'but Cook said this letter arrived in the morning. Why she didn't mention it before I can't imagine.'

'A letter? They're still delivering mail in spite of everything?'

She handed him the envelope waiting for him to open it. Instead, he looked for a sender's name and address on the back. There was none. Then, to his wife's irritation he studied the handwriting to see if he recognised it.

'Open it for heaven's sake, Carl.'

He slid his finger under the flat and took out a single sheet of paper.

Greta watched him as he read. Slowly a smile began to spread across his face.

'Well? What's there to be so happy about?' she asked.

'It's from the Arndorfer boy. He's asking for Gretchen's hand in marriage.'

Berlin, April 11, 1945

I t was 7.30 pm on a dark early spring evening when Albert Speer and Kurt Andorfer entered the Old Reich Chancellery garden.

Speer carried a rolled-up elevation plan of the Führerbunker and its air intake system. Kurt had a leather pouch slung over his shoulder. It contained the vial of Saran gas in its protective aluminum housing.

They tried to act nonchalant as they walked slowly along the gravel path to where the iron grill covered the ventilator shaft leading down to the lower bunker and Hitler's personal quarters.

But something did not seem quite right to Speer. He noticed that there were guards posted on the roof of the blockhouse and on each of the emergency exits from the bunker – guards that he had not seen before.

Had his plan been discovered?

But there was no turning back now.

'The grate should be up ahead,' he said quietly. 'Just pretend we're having a stroll to get some air.'

Kurt nodded.

The gravel crunched under their feet, a sound that would alert the guards.

'Try to walk on the grass verge,' whispered Speer.

Suddenly, he stopped.

'What's the matter?' asked Kurt.

Speer unfurled the roll of architectural drawings.

'That chimney! It wasn't there before. I didn't design that.'

In front of them was a four-metre chimney that stood on the exact spot where the iron grill covering the air-vent should be. They would need a ladder to scale it and drop the vial inside.

A metallic clang rang out shattering the silence. A powerful beam of light swept the garden until it found the two men.

'*Halt! Bleib wo du bist*,' commanded a voice over a loud hailer.

Blinded by the light, Speer shielded his eyes with his hand.

'I am the Minister of Armaments and War Production,' he shouted in the direction of the voice. 'Turn off that light, you idiot. Don't you know there are enemy bombers in the air right now.'

The searchlight was switched off.

'I'm coming down, Herr Minister,' shouted the voice.

As they waited for the guard to arrive, Speer said to Kurt, 'Don't speak. Let me do the talking. Hand me the bag and you take the blue-prints.'

Two uniformed guards, their Walther PP pistols drawn, came running towards them. Before they could say a word, Speer shouted at them: 'Who is the ranking officer here?'

'I am, Herr Minister?'

'Your name?'

'*Oberscharführer* Rochus Misch, *mein Herr.*'

'Here is my documentation,' said Speer, flashing his identity card. 'I want an explanation, Misch. On whose authority was this chimney built? It was not in my original design.'

Turning to Kurt, he said: 'Show him.'

Kurt unfurled the blueprint and held it open with both hands spread wide.

Speer stabbed at the drawing with his forefinger.

'Here. Do you see a chimney here?'

Rochus Misch leaned in and squinted at the drawing.

'No, Herr Minister.'

'Then explain to me why there is now a chimney here.'

'You will have to speak to Cheftechnicker Johannes Hentschel who is responsible for the workings of the Führerbunker, Herr Minister.'

'I want an answer now,' shouted Speer.

Rochus Misch shifted uncomfortably from foot to foot.

'This is not official but I overheard the Führer speaking to Cheftechnicker Hentschel a couple of weeks ago. The Führer was saying that in the First World War he was blinded for a time by poison gas. As you know, Herr Minister, poison gas is heavier than air. The chimney is an added precaution – if the enemy sprayed poison gas here. And he also ordered a 24-hour watch on the grounds.'

****

Albert Speer and his nephew Kurt walked slowly back towards the emergency entrance.

Kurt could see how dejected his uncle was.

'I'm sorry it didn't work out, uncle.'

'Sorry,' snapped Speer. 'Sorry. It's the German people who should be sorry.'

'I meant, after all your planning.'

Speer ignored him.

'There has to be another way,' he muttered, talking more to himself than to Kurt.

'I don't know if I should tell you this, uncle…'

'What? There are no secrets between us now.'

'For several weeks now Gretchen, my girlfriend, has been feeding him poison.'

Speer stopped. He glanced around to ensure there was no one within earshot.

'What are you talking about?'

'She's been putting strychnine in his food, a little at a time, whenever she's on duty.'

No wonder he's looking like he does, Speer thought. This could be the answer. The girl must carry it through, double the dose if necessary.

'The problem is,' whispered Kurt. She has to eat the food too. There's a doctor who has told her how to lessen the effect of the poison, but it's beginning to tell on her now.'

'How does she do it without being detected?'

'I don't know. She wouldn't tell me. In case she was caught and interrogated. But she's lost a lot of weight and I'm worried about her.'

'You must tell her not to give up, Kurt. This could save a lot of lives. We must increase the dose.'

'I'll tell her, but if she ingests more it could make her sicker. I love her, Uncle, and I want to marry her.'

Speer sighed.

'I will do what I can to protect her. In the meantime, give me the satchel. I have to have it disposed of.'

Berlin, The Führerbunker, April 27, 1945

The persistent drone of the bunker's ventilation system was punctuated by the sound of steel blades tattooing wooden chopping boards.

Gretchen and Constanze Manziarly were dicing vegetables for Hitler's soup.

'So, tell me about that handsome young man downstairs who seems to be madly in love with you,' teased Constanze.

Gretchen blushed. 'Oh, we've just been seeing each other for a while.'

'And what are his intentions?'

'Do you mean, are we going to get married?'

'OK, let's start with that.'

Before Gretchen could reply, the air vibrated with screams of anger that rose from the lower bunker and echoed along the corridors.

Hitler, thought Gretchen.

The women looked at each other and neither spoke. Knives poised, they waited.

Then from the floor below came the sound of heavy boots on wood floors and a man struggling and shouting as he was being dragged along, resisting and howling as he went.

'What's going on?' asked Gretchen.

Constanze put her finer to her lips. 'It's Lieutenant General Fegelein,' she said in a whisper.

'Who?'

'Eva Braun's brother-in-law. He's married to Eva's sister, Gretl. The guards call her 'The nymphomaniac of Obersaltzberg.'

'What are they doing to him?'

'He's being court-martialled for desertion.'

'Desertion?'

'Yes. It's a good thing he didn't see *you*. He'd chase anything in a skirt. His nickname is *'der Flegelein,'* you know, 'the lout.' He kept a bachelor flat on Bleibtraustrasse for his mistress. Some red-haired Irish woman and this with his wife eight months pregnant. They were planning to run off together and fly to Switzerland.'

'That's terrible.'

'I was told by one of the guards who arrested him they found a suitcase. It was full of false passports, road maps, lots of foreign currency and jewellery – some of it was Eva Braun's.'

'What happened to the woman?'

'She got away. Jumped from the kitchen window while they were getting him into the car. They think she was a British spy, reporting their pillow talk back to London. Well, at least they found the leak. We were all suspects, you know.... Are you all right?'

Gretchen began to sway. She dropped the knife and her knees buckled under her. The steady accumulation of cyanide in her system was beginning to take effect.

Berlin, Gestapo Headquarters, April 27, 1945

Othmar Veigl checked the file one more time. Everything had been meticulously documented for the Führer. It had to be perfect.

There were photos of Gretchen, wedding certificates, transcripts of his interviews with Dr. Bidermann, Greta von Bismarck, Sturmbannführer Fritz Suhren's report from Ravensbrück, speculations on the girl's Swiss connections and notes from Kurt Andorfer. Although these notes were innocuous enough they would attest to the thoroughness of his investigation.

But one thing was missing. There was no image of Gretchen von Bismarck's Jewish grandmother.

He decided he would pay a visit to Dr. Bidermann's house with a staff photographer.

It was the doctor himself who opened the door. The old man's first reaction was one of relief.

'You have news of Krista Becker?'

'Unfortunately not, Dr. Bidermann. In order to pursue our inquiries we need a photograph of her mother as we have none of the woman in question.'

'I can't see how that will help in your search for Frau Becker, Herr Kriminal-Oberassistent.'

'There is a family resemblance. Now, if you'll kindly step aside we will be in and out in the flash of a light bulb so to speak.'

'And if I refuse?'

'You are in no position to refuse, Herr Doktor. You have my word that your guest will not be transported to a less agreeable accommodation if you cooperate with me. Do I make myself clear?'

'Crystal clear,' said Bidermann, opening the door wider. 'Just let me prepare her for your arrival. She may be sleeping and she is not used to strangers.'

Veigl nodded as he and the photographer stepped inside, closing the door behind them.

'Please wait here,' said Bidermann as he climbed the stairs.

Veigl and his photographer stood impatiently in the hallway as the minutes ticked by.

'Enough of this,' muttered Veigl as he headed for the stairs, beckoning the photographer to follow him.

Veigl put his ear to each of the closed doors he passed until he heard the low buzz of Dr. Bidermann's voice.

He motioned the photographer to have his camera poised when he opened the door.

'Ready?' he mouthed.

The photographer raised the camera to his eye and looked through the viewfinder.

'Ready,' he whispered.

Veigl flung open the door to reveal Dr. Bidermann sitting on the bed next to Ruth Rosenberg. He was brushing her hair.

The light bulb flashed and the woman screamed. She clung in fear to Dr. Bidermann.

'The Beast of Ravensbrück!' she cried out, burying her face in Bidermann's shoulder.

'Get out,' hissed Bidermann, 'Get out you Nazi swine.'

'You will pay for that, Herr Doktor,' said Veigl, as he closed the door.

He rubbed his hands.

'Good job, Dietrich. Now, how about some coffee and a pastry?'

Berlin, The Führerbunker, April 27, 1945

G retchen tried to focus. She was lying on her back in an unfamiliar room staring at the ceiling and trying to remember what had happened.

Instinctively, she reached for the top button of her blouse, terrified that someone had unbuttoned it or had felt for her pulse and discovered the rubber tube strapped to her arm.

'It's all right,' said a voice that whispered in her ear.

She turned her head and saw Kurt kneeling at her bedside.

'Where am I?'

'You're in the Reich Chancellery where they bring the wounded. I carried you here. The woman in the kitchen came down looking for me. She told me you'd fainted…. How are you feeling?'

'A bit woozy still. I don't know, I just passed out. Did anyone look at me? I mean, a doctor or anyone?'

'No, but I called Dr. Bidermann. He's on his way. I have to meet him at the gate to escort him in.'

'I'm so sorry, Kurt. I'm just so tired. I've never fainted before.'

'You rest now. My uncle is in the bunker too. He told me he's come to say goodbye to the Führer. I don't understand why he'd do that. I have to get back to my post now. As soon as Dr. Bidermann arrives I'll bring him to you.'

****

Albert Speer knocked on the door of Hitler's study. The voice bidding him enter was the high-pitched quaver of an old man. The leader of the Third Reich was seated, hunched over in his chair, gripping the padded arms to stop his hands from shaking. His cheeks were sunken, his eyes dull and his skin a waxy yellow.

Speer had already heard of the volcanic rage that had consumed the last of Hitler's energy when Martin Bormann told him of the telegram sent by Hermann Goering. The carefully worded message had asked for permission to assume the leadership of the country. Hitler had interpreted this, with some prompting from Bormann, to be Goering's efforts at a coup d'état.

And here sat the man Speer had intended to gas to death, the empty shell of the leader he had followed with devotion for twelve years.

What had compelled him to risk his own life by coming to see Adolph Hitler for the last time? Was it the memory of the endless hours they pored over blueprints of the master plan for Linz, the city where Hitler had lived as a boy? Or the discussions they had had far into the night of building a capital that would be the envy of the world? Those heady days of victory, the annexation of Austria, the invasion of Poland, the taking of Paris, the Nuremburg rallies, the adoration of the German masses…and it had all come to this: defeat and disintegration.

Speer realized it was pity, not loyalty, that had brought him here to make his peace with the man who had destroyed his own dreams.

There was no warmth in this final leave-taking, only a profound sense of impending doom. Hitler had intimated that he would die in Berlin by his own hand rather than fall into the hands of the Russians. And he ordered that his body be cremated along with that of his newly wedded bride, Eva Braun. And his dog, Blondi.

****

A few minutes after Kurt Andorfer arrived back in the duty room, the phone rang.

'There is a man at the south gate demanding to see the Führer. He is not on our list,' said the voice at the other end of the line.

It must be Dr. Bidermann, thought Kurt. 'Has he shown you his identity card?'

'Yes. His name is Veigl, Kriminal-Oberassistent Othmar Veigl from the Berlin SS. He says he has urgent information for the Führer's eyes only. He says it concerns his personal security.'

Kurt thought fast. Why would Veigl bring information to Hitler? Did he know of Gretchen's plans?

'Let me check with my list here…Veigl, you say. How does he spell it?'

He could hear Veigl in the background remonstrating with the guard, trying to snatch the phone from him.

'Veigl. V- e - i- g-l. Dientaus Weis Nummer 223.'

'Veigl, Veigl'…Kurt repeated the name as if consulting a log-book. 'He is not on my list either. The only one for today is a Dr. Bidermann.'

'Yes, I have a Dr. Bidermann.'

'Good. Then hold this Veigl there until I come up.'

Kurt strapped on his holster and mounted the bunker's forty-four steps up to the emergency exit.

When Veigl spotted him he began to dance from foot to foot in impatience.

'What is the hold-up? This is of national importance. The life of our Führer is at stake,' he shouted, attracting the attention of the guards on the roof of the blockhouse. 'I must see the Führer immediately.'

'What do you have for the Führer?' asked Kurt, calmly.

'This!' shouted Veigl, waving an envelope. 'I must give it to him personally.'

'I'm afraid that is not possible,' said Kurt, his hand on his holster. 'The Führer is in conference with the Minister of Armaments and War Production.'

'That is precisely why I have to see him,' fumed Veigl.

'Whatever it is, give it to me and I will see that it is delivered to the Führer.'

'You don't understand, you young fool. You are a traitor!'

From his vantage point on the blockhouse roof, sixteen-year-old Erik Hausner, newly pressed into service as a bunker guard, witnessed the encounter of a short, round man in a shabby wool overcoat threatening a Wehrmacht-uniformed officer.

He dropped to a prone position and pressed his eye to the telescopic sight of his Mauser Karabiner Kar 98F sniper's rifle. He could not hear the exchange between the two men, but it was obvious that the civilian was angry and potentially dangerous.

His reading of the situation was confirmed when he saw Veigl draw a Luger from the pocket of his coat.

Veigl's eyes bulged and his lips were wet with spittle. He pointed the pistol at Kurt, holding it at arm's length.

'*Schnell,*' he ordered.

A shot rang out. A plume of smoke rose from the blockhouse roof. Othmar Veigl dropped to the ground. The bullet had struck him at the base of his skull.

Kurt knelt down, grabbed the envelope and stuffed it into the jacket of his uniform. Then he felt for a pulse in Veigl's neck but there was no sign of life. He signalled to the guard on the blockhouse to come down.

'Thank you,' he said to the young marksman. 'You saved my life. This madman would have killed the Führer. What is your name? I will see that it goes on your record. Now get his body out of here.'

****

Once back in the bunker, Kurt headed for the washroom and locked himself in the toilet stall.

He took out the file he had secreted in the jacket of his uniform and leafed through it. The more he read the more he became convinced that both he and Gretchen were in great danger. Veigl had all the supporting documentation to prove that Gretchen's mother was Jewish and there were detailed notes about himself and his liaisons with her – dates, times and places.

He realised that his only protection now was his uncle. He had fed Veigl with useless scraps of information about Gretchen to throw him off, but the detective was using his association with her to incriminate him and his uncle, Albert Speer.

The file had to be destroyed. But what if there was another copy held in Veigl's Gestapo files? He had to get Gretchen away – out of Berlin...out of Germany.

Kurt made his way to the kitchen. Frau Manziarly was nowhere to be seen. He crossed quickly to the stove, opened the firebox door and was about to throw the file in when the cook appeared, carrying a tray of fresh vegetables.

'What are you doing?'

Kurt whirled around.

'We have orders to burn the files. They must not to fall into the hands of the Russians,' he said, improvising.

He watched with satisfaction as the file went up in flames. Closing the iron door, he burned himself in his haste.

'Well, as long as you don't make smoke in here...And how is Gretchen?'

'I called her doctor. He is on his way.'

****

Dr. Issac Bidermann stood in front of the sentry box at the entrance to the Reichstag Gardens. In answer to Kurt Andorfer's frantic call, he had grabbed his leather medical bag and hurried over to the Führer bunker as fast as he was able to traverse the ruined city.

He approached the window with trepidation and held up the identification card that showed he was an honorary Aryan. The guard consulted his log and beckoned him inside.

'Your bag. Open it.'

Bidermann unclasped the bag and pulled the handles apart. The guard rummaged around inside, feeling for metallic objects. He pulled out a stethoscope.

'For listening to the heart beat,' Bidermann offered.

The guard nodded and handed it back to him.

'Open your coat and put your arms up so.'

Bidermann did as he was ordered. The guard patted him down thoroughly – his trunk, his arms and legs. Satisfied that there was nothing on his person or in the medical bag that could harm the Führer, he turned the crank on the field telephone.

'There is a Doctor Bidermann here. Will you send someone to escort him in.'

Kurt had been waiting by the phone for Bidermann's arrival.

'*Unteroffizier* Kurt Androfer here. I will come personally.'

'You will wait,' said the guard as Isaac Bidermann buttoned his coat. Tired from the exertion of crossing the city under the distant sound of shellfire, he looked around for a seat.

'You will wait outside,' said the guard.

Bidermann stood by the gate. The boy had given him little information about Gretchen over the phone, speaking in coded language. He understood that she had collapsed. She had been taken to a room in the Reichs Chancellery that had been requisitioned as a temporary emergency room to receive soldiers wounded in the defence of Berlin.

He wondered whether the accumulation of strychnine in the girl's system had finally taken its toll and what he could do to help her. But what concerned him more was whether the means by which Gretchen had been slowly poisoning Hitler had been discovered, and that the Gestapo had used Kurt to lure him into their grasp.

He did not care about his own safety. He was an old man and he was ready to die. In fact, there was nothing for him to live for now. With Hitler's accession to power the Germany he knew had ceased to exist. No, it was the young people he must protect.

Seeing Kurt striding towards him in his Nazi uniform he felt a frisson of disgust. Where were the boy's loyalties? Was he walking into a trap?

Kurt made no show that he knew or even recognised the man he had to escort into the Reichs Chancellery.

'Follow me, please, Herr Doktor,' was all he said.

When they were out of sight of the sentry box, he slowed the pace and spoke quietly.

'Gretchen fainted in the kitchen, Doctor. Luckily, the woman who cooks for Hitler knows I'm her boyfriend and she came to me. I carried her from the bunker to the Reichs Chancellery where they've opened a field hospital. She has a bed there now.'

'Is she conscious?'

'Yes, but very weak and tired.'

'Were there any other symptoms? Was she convulsing?'

'I don't think so.'

'Did she complain of muscle pain?'

'No,'

'Was she arching her back or her neck?'

'I didn't see it. She's resting now.'

'Take me to her.'

Dr. Bidermann found Gretchen at the end of what appeared to be a dormitory full of wounded soldiers being attended to by nurses. He looked for the most senior-looking nurse and introduced himself.

'My name is Dr. Isaac Bidermann. I am the family physician of your patient there, in the first bed by the door. Her name is Gretchen von Bismarck. It is unseemly that a young girl should be in a ward full of wounded men. I want her screened off immediately.'

'Yes, Herr Doktor.'

Bidermann and Kurt watched as nurses scurried to erect linen curtains around Gretchen's bed, effectively screening her off from the rest of the room.

Gretchen smiled wanly when she recognised her doctor. Bidermann crouched down at her bedside and took her pulse. But rather than feel for a pulse he moved his fingers along her arm to see if the tubing was still attached.

'Did anyone examine you?' he whispered.

Gretchen shook her head.

'Good. Help her sit up, Kurt. Unbutton your sweater and your blouse, young lady. I'm going to remove the tubing and the bulb. Kurt, make sure nobody comes in.'

Using a pair of surgical scissors, Bidermann cut through the tapes that secured the rubber tube to her left arm. He removed the bulb from her armpit and wound the apparatus up in a ball, stowing it in his medical bag.

'Now let's have a look at you. You are a very brave girl.'

For all his warmth and reassurance, Isaac Bidermann could not hide his anxiety over the condition of his patient. She looked anorexic;

there was no colour in her cheeks; there was a tightness in her jaw and she appeared to have difficulty breathing.

'I shouldn't have doubled the dose,' she whispered. 'But it seemed to be taking so long.'

'That's all right,' said Dr. Bidermann. "You lie still now.'

He turned to Kurt, indicating he wanted to speak confidentially to him.

'She must get to a proper hospital. She needs her stomach pumped.'

Kurt shook his head in confusion.

'I don't know what to do. With the Russians coming, how can I get her to a hospital?'

He pulled Kurt away out of Gretchen's earshot.

'She could die without the proper treatment.'

With a swishing sound the curtaining was suddenly pulled back. Everyone turned to see Albert Speer in his battlefield grey uniform step into the 'private' ward.

'Uncle,' said Kurt, 'she is very sick. This is her doctor, Dr. Bidermann. Remember your promise.'

Speer took in the situation immediately and addressed himself to Bidermann.

'What is the prognosis, Herr Doktor?'

Bidermann stepped outside the curtain, beckoning Speer to follow him.

Before he began to speak, Speer held up his hand.

'I know what she has been doing, Doctor. Kurt told me. I'm here to help her, believe me…. It was I who told her to double the dose.'

'Gretchen is very sick, Herr Speer, and she needs hospitalisation immediately. I cannot do much for her here. She needs her stomach pumped and an oral application of an activated charcoal infusion to take up any poison in her digestive tract that hasn't already been absorbed into the blood stream. In my bag, I have phenobarbital, which will control her convulsions. I can give her dantrolene, a relaxant to combat muscle rigidity. If she survives for 24 hours, then recovery is possible.'

'Then she must be moved to a hospital immediately.'

'There are no hospitals available. Her only hope is a clinic in Switzerland. She knows the daughter of the physician who owns one. Apparently, they roomed together at school.'

269

'Switzerland?'

'Yes, a clinic in Zurich.'

'But that's a 10-hour drive.'

'She might not survive that even if the roads were clear. But they're already clogged with Berliners fleeing the city.'

'At least she'd be going towards the Americans.'

'She needs a plane.'

'A plane?'

The two men stared at each other.

'It's a four and half hour plane ride,' said Speer.

'If you believe what this girl has gone through for the sake of Germany, no, for the sake of all that is good and honourable in mankind, you will find a way to save her life. Now, I must get back to my patient.'

Speer watched him disappear behind the curtain. He could see the doctor's shadow as he bent down over the prone figure of the girl.

He thought for a moment, consulted his watch and then returned to Gretchen's bedside.

'Young lady,' he said in a low voice. 'We are going to get you to Switzerland.'

Gretchen smiled and nodded her thanks.

Speer pulled Kurt aside and whispered to him.

'Come outside for a moment. There's an emergency airstrip near the Brandenburg Gate. I have a Fieseler Stork, a small observation aircraft, waiting for me on the runway. That's how I plan to get out. I'll send an order to the pilot to fly you and Gretchen to Geneva, but you have to get her safely to the plane.'

'Thank you, uncle, bless you.'

Kurt, in an uncharacteristic display of affection, hugged his uncle.

'Now I must go and get that order off,' said Speer. 'Take care of her. She's a remarkable girl.'

They embraced, both knowing that this probably was the last time they would see each other.

When Kurt returned to Gretchen's bedside, Dr. Bidermann was writing on a prescription pad.

'This is my phone number. As soon as you get to the clinic in Zurich have the receiving doctor call me and I will give him the case history and my course of treatment.'

Kurt took the piece of paper, folded it and placed it carefully in his wallet. It was then that Dr. Bidermann noticed the bloodstain on the arm of his uniform.

'What is this? Blood? Are you hurt?'

'It's not mine. It's Othmar Veigl's. He was shot by a guard. And if he hadn't been, I would have shot him myself.'

Bidermann nodded.

'Come with me for a moment.'

Bidermann led Kurt out into the ward.

'It's good that Veigl is dead. Because I believe he was instrumental in the death of Gretchen's mother.'

He put his finger to his lips to prevent Kurt from speaking.

'You must not tell Gretchen until she is strong enough to handle the news. Promise me.'

Kurt nodded.

'But you can tell her that I'll be in contact with her father. I will let him know where she is and how he can reach her. You have no time to say goodbye to your family. You must leave immediately.'

'You've been very kind, Dr. Bidermann. Thank you.'

'Nan nah nah. Thank that young lady in there…. I'll get a wheel chair. It'll be difficult moving it in the streets but she's in no condition to walk. On that prescription I gave you you'll see instructions on when to give her these pills. The white ones are phenobarbital and the orange ones are dantrolene.'

Kurt slipped the tiny jar into the pocket of his pants.

'And I would lose that jacket and hide the pistol. Here, take my coat. It's a bit big but we can't have you arriving in Switzerland in a Nazi uniform.'

Kurt was in the process of removing his jacket when there was a commotion at the far end of the room.

Wounded soldiers dressed in bloodied bandages rose from their beds and stood with their arms raised.

'Heil Hitler!' they chorused in unison.

Hitler shuffled into the room, moving slowly from bed to bed shaking hands with the soldiers and commending them for their bravery in defence of the city.

Kurt and Dr. Bidermann watched in stunned silence as the Führer progressed through the room towards them.

Bidermann noted how the man's hands trembled as he moved, hunched over as if he carried on his back the weight of the crimes he had inflicted on humanity. His skin was yellowish-grey, his eyes dull from lack of sleep, his body jerking with muscle spasms and his back arching.

The strychnine is taking effect, he said to himself with satisfaction.

Involuntarily, Kurt had snapped to attention and looked fearfully at Bidermann who shook his head and whispered, 'Relax.'

He heard Hitler ask a nurse, 'Where is the girl?'

The nurse, flustered and dumbstruck, curtsied and pointed to the curtained-off bed at the end of the room.

Kurt hastily ducked behind the curtain and began buttoning up his uniform. He knelt down by the bed and took Gretchen's hand.

'What's happening?' she said, her eyes half-closed.

'Hitler is here,' he whispered. 'He's asking for you.'

Kurt felt her hand go limp.

'Don't worry, my darling I'm staying with you… whatever happens. I love you.'

Hitler nodded to Dr. Bidermann as he approached.

'You are the doctor?'

'Yes,' replied Bidermann.

Hitler turned away and reached for the curtain.

The rings on the rod rattled as he jerked it aside.

Kurt stood up and saluted but Hitler ignored him and approached the bed.

'Frau Mozart told me you were here, young lady.'

Gretchen tried to sit up but the effort was too great and she fell back on the mattress.

'Don't overexert yourself, my dear. We are both not at our best it would seem. You must be strong for the sake of Germany, as must I.'

He leant over her and kissed her forehead. She could smell the acrid breath and the rancid smell of sweat. For a moment their eyes locked and in that instant Gretchen had the feeling that he knew. Tears welled up and she tried to stop them by squeezing her eyes shut. She heard the creak of his boots as he turned to speak to Kurt.

'Andorfer, you must look after this young woman. The new Germany will need women of her courage.'

Without another word, Adolph Hitler moved out of their lives.

Potsdam, April 27, 1945

C arl von Bismarck tuned his radio to the BBC World Service. He no longer used headphones and his wife Greta listened glumly to the triumphal voice of the newsreader.

'*The Soviet offensive to capture Berlin continues. Two Russian armies are attacking Hitler's capital from the east and the south while a third has overrun German forces positioned north of Berlin. The Red Army has effectively encircled the city after the successful battles of the Seelow Heights and Halbe. Russian tanks have been spotted on the runways of Templehof airport. The 1st Belorussian Front led by Marshal Georgy Zhukov, is shelling Berlin's city centre, while Marshal Ivan Konev's 1st Ukrainian Front has broken through Army Group Centre and has advanced towards the southern suburbs of Berlin. The Russians report fierce house to house fighting with German defence militia aided by conscripted Hitler Youth members....*'

'Please, turn it off, Carl.'

Von Bismarck acceded to his wife's request.

'We must only pray that Gretchen is safe and doesn't fall into the hands of the Russians.'

****

Before the war it would have been a three-minute walk from the Reich Chancellery to the Brandenburg Gate. Gretchen and Kurt would have strolled hand-in-hand north on Wilhelmstrasse and turned west on Unter den Linden. But this journey for Kurt – pushing the semiconscious Gretchen in a wheel chair – would take much longer.

For thirty-six nights in a row, until April 21, RAF de Havilland Mosquitos had bombed the German capital.

Five days later the Russians began their own bombardment of the city with Katyusha rockets and field artillery. No structure was left intact.

The skeletal facades of bombed-out buildings had shed their bricks like dead scales, forming hills of rubble and twisted iron that clogged the sidewalks and spewed out onto the roadway.

They passed a dead horse lying in the gutter, still tethered to the shafts of its cart. Water gushed from a nearby hydrant.

It was under these conditions, and in a constant light rain, that Kurt had to navigate Wilhelmstrasse, pushing Gretchen's wheel chair in front of him. She had a blanket over her legs. Under it she held Kurt's revolver.

Skirting the rolls of barbed wire and tank traps, Kurt pushed the wheel chair along a road that was more like an obstacle course than a thoroughfare. The stench from the broken sewer pipes mixed with the smell of sulphur and cordite from exploded ordinance was nauseating.

Kurt could feel shards of glass cracking under his boots wherever he stepped.

Their passage was further impeded by wild-eyed civilians, carrying bundles of clothes, rushing to the Wilhelmstrasse S-Bahn subway station to escape the Russian bombardment.

The young couple weaved their way through the tide of Berliners streaming towards them, ever alert to the whine of Katyusha rockets – more menacing than the staccato sound of small arms fire that was so near it could be coming from the next street over.

Kurt pointed to graffiti scrawled in white paint on a door that hung off its hinges: 'Every German will defend his capital. We shall stop the Red hordes at the walls of our Berlin.'

'Goebbels,' he said, 'defiant to the last.'

When they reached Unter den Linden, they heard an enormous explosion and the ground shook under them. The vibration caused the budding leaves on the lime trees to shake off their dust.

Kurt could see Gretchen beginning to tremble. He placed a reassuring hand on her shoulder.

'Not far now, my darling. You can see the Brandenburg Gate.'

'And there's the Adlon Hotel where I used to work,' smiled Gretchen weakly.

She noticed the windows on the first floor had been walled up. 'It's a military hospital now.'

She wondered about Herr Spangler, the director, Chef who taught her knife skills and the libidinous Joachim. She hoped they had survived the war somehow.

'Halt!'

Suddenly, they were confronted by a boy in uniform who stepped out of a doorway and pointed a Gewehr 98 bolt-action Mauser at them.

He could not have been more than fourteen and his weapon looked as if it had been used in the First World War.

'Where are you going and why are you not in uniform defending Berlin?' he demanded in a high-pitched voice.

'My wife is sick,' said Kurt. 'I'm taking her to the Adlon. There's a hospital there.'

'You have papers?'

'Yes,' said Kurt.

He put the brake on the wheel chair and positioned himself in front of the boy, blocking his view of Gretchen.

Kurt reached into his pocket pretending to look for his pass.

Instead, he knocked the rifle sideways and twisted it from the hands of the frightened boy. Then he opened the bolt and emptied the magazine of its five rounds. Placing them in his pocket, he threw the rifle back to the boy.

'Now I suggest you go home. You're too young to die. There is nothing left to defend.'

The boy burst into tears and slunk back into the doorway from which he had appeared.

Kurt took the brake off the wheel chair and began pushing it in the direction of the Brandenburg Gate, negotiating around the tank ditches and the network of trenches and bunkers.

'I can see the airstrip!' he exclaimed.

Gretchen's eyes were closed.

The wind had picked up and it drove the rain into their faces. But above the wind they could hear the throaty revving of an aircraft engine.

'I don't think I can make it, Kurt. I feel so weak.'

'We'll make it together. Trust me.'

He began to run, propelling the wheel chair forward. He could see the Fieseler Stork on the runway, just as Speer had promised. The pilot was waving frantically from the cockpit, its single propeller already turning.

The pilot was shouting something and pointing behind the aircraft.

In the distance, at the end of the runway, Kurt could see a Russian tank lumbering like a giant dinosaur directly towards the plane.

Kurt lifted Gretchen from the wheel chair and carrying her he raced towards the aircraft. The three-seater was already turning away into the direction of the tank to face the wind, ready for take-off.

The pilot had opened the side door and was shouting at them to hurry.

Kurt saw the swastika on the plane's vertical stabiliser and the iron cross emblem on its fuselage. He could hear the clanking of the tracks of the T-34 tank as it closed in on the light plane.

He hoisted Gretchen up and the pilot guided her into the seat behind him. Kurt leapt aboard and slammed the door.

'Buckle up,' the pilot shouted over the roar of the engine.

The tank's turret turned and its 3-inch high velocity gun took aim at the plane. There was a puff of smoke and a shell whistled by the cockpit.

The pilot took evasive action by swerving onto the grass before righting the plane back onto the flight path. He accelerated and the plane gathered speed for take-off.

Gretchen buried her face in Kurt's shoulder.

'There's nowhere I'd rather be than with you,' she whispered.

He kissed her forehead. 'I love you.'

The tank commander had raised the hatch on the turret and had levered himself up. He had an automatic pistol in his hand and was taking aim as the Storch lifted off before it could collide with the tank.

Kurt saw the Russian smile and salute as the plane made a steep climb and entered the low cloudbank. The last thing he saw was the tank crushing the wheel chair that had brought Gretchen to safety.

'Are you all right back there?' shouted the pilot over his shoulder.

'We're fine,' Kurt shouted back.

'Next stop, Zurich,' said the pilot.

As they climbed above the clouds heading southwest, the sky was blue and the sun was shining.

'I can't wait to see Soshy again,' said Gretchen, as she closed her eyes and reached for Kurt's hand.

Epilogue

At around 3.30 pm on April 30, 1945 – three days after Gretchen and Kurt's flight from Berlin – Adolf Hitler purportedly shot himself with a Walther Polizeipistole 7.65 in the private sitting room of the Führerbunker.

Most historical accounts suggest this is how he died, however some historians have theorized that Hitler killed himself by biting down on a cyanide capsule – the same fate of his new bride, Eva Braun, who was with him in the living room.

Nothing was ever proven, nor will it ever be. After their double-suicide, the bodies of Hitler and Eva Braun were supposedly burned in the Reich Chancellery garden outside the bunker in accordance with Hitler's prior instructions.

The newly-weds' charred remains were seized by the Russians, who, if they ever performed autopsies, never released the results.

In 2009, American scientists were able to do a DNA analysis on a skull the Russian government believed was Hitler's. It turned out to be that of a woman less than 40 years old.

Evan Braun was thirty-three when she died.

.

.

.